IN THE SHADOW
OF THE SON

IN THE SHADOW OF THE SON

A NOVEL

MICHAEL SIMANGA

THIRD WORLD PRESS
CHICAGO

Printed in the United States of America
First Edition 2000

05 04 03 02 01 00   5 4 3 2 1

Cover design by Taahira Mumford

Library of Congress Catalog-in-Publication Data

Simanga, Michael, 1954-
    In the shadow of the son: a novel/by Michael Simanga.
    p. cm.
  ISBN 0-88378-206-5 (alk. paper)
  1. Afro-Americans--Fiction. I. Title.
PS3569. I47235615 2000
813' .54--dc21   98-37071
                                                            CIP

Third World Press
7822 S. Dobson
Chicago, IL 60619

For my Father
Richard Adisa Humphrey
And my grandfathers
Howard Holly and Richard Humphrey Sr.
and my son
Malik Simanga

From this window, I have seen the seasons change. Brown leaves blown across asphalt basketball courts were crushed into dust under nike and reebok and fila athletic shoes. Children have braced themselves against the wings of the wind and fallen on the ice that covers the broken glass and empty shell casings frozen like prehistoric fossils forming a mosaic of modern urban existence. The pages of school books have soaked in spring rain and the summer sun has bathed the crap shooters and shit talkers with sweat and hot blood and cold beer.

From my classroom window I have watched the seasons change and the children of this community grow and reach for life beyond the limited sight of this window. From both sides of this glass I have seen our children eager to be educated, determined to succeed, bold in their defiance, brilliant in their perceptions, battling for an existence in a place that screams hatred at them while demanding their allegiance.

From both sides of this window I have watched our children confirm the duality that W.E.B. Du Bois spoke of. At the end of the twentieth century we remain the people of dual identity, every generation struggling to reconcile the African and the American. Our need to be accepted in the land of our birth beckons us to citizenship and patriotism. Yet, our historical memory whispers to our consciousness from the bottom of the Atlantic and from the dust of southern soil and from the branches of hanging trees and from the concrete of northern cities and from the broken promises of politicians and from our own children's questions.

CHAPTER ONE

It was the beginning of the end of the day. The classroom was finally empty. The halls outside the door were finally quiet and the weekend waited to be welcomed. Isaiah Bishop stood at the window and surveyed the playground below the second floor classroom where he'd taught for the last ten years of his fifteen year career as a high school history teacher.

His gaze stretched beyond the playground into the streets lined with old, single family, wooden homes that had once been the pride of the city's neighborhoods. Now, almost all of those old houses were desperately in need of repair and painting. Owners who no longer lived in the community had divided most of those houses into duplexes and small apartments, causing the population of the area to be three or four times what it had been originally planned for. Bishop's eyes roamed up and down the streets until they were halted by the gray, concrete structures looming over the houses in the neighborhood. His eyes rested on the tops of the huge housing project that stood just past the old homes and only nine blocks from Frederick Douglass High School.

Standing there in the window of the old school, he thought about the more than two thousand students he'd taught in those ten years and the thirty-eight that had just bolted out of his classroom when the bell rang, like they'd been shot out of a gun.

It was always like that on Friday afternoons. As much as his students liked his class and as much as Bishop enjoyed teaching, the anticipation of the weekend was always a distraction on Fridays. The students stared at the clock and out the window and Bishop stole glances at his watch. Both teacher and students were thinking about their plans for the two days that separated them from each other and a weekly routine that included fighting through Mondays, trying to restore and revive the attention of the students, hoping that Tuesday, Wednesday and Thursday did not include any major acts of violence, arrests or fires, and making sure that by Friday they'd actually learned something in his class.

It was an unseasonably warm October and the school had been unusually hot. For some unexplained reason, the furnace kicked on two weeks earlier and no one had figured out how to turn it off. All week Bishop had to come in early to open the windows so that his classroom would at least be bearable by the time his students arrived.

Looking out the window and past the steel grate that keeps students from throwing things out and vandals from breaking in, thoughts of a quiet weekend spent writing caused him to sigh with contentment. He felt fortunate. Teaching had saved his life and writing had saved his sanity.

Bishop bolted the windows, straightened a couple of chairs, picked a candy wrapper off the floor, erased the blackboard behind his desk, locked the eraser and chalk in his drawer and packed the papers that needed checking into his briefcase before stepping into the hallway. At the end of the hall near the staircase, Mr. Hopkins, the school custodian, slowly shoved a large pile of trash with a push broom and waved as Bishop locked his door and headed down the hall toward the old man.

Employed with the school for almost forty years, Mr. Hopkins started working there one year after it was built. Back then it was called General George Armstrong Custer High School and was the top all-white school in the city. The children of the politicians, business leaders, doctors, important lawyers and an occasional working class student who showed promise were all sent to the high school a few blocks south of downtown.

About twenty-five years ago, integration occurred. Whites began abandoning the area and built new communities for themselves on the north side as middle and working class blacks moved into the neighborhood around the high school. Shortly afterward, the government built a housing project a few blocks away that brought in lower income blacks and whites, causing the last of the affluent whites to run for the north side and the suburbs. By the early seventies, even the housing project whites had moved out and most of those middle-class blacks who could had moved on, too. By the end of the seventies, the high school was surrounded by a crowded, low income, black community. Black political power took hold of city government about that same time and, as part of their reforms, changed the name of the school to Frederick Douglass High.

Mr. Hopkins, the resident historian of Douglass High, would tell anyone who would listen the entire pre- and post-integration story of the community and the school, including every principal, every teacher, every major sporting event and at least a couple dozen students from each class who had graduated since he'd been there. His incredible memory was legendary at the school and he was always willing to share it. It was suspected that he must be close to seventy, but he wouldn't tell anyone his real age. The steady, physical work he'd done his whole life kept his body muscular and lean, further disguising his age.

Although Mr. Hopkins never went past the sixth grade, he was well read and conversed easily with teachers and students about every subject taught at Frederick Douglass High. He was one of those black men born and raised during the segregation era who were the stalwarts of the community. He had been married to the same woman for forty-three years and their four children all graduated from college. A member of the deacon board at Shady Grove Baptist Church, he had voted in every election since he had the right, his shoes were always shined and he showed up for work on time. The students called him Pops and he dealt with them as if they were all his grandchildren, praising their accomplishments and admonishing them when they got out of hand.

As Bishop approached Mr. Hopkins, he remembered the book, *American Negro Poetry*, that the old man lent him the previous week and that he should have already returned. He grinned sheepishly as he greeted the elder. "How you doing, Pops?"

Mr. Hopkins pushed his broom forward while saying, "Fine for an old man with nothing to read this weekend." He looked up at Bishop and grinned. "How you doing?"

"That's cold, Mr. Hopkins. You know I forgot your book."

"Yeah, I know." Mr. Hopkins pushed his broom forward guiding the pile of trash toward the wall. "Just bring it in Monday. Did you read that poem?"

Bishop answered quickly as if he were being tested. "The one by Richard Wright?"

"Uh huh. It's called, 'Between the World and Me.' You should use it in your class when you trying to teach them kids about what it was like before the civil rights movement. Just because you teach history don't mean you can't be creative." He shook his finger slightly as if giving a mild scolding.

"You're right and I am going to use it. It's a great poem."

Mr. Hopkins raised an eyebrow and cocked his head slightly to the side. "Of course it's a great poem, why else would I give it to you?"

Bishop smiled. Pops always amazed and amused him. The old man knew so much, but his method of teaching often came with that old man attitude that was just a little contemptuous of others' ignorance. Bishop watched as the old man looked back down toward the pile of trash and shook his head as if reading some disturbing news from the debris on the floor.

"I don't know why these kids can't put their trash in the damn can," Pops said as he pushed the broom hard into the pile.

Bishop shook his head. "Me either, Mr. Hopkins."

"You want me to tell you why?"

Bishop really didn't want to know. He was ready to go home and knew that Pops loved to tell stories and could have you hemmed up for quite a while if you got him started. But he couldn't be rude to the old man, so he asked, "Why?"

"They need more love. That's all. They need more love."

The simple wisdom of the statement grabbed Bishop like a firm hand-shake. He looked at Mr. Hopkins who continued studying the debris and patted him on the shoulder as he stepped over the pile of trash. "We've got a lot of work to do, don't we?"

"Yep."

"I'll see you Monday, Mr. Hopkins."

Bishop started down the hallway and Pops pushed the broom with one hand while waving with the other. "You have a good weekend, young man, and don't forget my book."

Mr. Hopkins' words and the playful laughter that came with them chased Bishop down the stairs and out into the parking lot where his 1985 black Volvo awaited him faithfully as it had every day from Reagan to Clinton. He unlocked the doors, threw his briefcase in the back seat, jumped in and turned the ignition confidently. He knew it would start up. He kept it in top condition and made sure it did. He couldn't afford to get stranded, especially at the school. Leaving a car overnight in the school parking lot was like sending out invitations to have it cannibalized.

Pulling out of the teacher's parking lot, Bishop turned on the radio in time to catch the news that there had been yet another drive-by shooting in the city. Announcement of the tragedy on the local black radio station was followed by an advertisement for a personal injury lawyer and one for Kelly's Soul Food Kitchen where they were having a two-for-one special.

As was his habit, Bishop began talking to himself out loud when he stopped at a traffic light. "Now what am I going to eat tonight? Jamaican. Yeah, that'll do."

He reached over and turned up the radio and the new Mint Condition song came on as he pulled away from the light. The woman in the car next to his had been watching his private conversation and *gave him a funny look* before she drove off. He sang along with the radio, reached the Kingston Cafe and picked up his food and a six pack of Red Stripe from the corner store. It was going to be a good weekend and he was hungry, ready to eat, relax and get to work.

I am stimulated by the quiet beauty of the night. Its mystery seduces me and the sound of music in its darkness forces away the demons that scare me.

The night frightens me sometimes. The last year of my youth was spent in the last year of the Viet Nam war and even though it has been more than twenty-five years, I still can not sleep soundly at night. One year of hating the darkness. One year spent fearing the possibility of some horrible, tortuous, unexpected death. Afraid to fall asleep for fear that an attack wouldn't be heard. Afraid to piss in the stillness of the night for fear that the enemy would hear it and kill me with my dick in my hand.

Even now, after all these years, sometimes when drifting into my dreams, the night surrounds me with images so horrible that I am assaulted by nightmares, bloody fantasies or fear. Those are the times when I must wait and wander in the darkness until dawn rescues me because nothing else can.

I came home in 1972, nineteen years old, a warrior who had come through the war without a serious wound on my body. Arriving not as some noble crusading soldier who had returned from fighting to welcoming and thankful masses, but as a warrior engaged in battle and had killed men and probably women and children. Returning to the States, my survival was dependent upon me always remembering the fact that I would and could kill.

CHAPTER TWO

The smell of curry lingered in the house. An empty beer bottle and the take-out container sat on the dining room table with some scraps of curry chicken left. The only light in the house came from a small lamp and a computer monitor in the study next to the living room. It was so quiet you could hear the hum of the refrigerator in the kitchen. The only other sounds present were the punching of keys on a computer keyboard and the almost inaudible sweetness of Miles Davis and John Coltrane blowing "Blue In Green" gently through the rooms. This was the quietness that gave peace to his life. It was the quietness that Bishop needed.

On a personal deadline and behind schedule, he had worked steadily for the last four hours, pausing only for reflection and to take an occasional swig from the bottle of beer that sat on the floor next to his chair. The phone rang and the sound was so abrasive it scared him. He had forgotten to turn the ringer off and the unexpected intrusion broke his concentration and annoyed him because he had also forgotten to turn the answering machine on. At first he tried to ignore it, but by the third ring Bishop looked across the room at the phone on the table next to the old leather arm chair and as he got up to answer it mumbled, "Who the hell is calling me?"

"Hello."

"Isaiah?"

"Yes?"

"It's Juanita. Are you all right?"

Her question made him realize that the interruption had put a hostile edge on his voice. "Juanita...hey...I'm sorry, the phone kinda startled me."

"I'm sorry to call you so late."

He dropped down into the leather chair. "What's wrong?"

"Well, I just got home from work and Billy left a message on my machine asking me to call you."

"Why didn't he call me?"

"I don't know. He left the message about five o'clock this afternoon."

"Oh. He probably called here, but I didn't get in 'til six and I forgot to leave the machine on. What did he want?"

"He just asked me to tell you to meet him at his apartment around midnight."

Bishop looked at his watch. It was 11:45 and he wanted to get back to work. "I'll call him."

Juanita hesitated as if waiting for Bishop to say something else. There was a tone in her silence that revealed a mother's concern, followed by a tone in her statement that revealed a woman's power to move a man into action. "I already did. He's not home."

Bishop understood what she meant. "I'm busy. I'll catch him tomorrow. I'll call him back in a little while" were not acceptable options. He had to go over to Billy's house to reassure Juanita that her son was okay.

"All right. I'll shoot over there in a few minutes."

"Thanks, Isaiah."

"No problem."

Hanging up the phone and looking around his study for the shoes he discarded sometime in the last few hours, Isaiah Bishop thought about the strange relationship he had with Juanita King. She was the mother of Billy King, Bishop's friend and former student. Bishop met her ten years ago, shortly after her son began attending Douglass High. Back then she was a thirty year old single mother with a fourteen year old son in high school and a daughter two years younger. He thought about her smooth brown skin, the way her dread locks fell on her shoulders and how she surprised him the first time he saw her at a reception for a Senegalese painter sponsored by 100 Black Men.

At the reception, Bishop spotted her across the room speaking fluent French with the artist. Her hands moved gracefully in the air when she talked and although he could not understand what she was saying, there was so much passion in her delivery, that whatever she was telling the artist made believers out of all who observed her. There was a magic about her. It made him feel like one of the boys in his class with a crush on a new girl.

He couldn't stop watching her, didn't want to stare, but didn't want to take his eyes off her for fear she'd slip away and he'd cuss himself all the way home. Bishop wanted to meet her, needed to meet her, had to meet her. He was excited, but felt uncomfortable and clumsy and therefore hesitant about approaching her.

After a few minutes, one of the sisters at the reception interrupted Juanita's conversation with the artist and led him away to introduce him to other guests. Isaiah took a deep breath and moved across the space between them as if music were pulling him toward a singer on a stage. He approached her with anticipation and apprehension and was met with a smile that spoke peace, causing all of his anxiety to wither. Juanita immediately made him feel comfortable, welcoming Bishop in a way that cracked opened his awkwardness and surrounded him with a feeling that this was the way they should be, men and women at peace, unafraid to speak to, or listen to, or see each other.

Standing there lost in the seconds that followed her smile, she watched him and then broke his trance by introducing herself. "Hi, I'm Juanita." She extended her hand, looked deep into his eyes and noticed the small scar at the corner of his left eyebrow.

Bishop shook her hand robotically while his mind raced to find something that would give back to her what her smile had just given to him. In the flash of time he had to respond, he couldn't find it and settled for his name. "I'm Isaiah Bishop."

Her face became even brighter as she repeated, "Isaiah Bishop."

The way Juanita slid his name through her smile made it sound informal and familiar. Bishop tried without success not to stare at her, but she was beautiful and he was getting lost looking at her. Juanita continued looking up at his face and liked it. She noticed his neatly trimmed mustache and beard and thought his eyes were kind, but somewhat sad. His hair was neat but still a little long and a little wild and she thought that the brother standing in front of her was probably a little wild, too.

"Are you the Mr. Bishop who teaches history at Douglass High?"

He wondered how she knew him, but he was so lost in his desire to talk to her that his mind was not accessing his memory. So many things about her were recognizable, yet he was sure that if they'd met before, he couldn't have forgotten her. "Yes, I am."

"Well, I'm Billy King's mother."

That night, Isaiah Bishop was both lost and found. Of course she was familiar. She had to be King's mother. There was the same intensity, the same intellectual power, the same kindness and commanding presence. She was the same force of nature that could blow gently across your skin and soothe you or come forward with enough power to bend trees that had stood for hundreds of years. King was definitely her child, her son.

"Billy talks about you all the time, Mr. Bishop."

"Your son is a remarkable young man."

They dove into words about King and his school work and his future and the Senegalese artist and how she learned French as a child because her mother had taken in a student from Mali who wound up living with them for five years. They talked and listened and looked and noticed. She liked his coffee with just a little cream-colored skin. He thought her dark brown locks made her dark brown eyes even more commanding. They raced through subjects as if they were talking for hours, when in reality only a few minutes had passed when a well-dressed, pecan colored, powerfully built brother approached them and Juanita said, "Isaiah Bishop, this is my friend, Lonnie Carlton."

Bishop stuck out his hand and said, "Glad to meet you." He played it off but was disappointed. He could have stood there and talked to Juanita all night, but the interruption and the way she said, "this is my friend" ended his dream abruptly.

Lonnie's face was familiar from the news. He was a well-known, politically connected, police detective often in the papers as the head of "Blue Fire," a special police unit assigned to deal with drug dealers and gangs. They had gained notoriety for their raids into the notorious drug infested projects in the city. In the neighborhood of Frederick Douglass High, they were praised by some for their arrest record, and despised by others for their often brutal assaults on young black men.

It had been ten years since that initial moment with Juanita. Those first few words, that immediate attraction, that fire between them had remained a constant, warm thought in Bishop's mind. He played with it often, wondering what would have happened if they had finished that first conversation. Juanita continued to see Lonnie, and Bishop became her friend and continued to speculate and admire her from a safe distance.

The memory of that first meeting with Juanita and the years of their friendship since did not soothe a growing uneasiness in Bishop as he finished tying his shoes and thought about the implications of what she had just told him over the phone. It wasn't unusual for Bishop and King to get together late. Neither of them slept well at night. They'd often call each other at ten or eleven o'clock, hook up and play chess, listen to jazz and talk until dawn. What was unusual was for King to have Juanita call. Although he was certain everything was fine and he'd tried to convey that to her, Bishop's own concern was causing him to hurry up so that he could confirm his optimism.

11

King's apartment was in a section of town full of old apartment buildings with wood floors and high ceilings, newly restored Victorian homes, tree lined streets, industrial buildings turned into lofts and trendy restaurants and boutiques. It was where all the hip, young, black professionals moved. Young lawyers and CPAs, doctors and entrepreneurs and those who aspired to be vice presidents of the insurance companies lived in the neighborhood with some interesting young musicians, artists and writers. As Bishop drove into the neighborhood, he thought about his young friend.

Billy King was twenty-eight years old. He had the same dark brown eyes as his mother. He was tall and muscular with long limbs that made him seem even more graceful when he moved. Bishop met him during his first year of teaching at Frederick Douglass High. When they met, King was tall for a fourteen-year-old freshman, almost six feet, slim and muscular, with copper-colored skin and intense eyes that pulled you into an inner light that burned beauty and broadcast brilliance. He had a kind smile and was a rising leader of the school. He was respected and respectful, held no school offices, participated in no extracurricular activities and attended no school functions, except an occasional basketball game. The students loved him.

They all called him King, not just because it was his last name, but because there was a regal quality about him and he settled the disputes amongst his peers like some young monarch of the inner city. In his studies he was completely focused. Often quieting other students who disrupted the class, he did it calmly, without ridicule or recrimination, and it always worked. This child lived in the city's most dangerous neighborhood, yet walked the streets without fear. Even the criminals, the drug dealers and crack addicts, the pimps and prostitutes admired and looked out for him. Bishop was fascinated by the power and the promise of this young boy. King became his best student and Bishop became his friend and mentor.

King's father was also a veteran of Viet Nam and that made the bond with Bishop even stronger. He was killed when King was very young. He didn't die in Viet Nam. He made it home but was labeled crazy and spent time in and out of government mental institutions.

During the first few years of their friendship, King spoke very little about his father. Bishop didn't press him and was surprised a couple of years ago when they were playing chess one night and King began talking about him. As Bishop drove toward King's apartment, he recalled that conversation. He remembered that it happened just as King placed him in checkmate, then slumped back in his chair and started talking.

"I never told you about my father, did I?"

Bishop was gathering up the chess pieces, throwing them in a box when he answered, "No. The only thing you've told me is that he was in the war."

King hesitated, then pointed to the chess board. "Let's play another game."

Bishop nodded and started resetting the board when King continued, "When my father came back from the war, he wasn't right in the head. The first few years he was just kinda quiet, didn't say much to anybody but my mother. I was little so I don't remember much, but I do remember that he read a lot and he used to leave the house and sometimes be gone for days."

Bishop listened as the words flowed slowly, deliberately out of King's mouth as if they would leave a terrible taste if he let them pour out the way they felt inside.

"I remember my mother being really worried and looking out the window hoping that the footsteps she heard on the sidewalk were his. Sooner or later, he'd show up and he always had a big bag of books."

King smiled as if recalling an amusing incident, then continued, "He'd have all these books by black authors. He brought home Du Bois, Frederick Douglass, Hurston, Nkrumah, Garvey, Cabral, Malcolm X, George Jackson, Angela Davis, the Panthers, Baraka and anything else he could find. It was kinda weird because when I think about it, he was like some kind of mad scholar. I was always glad when he came home, but after he got there he'd just sit at the table in the kitchen, staring into those books for hours."

Bishop remembered King's description of his father and knew that his old man was sitting there staring into those pages, condemned and confused, trying to clarify his concerns and redirect his rage. It was too late. There was too much blood on his shoes. Bishop knew that King's father had seen the seriousness of stalking an enemy. He'd heard the noise of battle and befriended men who died beside him.

As Bishop turned onto King's street, he could still hear the pain in King's voice as it dropped to a whisper and he described the terrible secret his father had told him.

"Once, my father looked up from one of his books and saw me standing in the doorway watching him. He called me over and told me he had something to tell me."

King swallowed hard and paused before continuing, "He told me that he

13

was afraid that someone would discover he'd killed a white captain during the war. He shot him in the head and blamed it on the Viet Cong. After that, he said that he would be murdered. That it was the price for killing a white man. It scared the shit out of me. I was a little boy and my father was telling me that he'd killed a man and that he would be killed himself. I ran out of the kitchen screaming. My mother caught me and held me and asked me what was wrong, but I didn't tell her. I never told her what he'd said.

"After that, whenever I was alone with my old man he would say crazy shit like he was Nat Turner reincarnated and that he was destined for martyrdom like Malcolm, Martin or Fred Hampton. One day, my mother came home and told me he was dead. I went to his room and packed all his books in a box and kept them under my bed. When I got older, I read them all."

King's father was killed in a shoot out with the police when King was eight. Bishop remembered the incident. It was all over the news and there was a minor uproar in the community about the killing of a war veteran. The uproar died down quickly and quietly because everyone knew Billy King's father was crazy.

By the time King revealed those things to Bishop, he'd read all of his father's books and had written down all that he remembered about him. He later showed Bishop what he'd recorded. The intense but brief images of the father were planted deeply in the mind of the child. His recollections were precise and often poetic phrases. Sometimes they were several pages long, sometimes just a few words. His words were stark and real, but never romantic. He wrote them as if they were a long, disjointed suicide note from his father. He wrote about how he was teased as a child for having a crazy old man, and how he'd fought boys and men for dishonoring his father's memory.

King's revelations about his father reminded Bishop of other veterans he knew who walked around waiting to explode. When he returned from Viet Nam, he was one of them and had to rescue himself by becoming a teacher. He'd gone to the war, came home and hoped that doing something useful would save him from the horrible things he'd seen and felt and done.

I don't recall exactly what thoughts occupied my mind when the letter came June 30, 1971, telling me to report for induction. I remember sitting down in the living room watched over by a silent color television. My parents were on the brown sofa and I sat in my father's recliner while they listened to me say the draft had caught up with me. When she saw the letter and heard the resignation in my voice, my mother cried and offered me money to go to Canada. My father, a veteran of the Korean War, stared silently like the TV. After a while he spoke solemnly about the three years he had spent in prison after coming home from that war. I had never heard either of them discuss this and his incarceration had been unknown to me.

That day was the first and only time I witnessed my father's tears. He is a strong and dignified man. A black man who never took shit off people, he never gave shit either. Consistently, without complaint, he went to work every day on an assembly line in an auto plant to provide for his family. It is still easy to recollect the smell of sweat and oil and pain on his body when he'd come home exhausted. He always hugged me as if he had thought about it all day and wanted to reaffirm how much he loved me, how much he loved us.

The day the letter came, I didn't know what to expect from him. My mother's reaction had been easy to predict. She had been an outspoken opponent of the war, making it no secret that she hated it and the military. She was one of the first and few black women active in demonstrations against U.S. involvement in Viet Nam.

My father had always remained curiously quiet and never went with her to opposition meetings or demonstrations. He would only gaze at the television, watching news of young men dying, killing and limping home physically maimed and psychologically wounded. Sometimes after seeing those images of the war, he would just get up out of his chair and leave the house for hours without saying a word. When I wondered aloud where he went, my mother would say, "Your daddy's gone to walk with the spirits a while." He would come home quiet, just as he left, never speaking about the carnage of Viet Nam that shook something deep inside him.

Because he was a veteran, when he asked me not to go to the war, it stunned me. His voice crashed into my head like a mournful choir of a thousand spirits of black men who had never revealed their scars. I saw the scars on my father's soul that day. Growing older, my own scars would begin to resemble his.

For reasons yet to be revealed to me, my father didn't fear my dying in

Viet Nam. He was afraid I'd be murdered upon returning. His son, his only son, had come to manhood at a time when our people were engaged in battle all across America.

This proud man, my father, had taken me to hear Malcolm X speak right after he left the Nation of Islam. We had ridden together to Atlanta to attend the funeral of Martin Luther King. He put a gun in my hand during the rebellions that followed King's assassination, and told me to shoot anyone who tried to come into our yard. Anyone, even the police. That same night he got in his car and drove out into the smoke and fire and gunshots, looking for wounded or trapped people who needed assistance. He left me, a fifteen year old, to defend our home. It was his first recognition of my manhood.

The day my letter came, my father, still wearing his uniform from the factory, sat in the living room and cried. His tears were like a river flowing, leading me into an ocean of understanding about all that he had taught me about being a black man in this place. He feared I would return home like him, unafraid of this country's propensity for murder and fully aware of my own power to kill. He was right. My only question upon returning home from Nam was whether my capacity to unleash precise, unemotional murder could be controlled. Coming home from the war, to my own country, as a black man and a veteran, there seemed to be no place for me. I had to rescue myself or surely I would kill and be killed.

The day my letter came, my father told me that like every other black man, my life, my entire life, would be spent trying to avoid being physically, psychologically or emotionally murdered while trying to be a man at the same time. He said going to war would make me that much more determined not to be denied what was my birthright. He stated it simply, yet in the most eloquent way I've ever heard. "You have the right to live in this place without being fucked with."

His warning made me remember that for years there were whispered rumors in my family, stories told after late night parties when the adults were drunk and the children eavesdropped on their conversations. Tales had been told that my father and black veterans like my father had fought and sometimes killed white men who attempted to deny them or refuse them or confront them.

The day that letter came, my father said he'd been to prison for beating a white man who had called him a nigger in front of my mother. He beat him down in the street, in daylight, in front of a crowd of people. He didn't run *afterwards. He stood there and waited for the police. He went to prison, and had never spoken of it again, until that day.*

He knew that his son was heir to his anger. He knew I would come back like him, with disciplined, controlled rage, capable of killing without concern for consequences. He knew that war causes you to discover that the thing that finally makes all men equal is violence. In war, surrounded by pain, noise and death, you realize that money, class, education, social status and race privilege are all rendered useless when you are face to face with a man whose only intention at that moment is to slay you. War teaches you the terrible equalizing power that comes from killing.

CHAPTER FOUR

The latest song by Rahsaan Salandy had just finished playing when Bishop turned the radio off. It was just after midnight and he sat in the black Volvo across the street from King's apartment, listening to the sounds of the night outside his car, listening for the sounds of danger in the blackness. He also heard his own breathing accelerating, rising, growing louder. Sitting there, thousands of miles and what seemed like a hundred years from the war, his thoughts kept drifting to battlefield memories, making him hesitate before getting out of the car. Trying to shake off the violence attempting to creep into his consciousness, he opened the door and stepped into the street. His hands were sweating, a sudden tension pulled at his neck and waves of nausea started rolling around in his stomach. There was some unseen danger and he'd learned a long time ago that unseen danger was the downfall of human beings.

Bishop thought, "We sense danger like other animals, but too often if we can't physically see it, our intellect dismisses it and blinds us. We should run away and seek refuge like other animals. They don't have to see it. Unlike us, they respect their instincts."

Bishop's first impulse was to retreat to the car. His eyes scanned up and down the street, in the shadows of the buildings, between the trees and behind the hedges. Glancing into the cars parked on the street, the alarms wailing inside him grew louder because he was unarmed and if someone or something attacked, he didn't have the fire power necessary to respond to a modern urban confrontation.

Deciding to bluff as he moved closer to the building, Bishop slid his hand inside his coat hoping whoever was stalking him might hesitate, wondering whether he was strapped or not. Carefully, cautiously he made it to the door. Slowly, he opened the outer door, entered the building and climbed the stairs to the second floor where King lived. His heartbeat pounded at his temples. Instincts honed by years of experience told him that confrontation was lurking nearby, even if he couldn't see it.

In the hall outside King's apartment, music floated out from under his door. It wasn't too loud and Bishop could hear the buzzer when he pressed it. There was no answer. Ring...listen...wait. Ring...listen...wait. The cycle repeated itself two or three times. "Shit!" Bishop mumbled while checking his pockets for the key King gave him when he went out of town. Realizing that it was in the car, he repeated, "Shit!" and rang again...listened again...waited again. Nothing but the music responded from the other side.

As he turned to walk away, something told him to try the door. He turned the knob slowly and pushed. It opened.

Bishop stuck his head in slightly. Nothing seemed disturbed. He surveyed the living room then stepped in. Bob Marley's "Natural Mystic" was the background music as he moved quietly until he reached the stereo, turned it off and stood in the silence, waiting and listening. Nothing moved until the ice maker in the refrigerator dropped some cubes into the tray, causing Bishop to jump as if someone had tapped him on the shoulder. He took a deep breath, calmed his nerves after realizing there were no other sounds and moved through the apartment quickly, looking for signs. Of what, he wasn't sure. Perhaps there was a message, a clue that would tell him what was going on. Methodically, he searched the living room, bedroom, bathroom and finally the kitchen where he saw the note lying on the table. It was in King's writing.

Gone to watch the game.

Bishop snatched the note off the table and left the apartment with the intention of getting out of there quickly. He shut the door behind him and realized that it has a dead bolt that must be locked from the outside. He had to go to the car to get the spare key to lock the door. The alarms sounded again. The animal voice, the instinct voice, yelled in his ear. He left the building with his hand inside his coat, moving steadily toward the car. Scanning the street, trying not to appear panicked, he unlocked the car door, got in and reached in the glove compartment for King's key.

"Fuck this!" he whispered to himself as the alarms screamed louder inside his head and his pulse sped up. He started the car and drove down the street looking back at King's building as if he'd just escaped some evil force in a horror movie. At the end of the block, Bishop made a U-turn, pulled over at the corner, turned the lights out, waited and watched.

He wasn't quite sure what he was looking for, but wanted to make sure that it was safe before he returned. The wind blew softly, rustling through the trees, making the leaves sound as if a crowd was applauding politely. The fall was his favorite time of the year because everything and everyone seemed to be slowing down, preparing to retreat, to rest, to be still for a while. The wind, the leaves and the smell of the fall began calming him down as he kept watch.

After about ten minutes, a young, well-dressed couple came out of King's building. They were laughing in the spotlight provided by the street lamp. The woman smacked the man on his butt. He grabbed her playfully and they kissed. The young lovers displaying their affection so openly, so freely, made Bishop smile. When the young man released her, she smacked him again and ran toward a Range Rover parked at the curb. He caught her, leaned her against the car and they kissed again.

Suddenly, a shadow came from between two of the buildings moving quickly behind them. A darkened van without headlights raced from the other end of the street. The man seemed to sense something behind him and turned around abruptly. The woman screamed as her boyfriend pushed her to the ground just as the van reached them. The door slid open, two more figures jumped out. Light flashed in the darkness. Dozens of shots from automatic weapons reported rapidly, loudly. The woman screamed louder. The three shadows jumped back in the van and raced down the street. They were racing toward Bishop.

Stunned by what he'd just witnessed, it took a second for him to realize that they were almost at his car. When they were a few feet away he slumped down hastily, hiding in the darkness waiting for them to pass. The woman was still screaming, sobbing in the distance as the van reached the front of the Volvo. The driver slammed on the brakes and the thought slammed into Bishop's head, "They must have seen me!"

He was frozen, listening, waiting. The car windows were slightly open and the fall breeze blew across his face like the darkness exhaling mystery into the car. Lying across the front seat, his body was contorted, his legs twisted awkwardly under the steering wheel. "Fuck! I'm trapped," he whispered. There was a siren in the distance. He prayed that it was coming his way!

The van crept toward him, its engine breathing like an animal. It stopped alongside his car. He waited. They waited. The sound of his heart-beat seemed so loud that he was sure it would give him away. Sweat ran into his eyes and the salt burned. He couldn't see what was going on outside because of the darkness and his angle from the car seat. Listening, trying to think of a way out, he extended his left hand over his head probing the pas-senger door for the handle, preparing to take a chance to get out of the car and run.

Finally, Bishop's fingers found the handle and just as he was about to yank it open he realized that he would have to reposition his body to get out of the car quickly, otherwise, when the door was thrown open, they'd have a well-lit target. Moving his legs without making any sound, he pulled them up onto the seat, bracing them against the driver's door.

He snatched the handle ready to spring out onto the ground. "Oh Shit! The damned door is locked," he mouthed silently, talking himself through the fear. Hearing the sound of a motor slowly pulling the van window down, he reached for the lock at the top of the door. Voices spoke vulgar, deadly instructions while a clip was slapped into the handle of an automatic weapon and a bullet slid into the chamber and the hammer locked into the firing position. Fumbling around for the lock, his internal voice shouted warnings and instructions, "Oh Shit! Come on! Find it!" His fingers located the lock, pulled it up and reached for the handle.

POW! POW! POW!...TAT-TAT-TAT-TAT!

A burst of gunfire exploded the silence. The van screamed away, tires screeching, engine roaring, profanity flying from the windows like trash thrown in the street. Staying down, he heard more shots and realized they were being fired from a distance, not from the van. The gunfire got closer for a few more seconds. Angry voices shouted more vulgarities.

Finally, the shooting stopped. New voices and footsteps ran away from where his car was parked. Slowly raising his head, he sat up under the steering wheel and watched two men with guns drawn running back toward the woman. Whomever they were, they had saved his life.

Within minutes, police cars flooded the streets from all directions. Members of the Blue Fire unit jumped out of the squad cars with weapons drawn. They were dressed in their trademark black military looking uniforms and ski masks. Other cops combed the street. A voice was yelling at Bishop.

"PUT YOUR HANDS WHERE I CAN SEE THEM!"

Placing his hands on the steering wheel, his car door was snatched open. Two Blue Fire cops were aiming their guns at him. Another one was in the mirror.

"GET THE FUCK OUT OF THE CAR!... NOW, MUTHAFUCKA!

Bishop got out slowly, keeping his hands in sight.

"ON YOUR FACE! LACE YOUR FINGERS BEHIND YOUR HEAD!

Following their instructions, he lay down in the street. One cop stepped to him, kicked his legs apart, and searched him. Taking his wallet out of his pocket, the cop threw it to another officer, then grabbed Bishop's right hand, put it in a pressure hold, pulled it behind his back and cuffed his wrist.

"GIVE ME YOUR LEFT HAND!"

He cuffed the other wrist and pulled him up to his feet. Another one searched him again from the front, emptying his pockets onto the ground. Two others rummaged through the car. Silently Bishop stared at them, noticing that their faces were covered with smudge. A light skinned black cop who looked like Ron O'Neal from *Superfly* had his wallet and came over to him while reading the information on his driver's license.

"WHAT ARE YOU DOING HERE?" the cop shouted.

Bishop didn't answer. He started to, then stopped, realizing that it was a trap. Anything he said could put him in more jeopardy. Silence settled over everything for a few seconds. The interrogator walked around him in a circular movement, first clockwise, then back the other way, measuring, testing, toying with him. Then, as if he'd seen enough, the cop grabbed Bishop by the throat, dragged him to the sidewalk and pushed his head down while kicking the back of his leg, forcing him to his knees. Glancing to his left, Bishop could see other black men on their knees all the way down the sidewalk.

The police were everywhere. Regular cops and members of Blue Fire. An ambulance arrived. The paramedics hovered over the body lying beside the curb. Detectives were talking to the woman.

"WHAT THE FUCK ARE YOU LOOKING AT?" A fat cop with slick hair barked at Bishop. "KEEP YOUR EYES TO THE FRONT!" The same cop yelled at another brother twenty yards away.

As the commands were being screamed at him, Bishop looked straight ahead, took a deep breath and began to relax, knowing he would survive and wouldn't be murdered, at least not that night, not there, not by those cops. It was still unclear if he were going to get an ass whipping. While considering the possibility of being beaten up, his knees began to hurt from the sidewalk just when he heard another man's voice behind him. Bishop recognized it, but couldn't place it until the voice said, "Uncuff him."

It was Juanita's friend, Lonnie Carlton. One of the cops standing nearby pulled Bishop up, unlocked the handcuffs and turned him around. Lonnie was standing there. He wasn't in the military uniform and ski mask. He wore an expensive suit that smelled of cigar smoke.

"What's going on here, Lonnie?"

"A drive by."

"Do you know who the victim is?"

"Naw. Not yet. Probably some dealer or gangster, it's always the same shit. A lot of them keep apartments for their girlfriends up here. Why are you here, Bishop? You looking for King?"

"Yeah."

"Did you see him?"

"No. I was on the way to the apartment when the gunfire started. I pulled over and took cover."

"Well, he's not there. I checked when I got to the scene."

Lonnie turned to say something to one of the cops watching their little exchange, then turned back to Bishop. "You'd better get out of here. And if you see King, tell him to give me a call."

Lonnie turned away again. Nothing else was said. He just turned and walked back toward the dead body. No comment on the behavior of his officers. No apology. No explanation. As Bishop got in his car to leave, he knew he had to find King.

Juanita's call about her son, the open door, the note, the attack, and the appearance of the police–especially Lonnie Carlton–were all too coincidental. Instinctively, Bishop knew something was wrong. Terribly wrong.

I have been warred against
and have waged war.
I have faced and fought
fierce enemies.
I've bled and died
in the lands of strangers
and returned home
to live
as a stranger
in the land of my living.
I've returned home to
familiar battlegrounds
again and again
and again.
Darkened by the sun
hardened by war
that always returns to my life
inspite of progress
and promises
and temporary peace
there has never been a truce
for me
there has never been
a time
when my existence was not
challenged
no cease fire is called
on my behalf.
The siege that masquerades
as misunderstanding
continues
generation after generation
after
generation

CHAPTER FIVE

Driving out of King's neighborhood, Bishop thought about Lonnie Carlton and the first time they were introduced at the reception where he also met Juanita King. At that time, he was sure he wouldn't like Lonnie and there were a whole list of reasons why. First and probably the main reason, he was with Juanita and his continuing presence in her life interrupted Bishop's dreams just as he had interrupted Bishop's first conversation with her.

Second, he was a cop. Until they met, Bishop's contact with the police was always based upon some kind of unpleasant business or unwanted confrontation. Dealing with traffic tickets, getting one of his students or their relatives out of jail, or getting pulled over for looking like a suspect was usually the reason for the contact. He generally tried to avoid any interaction with them altogether.

When Bishop was growing up, almost all the police were white. When he returned from the war, the movement to elect African Americans to local offices was sweeping the country. Almost every black mayor elected in the early 70s came in on a promise to hire more black police and to make the force responsive and sensitive to the needs of the community. The promises were repeated in Newark, Detroit, Cleveland, Atlanta, Los Angeles, and dozens of cities all across the country. For a while it seemed as if one of the few tangible results of electing these people was a decrease in police violence against black people. That was twenty years ago and since the black power movement, there have been mayors and black majority on city councils, police chiefs and integration of the police forces.

Bishop remembered listening to Lonnie one night at a party at Juanita's. For some reason, he was trying to explain the dilemma of the African American cop. He was not appealing for sympathy and didn't even seem to want understanding. He just sort of stated his views as a fact and didn't give a fuck if people liked them or not. It was the first time Bishop heard him talk about who he was or what he did.

Lonnie argued that night, "I'm telling you, black cops are the only real evidence of the political progress of black people."

Thinking the notion was ridiculous and perhaps Lonnie was a little drunk, Bishop responded, "What about the mayor and all the others who've been elected?"

Lonnie continued his explanation, "Look, out of all the elected and appointed positions, the cops are the only ones with real power. They and they alone hold the power of life and death in their hands and can apply it to anyone, white or black. They and they alone hold the future of the city in their hands.

"Every politician caters to us. Every major criminal wants to bribe us. All the top business leaders need their own private army to keep the masses at bay. We deal with the worse elements of every community. We know the most ruthless inner city gang leaders and their sociopathic killers and the most ruthless north side businessmen and their psychopathic assassins. The cops know the underworld bosses who pull strings silently and we know the politicians who take bribes."

Bishop thought, "Maybe he wasn't drunk."

Lonnie had always been a favorite of the politicians. At one time he headed the mayor's personal security detail. He was the top assistant to the chief of police. Whenever a need arose for a polished, politically savvy cop, they always called Lonnie.

The funny thing was that most black people liked and respected him. He made his reputation twenty years ago as a tough but fair street cop. He took no shit, would lock you up if you broke the law. But if it wasn't too serious, he'd often give you another chance. Lonnie was known to whip some ass on occasion, but folks always said he was justified. Often after kicking your ass, he wouldn't arrest you; he figured the point had been made. He would talk to your kids if they seemed headed for trouble, go get a husband out of the bar and send him home before he drank up his paycheck or make a store owner apologize for disrespecting an elder.

Lonnie joined the police force when he was twenty-one. He'd gone to college for a couple of years and when Sam Packard was elected the city's first black mayor, he applied to the police force when they started recruiting black officers under a court mandate to integrate.

He rose steadily. Affirmative action and his own performance made him a favorite candidate for promotions and a favorite target for resentment from a lot of white officers. He was politically astute and moved amongst the newly elected African American politicians with ease. He understood his role as an example of black political power. He also understood his community's need to be represented on the force. He believed he was part of the progress of his people and this nation.

That was twenty years ago. For the last few years, he had spent most of his time investigating the deaths of young black men and assaults on young black women. The mayor and the chief made him their spokesman and pushed him out front to give press conferences and talks about the war on drugs and how the gangs must be stopped. He also lunched in exquisite restaurants with powerful lawyers who had gotten rich chasing ambulances in poor communities, or doing development deals with the help of city hall or funneling crack money into businesses on the north side and bank accounts in the Caribbean.

He was sickened by what he saw. He was frustrated by how little he could do. He hated them all, the politicians who played the "get elected" game of public pronouncement and lofty promises that produce no results, the gangs who terrorized their own neighborhoods, the lawyers who sipped cocktails at respectable receptions in Armani suits bought with the money paid them by young uneducated crack dealers and the press who sold papers and stereotypes of the black community as some jungle full of animals who should be confined and contained and hopefully locked up and out. He hated them all, and he hated himself for being a part of their bullshit.

Bishop really didn't want to like Lonnie but felt a kinship with him as a fellow warrior. Listening to him at the party that night, he gained a new respect for him but still could not understand the thing between Lonnie and Juanita.

Watching her face as Lonnie talked about the power of the police, puzzled Bishop. She seemed distant and disturbed by his soliloquy. That was the moment when it dawned on him that Juanita always looked at Lonnie with great affection, but there was never any heat in her eyes. Maybe Juanita saw the contradictions and despised them in him. Maybe she saw that he used to be full of hope and tried to use his position to help push his community forward and then became a pawn of the politicians, spending most of his time protecting them and his own position. Maybe she remembered his promises to himself to not become corrupt or callus about his responsibility. Maybe she looked at him and was disgusted by the sight of so many cracks in his armor.

Bishop's reminiscence was interrupted when he remembered that he still hadn't locked King's door. He pulled the car over to the curb to decide what to do. Should he go back to King's apartment, go to Juanita's or go home and get his pistol? The last option sounded more and more sensible. The night was scaring him.

After thinking about it for a minute, he turned the car around and headed back toward King's apartment. It'd only been about fifteen minutes since he had left there and it would take a while longer until the cops were done and the morgue had retrieved the body and taken it away from the scene to prepare it for the morning news. He didn't want any problems. He just wanted to walk into King's building, lock his door and leave. That meant he had to sit tight until they were finished.

Stopping by a diner a couple of blocks from King's apartment, Bishop took a seat in a booth near the back and stared out the window into the street wondering, "Do the people sitting in here know all the shit that just went down a few blocks over? Who are these folks who like to move in the spotlight of street lamps? Aren't they afraid of the criminals who strike in the darkness? Aren't they afraid of the police?" He looked around the diner and saw that it was full of the late crowd, the night workers, the nocturnal creatures like him who loved or hated the darkness and seemed to welcome the hazards of the night.

He observed a young couple squeezed into the same side of one booth sharing a big plate of french fries and a triple decker club sandwich. Bishop caught the woman with her mouth stuffed after taking a bite out of the huge sandwich. She looked slightly embarrassed, then the woman and her boyfriend both burst into laughter. After what just happened on King's street, Bishop welcomed the comic relief. A waitress approached him.

"May I help you, sir?" She pulled a pen from behind her ear and a pad from the pocket on her apron.

"Yes. I'd like a cup of coffee and what kind of desert do you have tonight?"

"The best is peach cobbler."

"All right. I'm going to have some of that."

"You'll like it. Trust me."

The waitress disappeared around the corner to place his order. She was young, like a freshman in college. Her hair was cut real close so her face had no distractions around it. She reminded Bishop of his daughter, Sheila, and it made him miss her. Sheila and Juanita's daughter Carolyn were roommates at Howard University. He wanted to see her and made a mental note to call her.

Four young black men sat in the booth across the aisle. They were very neat in their appearance wearing gray and blue business suits, and they had a kind of corporate nasal tone in their voices that so many young brothers assumed while trying to assimilate. Their Young Republican conversation got louder and slid over to Bishop's table.

A dark brother with some kind of texturizer in his hair said, "Affirmative action programs are not needed any longer. We've got to stop expecting handouts and special treatment."

The chubby guy next to him replied, "You weren't saying that a couple of years ago when you wanted that contract with the state."

"A couple of years ago I needed that contract..."

Their conversation continued on in circles, extolling the virtues of Republicanism and detailing the failings of black businesses. Bishop's dessert and coffee arrived. Sugar and caffeine sped him away from their conversation. The waitress was right. The cobbler was good.

After forty-five minutes at the diner, Bishop drove back to King's apartment and parked right in front of the building. The authorities were wrapping up. The hearse from the county morgue passed by as he drove down the street. The few remaining cops stood around talking. There were no signs of Lonnie, but Bishop waited in the car just to check everything out. He couldn't break the old habits developed from being in a war and living in the city.

After assuring himself that Lonnie was not there and that there was no imminent danger, he grabbed King's key and headed for the building. The cops were getting in their cars and driving away. One of the white cops gave Bishop a hard look as he pulled off. It was the Officer Friendly look that all black men know. The "I can fuck you up" look. The "I am in charge of the plantation" look. Bishop kept walking.

As Bishop climbed the stairs to King's second floor apartment, the alarms started screaming in his head again. Turning around sharply to see if there was someone behind him, he found no one, but the anxiety intensified. He looked up the stairs. Nothing. Hurrying to King's door, he reached out to lock it and discovered that it was slightly opened. At that moment he realized he should have passed on the peach cobbler and gone to get his gun.

Bishop pushed the door open and peeked inside the dark room There were no sounds or signs of movement inside. Waiting in the silence of the hallway, his heart beating like a Max Roach solo, he knew that he couldn't leave the apartment open and couldn't call the police without them asking why he was there. He had to go in and see who or what had been or was inside.

Slipping his jacket off and letting it slide quietly to the floor, Bishop removed his belt and wrapped it around his fist with the large silver buckle dangling loose. He waited, listened, then crouched down and moved into the living room closing the door behind him. He closed his eyes for a few seconds to adjust to the darkness while listening intently. Still dead silence. He moved low to the ground from one room to another. Still nothing. There was no one in there. He turned the lights on and looked around for signs until he saw one in the bathroom. There was another note lying on the sink. It looked identical to the previous one.

Gone to watch the game.

King must have been there since he'd left. It was his handwriting. The note wasn't in the bathroom the first time. Questions flew around in Bishop's mind. Why did he leave the door open? Why leave this cryptic note? What was going on? The silence was disturbed by a soft sound that put the questions on hold when he realized he hadn't locked the door and someone was turning the knob. Bishop grabbed the note, turned off the lights and crouched low to the floor, preparing to strike when the light from the hallway fell into the living room.

"Bishop." The familiar voice again. It was Lonnie Carlton.

"Bishop, I know you're here."

Lonnie stood cautiously in the doorway and Bishop focused on his silhouetted hands trying to determine if his gun was drawn. It didn't look like it and Bishop called out, "Lonnie."

Bishop had called his name before revealing himself to avoid becoming a statistic. He didn't want to startle Lonnie by standing up abruptly. Lonnie turned toward his voice as Bishop turned on the light and they faced each other, anticipating the questions and answers that would fly between them.

"Bishop, I was waiting for you to come back."

"What do you mean you were waiting for me?"

They did not move. Lonnie glanced quickly and casually at Bishop's hands and noted the belt still wrapped around his fist.

Glancing at Lonnie's hands too, Bishop saw that in the dark he had been mistaken. Now, in the light, it was obvious that Lonnie did have something in his hand. He was cupping it, partially concealing it, but it was definitely a gun—a derringer. What they called a drop gun in the community. It was the kind of weapon that some cops carried in case they shot someone without justification and needed a self-defense alibi.

They waited for the questions and answers to start dancing between them. There was a fierceness in Lonnie's eyes. Years of deadly confrontations on the streets, of interrogations, of politics at city hall had taught him to look at another man with such intensity that he could read whether the man was weak or strong, an ally or a foe, passive or aggressive. He stared at Bishop and was astonished to find the same eyes looking back at him.

Lonnie's tone was calm and even. "I knew you'd come back looking for King."

"Is he in trouble?"

"We all are."

Bishop's eyes darted down to the small gun in Lonnie's hand then back up to meet his eyes. Lonnie was aware that his answer had unnerved Bishop. Used to interrogations and mind games, danger and murder, Lonnie could see the power shifting his way as he prepared for the attack. Bishop felt the need to place them back on even footing. He had to go on the offensive.

"Lonnie, where'd you get the note?"

A faint smile crossed Lonnie's lips for a fraction of a second before he caught it and pulled it back in. That hint of a smile made Bishop realize he'd made a mistake. The note must have been the same one that was in King's apartment earlier. One of the cops who searched him must have taken it and given it to Lonnie. Bishop had been so caught up in what was happening on the street that he didn't even notice it was gone.

"Is that what you came back for?" Lonnie asked.

"I came back looking for King and saw that his door was open."

"I left it open for you."

Lonnie's words hung in the room. He walked over to the window and studied something on the street for a minute as he placed the small pistol back in a holster inside his belt. Bishop knew his movement was obviously for dramatic effect, so he waited to allow him to present the full performance.

Lonnie turned from the window and looked at Bishop again. "I've got to talk to King. He could be in great danger and Juanita has asked me to find him."

Bishop let the belt uncoil from around his fist and began pulling it through the loops on his pants. "What kind of danger?"

"I'll tell you later. But right now, I need you to tell me where King is."

Bishop fastened the buckle of the belt and said, "Lonnie, what are you talking about? I don't know where King is."

"Well then, you'll have to come with me."

It was a threat. A threat made more potent because he didn't specify where they were going. Bishop's options were limited. Attack him and risk getting shot. Wait until they were outside and try to run. Again, risk getting shot. Continue to plead ignorance when it was clear that he wasn't. They both knew there were no real choices. He had to go with Lonnie and play out the hand.

Outside the apartment, Lonnie picked the jacket up off the floor while Bishop locked the door. They walked down the stairs and out into the street where Bishop saw the silhouettes of two cops in an unmarked police car double parked next to his Volvo. Instructing him to follow them, Lonnie got in the lead car with the two silhouettes and pulled off. As Bishop followed them, in his rear view mirror he noticed another car with four more figures pulling in behind him, and thought, "Lonnie is very good at his job."

CHAPTER SIX

The three-car caravan drove out of King's neighborhood, through downtown and into the streets surrounding Frederick Douglass High. Bishop's uneasiness grew with his curiosity as the street lights became fewer and dimmer and the street sounds increased when they drove deeper into the community where he taught. He wondered why Lonnie had brought him there.

The late busses rolled, making their occasional stops to drop off the tired bodies of those working the late shift. Sirens from police cars and fire trucks wailed under the dim lights, sometimes close, sometimes distant. Children who should be home roamed the streets weaving their way in and out of danger and adventure, while avoiding the drug addicts and running errands for the drug dealers. Sisters with a few hours before they had to get their young ready for school talked to white men from the suburbs looking for an exotic but cheap good time.

The door to the all night store with dusty cans and fresh prices opened and shut relentlessly. The man the kids called Homeless John guarded it and collected coins for doing windows or dispensing advice or greeting people with a smile. Music boomed from the confined spaces young people control as they rolled by. Occasional gunfire pierced the air. From the cracks in the concrete came voices screaming and whispering, begging and commanding, inquiring and answering, moaning and laughing. The sounds and the rhythms of the inner city were rising up around them.

They drove until they reached the edge of George Washington Homes, the most notorious housing project in the city. Behind those walls, the average age of a grandmother was 29. The average age of a mother with more than one child was 16. The women outnumbered the men 10 to 1. The unemployment rate (if you exclude drug-related work and other illegal activity) was 85 percent, and 75 percent of the males dropped out of school by the eleventh grade. It had the most concentrated violence of any place in the city. Shootings, stabbings and assaults took place there on a daily basis. No newspapers or packages were delivered there, but the coroner came often. It was six blocks north and south and twelve blocks east and west. Fifteen thousand people packed in, cut off and too often cut down. At that time of night it appeared quiet. The residents had their lights off and their children slept on the floor away from the windows. It was off limits to anyone who wasn't recognized at the gates of that ghetto kingdom. Even the police wouldn't go in there without an escort or permission from the king.

The monarch of that misery was Catrell Merit, the leader of the Egyptian Cobras. The Cobras had controlled George Washington Homes for more than nine years. They began as a small group of thirteen-to-fifteen-year-old teenagers who ran together for safety and salvation. They fought other gangs, out maneuvered the police, buried their friends and found ways to make money and to take money. They grew older, stronger, smarter, slicker and further away from the hopes of their parents and their people.

They made babies and made bail. They accumulated reputations and police records. They gained momentum, gathered guns and gave up on ever getting out of George Washington Homes or the life that demanded change or sacrifice at an early age. Eventually, the Egyptian Cobras got strong enough to drive all the rival gangs out. They began dealing drugs and death and ruled George Washington Homes with corporate efficiency and military effectiveness.

Years ago Bishop had the chance to briefly interact with Catrell. He had him for a student for about six weeks. When he was in the eleventh grade. Catrell had dropped out once before but decided to return. After about eight weeks that decision was altered when someone walked up on him in government class and shot him in the back. The young man who shot him was trying to make a name for himself with a rival gang, but instead wound up dead in a dumpster in back of the school. Catrell survived the shooting but never returned to class.

The rise of Catrell Merit and the Egyptian Cobras happened in the shadow of City Hall. You could look out the window of the mayor's office and see the brick wall that closed off the back of Washington Homes. It was a wall that ran six blocks from north to south. The city built it five years earlier under the premise that it was a sound barrier for a parkway that would pass behind the project. It was supposed to be a wall to protect the Washington Homes residents from the sounds of a parkway that was never built. A wall to protect them from the sounds of progress that never came.

When the wall began to go up, there was an outcry from concerned community residents, those in Washington Homes and those outside. The plan had never been presented to the people it would affect. They just saw the construction crews pulling in and the wall going up. The mayor assured everyone that it was for the good of the community. After all, he had only been elected for one term and had served the community well since taking office.

Near the end of his first term, the parkway was the cornerstone of his economic development package for the city. The parkway would be a direct route to the suburbs where most of the light industry and new offices had relocated. He said he was determined that the residents of his city, particularly those in the inner city, had access to those jobs. The parkway would have excellent bus service. There was even talk of a light rail system running alongside it. They would have access to the suburban jobs and he would ensure that some of the new industry located inside the city limits.

His performance was classic, his words spoken with a preacher's eloquence and a politician's evasiveness. He told the community how his first term had been a fight to extend black political control over the city. He had appointed a new black police chief and 60 percent of the department heads were now black. Minority contractors did business with the city and standing next to him were five of the most successful black business leaders who had become rich doing business in his first term. When it was their turn to talk, the community was assured that they would be instrumental in building the parkway and in becoming partners in the new industries that were coming to the city. They lied. The parkway was never built and the only people who benefited from the wall were the contractors who built it and Catrell Merit.

When the wall went up five years ago, Catrell was twenty-three. He attended the community meetings with the mayor and sat attentively, studying, watching, analyzing. Members of the community thought it was good that one of the young men from the neighborhood was interested in the issue. They all knew Catrell as the leader of the Egyptian Cobras. They feared him, but his presence at the meetings made them cautiously hopeful that he was rejoining them and abandoning his life of crime.

A young, community-based minister, Reverand Langston Canada, was the spokesperson and principal organizer for the opposition to the wall. He always made a point of talking to Catrell and they became friends. Back then, Catrell even went to his small storefront church with the black Jesus, African icons and liberation theology. It was located in the heart of the black community and served as a place of worship and a community center.

When the Reverand Canada led a demonstration outside the mayor's office in opposition to the wall, Catrell brought scores of his troops out to the picket lines. It was the first and only time that Catrell thought it was possible that the people from his neighborhood might get the attention of the politicians peacefully.

When the fight was lost and the wall was installed in spite of the com-

35

munity's wishes, Catrell and the Egyptian Cobras had no more illusions about the government's concern for inner city black folk and they became even more aggressive in their domination of George Washington Homes. Rev. Canada tried to talk to Catrell about the immorality of dealing drugs and was told he would make his way to heaven quickly if he ever brought his ass back down there. Frustrated and disillusioned, he left the little storefront and now pastors a huge 2000 seat church on the north side with a flock that worships his words and pays him a nice salary.

Catrell Merit understood that the defeat of the community meant that the mayor had just given him complete control of his kingdom. The way Catrell read it, the move to build the wall was an acknowledgment that a large segment of the black community was uneducated or undereducated and therefore unable to meet the demands of the new technological workplaces. The manufacturing jobs that used to sustain the black community had gone to the third world and it was time for a new era in America's relationship with its dark children. Close them off, contain them and hide their wretched souls behind a concrete wall.

George Washington Homes was the first place that the mayor had abandoned. Ironically, it was also the precinct that had given him a narrow margin of victory in his first election. He abandoned it right after the parkway fiasco. Catrell and the Cobras became too powerful and the cost of running them out of Washington Homes was deemed too expensive. It would require massive amounts of police funds allocated to an ongoing assault on the drug trafficking by the Cobras. The financial cost would be high and the human cost would be just as high. Surely the Cobras would kill some cops in the process. They would not give it up peacefully.

Even if the city succeeded in closing them down, Catrell would just adapt to the new environment. He would be back in a few weeks, perhaps months. But he would be back, in control, and the mayor would look like a fool because he would have lost after lofty promises, millions of dollars and the lives of at least a few cops.

Catrell hated the mayor and his cronies because they victimized people in slick and subtle ways, while portraying themselves as saviors because they'd joined an all-white country club or dined with the governor or some other shit that had no relevance to people forced to live in Washington Homes or other places like it.

Catrell hated their hypocrisy. He was branded a public enemy, a drug dealer, a murderer, a criminal who corrupted his own community and sold out the lives of his own people. But the politicians who danced and dined and did their deeds selling out the lives of their people behind a wall of lies were applauded.

Catrell hated them when he sent drugs or women to the private parties of the powerful. He despised them when they accepted his campaign contributions. He hated their respectability because he knew they were just like him and in other circumstances he could have been respectable. He could even have been the mayor.

Bishop leaned his head against the headrest and contemplated the consequences of sitting outside the stronghold of the Egyptian Cobras with the police. He wasn't sure why they were there, but he knew it was not healthy to be seen with the police. Across the asphalt filled with broken glass, he saw into a dark, narrow alley that led into the projects. Lonnie was talking to his men. The four cops in the second police car did not move. Just past the opening of the alley, shadows shifted.

Lonnie tapped on Bishop's window, gesturing for him to get out. They stood shoulder to shoulder in the street leaning against the car, looking into the alley. Lonnie took out an expensive lighter, struck it and sucked on his cigar drawing the fire into the tobacco and blowing the smoke out of his mouth.

"Lonnie, what's going on?" Bishop looked over at the alley, hoping no one would take a shot at the cops while he was standing there.

Lonnie puffed on the cigar and said, "I need you to do me a favor."

A sly, wicked smile crossed Lonnie's face. Bishop wondered if he'd heard him right. "What's the favor?"

With his index finger wrapped around the cigar, Lonnie pointed with his other fingers across to the alley. The smell of piss from the hallways and garbage from the alley mixed with the cigar smoke and filled their nostrils with a decaying stench. The darkness down that corridor called up bad memories. The shadows shifted back and forth and seemed to multiply as Bishop stared into the darkness.

"I've got to get to King." Lonnie pointed toward the projects. "Someone over there might know where he is."

Bishop looked at Lonnie then back at the alley. "What makes you think that?"

"Just a hunch."

"You have to come better than that, Lonnie."

"It's just a hunch." Lonnie replied and sucked on the cigar. "You know, cop intuition."

"Naw, I don't know," Bishop, said. "I think you're bullshittin' me."

"Come on, help me out."

"What do you want with King?"

"I just want to talk to him."

"About what?"

"I can't tell you right now, but if you don't help me there will be consequences."

Bishop moved off the car and turned to face Lonnie who continued smoking. Bishop held up two fingers, aimed them at Lonnie and said, "That's the second time you've threatened me."

Lonnie lowered the cigar, flicked the ashes into the street and met Bishop's gaze. Bishop's eyes showed the kind of wildness that Lonnie had seen in men who had no fear. He knew that he and Bishop were becoming trapped, locked in that space where men can not or will not back down from confrontation. For the second time that night, they stood inches from each other, inches away from something that didn't need to happen. Bishop and Lonnie weren't friends, but they had known each other for years and there was mutual respect. Maybe the tension had always been just beneath the surface. Perhaps it was because they both wanted the same woman. Maybe it was just the growing sense that something terrible was happening to King and they both felt powerless to help him. Whatever it was, they had placed themselves in familiar but hazardous territory.

Lonnie dropped the cigar in the street and started grinding it with his heel. "This ain't about threatening you. It's about finding King."

"Is that right?" Bishop kept his eyes on Lonnie, measuring him, becoming acutely aware of the distance between them.

Lonnie looked up from the crushed cigar and replied, "Yeah. That's right."

They read each other's eyes for a few seconds, both realizing that this was the moment that they could back off without losing face.

Bishop took the initiative to ease the tension. He took a step back from Lonnie, looked back over toward the projects and said, "And you think he's in there?"

"I think somebody in there knows where he is."

"Why me? Why do you want me to go in there?"

"King trusts you." Lonnie looked at Bishop and chuckled. "Besides, everybody around here knows you're the teacher so you're relatively safe."

"You are so full of shit." Bishop walked toward the middle of the street then turned back toward Lonnie. "What do you want me to say if I see him?"

"Tell him to call me. That's all. Just tell him to call me."

Bishop thought about King's note. *Gone to watch the game.*

It suddenly occurred to him why King would go there if he was in some kind of danger and needed to hide. It was the only place that the kids at the school said a black man controlled the game. George Washington Homes belonged to Catrell. It was his kingdom and everyone in the city, black or white, poor or powerful, knew it. Catrell and the Egyptian Cobras owned George Washington Homes and from there ran most of the drug trade in the city. Everyone knew it. The mayor, the chief of police, the DEA and the other federal agencies, the local newspapers and television stations all knew it, yet no one stopped it.

Catrell was arrested twice and beat both charges. He was tried and acquitted on a murder charge and then a racketeering charge. During his first arrest, the city's business paper did a story on him. It detailed his empire of stores, nightclubs, strip joints, limousine companies and car washes. It also printed his arrest record and talked about his violent past and continuing leadership of the Egyptian Cobras. It discussed his intelligence and how tragic it was that a young man so obviously gifted would be on trial for murder and the reputed head of a multi-million dollar drug kingdom. The journalist who wrote the story was shot in the face the day after it was published. There was no story in the newspaper when he was arrested the second time, only a mention on page twenty-eight that he had been taken into custody and charged with racketeering.

Although Catrell was an outlaw, he was also a powerful ally. He could provide protection for King and he had an army that could wage war if necessary. Bishop wondered why King needed the protection of Catrell Merit. He had Lonnie and he was also a powerful ally.

39

The day I told my parents I had been drafted and was going to the war, my mother listened to my father trying to persuade me not to. She sat still except for the movement of her hands that folded and unfolded a napkin she used to dry her tears while watching the effect of his words. She studied my face and read my eyes as she'd done my entire life. It was already clear to her I wasn't going to try to avoid the draft. She stopped crying. When my father finished talking, he looked at my mother and spoke that silent language that couples speak when they've loved each other and lived together for years. Her face told him he had failed to convince me. He walked across the room, touched my shoulder lovingly and left to walk with the spirits. My mother came to me, kissed my face and sat on the arm of the chair. I leaned my head against her and she whispered a secret of her sisters.

"For hundreds of years, every time our sons leave home, black mothers fear the violence will steal them. In the war, I can't reach you. I can't protect you. There will be no mothers there to save you and your brothers."

CHAPTER SEVEN

Lonnie didn't know for sure if King was in George Washington Homes, but Bishop knew. He could feel it. King was there because he needed protection and it was the one place that no one could get to him unless he wanted them to and no one could get inside George Washington Homes unless the Cobras allowed it or they brought an army.

Bishop took one last look at Lonnie and started walking toward the alley without saying another word. The note had been a sign. King wanted him to know where to find him. He entered the darkness of that narrow opening and walked maybe ten steps when a voice spoke to him from the shadows.

"Mr. Bishop, do not turn around, drop your keys and keep walking straight then turn left into the first alley."

Bishop was right. He was asked to come. King was there and expected him. It was safe. For the time being. He dropped his keys, heard them bounce on the concrete and kept walking. He hadn't planned to turn around anyway. He didn't want to reveal anything to Lonnie or his men. They were watching him. They measured his movement, smelling the footprints being left in the dark.

Bishop reached the end of the street and saw a narrow opening on his left with dumpsters overflowing with garbage on both sides. Turning into it, he heard the sound of automatic weapon fire and the screeching of tires. Looking back toward the street, he saw Lonnie and his men speed off under a barrage of gunshots. No one was hit. It was just a warning that they were a little too close. The thought of them running for cover made Bishop chuckle. He proceeded into the alley and hadn't gone more than five steps when he heard another voice.

"Mr. Bishop, follow me."

A shadow came to life and a small youthful body came out from behind a dumpster. He was covered in clothes too large for him, with a dark hood pulled over his head. By the sound of his voice, his height and size, he couldn't be more than twelve or thirteen. It reminded Bishop of the youth of Viet Nam. It reminded him that too often children are the soldiers.

Further down the alley the young boy stopped abruptly. Bishop listened and looked for the danger signs. The boy seemed completely still. Then, with just the slightest movement he slid into the shadows near the wall. Bishop mirrored his movement, staying close enough to grab him if needed, though hoping he wouldn't have to. There was an almost certain chance that under those baggy clothes was a weapon capable of swift slaughter. They reached the wall and sat down on their haunches. It was time to wait in the darkness.

They didn't wait long. Shadows started to move in the alley. One, then two, three, four, many. They were the Egyptian Cobras. They came from all sides, stopped at various positions and waited. Bishop studied their placement and realized they were tactically deployed and had set up a perfect crossfire zone. They controlled the alley from every angle. Someone knew what they were doing. Fascinated, he sat still, watched and didn't panic. Yet.

To the Cobras who filled the alley, his presence seemed unimportant. No one said anything. They were perfectly still and maintained their positions. Some distance away you could hear the fluttering of the ghetto bird, Ice Cube's term for a police helicopter. In that part of town it was so commonplace that it didn't even warrant notice. He wondered how many of the faces hidden in the darkness were his current or former students. How many of their faces would be seen in a casket soon? How many of their mothers would weep for their lost sons?

There was a sudden tension amongst the Cobras. Bishop couldn't see their faces, making it difficult to read their reactions. Footsteps echoed against the concrete. Several people were running. A voice seemed to be whispering behind him. No, two voices. He turned slowly to see them. Their faces were hidden but he knew one of them was King.

King moved toward Bishop quickly, took him by the arm and pulled him toward an opening in one of the buildings. It was completely black inside. He couldn't see anything and King told him to stay still for a moment. He was temporarily blinded by a flash of light. As his eyes adjusted he saw that they were in what looked like a storage room. There was nothing special about it except the walls were completely black and so were the windows, the ceiling and the floor. King stood in front of him and Bishop was relieved to see that he was all right. They grabbed each other by the right hand, pulled close and embraced like brothers. When they stepped back, King looked at his mentor and said, "Bishop, I'm in trouble."

His words had rushed out like a wave of disaster, causing a surge of panic in Bishop that required him to take a deep breath before responding. "Tell me what's happening."

TAT-TAT-TAT-TAT-TAT-TAT-TAT-TAT-TAT-TAT-TAT!!!!

The words were barely out of his mouth when automatic gunfire seemed to come from all directions, crashing into concrete, glass, wood and probably flesh. They both fell to the floor. King made it to the wall and cut off the lights. It was pitch black inside when the gunfire stopped as suddenly as it started. The silence was eerie, deadly. It was the shit Bishop hated.

They lay still listening to the sound of the ghetto bird's propeller getting closer. A sliver of light came into the room, sliding underneath the door when the helicopter trained its spotlight on the alley.

In the darkness Bishop whispered, "King, what the fuck is going on?"

"I don't know. We've got to get out of here."

TAT-TAT-TAT-TAT-TAT!!!

Gunfire erupted again. The light disappeared. The sound of the helicopter got further away. The door to the room flew open. A voice in the darkness shouted, "King! Follow me." They both scrambled to their feet and out the door running behind another young Cobra wearing a black hooded sweatshirt.

They ran through the alley and into a door leading down into the basement of one of the dozens of tenement buildings. They ran in darkness over glass and dog shit and old cans. They heard rats scurrying, saw Cobras running past them and heard more gunfire. Their guide stopped at a door leading to the basement of another building. King stepped through the door and Bishop started to follow, but the guide put a hand on his chest stopping him. It was a small but strong hand, a woman's hand. He was surprised because he had assumed the guide was male.

King turned to him, shook his hand and said, "I'll be in touch with you, Bishop. Tell my mother I'm all right. Don't worry, my friends will get you out of here safely." And then he was gone into the darkness.

Bishop didn't have time to respond to his words. The young woman grabbed his arm, turned him to the right and started running again. They ran through a maze of rooms and interconnecting tunnels underneath the buildings of George Washington Homes. He'd seen tunnels like these before in Vietnam and he knew whoever was chasing them would never catch those young people down there. Never.

She led him to a doorway that opened out into a small alley. The alley was only thirty yards long and ended at the wall. She pointed to the wall and through the darkness he saw another shadow gesturing, beckoning him to come.

He looked back at the young woman whose face he could barely make out by the light from the broken street lamp. Studying her face for a few seconds, his mind searched for the connection to her familiar features. He was either too tired, it was too dark or his mind was too overloaded with all the events of the night, but he could not remember who she was. As he turned to go, she spoke for the first time.

"Mr. Bishop...you were my favorite teacher."

He looked at her again and she was smiling but holding her head downward. Bishop recognized her. It was Cora Davis, a tremendously gifted student who had gotten pregnant when she was fifteen and had a little girl. Her academic life came to a halt because the principal at the time was embarrassed by young people like Cora. He convinced her to leave Frederick Douglass High. He drove Cora and many like her out of the school.

Disturbed by the memories, Bishop tried to smile back at Cora when he said, "Thanks, Cora. You were a good student."

He wished he had something more to tell her. He'd heard that she was lost, that she had three children now and wasn't even nineteen, that she had been on welfare for several years, sometimes sold herself for extra money and was a runner for the Egyptian Cobras.

Bishop looked at the young woman again, put his hand on her shoulder and said, "Thanks for helping me out. You take care of yourself."

With her head still lowered, Cora raised her eyes and looked at Bishop's face. "I'll try, Mr. Bishop."

He turned away and ran towards the wall and away from the gunfire echoing off the buildings of George Washington Homes and away from the thought of Cora Davis having the future stomped out of her young life. At the wall a young man led him to a hole that was just large enough to get through on all fours. Going through the wall and standing up on the other side, he saw his Volvo parked a few feet away. Relief. He stumbled to the car, opened the door and saw his keys and an envelope lying on the driver's seat. The night had been an almost unbelievable whirlwind of events. He fell behind the wheel completely confused and wondered, "What just happened?"

CHAPTER EIGHT

For the first time in hours, Bishop noticed how late it was as he drove away from George Washington Homes. It was 4 a.m., he was dead tired and his knees were really aching. He felt as if he'd been kneeling and crawling on concrete all night.

He couldn't go home. Lonnie or one of his men would probably be there waiting for him and he didn't want to deal with that yet. He needed to get in touch with Juanita, but couldn't go there either, right then. He decided to go to a hotel, get some sleep and figure out what to do next.

Bishop drove to the airport just outside the city and checked into a motel. While undressing, he discovered his knees were not only aching from being on the concrete but there were several cuts on his legs and his pants were stained with blood. Luckily, there was a gym bag in the trunk of the car with some sweats and toiletries in it. Dragging his tired ass back out to the car was not an appealing thought, but he'd need the clothes in the morning.

He put the blood-stained pants back on, retrieved the gym bag from the car and stopped by the vending machine to get a Coke. Back in the room, he stripped, stepped into a hot shower and thought about the bed waiting for him in the other room. He stood there and let the hot water run down on him, washing away the blood, soothing the aching muscles of his middle-aged body.

After standing in the shower for thirty minutes, Bishop threw his body on the not so firm bed. He looked at the unopened enveloped, thought about the shit that had brought him there and as he closed his eyes whispered, "Daylight will arrive soon. Thank God."

When King was a in high school, Catrell was already established in Washington Homes. Only twenty-two, Catrell was the rising star of the street idols. He was revered by young men who felt his power as they watched him impose his control over the local drug trade. He was reviled by many older people who saw him poison their children. He was worshiped by young sisters who wanted to be rescued and taken away from welfare and to a life on the other side of the wall. He was wanted by the police who tried but couldn't stop his reign.

Years ago he moved out of George Washington Homes into an expensive penthouse apartment in midtown. He dressed in exquisite clothes, always had his shoes shined and was groomed perfectly. He was meticulous in his appearance, never wore gaudy jewelry and if you saw him you would assume he was just a successful young lawyer or businessman. But the most outstanding thing people noticed about Catrell Merit was that there was always a book with him. All kind of books. History, business, fiction, poetry, science. It didn't matter what the subject was. Everything seemed to interest him.

Billy King walked by or through George Washington Homes every day. He had many friends and classmates who lived there and his house was just down the street. Like everyone else, he knew Catrell's reputation. King was never afraid of George Washington Homes because he was a fearless child and because he had visited and played with friends there all of his life. He grew up in the shadow of the wall surrounded by constant reminders that he was just one step away from the same kind of confinement, the same kind of imprisonment that trapped so many of his friends. He saw no difference in himself and those who had to live there. It was just circumstance–not some mark of shame–or destiny.

Destiny. Is that what brought two of the brightest young men in that neighborhood together? Destiny. No one could explain in any other way why two of the strongest would become so close to each other yet so different in how they faced a world that hated the fact that they even existed. Destiny. That would have to do as an explanation.

During his senior year at a local college, King heard that Catrell had met his sister, Carolyn, at the mall and was interested in her. She was sixteen, seven years younger than King, and looked almost exactly like Juanita, except she didn't have dread locks. Instead, she had her hair cut in a short stylish way like many of her classmates. She was free and bright and completely aware of the power she had as a young woman who was beautiful and intelligent.

She carried herself in a way that made her physical appearance seem incidental because she always commanded attention with the power of her tremendous intellect. Catrell's interest in her was made at least mildly alluring because she was curious about the world outside her neighborhood and the world of powerful and fearless young men she saw in her neighborhood. Her brother, who had behaved like a man for as long as she could remember, and Lonnie Carlton, her mother's lover, were both smart and streetwise. The fact that Catrell reminded her of these two men made his interest more fascinating.

She was mature enough, even at sixteen, to understand that Catrell, a grown man, leader of the Egyptian Cobras, wasn't a likely date for the prom and probably would not be in her future. She was also immature enough to underestimate the danger of playing in an alien world. She liked Catrell. She was drawn to his power and impressed by the treatment he received in the neighborhood.

The day she met him it was like meeting a movie star. She worked at a men's boutique in the mall and was closing up one Saturday when he came into the shop. She thought he was beautiful. Tall, with smooth dark skin, he wore a dark blue suit, the whitest shirt she'd ever seen and a red tie that made you notice the rich texture of his dark skin. He had two small, gold hoops in each ear, short hair and a walk that was so confident you would think he ruled the earth. He reminded her of Michael Jordan.

"You aren't closed, are you?" Catrell asked.

She thought, "He sounds like Michael Jordan, too." Carolyn soaked up the rich bass sound of his voice like something warm had just rained down on her.

Catrell walked toward the cash register where Carolyn stood staring at him. "Excuse me." He asked again, "Are you closed?"

"No...yes...I mean it's time to close but officially we don't close for another five minutes." She picked up an already folded sweater and refolded it.

Catrell asked, "You mind if I look around for five minutes?"

"Not at all. Take your time. Please." Carolyn tried not to smile too broadly but found herself unable to avoid it.

Catrell smiled back and said, "Thanks. Just let me know when you're ready for me to leave." He walked over toward the Armani and Hugo Boss suits hanging on the rack.

Carolyn tried to go about her work, tidying up the store, refolding merchandise, closing out one of the two cash registers. Catrell left the suits and tried to check out the shirts stacked neatly against the wall. He caught her watching him as he moved from one side of the store to the other. She caught him pretending to look at the sweaters while he was looking at her.

She finally gave up pretending and stopped busying herself. She stood at the counter and stared at him. He finally stopped pretending to shop and came back to the counter.

Looking deep into her eyes, Catrell said, "I keep trying to figure out where I know you from."

"I don't think I've ever met you," Carolyn replied, smiling again.

Catrell's hands moved through the air in smooth gestures that reinforced what he was saying. "You're right, but I think I've seen you before."

"I don't know. Maybe." She turned to pick up the sweater she was folding a while ago.

Catrell watched her then asked, "Where do you live?"

"Over by Douglass High." She looked at the sweater to keep from looking at him.

"That's it." Catrell pointed his finger at her and smiled. "You're King's sister, aren't you?"

She looked up at him and said, "You know my brother?"

"I know who he is." He extended his hand to her while looking at her in a way that none of the boys she knew ever did. "My name is Catrell. Catrell Merit."

She took his hand and shook it firmly. "I'm Carolyn King." And that was the beginning.

At first, nothing happened. He gave her a ride home from work, well, almost home because she had him drop her around the corner so the neighbors wouldn't tell Juanita. They talked on the phone a couple of times, and for the first couple of weeks there were no real dates or physical intimacy.

Catrell really liked Carolyn. She was smart and he liked the fact that she was unafraid of him. He actually thought she was unafraid of anything. He knew that if he had a different kind of life, he would want to be with a girl like that. He was drawn to her, yet kept his distance most of the time because he knew if he didn't he would want to be with her all of the time. After six weeks of stopping by her job occasionally, after calling her once or twice, and on those occasions talking to her for hours, after giving her a ride home a couple more times, he wanted to see this girl, this young woman, this bright, beautiful, female spirit.

It was whispered amongst the girls in school at first. "Carolyn is Catrell Merit's girlfriend." They didn't ask her directly in the beginning. Bishop heard it in the bits and pieces of rumors that drifted into the places where the teachers hung out. He didn't have to rely on rumor. He had a source that would know the facts. He'd been a single parent for eleven years and his daughter, Sheila, had been best friends with Carolyn since eighth grade. He asked her about the rumors at dinner one night.

"What's this I hear about Carolyn and Catrell Merit?" Bishop asked in an off-handed way while continuing to eat.

Sheila took a bite of snapper, looked at her father with a puzzled expression and said, "What?"

"You know what." Bishop looked across the table at his daughter and frowned. "There's a rumor that she's his girlfriend."

"It ain't that deep. She just hangs out with him sometime."

"Does she know who Catrell is?"

She sucked her teeth and made a face like the question was stupid. "Everybody knows."

Bishop became alarmed by the casualness of her answers. "Well, what do you think, Sheila? Don't you feel like it's dangerous for Carolyn to be going out with the head of the Egyptian Cobras?"

"Daddy, a lot of girls at school go out with Cobras. I don't see why it's a big deal."

Sheila recognized the look on her father's face and realized she was treading close to an inquiry about her own choices in young men. "No, I don't think she should be dating Catrell. I told her that."

Bishop let it drop and started eating again, but wondered how long it would be before King heard about it, and what his reaction would be. He and Carolyn were very close. He wondered if she had told him. Apparently not, because King would have intervened by now.

Carolyn had begun talking to Catrell on a regular basis. She had made him aware of the best times to call her when Juanita would be at work. She cut classes a couple of times to hang out with him. She liked the flirting and the kisses.

Catrell liked her, a lot. More and more time was required to feed his need to see her. She was something special in his life. He needed the light that she brought. He needed this girl who read as many books as he did. He started picking her up or sending someone to pick her up from school or work. He began calling even when Juanita was there. He wanted her to miss whole days of school to be with him. She wouldn't and it made him both proud and

49

disappointed.

The last time they were together, she left school an hour early. He took her to his penthouse on the other side of town. He explained to her that he kept his old apartment in George Washington Homes to do business and run his organization, but this was where he lived, where he liked to relax. He wanted to make love to her. She knew it before they got there and the anticipation both excited and scared her as she looked out his twenty-first floor window overlooking the city.

Maxwell's sweet tenor voice played in the background stroking them. Catrell talked to her. Carolyn talked to him. They both liked that about their relationship. They always talked, seriously, deeply, intimately. He kissed her. She liked his kiss. His heart beat faster. He wanted her. She felt his lust. She kissed him and touched his face and whispered to his eyes how beautiful she thought he was. He touched her breasts and unbuttoned her shirt and kissed her neck and teased her nipples with his tongue.

She told him to hold her and whispered to his ears that she didn't want to make love, not now. He didn't ask for it or try to take it. He held her and kissed her and touched her thighs and she kissed his chest and reached inside his pants and gently touched him and he kissed her neck and her breasts and her stomach and felt her wetness through her panties. For an hour they danced at the edge of intercourse and dreamed of loving each other, knowing every moment was stolen and that they could never be more than what they were right then.

It was not clear when King found out, but that day, the day Catrell touched Carolyn softly and gently in the peace of his penthouse, became a day of decision and destiny. For Carolyn, for King, for Catrell, for Juanita, it became a day of decision and destiny.

When Carolyn got home, King was waiting for her. She was late and someone had told him that she had skipped class to be with Catrell. He confronted her with the concern of an older brother who didn't want to see his baby sister hurt. She told him about her relationship and her feelings for Catrell. She told King that she was in over her head and knew it was time to end it. Carolyn was afraid that Catrell would not let her go and she was confused and didn't want to tell him it was over because she cared so much for him.

King listened and his heart swelled with love for his sister and his mind ached trying to control his emotions. He knew he had to go see Catrell. He knew that his sister, his only sister, his baby sister, could get more than her heart broken. He knew that she was in a relationship that could spin her life into a sea of confrontation and confusion and that she could be killed by just being with Catrell. He knew his own life was about to be put on trial.

King left Carolyn at home with explicit instructions to stay there until their mother got home. Carolyn watched him from their porch as he walked toward George Washington Homes, the kingdom of Catrell Merit and the Egyptian Cobras. She watched him leave and knew her brother might never come back.

King walked through the gates of George Washington Homes and for the first time felt as he was walking through the gates of hell. He walked into Catrell's kingdom and he saw the anticipation of confrontation on the faces of Catrell's men. Some of the Cobras knew him from school or from the neighborhood. Others knew he was Carolyn's brother. They all read his face and knew why he was there. He was stopped twice by groups of these young men. The ones who knew him warned him and told him to go back home. His only response was that he had come to talk to Catrell. It must have been the determination in his eyes, but they finally took him to Catrell, who seemed to be waiting for him.

Catrell told his men to leave them alone when King walked into the room of the apartment that served as the Egyptian Cobras' headquarters. Catrell was sitting behind an old antique desk. King glanced around the room and realized it was furnished with beautiful old furniture, an antique rug and three bronze pieces of African warriors on wooden pedestals. The furniture was the kind King had seen at his grandmother's house. It was strange that the elegant beauty of that apartment sat in the middle of a place where the playground was littered with crack vials, used condoms, beer cans and discarded furniture. It was also strange because there was a peaceful, quieting nature to this apartment with the old furniture and Gangstarr playing on the stereo.

Catrell sat there watching King observe his office. He didn't say anything, he didn't move. He just watched, listened to Guru's rhymes and Premiere's beats and studied the young man whose sister he loved. King didn't say anything either as he turned his attention to Catrell and noticed that they were completely alone. At least none of his men were visible.

As the moment grew longer and the tension grew tighter, the time for confrontation arrived. In what seemed like a choreographed movement, King stepped forward and Catrell stood up. King moved closer and Catrell came around the desk in one long graceful step. Before King could blink, Catrell was standing directly in front of him.

They stood there frozen in the seconds that precede battle. Frozen in those seconds when warriors anticipate attack and evaluate the attacker. King noticed that they were physically about the same size. He was six feet tall and about 175 pounds. His body was hard and athletic. Catrell was about five feet eleven inches and around the same weight. Maybe 180 or 185. King had been in many fights and knew it was basically decided in the first few seconds. He also knew that Catrell had killed men and that this was not just a fight. Someone would die there, that day, and the other might go to jail. Both could be finished, removed from the set forever.

King fought hard to push those thoughts out of his mind remembering how as a young boy his father had told him to avoid all distraction when facing a man in battle. He'd warned that distraction would make you hesitate and hesitation would get you killed. King knew he was being distracted by the possible consequences of this confrontation.

Catrell's life depended upon his ability to read men and dangerous situations. He had been in battle since he was a little boy. He'd grown up in gang fights and learned to wage war. He had killed with a gun and with his hands. He knew the look of fear in a man's eyes. He knew the moment of distraction. He could read a man's mind when he started to think about backing down. Catrell knew that was the moment to strike. He also knew that King was not weak and that he would probably have to kill him.

"I'm in love with Carolyn," Catrell said, breaking the silence.

"But you can't have her, Catrell." King replied sternly. "She can't be with you."

"It's not your call, King."

"Maybe not, but she can't be with you and if I die here she will never be with you."

Catrell's left eyebrow rose slightly then lowered. King had just made an error. King bit down hard, tightening his jaws. He knew it, too. They both understood that King had inadvertently admitted that Catrell would probably win a physical confrontation. Even if King could take him, Catrell's men would not let him win. They were somewhere near. King doubted he would win anyway. Catrell had too much to lose. He could not get his ass kicked by a college student who was upset about Catrell, the leader of the Egyptian

Cobras, seeing his sister. If he lost, he would lose respect and power. King understood the laws of his neighborhood perfectly.

Catrell also knew that King had taken away his power. He was trapped. He, too, had already lost. King was right, if he killed him and he knew that was the only way it could end, he would never have Carolyn. He looked into King's eyes and saw the soul of a prince and knew it would sadden him deeply to take this young man's life and also lose the only woman he ever loved. But he had no choice.

They stood there, within reach of each other, inches from death, waiting, when Carolyn stepped through the door. Catrell saw her first over King's shoulder. King saw Catrell shoot a glance past him. He thought Catrell was signaling one of his men who had slid in behind him. King reacted quickly, instinctively. He grabbed Catrell's shirt with his right hand and fired a wicked punch into his face with his left. Catrell was thrown back against the desk. King's speed and fury surprised Catrell but his instincts and his history responded immediately. Catrell swung his left hand up and over the arm that was pushing him backwards. He brought his elbow down sharply breaking the hold King had on his clothes. King punched him again with his left hand just as Catrell was spinning out from his grip.

Catrell's move caused King's weight to shift and he felt himself falling. He grabbed Catrell's shirt again and felt something crash into the side of his head. The force of it drove him to the floor. He tried to scramble to his feet when he felt it again, this time across his face. He tasted the metal in his mouth and knew Catrell had hit him with a pistol. He tasted blood and saw his own hand folded up under him on the floor. Next he heard that fatal sound, the sound that had become too familiar in his neighborhood. The sound of a bullet sliding into the chamber of a 9mm pistol. He closed his eyes and waited.

"STOP!"

King's head bled into his senses. He was shocked and bewildered as he heard a voice, a command, in the distance. No, it was somewhere close, there, in the room. A voice. A familiar voice. There was also crying and breathing, heavy breathing like an animal. He looked up and saw the barrel of the gun pointed at him and realized the breathing was coming from Catrell. Deep powerful breaths–like fire–were coming from his nostrils.

"STOP!"

Again, the voice. The familiar voice and the command that had flown across the room and allowed him to live a few seconds more. He glanced back toward the door and saw his sister weeping and his mother's outstretched hand floating in the space between her and Catrell. Something in her voice, in her familiar voice, had stopped Catrell from doing what every instinct, every law he lived by, every battle he'd fought, told him to do. He stood there for a moment, breathing, sweating, trying to put his instincts under the control of his mind until he finally stepped back from King and lowered his gun.

Juanita spoke again. "Catrell, I've come for my children."

He knew who she was the instant he had heard her voice. Catrell also knew the forces that could be unleashed. He saw it in the eyes of the son. He read it in the face of the mother. Juanita held the power of God, of life and death, of order and chaos, in her hands. She commanded forces that could not be stopped or controlled once they were unleashed. So many feelings, thoughts, emotions, rushed through Catrell's mind and heart. He loved the spirit of the daughter. He admired the courage of the son. He respected the will of the mother. All she wanted was her children.

Catrell understood the other danger, the looming presence of Lonnie Carlton and the army of police that would be set upon him if harm came to this woman or her children. But that was a secondary consideration. Something in Juanita had called to a lost memory in his heart. His memory opened up to his own mother's voice calling to him as he left the house, her words warning him of dangers in the streets, her songs wrapping around him like the arms of an angel. He remembered her voice calling to him, but he had ignored it, choosing to live as a predator instead of as prey. He had chosen to dance the funeral dance, flirting with the grave diggers who paged him constantly.

In those brief seconds, something in Juanita had sung the life song to Catrell. He looked down at King bleeding on the floor beneath him, lowered his gun, walked past Juanita, paused to take one last look at Carolyn, then left the room. From that day on he left her children alone and warned everyone else to do the same.

Carolyn finished high school in South Carolina where Juanita sent her to live with her grandmother. King and Catrell began to talk about a year later. They saw each other at the funeral of one of King's friends who was a Cobra and Catrell suggested they get together. In subsequent conversations, they discovered what they probably always suspected, that they had many things in common and were in many ways alike. Periodically, they would get together away from the neighborhood to talk about their lives and their dreams. Catrell inquired occasionally about Carolyn but they never discussed the day of their confrontation.

Juanita knew about their growing friendship but did not worry about King falling into Catrell's world. But sometimes when she thought about that day in George Washington Homes, she would weep. She wept for Carolyn, her daughter, because she understood how she could love a man like Catrell in spite of the danger. She understood how his power and his strength and his genius created the illusion that he was a warrior prince fighting against his enemies. She wept for her boy, Billy, because she knew that he was willing to die to save his sister and she'd almost lost her son. And sometimes her tears would flow for Catrell and for all of us because she knew that he could have been her son, because he was our son...and he was lost.

Chapter Nine

Something warm fell into Bishop's eyes and he wished it would go away. His eyelids lifted slowly, squinting from the sunlight licking his face. "Shit, what time is it?" He grabbed his watch off the night table. It was 9:00am. He tried to focus his mind and everything from the night before started rushing back into his head. King, Lonnie, George Washington Homes, the police, the Egyptian Cobras, all of it rushed back to the front of his thoughts.

Stumbling out of bed and toward the bathroom, he looked terrible and felt worse. Hungry and needing some clean clothes, he pissed, washed his face and started to dress when he remembered the unopened envelope. Some more shit to think about. It was Saturday and he was thankful there was no work. He put on the sweats, packed the dirty, bloody clothes in the gym bag, sat down and opened the envelope. There were two handwritten notes. The first one was from King.

Bishop,
This is part of what Lonnie wants. Stacey Freeman has the other part.
King

Bishop remembered that King had introduced him to Stacey Freeman. She was one of the young women who worked in the mayor's office. Lonnie had gotten King a job there a few months earlier. Bishop read the second note.

M nds 2nd payment of $50,000 to insure deal. G will pick up, usual plce/tme, Nov 2. Process already in motion. Watch the news.

The writing was unfamiliar and it contained no signature. Bishop studied it over and over and could not make any sense of it. It was time to go see Juanita. First, he needed some fresh clothes and his knees were aching again.

Arriving at his house it surprised him that none of Lonnie's men were there waiting. Bishop was glad that they weren't because he wanted to get in and out as fast as possible before they came. Picking the morning paper up off the porch, he ran in the house and disrobed while walking toward the bedroom. He changed clothes and decided to pack some extra things, a shaving kit, toothbrush and a change of clothes just in case it wound up as another night in a hotel room. He also got his briefcase, grabbed a pistol and shoved a couple of extra clips, a sawed off shotgun and some shells into a small duffel bag. He didn't know what was going on, but didn't want to be caught wrong. Again.

Driving to Juanita's, he started preparing for the questions that Lonnie would ask if he was there. Bishop stopped at a pay phone, called her, told her he was on the way, asked about Lonnie and was relieved when he was not there.

She was sitting on the porch when he pulled up in front of her house. Juanita always liked it when Bishop came around. She still liked to look at him and loved his conversation, even though Bishop usually kept it brief. Over the ten years since they'd met, she'd watched him get a little heavier and liked the little specks of gray that had shown up in his beard. Most of all, she liked the way his deep set eyes looked right at her when they talked. As always Juanita was pleasant.

"Hey. You alright?" She greeted Bishop as he climbed the stairs.

"Doing just fine. How you doing today, Juanita?

She pushed the hair back out of her face. It was a gesture that always caused a little rush in Bishop. He tried not to let it show, but something in the way she was looking at him indicated that she knew.

"I'm better now that you're here." She smiled playfully having no idea what that smile did to him.

He looked down the street to keep from looking at her and said, "I saw your son last night. He's fine."

"I know. Lonnie told me he was all right."

Bishop wondered what Lonnie had told her, and how did he know? Did he see King after he'd left George Washington Homes?

Juanita leaned forward and asked, "Bishop, did you hear what happened in George Washington Homes last night?"

"No. What happened?"

"There was a gun battle between the police and the Egyptian Cobras. Ten people were shot."

"Anybody die?"

"One of the Cobras and two cops. They arrested 25 or 30 people. It's been all over the news this morning."

Bishop jumped up off the porch, went to his car, got the paper and returned to Juanita. He sat down on the step in front of her. His mind was speeding as his eyes scanned the front page.

POLICE BATTLE DRUG DEALERS IN
GEORGE WASHINGTON HOMES

Last night, the police department's elite anti-gang unit, Blue Fire, raided George Washington Homes in what Mayor Floyd Packard called the beginning of his administration's total commitment to eradicate drug traffic in the city's housing projects. George Washington Homes has long been considered the base of the notorious drug gang the Egyptian Cobras. As reported by police and residents of the project, a fierce gun battle raged for over an hour. Ten people were shot and there were three fatalities including two members of the police force. Dozens of arrests were made.

"Watch the news."

"What did you say?"

"Nothing." He folded the paper up and turned toward her. "I was just thinking out loud."

He didn't realize he had said it until Juanita asked him to repeat it. Watch the news. It had to be somehow connected to the trouble that King was in. He was about to ask Juanita about King and Catrell when Lonnie pulled up in her driveway.

Lonnie stepped out of his car looking sharp as usual even though he was in jeans and a sweater. His face was clean shaven except for the neatly trimmed mustache and he had his usual polished demeanor, but he was dead tired. Bishop could see it. He'd seen it before. It was the look that came from being in combat and fighting the effects of sleep deprivation. Blue Fire was under his command and he must have led the assault on Washington Homes.

"Bishop, what's happenin'?"

Bishop acknowledged him with a slight nod. Neither gave any indication of their contact from the previous night. There was something solemn about Lonnie's demeanor.

He stood on the first stair and said, "Bishop, will you excuse us for a moment? I need to talk to Juanita."

"Sure," Bishop said, and unfolded the newspaper searching for more information about last night.

Lonnie and Juanita stepped into the house to talk, leaving Bishop on the porch wondering about King. Wondering if Lonnie had sent him in there last night to get King out before the raid. Wondering why King was there hiding out and whether he should give Lonnie the second note.

When Lonnie came out of the house, Juanita did not return to the porch. Lonnie moved past Bishop and down the stairs about to leave when he looked back over his shoulder. "Bishop, I'll talk to you later. If you need to get in touch here's a number to page me. Put in the code 68 after your number and I'll know it's you." He handed Bishop a card with a number written on the back.

Bishop looked at the card, then back up at Lonnie. "Why 68?"

Lonnie flashed that sly smile and said, "Because your name is Isaiah." He jumped in his car and drove off. Bishop sat there for a moment before getting up and knocking on Juanita's door.

"Come on in, Bishop." She yelled from the kitchen. "I'm back here."

Juanita was in the kitchen pulling food from the refrigerator. Standing there watching her for a moment, Bishop's thoughts were filled with how much he enjoyed looking at her. Then it hit him. "Do you have a Bible?"

"Look on the table in the hallway."

He found her Bible and turned to Isaiah 6:8.

> Then I heard the Lord asking, "Whom shall I send as a messenger to my people? Who will go?" And I said, "Send me."

He wondered if Lonnie was trying to relay some hidden message or whether it was just his ironic wit. Juanita called to him from the kitchen again. "I'm making some breakfast, how do you like your eggs?"

Bishop went back to the kitchen and set the table while Juanita finished cooking. They ate breakfast and finally for the first time since meeting years ago at that reception, they talked extensively.

"Juanita, why'd you become a nurse?" Bishop asked.

"I come from a long line of women healers," Juanita replied. "The women in my family have been nurses, doctors and what some people call root workers."

"See, that's the South Carolina showing up."

"Uh-huh." Juanita rested her hand on her hip and cocked her head to the side. "Would you like some more of my cooking?"

"Naw." Bishop shook his head fiercely. "I think I'll pass."

They tried to remain serious but neither of them could keep a straight face. As if on cue they both started laughing.

"Don't worry, Bishop, I won't put anything on you."

"I think you might have already," he said, smiling slyly.

"Umm-hmm. Anyway...Why'd you become a teacher?"

Her question caused him to pause and consider ways to avoid answering. It was difficult for him to explain how much he needed teaching.

"You know I was in Nam."

"Yes. Billy told me."

"Well, when I came home I needed to do something different with my life. You know what I mean?"

She saw his mood change to a sudden seriousness and knew she'd unwittingly touched a nerve. She studied him and remembered why she was always attracted to him. He was very manly, even a little rugged and yet so gentle that he seemed soft. Not in a womanly way, but in a quiet way like, you had to get real close to hear him. "Maybe you were supposed to be a teacher. I hear you're very good at it."

"It's been good for me." He stood up and started moving the dishes off the table. "Have you heard from Carolyn lately?"

Juanita started to get up to help him but Bishop waved her off, so she sat back down and answered, "Two days ago. Seems like she and Sheila are doing fine. Hey, let me ask you something?"

"Sure." Bishop had his back to her as he rinsed off the dishes.

Juanita adjusted the salt and pepper shakers on the table and said, "It's very personal but I've wanted to know for a long time."

"Go ahead." Bishop turned around grabbed a paper towel from the counter and leaned against the sink. "Ask."

"How did you end up raising Sheila by yourself? I mean, I think you've done a great job, but..."

"But it's strange for a man to raise a daughter alone."

"Not strange, just rare."

Bishop finished drying his hands and tossed the used paper towel in the trash can. "It was another one of those things that I was supposed to do. You know?"

He hoped his answer would steer her away from the subject. He didn't want to discuss his relationship with his ex-wife. He didn't want to bring that there. Not then. Maybe later. At that moment, he just wanted to have one conversation. The one that got interrupted years ago. His attempt to sidestep the issue didn't work.

"What happened between you and Sheila's mother? Isn't she the jazz singer Belinda Hamilton?"

"Yeah, she is." Bishop went back to the table and sat down across from Juanita.

"So, what happened?" She rested her face in her hands and waited for his answer.

"Well, we'd met shortly after I came home from the war. We were young and wild and full of dreams. You know the story. We fell in love, got married, had Sheila and enjoyed our youth.

"She was learning how to turn the ideas in her head into music and I was learning how to teach history. We were good for a couple of years. Unfortunately, we never learned how to love each other in a way that would allow us to exist as a family.

"As Belinda's career grew, the room in her life for Sheila and me began to shrink and she developed some habits that I couldn't get with. So, when Sheila was five, her mother and I split up. Belinda moved to New York and has remarried a couple of times. We still talk. After time allowed us to heal, we became friends again. Sheila visits her when she can. I haven't seen her in a while now but when I hear her music on the radio, it makes me happy she got what she wanted.

"I was twenty-five, with a daughter to raise alone. It made me grow up. I dated some women off and on but never found that special one, you know, so I remained single and unattached for the last 19 years. And that is the story. I guess you got a little more than you wanted."

Juanita pulled her hair back, took a scrunchy off her wrist, wrapped it around the locks and said, "No. It's just the beginning. It's funny, we've known each other all these years but we've never had a chance to really talk."

Bishop was intrigued with Juanita. There was something in her that spoke to him. After all of the years of being friends with her son, he'd never gotten over how she moved him the first time they met. They talked for two more hours about all kinds of things without mentioning King or Lonnie. They both sensed something awful was happening and neither wanted to get into a subject that was full of questions but held very few answers.

They explored each other and laughed and enjoyed the peace between them. Bishop told her how the African American, Caribbean and African art that filled her house impressed him and she gave him a tour of downstairs that included a history of how she saved money to purchase various original pieces and limited edition prints.

61

He was completely taken with her. The feeling was nice. It was warm, like what he remembered from their first meeting. It was the way men and women should be, at peace with each other discovering what lies inside the heart and head and soul of the other. They sat there, learning, listening, teaching and often flirting mildly.

He didn't want it to end. He wanted to stay there and sit in her kitchen and talk with her and continue listening to Sade and continue looking at her and fall in love. Bishop didn't want it to end, but he needed to find her son and talk to Stacey Freeman.

Finally, he stood up, sighed and said, "I have to go."

Juanita's eyes said she knew it before it was mentioned. She walked him to the door. "Bishop, I appreciate you looking after King all of these years. You've been good for him."

He kissed her on the cheek. "Thanks, for breakfast and the conversation." He left and Juanita watched him bounce down the stairs and toward the street. Walking to his car, Bishop noticed a policeman sitting a few doors away, obviously watching Juanita's house. Lonnie was looking out or checking up. It was unclear which.

His first stop was a phone booth to check the book to see if Stacey Freeman was listed. He found two listings: one in a white suburb and one in the city. He figured she was the one in the city. He started to put a quarter in the phone, but decided to just drive over there. She lived in an upscale community near King's neighborhood.

Driving past George Washington Homes and out of the neighborhood surrounding Douglass High, he surveyed all of the empty lots, empty stores, empty bottles and empty lives of black men filling up the spaces on the corners in front of the liquor stores. So many brothers showed up there every day like it was a job. Emptiness filled up the streets of the neighborhood. So much talent crushed in the glow of the street lights. So much talent drowned in bottles or disappeared in clouds of smoke.

Arriving at Stacey Freeman's house, a sense of dread came over him. He reached into the duffle bag on the floor and grabbed his pistol, popped a clip in, tucked it in his belt, covered it with his jacket and got out. The street was peaceful and green, full of trees and well-kept lawns. A group of girls were riding their bikes and some boys chased each other up and down the sidewalk.

When he knocked on Stacey's door, there was no answer. Anita Baker played loudly through the walls and he wondered if Stacey could hear him knocking. Bishop decided to wait until the song was finished and knock again. It was cool because he was digging Anita and the peacefulness of the street after all of the shit from the night before.

The record ended and he knocked quickly. No answer. He knocked again, harder. No answer. The same song started over. Maybe she stepped out and left it running. Maybe she was in the shower. As he searched his pockets for a piece of paper and a pen, her next door neighbor stuck her head out.

"I don't think Stacey's home."

Bishop turned toward the elderly woman who was standing on the porch next door and asked, "You know how long she's been gone?"

"Must be quite a while because that song's been playing since last night. She must have forgot to turn it off before she left. It's not like her."

"I'll just leave her a note. Thanks." Bishop waved at the woman who hesitated a moment and watched him, then went back inside her house.

Lonnie Carlton drove up just as Bishop was about to write the note. "Is she home?" He called from the sidewalk as he approached the house.

"No."

"What are you doing here?" Lonnie asked while he tried the door.

"Just checking on something."

Lonnie gave him a strange look, tried the front door again then walked around the side of the house toward the back. Bishop was still standing on the porch when the music stopped, the front door opened and Lonnie was standing there.

"Come in here."

It was a beautifully furnished house. Expensive furniture. Very expensive. Too expensive for a single, city hall secretary. He followed Lonnie through the living room and past a dining room where the table was set for two with candles and good china. It looked as if she was planning a special evening with someone.

"Lonnie, is this legal?"

"It is now, but don't touch anything."

He was about to ask him why when he saw a woman's body lying on the floor with a plastic bag over her head. It was Stacey Freeman.

Bishop had seen to many dead bodies for it to freak him out. But he was shaken by this young black woman, maybe twenty-nine or thirty, whose life had been snatched away. Looking at her, he stared into memories of some-one struggling for oxygen, fighting for their life, choking, eyes bulging, dying.

"Lonnie, she didn't die because of the plastic bag."

"What?" Lonnie walked over and stood next to Bishop who was look-ing down at the woman's body.

"Someone killed her and then put the bag over her head."

Lonnie moved to the other side of the body and knelt down being care-ful not to disturb anything. "How do you know that?"

"I just know."

"Are you sure?"

"Yeah, I'm sure. I witnessed an interrogation once where a plastic bag was placed over a man's head until he started choking, trying to get the last bit of oxygen he could. He began choking and gagging, straining against his ropes, his body became spastic and he started flailing against the post he was tied to. Just before he passed out, someone cut the bag open. His wrists and legs were bleeding from the seizure like actions of his body fighting for oxy-gen. There is no sign of that kind of panic here. Believe me, Stacey Freeman didn't suffocate, she died quietly."

Lonnie was impressed with Bishop's observation but was preoccupied with something else. Nothing seemed disturbed in the house. Her jacket was hung across a chair in the kitchen and there were a few dirty dishes in the sink. Lonnie didn't touch anything at first. He walked around looking care-fully at everything in the kitchen, then went back into the dining room, picked her purse up off the table and thumbed through it.

Lonnie went back into the kitchen and was still holding her purse when he took a long look at Stacey. Then he looked at Bishop. "Do you have something for me?"

Bishop sighed. "What's going on, Lonnie?"

Lonnie's tone got more forceful. He put on the police voice. The inter-rogation voice. "DO YOU HAVE SOMETHING FOR ME?"

Bishop had already decided Lonnie wasn't getting shit until he gave him something. He was sick of games and it must have shown on his face because Lonnie started talking.

"I got King a job in the Mayor's office a few months back."

"Yeah, I know."

"But what you don't know is that he was getting information for me."

Lonnie squatted and looked closely at the body again. "Stacey was helping him."

"What kind of information?"

"Information about the mayor and some members of his staff."

"What?"

Lonnie stood up and walked over to the phone. "I asked King to help me get some files and notes."

"Are you crazy? You used King for that shit?"

"Look, I'm working with a federal task force and King was in a position to help me out."

Bishop knew Lonnie was only telling part of the truth and that the rest was bullshit. "I thought you and the mayor were friends."

Lonnie looked at him with a smirk on his face. "Fuck the mayor." He started dialing the phone.

Bishop asked, "Who killed Stacey?"

Lonnie put the phone down and turned toward Bishop. "I don't know, but they are probably after King, too."

"What was that shit last night at Washington Homes?"

"Orders from the mayor.

"I thought you said fuck the mayor."

"Look, I still have to do my job and right now I still work for him."

By the look on his face, Lonnie knew Bishop only believed part of his story.

Bishop reached in his pocket. "Somebody left this in my car last night." He handed Lonnie the note.

M nds 2nd payment of $50,000 to insure deal. G will pick up, usual plce/tme, Nov 2. Process already in motion. Watch the news.

Lonnie glanced at the paper, folded it and put it in his pocket. He picked the phone up again, called the police station and requested a crime scene team. He turned toward Bishop and said, "You'd better leave. I'll talk with you later."

Driving away from Stacey's house, Bishop's head was hurting from whatever madness was invading his life. He drove along those tree lined residential streets as far as possible trying to avoid the traffic on the main street. In a couple of blocks he'd have to deal with it but until then he wanted to let the grass and trees and quiet, calm him down. It was a nice peaceful neighborhood. Peaceful enough for Stacey Freeman to get killed.

At the corner before his turn toward the main road, he waited for the car in front to move when another car suddenly pulled in behind him. Two men jumped out from the front car. In the mirror he saw two more jump out of the car in back of him. "FUCK! I'm being jacked!"

Pulling the gun from his belt, he opened his door and took aim but also noticed none of them had their weapons drawn. When they reached the front of his car they all froze. He waited. They waited. Nobody moved.

"Mr. Bishop."

He still didn't move and kept his gun aimed at the one who had just called his name. "Who the hell are you?"

He laid an envelope on the hood of the car. "Mr. Bishop, I've got something for you." The young man backed away. The other men followed. They all jumped back in their cars and sped away. Bishop stepped out with the gun still in his hand and retrieved the envelope. After driving around for a few blocks he pulled over and read the note.

Bishop,

I am safe. The game has moved. Will see you soon.

It was from King. Immediately Bishop knew those men were Egyptian Cobras and that they must have been watching him all along. He assumed that meant King already knew that Stacey Freeman was dead. He decided to take his tired, confused, scared ass home.

By the late 60s, the Civil Rights Movement had given way to Black Power. When I returned home from the war, a sense of collective purpose seemed to run through the black community in answer to Malcolm's demand for self-determination. Everywhere, folks were registering to vote and run ning candidates for office. I remember the electricity that ran through the national black community during the election of that wave of first mayors, city council people, state legislators, county commissioners, county sheriffs and judges.

Martin Luther King and others had defeated legal segregation. Now it was time to exercise our hard-won rights. We hoped for and organized for change. We wanted change in the way business was done in the city and change in the way services were delivered to our neighborhoods. We were tired of being denied those services and being shut out of opportunities. It was a time of change and promise.

There was a sense of power amongst our people. When I came home my mother and father got me involved in a voter registration drive and campaign to elect Sam Page, the city's first African American mayor. It was 1973 and the city was full of tension and expectation and on election day the vote split almost evenly along racial lines. Eighty-five percent of eligible blacks voted. It was the first time that black folks had voted in such large numbers. It was the first time that the fact that we were a majority of the population, meant anything. In addition to the mayor, we laid claim to half of the city council seats. We had organized and won. There was partying in the streets. We won. Black folks had taken "Audacious Power" as Adam Clayton Powell used to say. It felt good.

It was a different time and even the candidates were different then. For years Sam Page had been an activist in our community, fighting for improved schools, always first to confront the city about some act of police violence against one of us. He'd also been a "Freedom Rider" and had been beaten senseless by a mob in Alabama while trying to desegregate the busses and accommodations used in interstate travel. Sam was a veteran of the move ment like many of that first bunch of elected officials.

He rode into City Hall on a wave of black energy and fought on our behalf. He was always at odds with the business establishment who ruled the city and for decades had shut us out. He insisted on minority participation in all city contracts. He fired the chief of police, appointed the first black head of the department and pushed a rapid integration of the force until it was *almost half black. He had a lot of enemies and received threats all of the time but it never deterred him. Sam had come to do battle and we loved him.*

Every Sunday morning he'd be a guest speaker in some church in the community. On Sunday evenings he'd be on one of the two black radio stations explaining his position on some issue. City Hall was always full of folks coming down to tell Sam or his staff about a problem that they could never get taken care of and some just stopped by to tell him that he was doing a good job.

In his second term, Sam was responsible for creating a huge state-wide black voter turnout for Jimmy Carter and was welcomed at the White House where he was rewarded with a lot of federal money for the city. Construction began to boom. Highway and mass transit projects meant jobs. Businesses started moving in, money started pouring into the city and even some of the white business establishments started seeing him as an effective mayor and began to warm up to Mayor Sam Page and the young black folks running city government.

Then the first scandal hit. Councilman Delbert James was indicted on a tax evasion charge. He had been hired as a consultant to a real estate developer to persuade a group of mostly elderly black people to sell their homes on some prime land so that expensive condominiums could be built. He was paid over $250,000 in cash and gifts and failed to report it to the IRS. They couldn't get him on the Hobbs Act, for selling his vote, because every time a vote came up about zoning for the condominiums or some other issue related to the development, he shrewdly abstained or excused himself or was absent that day.

Delbert James was one of the most powerful men in city government and was a key ally of the mayor. He went to trial protesting and used as his defense that there was a conspiracy against black politicians and that the federal government was out to destroy him and other powerful black people.

It was the beginning of our disillusionment. Deep down everyone knew he had sold us out. Some rallied to defend him claiming he'd done nothing more than what the white politicians had been doing for decades. Others turned their backs saying, "That is exactly why we elected him because we wanted something different."

Delbert James was convicted and went to jail still claiming he'd done nothing wrong except maybe make a mistake on his tax return. Mayor Sam Page found himself in the position of having to defend all black politicians and yet distance himself from those who would sell us out. Typically of Sam, he did it by calling for the community to be more active in not only electing our people to office but in keeping the pressure on them to be responsible and honest once they got there. We didn't and the next generation would bring more of those who saw public office as a place to feed their lust and greed.

Sam Page died in 1980 just as he was preparing to run for his third term. He died just as Ronald Reagan became President and the federal money was about to be pulled out of the cities where black folks ruled. He died just when the cities were being abandoned and crack started flooding the inner city, becoming the drug of choice for the poor; and some white collar criminals plundered the national economy, crashing financial institutions; and some well-educated thugs raped the country, cannibalizing industries, leaving whole communities rotting on the side of the road. He died just when we started losing our children because they had no faith in us or the future.

CHAPTER TEN

Bishop arrived home thinking about Lonnie's story. He needed to know if Lonnie was really investigating the mayor with some federal agency. He only knew one person who could give him that information, his former sergeant, L.C. Gray. While in the war, Bishop felt as if his survival was due partially to luck or grace or whatever and due partially to the leadership of Sergeant L.C. Gray.

Sgt. L.C. Gray was doing his third tour of Viet Nam when Bishop came into his unit. Sgt. Gray was fearless and cold when it came to battle. Nothing seemed to rattle him. He knew the country as if he had been born there and spoke fluent Vietnamese. He was widely respected as one of the best in the field. He was also regarded by most of the white officers as slightly crazy, which is why he was never promoted even though he was highly decorated.

After the army, Sgt. Gray became a member of the Washington D.C. police force. He did undercover work in narcotics and later became a DEA agent. Bishop saw him about two years ago at the Wall in D.C. It was purely coincidental that they were both there that day. He had just driven Sheila back to school at Howard and decided to go over to the Viet Nam Veterans' Memorial for the first time.

When Bishop saw Sgt. Gray kneeling before the Wall, he couldn't believe it. Gray must have felt someone staring at him because he looked up and saw Bishop standing there. They shook hands, then hugged, then broke down and cried. They hadn't seen each other in the years since leaving Nam and all of the things they had felt but never spoken about poured out onto the ground between them.

They spent that whole day together talking about their lives since the war and remembering others who'd served with them. Sgt. Gray was glad Bishop was a teacher. Bishop didn't know if he was glad that Sgt. Gray had become an undercover cop or not. It didn't surprise him though that he would be in a paramilitary situation and was good at it.

Bishop needed to talk to him. He was the only person he could think of that probably had the connections to get the information he needed so he called Sgt. Gray in D.C. and left a message on his machine.

The raid on George Washington Homes was all over the Saturday night news. No mention had been made of Stacey Freeman yet. Bishop was tired but couldn't sleep. He spent some time writing then turned on the television and flipped through the dozens of channels over and over again trying to find something worth watching.

Bishop woke up on the couch Sunday morning about eight. He must have fallen off to sleep around four. That's the last time he remembered looking at the clock. The TV was still on and Mayor Floyd Packard was on a morning news show talking about his intention to stop the drug trade and run the gangs out of town, especially the Egyptian Cobras. Bishop listened for a minute then went to the porch, got the paper and saw the headlines.

MAYOR'S AIDE FOUND MURDERED
GANG LEADER SOUGHT

Stacey Freeman, a secretary in the office of Mayor Floyd Packard, was found murdered in her home last night. No suspects have been arrested, but a police spokesman said they are searching for Catrell Merit, the alleged leader of the Egyptian Cobras. Sources close to the investigation suggest that the murder could be in retaliation for the mayor's recent announcement of his intention to break up the notorious gang. When asked if there is any evidence of Merit's involvement in the murder, the police would only say that he is wanted for questioning.

They were living in a circle of lies. Billy King, on his way to a promising future, was now being dragged down into a sewer. His life was endangered by people who should be extending their hands to help him. Those who loved him thought he was safe, that he had gotten past his teen years without being stolen in the streets. They thought that because he was attending college and knew what he wanted to do with his life that he would not show up in the body count. They never thought that he would have to seek protection amongst the gangs.

War had been declared on Catrell Merit. War had been declared by people who had no moral authority, no honor amongst the youth. The young people of the south side had no respect for the hypocrisy of the so-called leadership.

Lonnie Carlton was hunting King and Catrell. He also claimed to be pursuing the mayor. Bishop wondered, "Was Lonnie the one who said

Catrell was the suspect in Stacey Freeman's murder? Was he really trying to find King and pull him out of some shit he got him in to? Who was he really working for, the feds or Mayor Packard?"

Waiting for some word from King, Bishop tried to keep himself busy. Twice he called Juanita and twice he hung up when he got her voice mail. He piddled around the rest of the day, raking some leaves in the yard, reading the rest of the Sunday paper, watching football and thinking about the drama that was unfolding. He had classes to teach the next day and settled down to prepare his lessons for the week. It was about 8 p.m. when he decided to call Juanita again before he started working. He was relieved when she answered the phone.

"Hey, Juanita, it's Bishop."

"I was just thinking about you."

"Have you heard from your son?"

"Nothing. I was hoping you had some news."

"Nothing new. I know he's safe, so you don't have to worry about that."

"Lonnie just told me the same thing. We were about to have dinner so I'm going to have to call you back."

"That's OK. I just called to see if you'd heard from King. I'll talk with you later."

Bishop knew that his tone had changed once he knew that Lonnie was there. As much as he tried to sound casual and unfazed, he was jealous. He wanted to talk to Juanita and feel like he felt yesterday when he'd sat in her kitchen. After a few minutes of disappointment, he thumbed through his compact disc collection, found an old Stevie Wonder disc, *Songs In The Key Of Life*, put it on and settled down to prepare his lessons.

The topic that week was the European invasion of Africa and the collaboration of some African chiefs with the slave traders. Stevie started talking to him. Bishop leaned back in his chair, closed his eyes for a minute and listened to the voice of the ancestors. The harmony was perfect. The rhythm was strong. He danced in his seat shouting, "That's right, Stevie, sing that shit."

There is nothing I have ever done in my life as rewarding as teaching except raising my daughter, Sheila. Teaching history saved me from my war-making self and introduced me to my healing self. I learn so much from my students. Their curiosity and concern opens my soul to the real beauty of life. Their perceptions are incredible. My reward is their ultimate discovery that history teaches us that no obstacle is insurmountable. I want them to leave my classes at the end of the year understanding that even people who seem to be in the most desperate and terrible conditions have power to make change.

The cycle of knowledge passing from old to young and from young to old constantly renews my faith and me. It renews my faith in what is good and what is possible. Every time I look at one of those children I see the future. I listen to them and know that we, the people who were brought here to be used, will never be rendered useless. When I look at them, I know that our gifts are too great, our spiritual resources too deep to be denied.

The young people I teach come from an environment that teaches them to fail. Yet, every year more come to say that they won't fail. Unfortunately, some will be lost, but as a group they will not fail themselves or us. They will discover their mission and fulfill it. Then they will be the old, teaching and learning from the young, passing on and protecting our legacy. The cycle of knowledge keeps expanding.

In my life, I've become highly skilled in two areas. Killing was the first thing I excelled at. It is the one I hate. Teaching is the second and the one I love. Teaching rewards me in a way I never imagined when I was killing other human beings and thought my life might end without ever finding a way to give some of what's right inside me. Once I found it, I was saved. Saved from all the signs, all the symbols, that told me that my options as a young brother were to die or go to jail or fail at being a man.

Chapter Eleven

It was right before sunrise on Monday morning when Bishop hopped up the stairs to his porch. He was breathing heavily and dripping with sweat from his early morning run. It felt good and had helped him clear his head. The sun was just coming up and he stood on the porch looking at the street coming to life and the colors of the autumn leaves and the freshness of the morning when he spotted the strange car a few doors down. It took a second to notice the two figures slumped down in the front seat, but he knew they were cops. Lonnie was watching him. He stepped into the house, peeled off his sweatshirt and headed to the kitchen where he poured a large glass of apple juice and threw a couple of slices of bread into the toaster when the phone rang. Bishop hesitated before answering. At 6:45 in the morning he figured it must be bad news.

"Hello."

"Bishop? It's L.C. Gray."

"Hey, man. What's happenin?"

"I'm coming through there today. I got a two-hour layover at the airport."

"What time?"

"Four o'clock. Universal flight 111."

"I'll meet you at the gate."

"Bishop, you OK.?"

"Yeah. I'll tell you about it when I see you."

Bishop showered, shaved and dressed for work as he began to feel that familiar Monday anticipation. Almost every week, one or more of his students would have some story to tell about an incredibly traumatic weekend. He laughed out loud thinking about it because his students would be shocked to hear how he had spent his weekend.

Bishop expected interesting discussion in his classes that day because every year when he got to the lesson about the slave trade the students were surprised to learn that some Africans had collaborated with the European slave traders. It always led to raging debates about "Uncle Toms" and those the kids called sellouts.

The students, like African Americans in general, were not used to open political criticism of the leaders of the black community. Yet, when the classroom discussion opened up, they always had a lot to say and Bishop loved it. He loved their struggle to understand what motivated the people and their leaders.

When Bishop walked into his classroom and took attendance, he knew it was going to be a good day and maybe a good week. All but four of his thirty-six first period students were there which was highly unusual for a Monday. After a few minutes of encouragement he almost got them to settle down when the questions started coming.

"Mr. Bishop, we heard you were in George Washington Homes Friday night."

"Mr. Bishop, do you know Catrell Merit?"

"Do you think he killed that girl?"

"Was you there when the cops came in shooting?"

"How come the police actin' like they gonna stop the Egyptian Cobras now? They ain't been doing nuthin 'bout em."

The questions came fast, leaving Bishop temporarily stunned. He had to collect himself and felt foolish that he had underestimated his students and the inner city news wire. He couldn't answer their questions. He was looking for answers himself.

"All right, settle down. We have work to do."

It was weak and he knew it. For many of his students he was the only adult they talked to. His classroom was not just a place of instruction but it was one of the few safe places where the young people of that community could express their concerns. But that day, instead of dealing with their questions, he opted to put them to work.

"Listen up. Last week I divided you into two groups to make presentations to the class. I want you to get in your groups now. Group One will explore the historical context of slavery in Africa prior to the European invasion. Group Two will examine slavery in African history after the invasion. Are there any questions?"

The students looked around the classroom at each other in the way students do when something needs to be said but they aren't sure yet who will have the nerve to say it. Finally, a hand shot up from the back of the room.

Bishop called on him. "Romero. You have a question?"

"Mr. Bishop, what's up with not discussing what happened this weekend. We always do that on Mondays. Besides, some of our friends was shot in G. W. Homes on Friday."

His question caused nods of agreement followed by comments that supported his statement. It was obvious to Bishop that he had seriously deluded himself into thinking this was not going to be a typical Monday. He went back to his usual Monday posture, which was to assume that he would only accomplish half of what was supposed to be done that day. The rest of the time would be spent shaking the weekend off the students so they could learn something Tuesday, Wednesday and Thursday.

"All right. We've got fifty minutes left in this period. We'll spend twenty minutes on what happened over at Washington Homes and after that, you'll get in your groups and start work on your projects."

It was his usual Monday morning tactic and it worked. The students told him which of their friends had been shot and their theories on why the mayor suddenly ordered the crackdown on the Cobras. They were animated and observant, but cynical. None of them believed that it would change anything in their community. After twenty to twenty-five minutes of discussing the big news of the weekend, they broke into their groups and did a little work.

Bishop repeated the tactic in his other five classes and it turned out to be a not so bad day. At three o'clock he was ready to leave and he wanted to make sure that none of Lonnie's men followed him when he left the school. Instead of going to his car in the teacher's parking lot, he went out on the other side, walking quickly away from the building hoping that the cops Lonnie had watching would be waiting on the wrong side of the school.

It should have worked perfectly. He wanted to leave undetected by Lonnie's men, get to the airport in time to meet L. C. Gray at the gate at four o'clock. This time he wasn't worried about leaving his car in the lot. It was in Cobra territory and he bet they were watching whoever was watching him. He'd be back in a couple of hours and hoped he was right and his car would be safe.

It was three o'clock and it would take about ten minutes to walk to the train station and another fifteen to twenty minutes to ride to the airport. As he walked down the street, the old homes seemed to whisper their past to him. Underneath their faded paint and broken stairs were memories of a time when black people could only make deliveries in the area. It wasn't so long ago, but the changes had been dramatic.

He passed four little girls jumping rope on the sidewalk and two elderly men playing chess on one of the large wrap around porches. A young couple held hands as they strolled across the street. Bishop's thoughts roamed from the street to the trouble he faced. He thought of King and the predicament he was in and Juanita and the time he'd spent with her and Stacey Freeman lying dead on her kitchen floor. Then when he was almost at the train station it dawned on him that he'd messed up. He remembered that his pistol was in the briefcase.

Too much was on his mind. If he went back he'd be late. Worse, he'd be seen by the cops waiting for him. He had no choice. He knew he couldn't take a gun into the airport.

Standing on the corner he tried to stop a cab to rush him back to the school. "TAXI!" He shouted at the empty cab. The driver shot a glance Bishop's way and kept going. He knew it was futile. For a black man, finding a cab and then getting one to stop in this neighborhood was always an ordeal. It wasn't going to work. His plan was falling apart. He turned around and started heading back down the street. He had to try to run back, precious time was being lost.

Bishop ran down the street about a half a block when those alarms started sounding inside his head again. He turned around quickly and spotted the source of his fear. A car was following slowly behind him about twenty yards away. He stopped running and walked quickly while he contemplated his next move. The porch where the old men had sat was empty as he passed. The rope was lying on the sidewalk but the four little girls were gone. The street was empty. People in that neighborhood knew the signs of the predators and had seen them before Bishop knew the car was behind him. He switched the brief case to his left hand and pulled the flap lose. If something went down he wanted to be able to get to the gun. The car sped up and so did his heart. It was on. In a matter of seconds the car was almost next to him. As he turned to face it, he grabbed the gun from the briefcase and moved toward the street. It took just a few steps to reach a car parked at the curb just as the stalkers came to a halt. Bishop raised his gun while crouching down taking cover. The car doors flew open in the street. A young man jumped out with a sawed off shotgun, coming right at him, raising the gun, aiming. The driver had a pistol and was pointing, aiming, too. Bishop had the one with the shotgun in his sights ready to fire if he took two more steps. There was a sudden burst of automatic gunfire from down the street. He ducked and heard the sound of metal on metal, bullets crashing into cars, glass shattering, cursing and screaming.

"GET IN! NIGGA GET IN!" The driver of the car yelled. The one with the shotgun turned away from Bishop and jumped back in the car. The door slammed. Tires screeched against the asphalt. More gunfire. A crash. More gunfire. Screams of pain and fear.

Bishop rose up to look, ready to fire. Another car came flying down the street past him. He looked up the street and saw his assailant's car lodged against a light post. Two men were standing along side it emptying their automatic weapons into the crashed car, then they jumped into a van. He heard a voice in back of him. Spinning around ready to shoot, he saw one of his eleventh-grade students, a short, stocky kid with a big afro, Carl Johnson, standing a few feet a way.

"Mr. Bishop, come on."

Carl turned and ran between two houses and Bishop sprung up from his cover to follow him. They ran through a backyard, across an alley and between two more houses before reaching the next street over. Bishop didn't know what just happened or why and wondered who was trying to kill him now.

On the next street, Carl jumped in the back seat of a waiting car. Bishop jumped in with him. There were two other young men in the front. He didn't recognize them.

"Mr. Bishop, are you all right?"

"Yeah. What the hell is going on, Carl?"

Realizing the gun was still in his hand cocked, Bishop released the hammer slowly and put it in the briefcase while Carl watched.

"They were Dexter Avenue Zulu Nation. They been riding down on people in the 'hood all day. They killed two of my homies this morning. But we got 'em. Yeah, we got dem muthafuckas good."

Carl was an Egyptian Cobra. Bishop hadn't known but wasn't surprised. Carl was a good student and probably a good recruit for Catrell. He liked them smart. Sirens flew toward the scene as they drove away. The young men in the car were as calm as if they'd just stopped at McDonald's and got a Happy Meal.

"I've got to get to the airport." Bishop watched the police cars and the ambulance as they flew by them. The driver and the other cat in the front were silent.

"Carl, I've got to get to the airport right away."

"Yeah. Don't worry about it."

Bishop wiped the sweat from his forehead as he caught his breath and began to relax. He realized that Carl and his boys must have been watching him, following him, too. He knew he wanted to lose the cops Lonnie had watching him but he hadn't considered the Egyptian Cobras. Fortunately, they'd shown up. They'd saved him again, but all of these confrontations were scaring the shit out of him. Inside the car, Tupac was bumping on the box while a thousand questions ricocheted inside his head.

Dexter Avenue Zulu Nation was a smaller rival of the Egyptian Cobras. They were a younger, less organized gang that had always been stifled by the dominance of the Cobras. As he led the Egyptian Cobras and dominated the drug traffic in the city, Catrell employed a strategy of allowing new gangs to form, letting them build up the drug market in their neighborhoods and then either incorporating them into the Cobras or crushing them and taking over their territory. The Egyptian Cobras were so strong that it was almost impossible to function in the trade without their acquiescence or approval.

The Dexter Avenue Zulu Nation had been growing and flexing, trying to expand and possibly challenge the Cobras. Rumor was that Catrell's men were angry over it and wanted to go to war, but Catrell held them back, waiting, studying the situation. Even though the Zulu Nation had gotten stronger, until that day they had not been bold enough to go into the heart of Egyptian Cobra territory and attack anyone. Clearly, their actions were based upon calculating the demise of the Cobras after the mayor's attack on them in George Washington Homes and his pronouncement that he would rid the city of them. The mayor had inadvertently caused a gang war to erupt.

Bishop lowered his voice and said, "Carl, I need you to do me a favor."

Carl didn't answer. He looked at Bishop but remained quiet.

Bishop lifted the briefcase and set it on the seat between them. "I need you to keep my briefcase and bring it to me tomorrow at school."

It was a gamble. Bishop couldn't get back to the school to leave the gun in time and couldn't take it to the airport. He had to trust him. They'd saved his life twice in a few days.

Carl took the briefcase without uttering a word. They arrived at the airport at 3:40. Bishop jumped out of the car and turned back to Carl. "Thanks and I'll see you in the morning. I'll be in my class at 7:45."

"I know, I've got you first period."

As they drove off, Carl's lighthearted, youthful laughter hung in the air and reminded Bishop that only a few minutes ago another group of black youths was gunned down in the street. As he made his way into the crowded airport, the lingering thoughts of Carl, the Cobras, the dead members of the Zulu Nation and his own narrow escape from death climbed up from his stomach and he began to sweat and his breathing got heavy. Bishop went into a restroom and washed his face with cold water to help regain his composure.

After a few minutes, he walked back out amongst the crowds and found the Universal Airlines monitors and saw that L.C.'s plane was running forty-five minutes late. Going through the metal detectors and the security check, he thought about the disaster that would have happened if the gun had still been in his briefcase. He made his way to the terminal where L.C.'s plane was coming in, found a bar near his gate, sat down and ordered a glass of scotch. The liquor calmed him and for some reason he thought about his daughter and how much he missed her. Sheila was absolutely his favorite person in the world and although her company was missed at home, he was proud of her and happy that she was doing well at school and finding her way in the world.

The bar had begun to fill up. It was after four o'clock and the business travelers were streaming in. He had been seated at the bar for about forty minutes when two young African American women came in and sat down next to him. They were dressed in elegant and expensive business suits and looked as if they'd just finished a long day of meetings. One of the women had neatly braided hair and seemed to be consoling the other one about something that had happened. He tried not to eavesdrop. Not really. He was actually trying to listen to every word. They had that music, that rhythm in their voice that sisters have and it was a relaxing diversion for him. The one being consoled had a short neat haircut. She looked at Bishop past her friend sitting between them and started laughing.

"Are we talking too loud?"

Bishop sipped his drink and said, "Can't even hear you talking about your problems, but if I was you..."

The other one turned around and looked at him. All three of them laughed. He extended his hand.

"Hi, I'm Isaiah Bishop."

The one with the nice braids shook his hand firmly. "Denise Michaels and this is my friend Sheila."

"Sheila. That's my daughter's name."

He was ready to enjoy the conversation that was about to unfold, a conversation seasoned with some light flirtation, when he looked at the clock behind the bar and realized he should make his way to the gate. He didn't want to miss Sgt. Gray.

"It was really nice meeting you two, but you'll have to excuse me. I have to meet a plane."

Sheila handed him a business card with her left hand, extended her right hand and said, "Well, if you're ever in Chicago give me a call."

Bishop thanked them, said good-bye and stepped out into the terminal where it seemed as if thousands of travelers were hustling back and forth. He walked over to L.C.'s gate just as the first passengers were coming off. He leaned against the wall and waited for his old sergeant, who came through the gate five minutes later.

Bishop always looked forward to seeing L.C. He thought it was funny that neither he nor any of the other men who were in Nam with him knew what L.C. stood for. They used to ask him but he always said that was it. His name was just L.C. They tried to guess but he would just laugh and say it was just L.C. After a while they just called him anything that began with those letters. Larry Cool, Lazy Coon, Little Creep, Long Cock and anything else they could come up with.

Usually this game took place when they were high and bored. Sgt. Gray never took offense but would come back at whomever was playing with some of the fiercest dozens any of them had ever heard. He understood how lonely, homesick and afraid they all were and that they played those kinds of games to take their minds off all the horrors they had to witness and participate in.

"Bishop, I'm glad to see you. We're not going to have much time before my next flight."

"We don't need much."

They walked back to the bar and found a table by the wall. The two women were still sitting at the bar and waved at Bishop. Sergeant Gray gave him a sideways look. "I see you've already pissed on this tree." They both laughed as the waitress came and took their order.

L. C. Gray got right to the point. "Bishop, you said you needed to see me."

He knew something was wrong. It was old instinct. He knew Bishop hadn't come out to the airport just to make a social call. As he spoke, the look in his eyes was intense and beckoned Bishop to tell him what this was all about. In a few minutes he had heard what had transpired the last several days.

L.C. listened without interrupting. He just sipped his drink and listened, occasionally asking questions about some of the details, but his expression never changed and he never took his eyes off Bishop. He watched him even when lifting his glass to his mouth.

When the story was finished, Sergeant Gray told him to sit tight and he got up from the table and headed out of the bar into the terminal. Bishop watched Denise and Sheila finish up their drinks and get up to leave. They turned his way and waved as they walked out of the door. He watched them and laughed. It was welcomed frivolity. Retelling the events of the weekend had made him tense again.

L.C. returned to the table to find Bishop staring at the space where the two women had been seated and were now replaced by two middle-aged white men whose neckties were loosened and whose faces were tight.

"What'd you do? Chase them out of here."

"I thought they'd gone to find you."

"I wish."

As they paid their bill and left the bar, the banter was loose and comfortable and helped to lighten up the space between them that had been filled with the violent events of the last three days. They walked toward the gate where his connecting flight was boarding and shook hands.

"Bishop, look. I'll find out what I can and call you in a day or so."

"I'd appreciate it."

"Yeah, but be real careful with this shit. I don't want to have to come down here and fuck somebody up."

The lighthearted way it was said did not diminish the fact that he was capable and probably willing to do just that. Bishop understood him. They shook hands again and Sergeant L.C. Gray passed on through the door that led to his plane. Bishop jumped in a cab and headed back to the city to pick up his car and back to the storm that was gathering.

When he arrived home, the unmarked police car was in the same spot. Bishop was tired even though it was only about seven o'clock. He went to the kitchen, warmed up some left over lasagna his mother had given him and ate in silence. Afterwards, he opened a bottle of Merlot, sat down on the sofa in the living room, sipped his wine, closed his eyes and faded into his memories.

I knew even before arriving in Nam that I was in some shit that I had no business being in. I had no illusions about it being adventurous or glorious like some John Wayne movie. My only concern was to get home alive, to do my tour and go home. I didn't even care who won. I wasn't buying all the shit they tried to teach you in boot camp. I understood that all the things they told you about the Vietnamese being some evil enemy leading the communist attack upon the Western way of life was just propaganda to make you fight.

Like thousands of young black men, I went because we were told to go. Like a lot of brothers, I was tagged as having an attitude problem. They said that I didn't seem to have any respect for white people in authority. They were right. The respect I had was for my parents and the elders in my family and my neighborhood. I respected Martin Luther King and the folks confronting the segregationists. I respected the men I knew who had been criminals and had followed Malcolm X and became Muslims and cleaned themselves up. I respected all the black folks who got up everyday and went out to work in a world that spit on them and still came home and loved their children and raised them to be men and women and created music and told great stories and smiled at the sun because they knew that it had kissed them thousands of years ago.

Even though I had problems with those whites in authority, I got to know a lot of enlisted white guys who were cool. In the first unit I was in, I met a young white guy we called Dallas. He was a country, redneck kind of cat, from Arkansas. I can't even remember his real name. All the brothers called him Dallas because he had this hard Southern accent and was just a country dude whom we thought was funny. We became friends, at least the kind of friends that you become when you are thrown into a world of sudden death and danger and in spite of the differences you find some commonality in your shared history in America and your need to stay alive.

Dallas was typical of a lot of white guys who were just getting there. He was full of patriotism and willingness to die for his country. He used to talk about how he enlisted to fight communism. Now remember, this cat was from the woods, and he was poor. I think his family was sharecroppers, yet his only ambition was to go die to stop communism. He didn't even know what com·munism was, but he thought it was noble to fight the war against it. Maybe he thought it would change the course of his life and he would return home a hero and wouldn't have to be poor anymore.

When we met, his hard Southern accent made me and the other brothers think he was the kind of young white guy who was probably in the Klan, but after a few minutes talking to him you knew right away Dallas wasn't one of those white cats who hated black folks.

For some reason, he was always around me, following me around like a puppy. Everybody called him my shadow. One day we were hanging out, me, a couple of brothers and Dallas. We were smoking some weed and drinking and everybody was high and talking shit about back home. Marvin Gaye was singing "Inner City Blues" on the radio when one of the cats asked Dallas why he was always with the brothers. He got this real strange look on his face and got real quiet. After a few minutes, he looked at us with this serious expression that made all of us lean in with great curiosity. For a long moment Dallas seemed suspended in deep thought and then he said, "I'm really black."

There was dead silence for about thirty seconds. Then we started crack ing up. That shit was so funny that we were rolling on the ground hysterical ly, tears coming out of our eyes, stomachs hurting. He didn't change his expression and said it again with even more conviction. "Really, I'm black."

Well, that just made it funnier and some of the cats started making jokes about him passing. Dallas got up and walked away. We were dying. In our herb- and alcohol-influenced hysteria I think we must have laughed and joked about it for half an hour. After a while he came back with a beat up little fold er about the size of a pocket phone book. He stood in the middle of us look ing so serious that we all sobered up for a minute and listened to what he had to say just in case it was some more funny shit.

"My grandmother was a light-skinned black woman who died giving birth to my mama. We was raised white. Nobody ever talks about it and we was never allowed to meet any of her family or anything. After my mother was born, my granddaddy moved to another town and nobody there knows that we got black blood in us. I was raised as a white boy. Some of my folks is in the Klan. Some of my folks hate blacks. My mama always told me not to hate nobody. Last year when she heard me call somebody a nigger, she told me about my grandmother, and that we was niggers too. I been around some black folks but you know I never really got to know none until I got here. I wanted to know my family, and y'all's the closest thing to it."

We were shocked. He showed us a picture of his grandmother. And it was unmistakable. There she stood, a light-skinned black woman who you would almost think was white except she had features that were clearly black, full lips, broad nose and a head of beautiful, thick, nappy hair. We looked at that picture like we were looking at one of our relatives. There was silence amongst us for a minute, then we started cracking up again. The shit was so absurd.

There we were in the middle of a damn war and we wind up with a white boy on a search for his roots. It was the ultimate confirmation of the insanity that we were dealing with. He would have never confessed his bloodline in Arkansas. But there, thousands of miles away from America, it was safe. He could reveal his ancestry and hang with his "brothers" and then go back home and be with his family digging in the dirt trying to scratch out an existence on somebody else's land while protecting their great secret. Whiteness was precious like money in America but over there the Vietnamese didn't give a shit about it. And neither did we.

Dallas didn't make it home. He was killed when we were on patrol one day. A sniper shot him while he stood right next to me. He could have shot me too, but he didn't. Instead I heard this Vietnamese voice shouting in broken English, "Brutha, go home, fight real enemy."

CHAPTER TWELVE

Tuesday morning at six o'clock the alarm rang and Bishop struggled to get out of bed. He'd had too much to drink the night before and was dehydrated and dragging when he needed to keep his head clear. He decided not to go for his morning run but did look out the window to see if the cops were still watching his house. They were and he wondered whether Lonnie was protecting him or just watching him. He thought about L.C. Gray and hoped he could provide him with some information about what Lonnie was doing. Bishop had been swept up in somebody else's intrigue and was tired of not knowing what was really going on and why. His head hurt a little from the wine and from thinking about all that shit. By the time he'd gotten dressed and ready to leave for school he acknowledged he had a slight hangover, took a couple of aspirin on the way out the door and hoped his students wouldn't notice.

When he started teaching in 1979 they had not yet entered the era of locked doors, police patrolling the halls and metal detectors. The teachers that he remembered in high school didn't give up on most of their students and expect nothing from them. Students didn't die because they were wearing expensive sneakers or jackets with the logos of sports teams or the wrong colors.

Every time he entered Frederick Douglass High School, he wondered where we split from our children, when did we leave them to wander in the wilderness of social contradictions. At each funeral he'd attended for one of those children, those young people on the brink of adulthood, he heard hysterical screams of history, vehement voices, pleading from the past for the lives of the children who were being sold away, never to be seen again.

Entering his classroom, he set his coffee on the desk and surveyed the empty seats. It would be a few minutes before the students started arriving. He hoped Carl would bring his briefcase and didn't get caught by the Zulu Nation or the police. The idea of Carl getting stopped with his gun made Bishop feel guilty for giving it to him. He pulled his chair out and was just about to sit down when he saw the briefcase under the desk.

He opened it. Everything was there. He looked around to make sure no one would see him, then pulled the pistol out under the desk to check it. The clip was still full, there was still one round in the chamber and the safety was still on. He relaxed a little as he placed it back in his briefcase and wondered how Carl got it back there before school opened. After learning those last few days how organized and far reaching the Cobras were, he didn't wonder too long.

As Isaiah Bishop sipped his coffee and thought about the Egyptian Cobras, he began to think about the history of gangsters in America and the possibility of a book on the subject. Maybe he'd do a historical examination of the parallels between the rise of the Italian American, Jewish American and Irish American gangsters in the first half of the century with the African American gangs of the last few years.

He thought about how other groups had taken illegally produced wealth and underworld violence and pushed their way into the political and economic mainstream. He believed that the end result of the money and violence of the black gangs wouldn't be the same. It would not result in a glorification of their behavior as part of American folklore.

He scribbled some notes. It is was an old habit. He was always scribbling notes about historical subjects that interested him with the intention of writing books or articles on them in the future.

The students started arriving. He looked up to watch them enter in their Karl Kani and Phat Farm clothes and boots. Their hairstyles demonstrated the diversity of the black community. Finger waves, braids, dreadlocks and perms, bald heads and Afros all came through the door. Bishop loved it along with the rhythm of their speech and the poetry in their bodies and hands as they moved through the air punctuating their language.

He thought, "Yeah, these are our children. Music and literature, science and math unfolding underneath their hair-dos while rap music records their lives. James Brown and John Coltrane, Bessie Smith and Robert Johnson, Louie Armstrong and Aretha Franklin all dance inside their cultural memory. They can not escape their lineage. We can not deny their logic. We must be who we are or die."

Carl came into the classroom and took a seat near the front. He gave Bishop a subtle nod, pulled out his homework and sat there ready. Carl was a good student and his mother came to the school often to check on his progress. It was ironic that he was in the Cobras, walking with one foot on both sides of the life of his community.

Bishop felt fortunate because most of his students seemed to like his classes and usually showed up. The absentee rate for his classes was only about 25 percent. That was good because some other teachers had a rate that was more than 50 percent.

In his first period class there were thirty-six students. Most of his classes had about that many. Thirty-one were present that day. Five were asleep. Some of them had jobs at Burger King and McDonald's and didn't get home until after midnight. Some of them had to get up early to get younger siblings ready for school and out the door because their mothers and fathers left before dawn to go work for low wages.

Some wandered the streets all night rather than go to troubled homes, returning to school the next day in the previous day's clothes. Some slept on the floor of crowded project apartments to avoid stray bullets. Four of the girls were mothers with small children. One of the boys was raising his two-year-old son and his younger brother. Still, they showed up there to learn, to hope, to look for something more in life than what they'd seen in the sixteen to seventeen years they'd walked the planet.

Bishop watched them stroll into his class while admiring their determination to come to school in spite of all the reasons they had not to. He had Carl pass out a study guide for the next week's test and after the usual early morning chatter, the class settled down. The topic for the day was Africa before the European invasion.

The discussion of ancient Africa always had a strange effect on the students. For some, it seemed to give them back some of what was taken hundreds of years ago. It seemed to hook them into a time when everything about black people didn't seem so negative, when they didn't seem so powerless, a time when they weren't the victims of constant abuse. A time when they ruled and prospered. A time when their contributions were recognized as more than just entertainment. It gave them a place to start piecing together themselves, their start in history. It said to them, "Yes, your ancestors were more than someone's servants. Yes, they did travel the world, trading and exploring and exporting their knowledge and culture. Yes, they felt the soil of the earth first and cultivated it and built from it." Some of them had heard things like that before, but they were almost like fairy tales until Mr. Bishop made them research and study it.

Bishop also wanted them to understand that Africa was not, as it was often presented, some mythical place without flaws or contradiction. He wanted them to understand its importance to the world, but not as fantasy. He made them examine it and understand that it was not just Europeans that led to its exploitation and subsequent underdevelopment, but its own internal conditions contributed as well.

The students came ready to deal with the discussion. They were generally surprised by the existence of slavery in Africa before the European invasion. They debated whether or not it had the same cruelty and dehumanizing qualities that American slavery had. They discussed the capture and treatment of the enslaved amongst warring African nations and the role of Arab traders.

Bishop pushed hard, throwing questions at them to make them think, respond, debate. He paced up and down between the rows of desks asking his students, "Does all slavery destroy the dignity of the enslaved? Why did it exist in Africa? Did pre-European African slavery open the way for the European slave traders? Was slavery in Africa different from slavery in Greece and Rome?"

The discussion got hot, their minds raced back and forth across the room. They searched Africa, the birthplace of their ancestors, trying to find themselves. The discussion led to a debate about the term African American. Some of the students said they should just call themselves Americans, some said African. Their questions and comments provoked more questions and comments.

Bishop gave them even more questions for homework and more topics for their research. The bell rang and he watched them leave in all their color and all their rhythm and all of their curiosity. For fifty-five minutes he was exhilarated and healed and taken away from all the craziness that had been swirling around him for the last few days.

He caught Carl before he left and pulled him to the side. "Thanks for taking care of that for me."

"It ain't nuthin, Mr. Bishop."

"I need another favor," Bishop said. "I need to see Catrell."

Carl looked around cautiously, checking to make sure they were alone. "Yeah, I'll see what I can do."

"Let me know. It's important."

Carl seemed pleased that Bishop had asked him to carry an important message to his leader. He saw it as a sign of respect that Bishop trusted him and needed his help again. He nodded his approval and put his hands across his chest folding and arranging his fingers in a sign of the Cobras that made Bishop wonder if his parents knew about his secret life and if he knew about the secret male societies in Africa and their hand signs.

"Thanks, Carl. And don't forget your paper is due tomorrow."

"Got it right here, Mr. Bishop." Carl raised two fingers and said, "Peace Out," then glided out of the classroom like a dancer. And, as if Carl's exit was a cue, Lonnie Carlton walked in.

Bishop saw him coming through the door and was annoyed by his unexpected arrival and decided not to try being cordial to cover up his irritation. "What's up, Lonnie?" Bishop asked as he turned his back to Lonnie, walked to the blackboard and erased it.

Lonnie strolled over to the first row of desks and leaned against the edge of one facing Bishop. "Where have you been, Bishop?"

Turning toward Lonnie, he replied, "Here."

Lonnie folded his arms, and continued, "Yesterday. What happened to you after school yesterday?"

Without answering, Bishop gathered the papers on his desk, stacked them neatly, placed them in a folder and put the folder in his briefcase. When he finished, he walked over to Lonnie until he stood just a couple of feet in front of him and said, "Look, am I a suspect in some crime? Because if not, you and your men should leave me alone."

Bishop turned and walked toward the door. His second period was free and he headed toward the teachers' lounge. The teacher for the next class arrived and students started filing in behind her. Lonnie hesitated for a moment then followed Bishop into the hall. The two men walked through the swarm of students in silence. The students moved past them, loud and energetic. As he walked beside Bishop up to the second floor toward the lounge, Lonnie calculated his response.

The lounge was almost empty when they entered. Only two teachers were there. One was a new student teacher, Karen Wills, a young, dark-haired white woman who taught math and looked beat down from her six weeks at the school. The other one was Hannibal Lowery, a short distinguished looking brother who'd been teaching for almost 40 years. Bishop introduced them to Lonnie, poured two cups of coffee and took a seat near a table at the back of the lounge. He placed a cup of coffee in front of Lonnie then sat down across from him and they made small talk.

"Bishop, do you get a lot of white teachers here?"

"Not many. We get a few like Karen." Bishop gestured toward her. "If she can hang, she'll probably be a good teacher because it's what she really wants to do. She wants it bad enough to put up with this shit everyday. We'll see if she lasts. Few do."

"What about black men? How many are on staff here?"

"Out of forty teachers and instructional staff, there are eight men. Five black and three white. And we're getting ready to lose one. Brother Hannibal over there is ready to retire. It would take five men to replace him."

Lonnie looked toward Hannibal. "He that good?"

"The best. He's an excellent math teacher and funny as hell. His students generally test in the top percentile in the state. Last year he got a special award from the governor for inspiring inner city youth to seek careers in math."

Bishop drank his coffee. Lonnie didn't touch his. He was just there, hanging out, waiting. Even though he really wanted answers to other questions, Lonnie's interest in the teachers and students at the school was genuine. He never had children of his own, but his long relationship with Juanita had allowed him to participate in the lives of her children. The phone rang in the lounge and Hannibal picked it up. It was for Bishop, who walked across the room, put the receiver to his ear and heard the voice of Sergeant L.C. Gray. "Bishop."

"Hey, how're you doing?" Bishop looked over at Lonnie and tried to remain casual. He watched Lonnie pick up a copy of *VIBE* magazine and flip through the pages.

"You know that investigation you asked me about?"

"Yeah." Bishop knew Lonnie was listening even though he appeared totally engrossed in the magazine.

"It's not true. There is no federal agency working with that cop down there. I don't know what your boy's into, but watch your ass. You understand?"

"Yes, I understand." He looked over at Lonnie whose head was hidden behind the *VIBE*. "Thanks for calling. We'll talk soon."

Bishop hung the phone up slowly trying to decide if he should mention the so-called investigation. The two teachers excused themselves and left. Lonnie closed the magazine and set it down on the table. Bishop came back over and took his seat. Lonnie slid his chair closer to the table and leaned forward on his elbows. "Bishop, I'm not your enemy."

Bishop had been waiting for this. He knew Lonnie's chatter about teachers and education was just to pass the time until they were alone.

Lonnie continued, "We're not watching you because you've done anything. I'm just trying to find King. He's in trouble and needs help. You know he's like a son to me. I've known him since he was twelve years old."

Bishop leaned forward, too. "What kind of trouble?"

They were locking into each other, their eyes becoming intensely focused, each one trying to read the other, trying to find the truth or the lies that they both carried about what was happening all around them.

"He hasn't broken the law." Lonnie spoke quietly, calmly as if what he was saying was no big deal. "I just think he saw something down at city hall that may make him dangerous to some people."

Bishop was becoming agitated by the casualness of Lonnie's answers and asked pointedly, "What people? What do you think he saw?"

"Don't know yet." Lonnie, leaned back in his chair and glanced over toward the phone, breaking the stare between them. He looked back at Bishop whose eyes had not moved.

"Lonnie, look, for the last few days you've been telling me basically the same thing, that King knows about some kind of conspiracy that could endanger his life. You're not really telling me anything, yet you want my help in finding him. I can't help you. I don't know where King is, who he's with or why he's disappeared. So why don't you leave me alone? I'm sure King will contact you when he's ready."

Without acknowledging Bishop's remarks, Lonnie stood up and asked, "OK if I use the phone?" He started in the direction of the phone as if permission had already been granted.

Bishop pushed back from the table. "Yeah. Go ahead." He watched Lonnie move to the other side of the room and tried to measure his sincerity. He knew that this was just a tactic, another practiced interrogation method. Lonnie's call was short. He was just checking voicemail messages and didn't even say anything. It took less than two minutes. When he came back to the table, Bishop sipped his coffee and watched as Lonnie took his seat, sat back in the chair, crossed his legs and brushed at some lint on his pants.

"Bishop, I know you're fond of King, but you can't help him in this shit. I can."

"Then you should go find him."

Bishop was deliberately trying to provoke Lonnie and studied his reaction. He saw Lonnie's jaw tighten and his eyes cut sharply his way. Bishop had intentionally put them at odds. They both knew Lonnie was lying or at least not telling the whole truth. Lonnie pushed his chair back and stood up abruptly. He had said what he came to say. He stared at Bishop who sat his cup down, looked up directly into his eyes and asked, "Who killed Stacey Freeman?"

Lonnie shoved his hands down into the pockets of his expensive, wide legged, pleated pants, and with frustration hung on him like the Armani jacket he was wearing, replied curtly, "We don't know."

Bishop stood up so that they were again face to face, eye to eye.

"Why are the police looking for Catrell Merit?"

"He knew Stacey." Lonnie spun toward the door.

Bishop walked behind him, continuing with his questions, "Do you think he killed her?"

Turning back to face Bishop, pissed off that the discussion had not only yielded no results, but had also been turned against him, Lonnie said sternly, "No. We think he might know who did." And as if it was an afterthought, he added, "If you hear anything from your students, call me. You know if you hold back any information that could help the investigation you could get in trouble."

Bishop didn't respond to his invitation to be a snitch or the implied threat. He just studied Lonnie and again noticed the fatigue and frustration. Lonnie was clearly agitated. Bishop didn't know if it was just his refusal to be helpful or whether it was something else. Lonnie tried to conceal it. He was used to hiding behind a veneer of control, but the cracks were showing.

He said nothing more to Bishop. Without uttering a word he just turned and left and walked into the hall and out of sight. Bishop was glad he was gone. Lonnie had seemed almost panicked by something. Time was becoming crucial.

Bishop thought about the call from Sgt. Gray and the questions that still had no answers. If Lonnie wasn't really investigating the mayor, why would he say that? He must have figured Bishop had no way of checking and that saying it was a federal investigation would make his need to find King seem more urgent.

It was a good story because it wouldn't have been the first time Mayor Packard had been under investigation. It was already the third or fourth. Each previous time he escaped without being charged with any crimes, but members of his administration had been indicted for taking kickbacks on city contracts and a couple were convicted and served time in jail.

The mayor was always accusing the federal government of trying to destroy his administration and his effectiveness as a black leader. While making those charges he would have to denounce the actions of the members of his own administration who were convicted. Oddly, the corruption in his office was excused by his constituents who rallied to support and protect him from the people who were supposedly out to get him. He was a master of rhetoric and could appeal to the deep need in the black community for heroes.

The bell rang for the next period. Bishop had another class to teach and walked out into the hall and into a crowd of youthful faces. They grabbed their things and slammed their lockers. A couple kissed in the stairwell as Bishop passed and told them to get to class. A member of the basketball team dribbled a ball while one of his friends tried taking it. Singing seeped out of the girls' bathroom in perfect four part harmony.

He reached his classroom feeling invigorated by the energy of the halls. He was ready to teach another junior class. When he arrived, the students were already in their seats. As he approached his desk, Bishop noticed that the room was eerily quiet. There was no sound except a muffled sobbing. He turned to face them and saw that the students were solemn. Some were weeping. He dropped down into his chair and thought, "Oh God, not again!"

A tear stained voice reached from the back of the room. "Mr. Bishop, Carl Johnson was just killed outside the school."

Bishop's eyes filled like a reservoir of sadness and his heart vomited pain into the wound opening up in his soul. Torn, snatched from his senses, his body was numbed by the sobbing and weeping that was rising inside the room. He could not speak. Frozen, suspended in the sound of grief washing over him, he could only look at his young students and watch some of the young men shifting around in their seats, struggling in silence to confine their emotions, pretending they were too hard for it to bother them. The young women cried, hiding behind their hands to mask the contortion of their faces caused by the terrible, terrible monster that was slashing its way through their friends. He had no words to help them or guide them or heal them and he was nauseated by the constant spinning of the cycle of destruction. Bishop sat there like an aging, almost beaten prize fighter slumped in his corner, contemplating whether to answer the bell or throw in the towel.

Carl was a popular student and had friends throughout the school. He was smart and witty and girls liked the way he behaved like a gentleman. His parents were two hard working people who didn't make a lot of money. His father drove a truck for a local furniture store and his mother cleaned up office buildings downtown. They taught their son manners and whenever he talked to them he said "yes, Sir" and "no, Ma'am."

Carl had never been in any trouble until he was caught writing Cobra

94

graffiti on the walls of the school. As Bishop thought about it, he realized Carl must have been a recent recruit of the Cobras. He was still excited about the deference that the gang members got. Being from a loving family didn't save him. Being in a gang didn't kill him. Living without dreams in the middle of a war zone did.

Bishop didn't even have to hear the details. What happened was clear and too familiar. Carl had left school and was walking down the street when someone rode up on him, blasted him with an automatic weapon and ended his young life.

Juanita was getting out of her car with some groceries when Bishop pulled up in front of her house. Emotional and physical exhaustion had ripped the energy out of him as he fought with his feelings about Carl and tried to console the students. He dreaded going over to Carl's house and offering condolences to his family. He was sick of going to the funerals of children.

Juanita was smiling and the setting sun was laying its warmth on her brown skin. He gave her a hand with the bags and followed her into the house and into the kitchen. She thanked him and started putting the groceries away. His eyes were fixed on her movement but his mind was broken from her image by the loss of Carl. Her hands touched objects, carrots and broccoli, collard greens, pears, grapes and a huge mango. His eyes recorded what he was seeing but his reactions were dulled by an aching numbness.

Juanita placed a pear on the counter, turned on the faucet and washed away the dirt and chemicals then turned toward Bishop and handed him the fruit as a reward for either his help or his company. She pulled the handle of the refrigerator and pushed it shut, putting things in their places. The odd rhythm of it caught his ear. The faucet dripped slowly. The wind blew the branches of trees against the house and rustled leaves fallen in the yard. A siren wailed in the distance. Bishop bit into the pear and heard the crunch of the skin as his teeth broke through. He chewed and swallowed but could not taste its sweetness. He rested his hand on the table and held the pear and stared at the hole he'd torn in its flesh.

Juanita finished putting away her groceries and sat down across from him. She was worried about Bishop and studied him closely. Almost the whole time he'd been there silence had been draped across his shoulders like a cape. Playfully, she questioned him, "Are you tired of talking to me already?"

Bishop sat silently. He looked up at her, then back down at his hands. Juanita continued, "We finally had one good, long talk and now you've got nothing to say. I don't understand you, Mr. Isaiah Bishop. What's wrong? I thought we..." Juanita stopped suddenly, her face full of alarm. She saw the pain painted on Bishop and it frightened her. Her body stiffened as if anticipating a blow.

"Has something happened to my son?" she asked covering her mouth with her hand.

Bishop looked up at her and very quietly replied, "No. Nothing has happened to King."

Juanita closed her eyes, said a quick prayer and exhaled heavily as if she'd been holding her breath. Her shoulders relaxed and she was visibly relieved but still concerned about the hurt in Bishop's face.

"Bishop, what happened to you today? There is such sadness all around you."

He told her about Carl Johnson and he began to cry. She came around the table, took his head into her arms, pressed his face against her body and cried with him. Her tears flowed down into his life and he stood up and held onto her and they wept together and there were no words for their sorrow and no other sound except the dripping of the faucet in her kitchen.

War pulls me away
from you.
It tears me away
and hurls me into
fire and blood and noise.
It rips me
from the softness
of your skin
and the warmth
of your eyes
and the comfort
of your voice
and the peace
of our love.
It slams me into
something brutal
and ugly and
loud.

Chapter Thirteen

It was night when Bishop finally left Juanita's house. They hadn't talked much. They just held onto each other for a long time and then sat in the silence of her kitchen while the darkness slid in.

Although Bishop felt a need to go on and make his visit to Carl's parents, he was afraid of his feelings and wondered what he could say. The same shit that was said to the others. Nothing. At least nothing that will fill the hole that was just burned into their lives. What are our children dying for today? What cause is worthy of this tremendous loss? What God requires this kind of appeasement and demands that we sacrifice their lives?

He spoke those thoughts to himself as he pulled away from Juanita's house and depression descended on him. No. He couldn't do it that night. He couldn't talk to Carl's parents. The morning would be better. His own grief would only add to their injury. He decided to wait until the morning and changed directions before he went somewhere and got drunk and more depressed. Ironically he headed into George Washington Homes.

Pulling up alongside the project, Bishop thought it seemed much too quiet. The usual shadows guarding the entrance weren't visible. The familiar gunshots, sirens and screams of pleasure and terror weren't heard. It was a dramatic difference from the other night. It was quiet, still, like the darkness was anticipating some eruption of heat and anger that would shake the buildings out of their foundations with such force that the people would tumble out of the windows onto the concrete.

He got out and walked cautiously toward the buildings. A young man in a long leather coat stepped out from the side of a building and directly in front of him. For a heartbeat or two they examined each other. The young man's face was not familiar and he seemed to be searching his mind to find something familiar in Bishop's.

Bishop gestured toward the buildings and said, "I'm looking for Catrell."

The man shrugged his shoulders and replied, "He ain't here." The man kept his right hand in his pocket and kept looking around behind him and up and down the street behind Bishop.

Bishop glanced around to see if there were others lurking in the shadows. "Tell him Mr. Bishop wants to see him."

"Mr. Bishop, yeah." He shook his head up and down. "You King's teacher."

"You know where King is?" Bishop asked.

"Naww." He shook his head and took his hand out of his pocket.

"Can you get my message to Catrell?"

"Yeah."

Bishop said, "Thanks." Then stood there wondering what he should say or do next. The young man scanned the area then finally stepped around Bishop and started walking back toward his car. It was an invitation to leave. Bishop followed a step or two behind him and watched the young brother look up and down the street where the car was parked. He stopped at the curb and watched Bishop get in and drive away.

He didn't know where to go. Driving out of the projects and into downtown, passing city hall, he pondered the accusations Lonnie made against the mayor. Bishop drove away from the black community but without a destination in mind until he finally rolled into the north end of town filled with white people and their restaurants, boutiques, stores and scores of folks walking and enjoying the casual night life that surrounded them. He parked his car and melted into the pedestrians strolling past the shops or coming out of restaurants. At a little cafe he stopped and ordered a cup of cappuccino. His best friend, Vincent Daniel, lived nearby and Bishop called him from the pay phone in back of the place and asked him to come there and have a cup of coffee.

While he waited for Vincent, Bishop took a seat by the window and counted the black people walking by. There were only a few. He played a game, trying to guess what they did. He figured some were doctors or lawyers, a few might be entrepreneurs and some must be college students and artists. He watched a homeless man cleaning windshields at the corner and one of the councilmen from the south side holding hands with a young white woman as they crossed the street. Everything seemed so far removed from the horrors thousands of people lived with every day on the other side of the city.

A history professor from the university came into the cafe with her husband. She and Bishop were friends and she stopped by his table and invited him to join them. He told her he was waiting for someone. It would have been nice at another time but Bishop was so drained he just wanted to sit there and play that silly game and be away from the fires burning across town.

His second cup had just made its way to the table when Vincent walked in. His family owned the local black newspaper, *The Crusader*, and since his folks retired, Vincent had become the editor and publisher. He spotted Bishop and went over to his table.

Bishop greeted him with a smile and said, "Vincent, what's happening?"

Pulling a chair out and sitting down, Vincent replied, "Hey, Bishop, I'm just trying to get in where I fit in."

That was Vincent, always poetic in the way of their people. In just a few words he had summed up their whole existence in this country. "Trying to get in where I fit in." Bishop thought, "Yeah, where is that? After all of these hundreds of years, where the hell is that?"

Vincent was always like that. In high school he wore a huge afro and wrote poetry. Fiery, beautiful poetry. He turned Bishop on to all kinds of words, by great word wizards. When Bishop was in Nam, Vincent sent him work from writers throughout the black world, as well as some of his own poems. He sent him the poetry of Aime Ceasaire from Martinique and it lifted Bishop up when he saw that Vincent had marked the lines that said,

> there is no place on this earth without my fingerprint and my
> heel upon the skeleton of skyscrapers, and my sweat in the
> brilliance of diamonds!

He hipped him to Mari Evans' "Speak the Truth to the People," Jayne Cortez's "There It Is," and Haki Madhubuti's "We Walk the Way of the New World." Bishop started writing his own poems and sending them to back home to Vincent. They'd end their letters with quotations from the works of Gwendolyn Brooks, Larry Neal, Margaret Walker, Sonia Sanchez and Askia Touré. And often the entire Claude McKay poem "*If We Must Die*" would be their post script.

When Bishop came home from the war he and Vincent would go hear the great poets whenever there were readings in town. Their favorite was Amiri Baraka, whose use of language and imagery was so musical and innovative it was as if his poems were notes pulled out of an instrument by Bird.

Bishop sat there, in that little cafe, consumed with pain about the death of his student and the danger surrounding King and the escalating gang war in the city and felt a great sense of relief that one of his oldest friends had shown up. At the moment Vincent walked into the cafe and with his first words sang poetry to Bishop it seemed as though there was nothing that rhymed or flowed with the beauty and power of their tradition. Vincent had reminded him that the key to their survival was to walk, to move, to dance, to sing, to live, as Baraka had said in one of his poems, in the tradition.

Vincent was dressed casually in jeans, a beautiful cotton shirt, leather jacket and some Italian loafers that looked soft as butter. Ever since he'd known him, even in high school, he'd always dressed well, draping beautiful clothes on his six-foot two-inch frame. He was like the Duke Ellington of their school. Vincent would have on some shit that made him look elegant like Duke. He had that royal manner about him, too, but it was cool in the way that black folks made even stiff shit cool. He hadn't changed. He still had that Ellington thing happening.

It had been two months since they last saw each other. Neither could offer a reason why except that their lives were so busy. They sat and talked for over an hour, catching up on the latest and each other's lives. Vincent asked about Sheila and gave Bishop a report on the latest progress of his two young sons. His wife, Michelle, was a painter and he invited Bishop to a show she was having in a couple of weeks. They fell into easy conversation the way only old true friends can. It was as if they'd just spoken on the phone yesterday. The familiarity of the company and conversation relieved Bishop and took him away from the contradictions screaming inside him.

"So, Vincent, do you plan to run for city council again?"

"Probably. I missed it last time by less than two hundred votes."

"You have a year and a half to put it together."

"If my close friends would kick in some campaign contributions I'd have a head start."

"Why don't you try being a little more direct?"

"I'll remember that." Looking at the dessert menu, Vincent asked, "You want a slice of carrot cake?"

"Hell no. You see how much weight I've put on." Bishop patted his stomach.

Pulling back his jacket and looking at his midsection, Vincent answered, "Me, too."

"What are you talking about? You look the same as you did twenty years ago."

"Plus fifteen pounds and I have to work like hell to maintain that."

"It's a motherfucker ain't it?" Bishop stated.

"Damn, Bishop, now I don't even want the cake." Vincent tossed the menu onto the table. "That's fucked up."

They both laughed and Bishop wanted to tell him what had been going on but hesitated. If he opened up the emotion he felt, he didn't know what would spill out onto the table. He knew Vincent had been watching the attack on the Cobras and the mayor's launch of the latest war on crime and drugs. He would report on it and analyze it in the pages of *The Crusader*. But, like most people in the city, Vincent didn't know how deep it was about to get.

They talked for over an hour allowing the spirits of two old friends to visit and renew the bond of deep brotherhood born in adolescent adventures and adult accomplishments. They finally said good-bye outside the cafe, on a street in the north end of town. Bishop noticed that none of the people passing on the street were walking in fear. The streets were brightly lit, there was no broken glass under his feet and the only siren was from an ambulance rushing to the scene of a car accident in the next block. They shook hands and hugged each other under a sky of fluorescent lights. Two forty-four year old African American men shook hands, embraced and promised to see each other soon.

Walking back to his car, Bishop was grateful to have lived to see forty-four years, grateful that he'd spent time with his best friend, grateful that Juanita washed his wounds with her gentle tears, grateful that he still believed they would rescue their children and save their people and this nation. He knew there was no other choice.

CHAPTER FOURTEEN

When he stepped inside his house it felt cool, like a window had been left opened. The thought led Bishop from room to room, checking to insure everything was in place and that he hadn't had an uninvited guest. Everything was fine, it was just that the nights were getting colder and he hadn't turned on the heat.

Passing through the house, Bishop realized how much he enjoyed it. It was an old two-story brick home in a historic black neighborhood. He loved the community with its teachers and factory workers, writers and doctors, young couples who grew up there, went away and moved back to start their families, and grandparents who had been there for thirty or forty years.

He bought the house about ten years ago, and had spent some time and money working on it. Slowly it responded to his touch and welcomed the art, books, music and furniture that began to fill it. Sheila told him recently that she had always enjoyed the eclectic feel of the house and that her friends had thought it was cool that every room was a different color and set a different mood.

As a little girl, she played a game in which she would move from one room to another, pretending each room was a different movie set. Even then it was evident she was headed for the stage. It wasn't a surprise when she started performing in school plays or that she was studying theater arts in college. She was blessed with her mother's artistic genes.

Bishop was about to make a sandwich when the doorbell rang. The stove clock said 11:00 p.m. It was strange to have an unexpected visitor at that hour. He retrieved his pistol and went to the door holding it behind his back. Standing to the side of the door, Bishop shouted, "Who is it?"

"Catrell Merit."

Bishop stuck the gun in the back of his pants and yanked the door open. There, standing on his porch alone, was the leader of the Egyptian Cobras, a man wanted by the police and marked for death by his rival, the Dexter Avenue Zulu Nation.

"Come in." Bishop let Catrell pass by him and then looked around outside before closing the door. "Are you alone?"

"Naww, but I'll come in by myself."

Bishop hadn't been that close to Catrell in the years since he was his student. Catrell seemed taller and a little heavier but handsome and polite like Bishop remembered him. They went into the kitchen where Bishop said, "I was just fixin' a sandwich. You want one?"

"Yeah, thanks." Catrell sat at the table and studied the three Vanderzee photographs on the wall.

Bishop hooked up two sandwiches of sliced turkey breast, some cheese, lettuce, tomato and mustard. Catrell watched patiently while Bishop pulled two beers out of the refrigerator, handed him one, then sat down at the old wooden table that used to be in his grandmother's kitchen and that she had said was handmade by a former slave.

Catrell twisted the top off the beer, took a sip and said, "Mr. Bishop, you said you wanted to see me."

Bishop pulled the top off his beer. "You know the police are looking for you?"

"Yes."

"Catrell, I don't know what's going on, but they've been watching me for the last few days. They probably have the house under surveillance now."

"Yeah, they do. But don't worry about it, I know the cops who are on duty tonight." He took a bite from the sandwich. "This is good."

Bishop was amazed that Catrell was so unconcerned about the police, but realized he shouldn't be. Catrell had survived as the reigning king of his trade for years. He probably employed dozens of cops. Surely, he knew they were looking for him before most of the police force had heard it on the radio. They both sat there in silence for a moment eating their sandwiches and drinking the beer.

After a few minutes Catrell said, "You've got a nice house here, Mr. Bishop." He pointed toward the backdoor. "Do you mind if we go sit on your back porch?" Catrell stood up with his half eaten sandwich in one hand and the beer in the other.

"Sure." Bishop grabbed a sweater from the back of the chair. "Let's go."

He wasn't surprised by the request. Catrell was calmly cautious like someone used to the possibility of danger any minute. He was like a soldier in a combat zone, always anticipating an attack, always making slight adjustments in what you're doing, where you're standing, trying not to let yourself relax into being an easy target.

They stepped onto the back porch. Shadows moved in the alley but they didn't startle Catrell. He didn't even react. Bishop and Catrell sat down on the steps with their sandwiches and beer, enjoying the crisp, fall night like two friends about to discuss the World Series. But what they were going to discuss was not about baseball.

"Tell me what you need." Catrell set his food down between his legs and rested his long arms on his knees.

Bishop felt himself admiring the power of the young man sitting beside him. He gulped some beer then said, "Two things. I need to know where King is and I need some information."

Catrell was chewing and waited until he had swallowed before answering. "King is safe, but you won't see him for a while. He's going to stay out of sight until things calm down. Don't worry, he'll contact you. What information do you need?"

He answered Bishop's first question with such absolute authority that there was no sense in probing deeper. Bishop liked his directness, his no bullshit responses.

"Did you know Stacey Freeman?"

"Yes."

"Why was she killed?"

"Because she knew me."

"Is King in trouble because of his relationship with Stacey or you?"

"No. King is in trouble because of his relationship with Lonnie Carlton."

"What?"

Catrell paused, took another bite from his sandwich, took a sip of beer and pulled out a pack of cigarettes. "Do you mind if I smoke?"

"Go ahead." He offered one to Bishop, who declined by waving his hand somewhat impatiently. He was eager to hear what Catrell was about to say. Bishop remained still and hadn't touched the beer or sandwich since the conversation began. Catrell lit a cigarette, stared at the magnolia tree in the yard and started talking, almost whispering, again.

"Stacey and I used to hang out sometimes. I'd been seeing her for about a year. Six or seven months ago, Lonnie Carlton got King a job in the mayor's office where Stacey worked."

"I know, but what does that have to do with—"

"No disrespect, Mr. Bishop, but you gotta listen. Listen very carefully."

Pausing and pulling hard on his cigarette, he looked at Bishop then turned his attention back to the tree as if it were a teleprompter with the information carved into its bark.

"Lonnie asked King to get some information from City Hall. Stacey

105

told me what King was doing and I asked him why Lonnie wanted it. He didn't know, he just did it as a favor because of Lonnie's relationship to him and his mother. I told Stacey to help him out and give me copies of everything that King took. I figured if Lonnie was looking for something on the mayor, it might be helpful to me in the future. There was nothing specific at first, just some memos from the mayor, records of meetings and things like that. Useless documents about nothing really important.

"Last month, King told Stacey about a particular file Lonnie was looking for. A file on a man named Greg Gatson. She'd never heard that name or seen a file on him. She told me about it. Again, I asked King what it was about. He didn't know who he was either or why Lonnie was interested. It made me curious because I'd heard this cat's name mentioned once or twice in the past.

"Two weeks ago, a man shows up at City Hall to see the mayor, says his name is Greg Gatson. He wasn't on the mayor's schedule so Stacey told him he'd have to call for an appointment and asked what it was about. He wouldn't tell her and just left.

"The next day she saw his name on the schedule. He came in and met with the Mayor for about an hour. Stacey told King what happened and King told Lonnie.

"Later that day, Stacey took some papers into the Mayor's office and saw a handwritten note on his desk. It said something about a $50,000 payment. She made a copy of it and gave it to King. Lonnie called King that same day and told him to look for a file under the name ENTAC Enterprise."

Catrell took one last hit on the cigarette, walked down the stairs and dropped it on the concrete walkway where he stamped it out. Still standing, he faced Bishop and continued. "A few days ago, Stacey found the file and called me, upset, scared about something she'd read in it. Something about me. She couldn't copy it because the office was full of people. She couldn't read it to me over the phone either. She took it home and called me. King and I went over to Stacey's house to meet her. When we got there, she was gone. Her house was empty, nothing had been disturbed, it was like she hadn't been home from work yet. The file wasn't there either."

He lit another cigarette and the reflection of its glow made his eyes seem as if they were on fire. The smoke drifted up past the smooth dark skin and sharp cheek bones and Bishop listened to his voice resonate in the darkness, almost hypnotizing him with a cadence and tone that was deeply musical.

"Hours went by and I didn't hear from Stacey. I knew something was wrong. King went home and later called me because he thought he was being watched by someone parked outside his building. I sent some of the brothers over to get him and bring him back to George Washington Homes. He left you the note so you could find him. We didn't anticipate Lonnie running into you."

"Catrell, what about the shooting outside of King's building?"

"Zulu Nation. They killed one of their own because they suspected him of spying for me. It was just a coincidence that you were there at the time. We knew Lonnie would be looking for King, but the shooting brought him to the house before we could get you to Washington Homes.

"Because King trusts you, we agreed to ask you to go back to Stacey's to see if she was all right and to get the file for us. Before he could tell you what was going on, we came under attack Friday night in George Washington Homes and Stacey was murdered."

"Catrell, why? What has triggered all of these things so suddenly?"

"Everything has something to do with that file."

Bishop sat there stunned and speechless. Some kind of hellish chaos had been unleashed. His mind stuttered, searching for coherent thought. Confusion was storming around in his consciousness trying to decipher everything he'd seen and heard recently. There was too much information to process, too many intense emotions to assimilate.

Catrell had never taken his eyes off the magnolia tree. The story was told clearly and calmly as if he had been prepared for the witness stand by an experienced trial lawyer. So many things had happened, so many questions were demanding satisfaction, yet answers remained absent. Like Bishop, Catrell was searching, trying to find out what had caused so much destruction and disorder to descend upon his life in the last few days.

Just as Bishop was about to ask him what he intended to do, one of the shadows stepped into the light falling out of the kitchen window. Catrell moved down the stairs to meet him. The young man whispered something to him, then melted back into the darkness and out of sight.

"I have to leave. If you find out anything about Stacey let me know. You can always reach me, just speak to the street. Don't worry about King, I'll keep him safe; but, you be careful. You're in the shit, too."

Before Bishop could respond, Catrell had stepped into the darkness, joined the shadows and merged with the blackness.

After Catrell left, Bishop sat there on the back steps of his house, listening to the leaves dance in the wind, watching them wave at the night sky. He sat there a long time as the sounds of his neighborhood at rest floated over to him. A few doors over, a dog barked at something unseen. A car door slammed down the street. Youthful footsteps echoed off the sidewalk and bounced up the stairs of a house across the street. Next door, the whispers of lovemaking slid underneath the slightly raised window. The fall wind danced with the trees and Bishop sat there on his back steps, wondering how the night could be so calm, so full of gentleness, so peaceful, and yet so full of madness.

Like a lot of brothers over there during the war, I had become the living embodiment of America's stereotype-fed anxiety, a young black man with a gun who didn't really care who got killed. To be universally feared, not just by those who were supposed to be your enemy, but also by those who were supposed to be your friends, is a very powerful experience. In the war, my violent attitude was tolerated because I was useful in the field, but here at home, there is nothing but destruction, fatal destruction for a young black man with the same posture.

In the war, many of the men had become such efficient killing machines that they completely disconnected from their own humanity. Some of them seemed to enjoy killing and decorated themselves with the ears or fingers of those they killed. Even though I killed, too, I felt that carrying someone's body parts on me as a trophy would confirm that my soul was lost. I fought with my mind, wrestled with it, to never believe that any human life was worthless, even if I thought they had to be killed. Somehow I felt that made my shit better, nobler. In my mind, I'd worked it out where killing you, didn't have to include hating you. To the victims of my actions, I realize now, my twisted logic didn't matter.

CHAPTER FIFTEEN

Perhaps going to see Carl's family before work was the coward's way, but it was the only way Bishop could get through the visit. He shaved, showered, dressed, drank his morning glass of juice and glanced over the headlines in the newspaper while listening to Me'Shell NdegeOcello on the Tom Joyner show. Bishop felt like a coward, but there was so much pain and confusion swirling around inside him, that he had to limit the time he could stay with them. Making the visit short would restrict the amount of his own pain that he tracked into their house like mud from his shoes.

Bishop's plan was to sit with them over coffee for a few minutes, enough time to offer condolences, enough time to show respect without exploding from the weeping going on inside him. He realized that his visit would not help them heal, but it would be a gesture to say that Carl belonged to him, too, and to their village, their tribe, their nation, to their people. It would say that he, we, also mourned because the child they gave us had to leave so early to join the ancestors' choir.

When Bishop arrived at their house he looked through the custom made security door that kept them safe inside but could do nothing to protect their children outside. He knocked on the door. Carl's father, Marcus, opened it.

Bishop stuck out his hand. "Mr. Johnson, I'm Isaiah Bishop. Carl's teacher."

Marcus Johnson's eyes were red and swollen. He looked at Bishop strangely then took his hand and shook it. "Come in, Mr. Bishop. My wife will be right out."

Marcus Johnson's hands reminded Bishop of his own father's. They were laborer's hands full of calluses and scars and aches and stories of a million hours working trying to feed a family. They were the hands of life, extended by machinery and tools and makeshift instruments of work. They were the hands of men breaking bricks and carrying concrete and lifting loads and bearing burdens so heavy that their strength sang centuries of songs of survival. Bishop shook Marcus Johnson's hands with both of his, hoping to convey his sense of respect for him as a man and his sympathy for him as a father.

Carl's mother, Mary, entered the living room and hugged Bishop. They'd met several times at parent teacher conferences. She hugged him and said, "Mr. Bishop, I'm so glad you came by. Carl loved your class."

Bishop fought the tears swelling up in his heart. He swallowed hard and said, "I'm so sorry, your son was a real light at the school. It is a great loss for all of us."

"We appreciate that." She patted him on the arm and walked toward the kitchen. "You want some coffee, Mr. Bishop? I shoulda cooked some breakfast by now, but..."

"Coffee's fine. Thank you." He took a seat at the dining room table.

Mary was a petite woman with long black hair streaked with gray. She was younger than Bishop, maybe thirty-three or thirty-four. Her husband, Marcus, was a big man with broad shoulders who looked to be about forty-five. After opening the door, Marcus sat down quietly in a chair covered with plastic, in a living room of furniture covered in plastic. He and Mary both looked tired and weary and worn and lost. They looked as if they needed someone to explain who the enemy was that killed their son. He wasn't gunned down in some war in a far off land. He wasn't caught on a dark night on a southern road by the Ku Klux Klan and lynched and mutilated. He wasn't beaten to death by a group of racist cops and then strung up in a jail cell to make it look like suicide. He was murdered outside his high school, in his own neighborhood a few blocks from his home, by young men like him.

Mary showed Bishop pictures of Carl as a little boy. He was a happy three year old in one photo, dressed up for church on Easter Sunday. In another, he was about ten, wearing a little league baseball uniform. There was a family portrait, the kind taken at Sears. Marcus and Mary were smiling, the proud parents of Carl and his two younger brothers.

Looking at that cheap family photo, Bishop thought, they are the best of who we are. A man and a woman, a family, hard working, loving folks, trying to raise their children to love and live and develop and create in an environment that encourages none of that.

Carl's grandmother came downstairs. They called her Miss Mae and she was small like her daughter, Mary, but with long straight silver hair. Bishop noticed that Mary's mother looked Native American except she had dark, black skin. The affection between Miss Mae and Mary was obvious when she walked behind the chair where her daughter sat and started combing Mary's hair. On the wall behind her, a white Jesus, Martin Luther King and John Kennedy looked over the grief in the room and watched Miss Mae combing her baby's hair while humming to heal her daughter's hurt.

Bishop sat there trying to lend whatever strength he could while struggling with what he would face once he got to school. It was going to be a long, painful day. His stomach was in a tight knot knowing that the eyes of Carl's classmates would search his face for answers. Their eyes would ask, "Who protects us?" Their angry, confused, mournful mood would melt all rational responses and reprimand the adults who had promised a better world for them. They would want to know how the march forward was turned into a constant struggle against forces of rage turned inward, unleashed in waves of murder, self-hatred and revenge. Sitting in the Johnson's home he wondered, too. Every day, he wondered.

After about fifteen minutes, Bishop rose to leave, offering his pre-planned excuse that his classes would begin soon. He thanked Mary for the coffee, promised to attend the funeral and headed toward the door. Marcus finally stood up, thanked him for coming and walked him out. Bishop made his way slowly toward the car while two women from the neighborhood and Mr. Hopkins, the school custodian, came up the walk bringing food to the Johnson's house. As he drove away, Miss Mae's humming filled the air as if she were conjuring spirits to come, now, to protect and surround her family with love.

Promises
pass through
pieces of memory
strewn across
hundreds of years
gathering themselves
to remind us
of a time
a place
a people
born in blood
lost on battlefields
and farmland
and cities full
of sin
seen through
sudden sun rises
and seasons
running from
the expectations
our experience
explains
in blues and
recalls in the rhythm
of souls singing
for salvation.

CHAPTER SIXTEEN

By the evening of the day after Carl Johnson was murdered, Bishop was exhausted. Teaching in the public school system was always difficult. Teaching through a wall of grief was almost impossible. All day, the sadness surrounding Carl's death kept heaving itself upon the entire school, splattering everything with a smell and a taste and a texture that was foul like rotting flesh on a battlefield. His classmates knew there weren't any answers, so they didn't ask any questions. And that was the only lesson learned that day.

In addition to his regular classes, Bishop also had to teach his once a week adult night school class. Like the day classes, he pushed through the evening classes distracted by his thoughts of Carl and King and all the black boys dying. For once, he was uninspired by the effort being made by the adults sitting in front of him trying to get an education. It was unusual for him to feel that way and shame crept up to remind him of the nobility of their efforts.

Arriving home about 10:00 p.m. Bishop's clothes felt heavy on his weary body and he shed them. Dropping his jacket on the couch in the living room, he threw Arthur Blythe and David Murray into the CD player. He left his sweater and shirt in the kitchen, where he stopped to pour a shot of cognac. Pants, socks, shoes and underwear were on the floor in the bathroom where hot water filled up the tub. His nakedness did not satisfy his need to be free of all the pain he carried inside, but it relaxed him like the cognac.

Before stepping into the tub, he paused at the mirror to look at the changes in his body. Though not fat, he was getting soft in spots and needed to work out. He'd always been in pretty good shape and since the army he'd tried to remain active and exercise, but recent laziness had interrupted his maintenance and it showed. He looked at his reflection and thought, "Damn, is that my stomach sitting there looking ready to be rubbed?" He rubbed it, shrugged his shoulders and said, "Fuck it." The hot water was calling him.

He slid down in the water recalling how much he loved that old tub with the claw feet where you could stretch out so the water came all the way up to your neck. The cognac reached his head, the music filled the house and the hot water pulled the tension out of his body. For almost an hour he lay there, warm and wet, washing away a day that should not have had so much pain in it. He wanted to sleep and dream of something peaceful. He wanted to dream of Juanita. He fell naked into the bed and into a hard sleep.

Tap-Tap-Tap.....Tap-Tap-Tap......

A noise started banging against his dreams. His eyes popped open and his ears reached for the sound coming from downstairs. Instinctively, he grabbed the Baretta from the night stand and cocked it. There was a tapping sound. Then it stopped. He swung out of the bed and landed lightly on the floor. More tapping, then silence. Bishop was naked but didn't want to waste time putting on clothes or risk making noise that would give himself away. Creeping to the top of the stairs he listened. The tapping started again. One, two, three times, then it stopped. He focused intensely on the noise. It sounded like someone was tapping on the door but they didn't want to make too much noise. It sounded like someone checking to see if anyone was in the house.

Moving quietly downstairs and into the hallway that led to the front door, Bishop stayed close to the wall, looked through the stained glass window and saw a man standing on the porch. Because of the contours of the glass, Bishop couldn't see his face clearly, but it was definitely a man, an unfamiliar man. He moved closer to the door to get a better look at the stranger. The person on the porch looked around nervously at the street. Bishop wondered, "Who the hell is he and where is the cop that was parked on the street watching my house?" In the shadows in the hall, Bishop crouched down and waited.

The man tapped again, lightly, then turned around and looked up and down the street again. He pressed his face against the window of the door and looked into the darkened house not knowing he was being watched. He couldn't see Bishop in the shadows when he turned the knob and the door creaked as he pushed his weight against it, not hard, just enough to test to see if the door was locked. Bishop kept his eyes and gun trained on the man and waited calmly, knowing whoever it was, he was going to shoot him the minute he came through the door.

A car passed the house and the man on the porch froze for a moment. There was silence on the street for several minutes. Bishop heard another car crawling slowly. The stranger moved away from the door and his Reeboks allowed his footsteps to hit the stairs quietly. The car stopped. Bishop heard a door open and close quickly, then the car move away rapidly. He figured the stranger must have gotten in and left. Bishop knew that there were at least two of them and possibly more.

He waited in the dark a while longer, listening, searching the night for sounds of danger. Trying to figure out who it was, Bishop considered several possibilities. It could have been one of Lonnie's cops or one of Catrell's men or some more predators from the Zulu Nation. It could even have been just an ordinary neighborhood thief looking for a VCR to steal. Whoever it was, their intentions were wrong and at some point they would probably be back. He moved through the house in the dark, checking windows and doors to make sure everything was tight. The kitchen clock read 4:00 a.m. He was too hyped to get back to sleep. It was time to act.

Bishop realized that up to that moment all his actions had been defensive, reactions to what others were doing. He went upstairs, pulled on some jeans, a sweater and some sneakers, stuck the Baretta in his belt and covered it with a black leather jacket. He went back down stairs, out the front door and scanned the street quickly before jumping into the car.

There was no sign of the unmarked police car that had been parked a few doors down for the last few days. Lonnie had pulled his men off. At that moment Bishop felt it was a very good thing and that it made what had to be done less complicated.

He drove around for a few blocks, quickly turning corners trying to insure that no one was following. After confirming that no one was, he drove back toward the house and parked one block over from his street. Getting out of the car, he slipped between houses, through a neighbor's yard, across the alley and between the two homes that stood directly across from his house. He sat down on the ground and waited.

The wait didn't last long, maybe ten minutes, before a car glided down the street slowly and stopped directly in front of him about ten feet away. The headlights were off but the street light outlined two men in the front seat. They sat there for a while, discussing something. Finally, the man on the passenger side got out, went to the trunk, pulled out a ten gallon can of gasoline, set it on the ground and searched for something else. The driver whispered instructions for him to hurry up, but in the stillness of the night, his voice carried over to Bishop who heard him say, "Burn the house!"

Bishop moved quickly. Adrenaline was pumping and his reflexes were still capable of carrying him into attack. In his rage he thought, "Stupid ass motherfuckers, I should do you both right now." Instead, he quickly and silently came up on the man at the back of the car. The raised trunk hid Bishop from the driver as he stuck his pistol in the back of the other one's head and reached around in front of him, grabbed his throat and put pressure on his windpipe. Bishop whispered, "Drop down and stick your hands under your knees."

The would be arsonist was shocked and fear flamed up quickly. Bishop felt his pulse quicken as the man complied without a sound. He released the man's throat and whispered to his prisoner asking, "Do you have a gun on you?" Bishop was next to him with his gun pointed directly at the man's head.

The man on his knees shook his head up and down while forcing a whispered, "Yes."

The driver called to his partner again, "Hey man, hurry up and do this before somebody comes."

Bishop took a 9mm out of the prisoner's belt, tucked it in his own and frisked him quickly. He picked up the gas can with one hand, placed it back in the car, twisted off the cap and set it down on its side so it would drain out into the trunk. The prisoner's eyes were wide with fear. Bishop worked fast and everything had occurred in only a few seconds.

"Give me your matches."

The prisoner started to say something and Bishop pushed the gun into his eye socket just hard enough for him to feel pressure without screaming.

"Get your matches."

Taking his right hand out from under his knee, the prisoner reached into his pocket slowly. Sweat dripped down his face even though it was chilly outside. He fumbled in his pocket before bringing his hand out. The intensity in Bishop's eyes and the pistol pushed into his eye socket must have told him that if there was anything other than matches in his hand he'd be dead. Holding his hand up slowly he showed Bishop a silver Zippo lighter.

"Light it and throw it in the trunk."

He did what he was told and just as the fire hit the gas spilling in the trunk, the driver opened the door and stepped out into the street to see what was taking so long. Bishop saw his head rising up next to the car. The gasoline ignited and the prisoner jumped in reaction to it. Bishop slapped him across the bridge of his nose with the barrel of the pistol and aimed it quickly at the driver who was coming around the end of the car.

"GET BACK IN THE CAR, MUTHAFUCKA!"

Terrified, the driver scrambled back to the door, jumped in and took off down the street with fire starting to shoot out the back. Aiming the gun back at the prisoner writhing in pain on the ground and holding his nose, Bishop grabbed him by the throat again, pulled him to his feet and dragged him back into the alley. He was bleeding from a broken nose, crying from fear and gasping for air when Bishop let go. There was an explosion a few seconds later. The car's gas tank had blown up. Looking at his terrified prisoner Bishop said, "You want to die like your partner?"

The prisoner's eyes were wide with fear as he mumbled, "N-n-o."

Bishop began his questioning. "Who told you to burn my house?"

The interrogation had to be quick. The explosion would have the police and the fire department there in minutes. Without emotion, the question was put to the prisoner again, calmly, quietly.

"Who told you to burn my house?" He didn't get an answer and it pissed him off. Bishop slapped the man in the face and said, "A few minutes ago, you cowardly son of a bitch, you were going to pour gasoline on my home and burn it. Now tell me who told you to do it."

Bishop pushed the gun closer to the man's face. Without being told to, the prisoner dropped to his knees and started begging. "Please, don't kill me."

Bishop was unmoved and remained focused and persistent. "Fuck you. Who told you to burn my house?"

"G."

He slapped the man again. "Who?"

"G....that's all I know...a...a man they call G."

"Where is he?"

Shaking his head furiously, the prisoner pleaded, "Please don't kill me. I don't know...don't know...swear....I don't know...please!"

The sirens were getting closer and the neighbors were stirring, looking out their windows and coming onto their porches. The whole thing had taken only two or three minutes, but seconds were all that was left. Looking down at that man on his knees, a man who a few minutes ago was about to set fire to his house, Bishop knew what he had to do.

He looked up and down the alley then lowered the gun. Relief swarmed over the man's face. He sighed heavily and wept. "Thank you, man...thank you...I'm sorry."

For the first time Bishop studied the prisoner's features. He was about thirty years old with small eyes, light skin and a thin mustache. He was shaking from fear and his mouth and mustache were covered with blood and snot from his broken nose that had swollen to an enormous size.

His small eyes looked at Bishop gratefully. He thanked him profusely for sparing his life. His mouth opened to say something else, but before he could speak, Bishop struck him across the temple with the barrel of the gun, smashing his skull, dropping him to the ground. Bishop leaned over the man's unconscious body, grabbed his throat again and with a hard downward push with the heel of his hand, crushed his windpipe. There was one sharp gasp, the man's body jerked, his small eyes bulged and then there was silence in the alley except for the sirens that had flooded the area.

Bishop walked swiftly back to his car. The neighborhood was lit with a huge glow caused by the flames from the crashed car. The smoke from the fire filled the air. His neighbors populated the streets in hastily adorned clothing and Bishop drove past them and into the darkness.

More than an hour had passed since Bishop arrived at the river on the edge of the city. The 9mm pistol he'd taken off the prisoner was at the bottom of the water. The night air embraced him and the sound of the river rocked him gently like soft music. His thoughts traveled through his life's history like the water flowing beneath him. War had forced him to kill countless people. In his memories they were all faceless corpses, the enemy, unknown people in a foreign land. He thought he should feel different about what he'd just done. For the first time in his life, he had killed a black man. There was a dullness in his body, but there was no moral response to the act of murder he had just committed. There was no struggle with his conscience about killing. Bishop dropped his head and closed his eyes, saddened that he felt no remorse. War had done that to him. One year of hating the darkness.

Sometimes after battle
I can't return home
I am lost.
I wander the streets
counting the cracks
in the sidewalk
and the cracks
in my life.
Sometimes I never return.
I stand frozen in front of
store windows
staring at my
battle scars
watching their strange pattern
wondering why
my wounds
won't heal.
Sometimes I never return
I wonder why
I'm not dead
I seem dead.
People drop their eyes
when they see me
as if they are mourning
the dead.
Sometimes I walk dead
Sometimes there is no feeling
except hunger
to be alive.

CHAPTER SEVENTEEN

The sun stirred Bishop back into consciousness. He'd been sitting in the car all night, staring at the water, waiting for the dawn. When daylight came it was time to move again. The feeling was returning slowly to his body. Things were spinning completely out of control. A woman, Stacey Freeman, had been murdered. A gang war had erupted in the city. The police were hunting desperately for Catrell Merit. Lonnie wanted King, and Bishop had killed the men sent to burn his house by some shadowy figure they called "G." And all of it had something to do with a mysterious file no one could locate.

M nds 2nd payment of $50,000 to insure deal. G will pick up, usual plc/tme, Nov 2. Process already in motion. Watch the news.

He turned it over in his mind. *G will pick up, usual place and time, November second.* It was October twenty-fifth. Eight days from now, what is going to happen? "G" must be Greg Gatson, the man who met with the mayor. *Watch the news.*" Bishop started the car, headed back toward town, turned on the radio and listened to the morning broadcast.

> "In a quiet residential neighborhood last night, fire fighters were called to the scene of a car engulfed in flames. It took them over an hour to extinguish the fire. One body was pulled from the charred vehicle and has yet to be identified. Also, another unidentified man was found fatally beaten in an alley less than a block away. Police are trying to determine if there is a connection between the two bodies and have no suspects. Meanwhile, the crackdown on the notorious drug gang, the Egyptian Cobras, yields additional arrests as police round up more gang members. The search for their alleged leader, Catrell Merit, continues."

It was early, only 6:30 a.m. Bishop stopped at a doughnut shop, grabbed some coffee, a doughnut and a seat at the counter. The Tony Rich Project was playing on the radio in the joint, adding all kinds of flavor to the morning. The place started to fill up with workers on their way to the job and students headed to school. Bishop decided that he wouldn't go to work that day and made a mental note to call in around seven.

Lonnie always stopped at Juanita's in the mornings. Even though his life and schedule were irregular, he was also ritualistic. He would stop at Juanita's in the morning if he hadn't spent the night there, which wasn't often. It started when she worked the night shift. He would meet her at the house for breakfast and help get King and Carolyn off to school. It gave them a short time together in the mornings before Juanita crashed and Lonnie hit the streets again. Once she started working the day shift, she didn't have to be at work until nine, but Lonnie still came by every morning to check on her and share the beginning of the day.

After parking a couple of blocks away, Bishop walked toward Juanita's. With everything going on, he was sure Lonnie would have someone watching her house. At the corner of her block, Bishop cut over to the alley and moved quickly past the rear of the first five houses until reaching her back yard. He waited to see if anyone had noticed. No one did and just as he'd thought, her back door could be approached without being detected by the cop out front. Some protection.

After hopping the fence, he saw Lonnie and Juanita sitting at the kitchen table. The same table where he'd sat with her a few days before and she had held him in her arms. It was time to wait again. Juanita's car sat in the driveway and there was a small space between the front of her car and the garage where he could sit and remain undetected until Lonnie left. He settled into the spot and leaned his back against her garage. One of the teenagers next door was listening to A Tribe Called Quest, and their rhymes bounced against the bass and over to him.

It was 7:48. In a few minutes his first class would begin. The school secretary seemed surprised when he told her he was sick and would be out the remainder of the week. Since he was hardly ever absent, she was very concerned about his illness. He was, too, because it was some ill shit he was dealing with.

Eight fifteen. The front door opened and Lonnie said good-bye from Juanita's porch. His car door opened and shut, his engine started. Looking out from the hiding place, Bishop's eyes barely caught him as he drove off down the street.

Juanita returned to the kitchen and was putting the dishes in the sink when she looked out the window and saw him coming toward the house. She didn't smile. There was just a curious look on her face. When he reached the back porch she was standing in the doorway. Something odd and restless was in her eyes.

Bishop came into the house and followed her through the kitchen, down the hallway and into her living room. The haunting sounds of Billie Holiday were floating across her wood floors, past the paintings, the African masks and pictures of her children. Juanita was wearing a simple blue dress that hung full and flowing on her body and off one shoulder. Her locks were pulled back and up, revealing silver earrings that hung next to her brown neck. Bishop could have looked at her forever and hoped she knew it.

There were no words between them for a long time. They watched each other and looked away as if neither of them wanted to get lost inside the spell that had descended upon them at that moment. Their eyes were repeatedly drawn back to each other and the magic, over and over. He caught her studying his hands. She caught him staring at and envying the blue cloth touching the smooth skin of her shoulder. She reached up and touched his face. He took her hand and kissed her palm. She knew. Minutes passed before they spoke and her hand was still in his when they cast their words against Billie Holiday's music.

"Bishop, why did you come this morning?"

"I needed to see you."

"My son is in trouble, isn't he?"

"Yes. But that's not what brought me here."

"I know."

"You are the one that heals me."

"I know. You heal me, too."

She stepped to him and again took him in her arms. His night had ended with such violence, such ugliness, that only Juanita's voice, only her touch, her look, could turn him away from the rancid taste of blood in his mouth. The feeling was returning to his life and the horrible acts he'd committed a few hours ago receded into the dark areas of his memory and he wished the world were different so he could love her in peace.

Bishop held Juanita for a long time and she rested her head on his chest listening to his heart beating for her. She pressed warm against him and he kissed her shoulder but was afraid to kiss her lips because there were too many things in their way right then. They didn't say much. Both of them seemed afraid to discuss the trouble and expose the fear and pain that was closing in. But they both knew that one day soon they would touch again.

As silently as his visit with Juanita began, it ended. They released each other and touched hands once more. He promised her everything would be all right, went out her back door and disappeared down the alley.

Walking back to the car, he wished he hadn't lied to her. Everything would not be all right, at least not right away. He'd been drafted again and sent back into war.

When I was discharged from the military, I was determined to push the whole experience as far back in my mind as possible. My friend Vincent helped me plunge into school and community work. Together we worked on voter registration, political campaigns and education reform, and hung out listening to poetry, jazz or reggae. For the first couple of years I never discussed my experiences in Nam, and he never asked.

One night Vincent and I were having drinks in a local blues bar when we ran into Cathy Haynes, an old high school classmate. She was one of the finest girls in school and all of us wanted to go out with her, but Cathy always dated older cats, men who were in college or had been out of school for at least a couple of years. She never went out with any of her classmates.

She spotted Vincent first, and when she came over to the table and saw me, she started crying. Cathy gave me a big hug and said how happy she was that I'd made it home safely. It moved me so much I almost cried. Her words meant so much to me. We'd been casual friends in school, but in spite of my interest in being more than that, like the rest of my classmates, she had kept me at a distance, too.

After a few minutes of standing there, crying and hugging and saying how good it was to see each other, Vincent invited Cathy to sit down and have a drink with us. She said she couldn't, she was meeting her boyfriend there and he didn't like her talking to other men. We were stunned by her words because in high school Cathy was always very independent and never seemed like the kind of girl who would be in a relationship with a cat like that. She had gone on to college, completed a communications program in three years and was about to enter a masters program in film. When she spoke of her boyfriend, fear flashed on her face and her eyes darted toward the door hoping that she wouldn't get caught talking to us.

It was too late. Before she could complete or explain her statement, the boyfriend came through the door. He was with another brother and both were big, muscular men in their late twenties. They looked like ex-college football players. They were well dressed and seemed as if they would have some kind of professional jobs. He saw her standing there with Vincent and me and started in our direction. Cathy froze when she saw her boyfriend come toward us. She spoke to him as soon as he had crossed the floor and reached the spot where she stood.

"Frank, these are some friends that I went to high school with."

"Hi, I'm Isaiah Bishop."

I extended my hand to Frank, but it was left hanging in the air while he just stood there staring at Cathy. His partner was just past his left shoulder, and a little shorter than Frank. They had arrived and planted themselves in the territorial posture that men assume. They stood in that position, feet slightly spread, shoulders squared, faces tense while confrontation hovered over the space and the wrong words could whip things into a disaster.

Pulling my hand back in, I reached over to the table, picked up my drink and downed it quickly, trying to contain the instincts that had been suppressed for the last couple of years. I tried not to look at Frank. His contempt for Cathy and me and Vincent might make me kill him. Vincent watched me, look ing for clues as to what we should do. Cathy studied Frank with frightened familiarity. She knew he was going to say something threatening to us, her friends. Vincent and I both knew from the fear on her face that this asshole would make her pay later. Frank's words broke the silence.

"Cathy, I told you about this shit." He shook his finger inches from her face.

Almost in tears, her voice quivering, she tried to calm him down. "Frank, Bishop was in Viet Nam and I hadn't seen him since he came—"

"Shut the fuck up!" Now his face was just inches from hers.

Vincent tried to intercede. "Hey brother, we're just old friends saying hi."

Frank turned his ire toward Vincent. "Motherfucker, was I talking to you? I don't give a fuck who you are. Cathy belongs to me. You under stand?"

At that moment, Vincent saw me as he never had before. We'd been friends a long time, had fought other boys as teenagers, chased girls, been harassed by the police and engaged in the stupid acts that boys engage in when they are in school. But we were men now, and we were trying to do seri ous things with their lives. The thought of fighting those big ass motherfuck ers in a bar was some weird shit, but it was unavoidable. That night, what Vincent saw in me was not a desire to fight, but a capacity to kill. He saw the thing that had been planted and cultivated in the war.

As we all stood there, I must have seemed somewhere else. My body and mind were submitting to my recent history. I became distant and serene as though at peace with whatever was going to happen. Everyone else was vis ibly tense. I was relaxed and calm when I spoke to the tough guy. "You like to beat women up?"

126

My question was casual as if I'd asked him if he liked to ride motorcy cles. My eyes pierced Frank's face demanding an answer. My hands were resting at my waist with my thumbs tucked inside the belt. Frank's friend stepped up beside him. Dumb motherfucker thought that would increase the intimidation. My demeanor did not change. Calmly, I asked again. "You like to beat women up?"

Now Frank was the one who was frozen. Cathy watched with amaze ment and dread. She had suddenly been removed from the confrontation. This was between us, the men. It was about our egos, our power, our man hood. When Frank finally spoke, his voice had lost some of the commanding edge it had before.

"Look man, this is between me and Cathy. It ain't got nothing to do with you and your friend."

Cathy had never seen Frank in a position where he was intimidated and forced to explain himself. Vincent had never seen me in a position where I completely dominated a situation psychologically and physically. It must have been strange for Cathy and Vincent watching us. Frank was about two inches taller and probably thirty pounds heavier than me. Yet, at that moment I knew something unspoken told him that someone was going to die. He looked like the kind of cat who had been a college linebacker and liked phys ical contact, the kind who had started and been in many fights. But I could tell by the look on his face, he'd never faced a man who was willing to kill and or die.

"I asked you a simple question."

"Hey, man, it's not like that. I just get jealous sometimes."

"Yeah, you like to beat women up."

That time it wasn't a question. It was a statement, an observation, an indictment. Frank's friend understood the implications and took a half step back as if anticipating a storm. I didn't move. I stood there gazing into Frank's eyes, reading his soul, sensing his body stiffening and his weight shifting to his left foot, preparing to strike or defend.

Everything seemed quiet, Vincent, Cathy, the muscle-bound friend and everyone in the room disappeared. It had come down to just me and him. The more we stood there, inches away from each other, staring into the tension between us, the more he made me sick. I'd had enough of his shit, he was a bully and a coward. Finally, in what seemed like one motion, I snatched my belt off, wrapped it around Frank's neck like a garrote and took one, short, quick leap that brought me behind him. The speed and force of the movement snatched Frank backward, down to the floor, choking and grasping for the belt. The ferocity of the action left his friend paralyzed while I tightened the belt until Frank almost passed out. Right before he lost consciousness, I released him and left him sputtering and coughing on the floor.

Every one's blood ran cold and the entire room was horrified. The bar tender grabbed the phone to call the police. The other patrons in the bar recoiled in terror. Frank lay on the floor spitting up blood from his throat, sobbing, a big, muscle-bound mass of punk.

I knelt down beside him and whispered in his ear. "If you ever even threaten her again, I will find you and kill you."

My voice still had the same calm tone. The same clarity and absolute authority of someone capable of murder. Shocked, Cathy looked at Frank as if he was a stranger. She looked at me like she was thankful. The friend had backed up about ten feet and looked at the scene as if he hadn't been in it. For the first time Vincent saw the demons of war screaming inside my head.

We left before the police came. In Vincent's car, I didn't say anything and neither did he. As we drove into the night, I stared out the window at the buildings and the street lights and the dark city sky, trying to remind myself that I was back in the world, that I was home.

We went to Vincent's house with a bottle of tequila, put Charlie Parker, Sarah Vaughn and Sly and the Family Stone on the box and talked until the next morning. And for the first time, I tried to describe to my friend the hell I'd lived in, the way death smells, the sounds of killing and the bloody scenery of war. That night, Vincent understood why I fought desperately to save myself, to heal myself, to rescue myself from the violence that had defined my existence that year in Viet Nam.

CHAPTER EIGHTEEN

The offices of *The Crusader* were in the Equiano Building, a small, free-standing, four-story structure just outside downtown. It was built in 1907 by a group of black people who pooled their money together. It was one of the first buildings built to house the professional offices of black doctors, lawyers and artisans at the beginning of the century. Downtown was segregated and blacks weren't allowed to work there unless they were cleaning up the buildings or running errands. Black professionals, doctors, tailors, lawyers, insurance companies, barbers, furniture makers and artisans joined together with churches in the community and founded the first black bank. Through that institution, People's Independence Bank, they borrowed money and built that building and others so they'd have a place to work and serve the people of their community.

When Bishop came through the door of the old building, a tall, young brother with tiny dread locks, a black shirt, red tie, baggy pants and Nikes, greeted him in the small reception area. He looked about nineteen and was pleasant and professional. The first floor was full of people at the desks, talking on the phone, discussing stories, writing, working. They were young and old, male and female, dressed in suits and some in jeans.

The young brother directed him to Vincent's office on the second floor and handed him the latest copy of *The Crusader*. Bishop glanced at the front page headline while climbing the stairs to the second floor.

MAYOR CRACKS DOWN ON CRACK

Vincent was on the phone as usual. He waved Bishop into the room and pointed to a brown leather chair. Sitting there reading the paper, the soft, worn feel of the seat induced a sudden drowsiness in Bishop. Vincent must have seen him wrestling with the feeling and finished his conversation and came around the desk to greet him.

"Bishop, what a surprise."

"I figured it would be."

"Well, after the other night, I didn't expect to see you again so soon."

"It's good though, right?"

"Always."

Vincent was smiling a sly smile, like he knew it was not just a social visit and Bishop needed something.

"Vincent, I need your help."

"Figured you did. Whatcha need?"

"Have you ever heard of a cat named Greg Gatson?"

"That name sounds vaguely familiar, but I can't place him right now."

Vincent went back behind his desk and started to key in something on his computer. "Let me see if he's anywhere in our files. Maybe he showed up in the paper at one time or another." They waited for a few seconds while the computer searched for his name. "Yeah, here he is. May 1987 we did a story on Greg Gatson in the business section. You want me to pull the article?"

"I'd appreciate it."

"Sit tight for a minute while I get it for you."

Vincent left his office and Bishop continued to read the copy of *The Crusader* he'd been given downstairs. It was a well put together weekly, covering subjects of interest to the African American community. There were articles on politics, developments in business, the arts, sports and education, as well as information about community meetings and reviews of books, films and events. The paper covered important developments in Africa, the Caribbean and the world. It also profiled African American success stories in politics, business, education, science and the arts. Overall it was a good publication and with Vincent as the publisher and editor it had taken on many challenges by printing stories that the daily newspapers would not run.

Within five minutes, Vincent returned with a print out of the article on Greg Gatson. It was a profile of a young man who recently moved to the city as a top executive of a major engineering firm, American-International Engineering (AIE). The article detailed his academic career, including advanced degrees from Stanford, his active charity work as a board member of the Boys and Girls Clubs and his growing involvement in the local black political establishment. In 1987 when the article was written, he was only twenty-seven years old and had been appointed a vice president of AIE. *The Crusader* called him one of the young professionals to watch and mentioned the fact that he had also been profiled in *Black Enterprise* and *Ebony*.

There was an attached article written in 1990. It was small and basically just a mention of the fact that he had resigned his position with AIE to start his own consulting firm.

Bishop looked up at Vincent who had been watching him read the material. He laid the clippings on the desk and asked, "Is this all you have on him?"

"Yes. It seems that after 1990 we didn't hear any more about him."

"What happened to his consulting company?"

"Don't know. He just faded off the scene. Why are you interested?"

It was time to talk. Bishop got up and closed Vincent's door, then told him all that had occurred in the last few days. Vincent listened to his tale of violence and intrigue. He studied Bishop's words and occasionally jotted down some notes on a small pad on his desk. When the story was finished, he leaned back in his chair and stared at Bishop for a minute.

"Why do you think they tried to burn your house?"

"Don't know. Maybe someone wants to scare me because of my relationship to King. Maybe they saw Catrell come to my house and want to send him a message or maybe the message is for Lonnie Carlton. Shit, I don't know."

"Do you think anyone saw you in the street or the alley?"

"No. Nobody knows what happened, though Lonnie might suspect."

"What are you going to do?"

"Find Greg Gatson."

"And then what?"

"Reason with him."

Vincent's eyes had been fastened on Bishop since he started describing the events of the last week. He hadn't moved, yet it was clear he was analyzing all that was said, looking for the information that would piece it all together.

"Do you know what's in the missing file? Or where it might be?"

"No. But the key to all of this has to be Gatson."

Bishop thanked Vincent for his help and told him that he would keep him informed, promising him that *The Crusader* would be the first paper to break the story to the public. Whatever the story turned out to be.

Before Bishop left his office, Vincent issued instructions to be careful and to stay in touch. Bishop was glad he'd told Vincent. Someone needed to know what was going on just in case it turned out badly for him. Vincent's deep concern for his community and their twenty-five-year friendship made Bishop feel confident that he could be trusted to do the right thing.

Passing back through the first floor, the sight of the newspaper staff working to produce an important voice of communication for the community was inspiring. Bishop walked out the door declaring to himself, "Everything is not fucked up."

From his second-floor office window, Vincent Daniel watched his childhood friend get in the car and drive away. He was worried, even though he had tried not to show it to Bishop. Whatever had caused all of that death and all of that fear had also caused Bishop to revert to old habits and instincts. More death was certain. The question had become, who else would die?

CHAPTER NINETEEN

He knew Lonnie would be looking for him after what had happened the previous night. Before going home he needed to get a message to Catrell and decided to seek out his former student Cora Davis. Bishop pulled up on the street that ran behind George Washington Homes and searched the wall for the hole from the other night. It took a minute to find it. The police were everywhere since the crackdown on the Egyptian Cobras. He hoped to get through the hole and inside without being detected. It would be difficult in the daylight.

Once inside the fence, there was an eerie feeling, an uneasiness that none of the usual clusters of Cobras were at their various posts, doing their business, protecting their territory. It was strange that without their visible presence it felt more dangerous. A girl with an infant on her hip came toward Bishop as he walked cautiously down one of the walkways that ran alongside the buildings.

Glancing around, checking for the police, Bishop called out to the young woman. "I'm looking for Cora Davis."

"Building 13."

She said it without stopping or looking back at him, almost as if she expected the question. On the building directly in front of him, the number 7 was carved into the bricks between the first and second floors. Given the police lock down of George Washington Homes, six buildings over was a lot of distance to cover with two cop cars and four other cops on foot between him and building 13. The Baretta was still stuck in his belt. If he got stopped with it, they would take him to jail. Walking slowly, evenly, he contemplated the next move.

"Mr. Bishop."

A voice to his left had whispered his name, causing him to stop and spin around. The cops were milling around nervously in the massive parking lot that sat in the middle of the projects. They seemed edgy and preoccupied as if anticipating some kind of retaliatory act from the Cobras. Fortunately they hadn't seen him yet.

"Mr. Bishop, come over here."

Turning toward the voice, he saw the small body in the big clothes from the other night standing in the side doorway of building 8. Watching the police, Bishop moved to the door and followed the little boy as he retreated inside. They went down a flight of stairs, through a tunnel and several rooms that were empty except for the broken bottles, fast food wrappers and pee-stained mattresses. Finally, they arrived at a room where six young men sat on crates, cinder blocks and pieces of broken furniture. They were all armed, heavily armed, with automatic weapons. The NRA would have been proud.

As they entered the room, the young brothers were playing cards and listening to a police radio. They were hiding down there in the catacombs of the projects. Their past experience assured them that the cops were just there temporarily. The police presence was just to give the illusion that the hell hole was now safe for the residents. Eventually, once the Mayor had scored his public relations points, they would leave and whatever was left of the Egyptian Cobras would regroup and take control again.

One of the men playing cards, a tall, slender, brown-skinned brother with a black bandanna tied on his head, studied Bishop for a few seconds then stood up and met him in the middle of the room. "You the teacher, ain't you?"

Bishop stepped closer to the young man, nodding. "Yeah. I'm Bishop."

"Yeah, Mr. Bishop from over at the high school. Whatcha looking for?" His question wasn't hostile or friendly, just a straight inquiry.

Bishop looked around the room, then back at the tall brother. "I need to get a message to Catrell."

"What's the message?"

"I need to see him tonight, at Juanita King's house."

The tall brother flashed some kind of sign at the little boy in the big clothes, then said to Bishop, "That it?"

"Yeah."

The little boy in the big clothes walked by and tugged at the sleeve on Bishop's coat, gesturing for Bishop to accompany him. The tall brother picked up a cellular phone and calmly gave orders to whoever was listening on the other end. "In two minutes we need some action in front of building 15." He hung up and turned back to Bishop. The other young men kept playing cards as if it were all routine. "Follow Little Man, he'll get you back to your car."

Little Man led him back through the tunnel, past the rooms, up the stairs and to the door leading to the side of building 8. After waiting there a few seconds, gunfire erupted in the middle of Washington Homes. The Cobras had created a diversion. The police scrambled for cover behind their cars and Little Man ran toward the wall with Bishop right on him. They reached the hole, Bishop crawled through on all fours, jumped in the car and drove off. Sirens screamed as squad cars came rushing past. He watched them and thought, "They're bringing in more troops. They never learn."

When he reached his block, Bishop spotted the police car immediately and placed the Barreta under the seat. The cops were sitting directly in front of his house. This time, there was no pretense, no unmarked car a couple of houses down. It was a squad car. As he pulled into the driveway, two uniformed officers, one white the other black, exited the squad car and approached him. "Isaiah Bishop?" the black one asked in a voice that sounded like a radio announcer.

"Yes." Bishop got out of the Volvo and stood facing the two officers.

The black officer spoke softly but firmly. "Detective Carlton would like to see you." He pointed toward the squad car. "Would you please come with us?"

Bishop asked, "Am I under arrest?" He looked at the black cop, then the white cop and could tell that they were both young and inexperienced.

"No, sir," the white one answered in a very courteous tone. "He just wants to see you. Now."

"All right." Bishop smiled and said, "I'll follow you in my car."

The cops seemed temporarily confused, but agreed and he followed them to Kelly's, a soul food restaurant nearby. The uniformed cops waited outside. Bishop went in and found Lonnie sitting at a table eating some fried chicken, string beans and yams. Lonnie wiped his mouth with a paper napkin. "Bishop, have a seat. You want some lunch?"

"Yeah." Eyeing Lonnie's plate he realized that all he'd eaten that day was the doughnut at the coffee shop early that morning. The waitress set a menu in front of him, but he didn't look at it. Instead he ordered the same thing Lonnie was eating plus a glass of lemonade.

Lonnie waited until the waitress walked away before he spoke again. "I know what happened at your house last night. But look here, I don't care. Fuck them. They were gang bangers and somebody would have killed them sooner or later anyway. I want to know what information you have about what's going on."

Bishop folded his arms, leaned back in his chair and wondered if Lonnie

135

thought he was a fool. Lonnie had prefaced his question with a statement that opened the door for Bishop to implicate himself in a murder, maybe two. Bishop answered him, "What are you talking about?"

"Come on, Bishop, let's not fuck around." Lonnie laid his knife and fork down and looked up from his plate. "King's life could be in danger."

Bishop rocked back in his chair so that only the back legs were on the ground. "Where is he?"

"Hoped you knew. We know you've been in contact with some of the Egyptian Cobras." Lonnie picked up a piece of chicken and started eating again.

"Lonnie, for some reason, everyone keeps putting me in the middle of whatever shit is going on. Right now, I'm just trying to stay alive."

Bishop's lunch arrived and they stopped talking while the waitress set it down in front of him asking, "You need anything else?"

"Just some hot sauce, thank you."

She brought it back and Bishop got with the food right away. Lonnie picked the conversation up where it had stopped, "I can't help you if you won't work with me."

Bishop didn't trust him. He knew Lonnie was just trying to use him to get information. He shook some hot sauce on his chicken and dug his fork into the yams while avoiding eye contact with Lonnie and ignoring his last statement.

Lonnie wiped his mouth again and continued, "So what are you going to do Bishop?"

Bishop looked up across the table and replied, "Lonnie, right now I'm going to eat this chicken." He took a bite then added, "Beyond that, I don't know."

"Listen, I'll keep you up on anything I find out, if you'll do the same. All right?"

Bishop kept eating and didn't answer. Lonnie was frustrated. More than usual. Things were also out of his control. Something or someone was moving events, manipulating people and situations for some reason neither of them knew or understood.

Lonnie pulled out a wad of money and peeled off a twenty and a ten, then asked Bishop, "You still have the number I gave you?"

"Yeah."

"Call me if you find out something. We don't have a lot of time."

Bishop had a fork full of string beans on the way to his mouth when he realized Lonnie had finally slipped. Lonnie's statement confirmed that they were up against some kind of deadline. Bishop realized it had to be whatever was going to happen on November second. Lonnie was unaware of the mistake and didn't catch Bishop frown slightly as he put the fork in his mouth. As Bishop chewed his food and watched Lonnie call for the check he thought, "Watch the news. Lonnie has to know that the key to this puzzle is Greg Gatson."

Lonnie paid the check and dropped one more warning on the table with a five dollar tip. "Watch yourself Bishop," he said. "Things will probably get very strange in the next few days."

Bishop took a swallow of lemonade and responded, "Shit, it's already strange."

"Brother, you ain't seen strange." Lonnie spun around on his heels and walked toward the door.

Bishop sipped his lemonade and watched Lonnie step out of the restaurant and onto the sidewalk where he discussed something with the two cops before they got in their cars and drove away. Bishop sat in silence and finished eating. The food was smokin' as usual.

By the time he arrived back home Bishop was dead tired. He'd been up all night and hadn't slept much in the last few days. The unmarked police car was back, sitting a couple of doors down from his house. He still couldn't decide whether Lonnie was protecting or watching him. Either way, with them sitting out there, at least no one would burn his house down.

Once inside, he made a check of all the doors and windows, walking through the house room by room. Everything seemed all right. Nothing looked disturbed or out of place. He lay down on the couch to take a nap and tried to think through the new pieces of the puzzle. "Why were those men sent here last night? Why was I their target?" His questions faded with the statement, "Me and Mr. Gatson are going to have to have a discussion real soon." It would have to wait because right then he needed some sleep.

When he woke up it was 7:30 p.m. and it was dark outside. The four hours of sleep felt good but it was time to get in motion. He looked out the window to see if the cops were still watching. As expected, they hadn't moved. As long as they didn't see him leave, they would keep Lonnie informed that he was still there.

He showered, put on some fresh clothes and thought about his plan. No telling what time Catrell would show up at Juanita's. He was betting it would be late. She had to be told what was going on. Her son was in danger and he wasn't sure what Lonnie had told her.

To reassure the cops, Bishop went out to the car, got some papers off the back seat and retreated back inside the house, making sure they saw him. The cops in the unmarked car watched him casually. He wanted them to think he was in for the night so he left the lights on upstairs in the bedroom and the television on CNN downstairs in the living room. He left out the back door and cut across the alley to the street behind his. It would take two buses to get across town to Juanita's.

At the bus stop, a young woman waited with her four-year-old daughter on the bench and an older man in a security guard uniform stood nearby. The bus came in a few minutes and as they boarded, the woman driver greeted the man, the young woman and her daughter by name. Bishop hadn't ridden the bus since college but it was a nightly routine for the rest of them.

Riding the bus had always been an education. The diversity of the passengers revealed the life of the city. The bus was a place where you were surrounded by discussions of politics, religion, sex, talk shows, sports, money and relationships. Lovers cuddled and kissed or argued and fought. Young women and men with their young children struggled with strollers and diaper bags and babies. Young brothers who wanted the world to notice them played their music so loud it filled the bus through their headphones while they shot looks and smiles at the sisters. Workers on their way to work complained about how little money they made, and those on the way home wore their fatigue like it was a uniform.

As the bus passed through the neighborhoods, idle young men talked loud on some street corners, while a few blocks over, BMWs, Jeeps and Volvos were parked in the driveways of tree-lined streets. They drove through communities that were well lit, quiet and clean, and others that were dark and the streets were full of glass and beer cans and noise. On the out-skirts of the business district, transvestite prostitutes were available on the avenue and as they passed downtown it was full of tourists and strip joints.

Bishop observed that in the car you tended to speed by the parade of people and endless interaction, focused only on your destination. On the bus, the constant stopping, the life and words of the passengers and the activity of the people beyond the bus window, made you look. And if you looked, you could smell and feel the life of the city. He hadn't been on the bus for a long time so Bishop stared out the window, drank up the scenes of the city on the way to Juanita's house and hoped he would get more time to be alone with her.

CHAPTER TWENTY

Juanita Ross was born in the 1950s. She grew up in the sixties and seventies. It was a time of change and an important time for a black girl to grow into womanhood. There was an awakening, an embracing of who she was, a brown-skinned girl celebrated as beautiful. Her African American features were extolled in the music, poetry, plays and prose of the Black Arts and Black Consciousness Movements. The Civil Rights and Black Liberation Movements were being forced by sisters and circumstances to confront the fact that African American women were not only important but critical to the progress made in the past, the fight occurring in the present and any potential for the future.

Juanita came to womanhood struggling with traditions that wanted her to remain a slave, but she had refused to be one or become one. In high school she was considered one of the smartest students and one of the most active. She participated in the Black Student Union. She played basketball, was a member of the debate team and at sixteen years old, in the eleventh grade, she met Sonny King.

Sonny was an average sized man, about five feet ten inches tall and about one hundred and sixty pounds. He was nineteen, with an afro, a light mustache and copper colored skin that seemed to glow when he smiled. His smile was the most distinguishing and captivating aspect of his face, besides eyes that seemed to always be intensely focused on whatever had his attention at the time. When they met, Sonny could not prevent them from focusing on Juanita.

Their first encounter was at a reception for a representative of FRE-LIMO, the Mozambique Liberation Movement. Sonny was a student at the community college and a member of the student organization that had brought the woman in from FRELIMO. As the program got underway, Sonny walked up to the podium about to give the opening remarks for the evening. He was met with applause by the students who had gathered and he raised his hand to quiet them down and said, "Good evening, sisters and brothers." It was at that moment when he first spotted Juanita sitting in the third row.

Sonny's eyes became fixed on Juanita. She distracted him so much that he stood there speechless for a minute. He tried to gather his thoughts and fumbled with the paper that held his notes. He kept looking at Juanita until someone in the audience said, "Take your time, Sonny."

He realized he had been staring at her and felt a slight wave of embarrassment creeping across his face when he began again, "Good evening, sisters and brothers....I have been asked by the uh...the uh...Black Student Union...to uh..."

Sonny fumbled with the paper, tried not to look at Juanita and saw the faces of those who knew him. Some of them thought it was funny, others found it unsettling and couldn't figure out what was wrong because Sonny was always a confident, articulate orator. He continued to force the words out of his mouth even though he could not quite concentrate on what he was saying.

"We are fortunate to have with us tonight, a sister who has traveled all the way from...from...uh Mozambique where she is a leading member of the liberation...the liberation struggle." Sonny wiped his brow and made himself not look at Juanita.

Juanita sat through Sonny's opening remarks hoping that the brother would relax, realize he was amongst family and let his words flow. He had a nice voice and what he said made people want to listen because it made sense. It was just that his pauses and slight fumbling kind of distracted her. She was sure that if he practiced he could be a good speaker because when he stepped to the podium people sat up and paid attention as if expecting something important to be said. If he would only relax. He didn't and she was happy that the audience encouraged him and applauded in support when he sat down after struggling through his presentation. When Sonny took his seat, he continued to study her from the platform.

Juanita was beautiful with, short natural hair and round, cat-like eyes that observed everything around her. Full lips gave way to a distinct, smooth, almost husky voice that commanded everyone's attention when she stood up to ask the FRELIMO representative a question about the role of women in Mozambique's struggle for liberation from the Portuguese. And all of it, the eyes, the lips, the voice, the beauty, was surrounded by brown skin set off by the royal purple shirt she wore.

Juanita felt Sonny looking at her from the platform. When she looked in his direction, he seemed to be staring at her, lost somewhere in his thoughts. Maybe he wasn't looking at her. Maybe he was staring into space trying to recover from that speech he had just given. Sonny couldn't stop. Occasionally, he'd look over at the speaker, but his eyes and thoughts continued to be locked on the woman sitting in the audience.

Finally, the program was over. Finally, he could say something to that young woman in the third row who had made him forget what he was supposed to say. After wading through the crowd of people standing around talking, enjoying the refreshments and greeting the guest from Mozambique, Sonny reached Juanita just as she was about to leave. Her back was to him when he said, "Excuse me, sister," and touched her gently on the arm to get her attention.

Juanita said, "Yes." Then turned around toward him and saw that it was the fumbling but handsome speaker. "Oh, it's you. Hi. I thought your speech was very..."

"Very...uncool." Sonny covered his face with his hands, feigning disgrace. "You know it's your fault."

Juanita put her hand on her hip and rolled her eyes at Sonny, saying, "Please. I don't even know you, how could it be my fault?"

"If you hadn't been sitting there looking at me like that, I wouldn't have messed up."

Her mouth flew open. "What! I was looking at you? I thought something was wrong with your eyes the way you were looking at me from up there on the platform."

They stood there and talked and laughed until the reception was over, then went to a cafe near the campus where they talked until midnight, then Juanita realized she had missed her curfew and had to get home. Sonny walked her to the bus stop and she caught the last bus home and watched him wave at her on the bus until she was out of sight.

That night was the beginning of a feeling Juanita had never had before. She and Sonny became best friends, supporters of the same causes, listeners of the same music, readers of the same books, dancers of the same dances, advocates of the same changes, watchers of the same movies, and lovers of the love they had for each other.

As she entered the twelfth grade, Juanita was pregnant with Sonny's baby. Her father demanded she have an abortion and banned Sonny from his house. Her mother criticized her for messing up her life and destroying her future. Juanita left her parent's house, moved in with Sonny and continued to go to school even though the principal wanted her to leave and attend night classes.

By the time she was six months pregnant, Sonny had dropped out of college and was working in a warehouse to support them. She objected to him dropping out at first, suggesting that they both get part-time jobs. Sonny argued that he could go back next year, but right now, it was important that she stay focused on finishing that last year of high school and having a healthy baby. He never got back to school.

When Sonny dropped out of the community college, he lost his student deferment and just before their child was born, he received a letter from the government saying that he was drafted. They discussed all of the possibilities, including going to Canada, trying to stay out as a conscientious objector and going in the Army. Juanita hated the military and thought the war in Viet Nam was unjust. She wanted to move to Canada. Sonny was also against the war and thought black people had shed enough blood for a country that treated them as second class. But with a family to provide for, no real skills and an uncertain future, he figured he'd do the two years in the army. His family would get benefits and he'd come home and let the government pay for the rest of his education. Sonny married Juanita and his son, Billy King, was born. Eight weeks later he was sent to Viet Nam.

While Sonny was in Nam, Juanita graduated at the top of her high school class and enrolled in the state university on a full academic scholarship. They wrote to each other every week. Juanita's letters described Billy's newest developments, how much she missed Sonny, what was happening in the community and how her studies were going. She also attached clippings of newspaper articles she thought would interest him. Sonny's letters detailed his love for her, how anxious he was to see Juanita and his son and some of the comical antics of the soldiers in his unit. He never mentioned the danger or the terror of the war.

He came home from the war after his one year tour of duty. He only stayed for two weeks. He told Juanita he had reenlisted to do a second tour of Viet Nam. She was shocked. He couldn't or wouldn't explain it to her and his mood was sullen and even hostile when she would try to discuss it with him. Where there had been comfort and confidence in their relationship, there was now confusion.

Sonny went back to Nam and his letters became infrequent. When he did write, the letters were long and incoherent, full of rambling rhetoric about black salvation and God's punishment of the enemies of people of color. Six months into the second year, Juanita got a call from the Army. Sonny had been wounded and was in a hospital in Japan recovering. She got her sister to keep Billy and flew fourteen hours across the Pacific Ocean to be with her husband. It took her two days to reach him and when she did, it wasn't his physical injuries that wounded her.

Sonny lay in a military hospital. His right leg had been amputated below the knee. He had been shot by a thirteen-year-old boy and a tourniquet applied in the field to stop the bleeding was inadvertently left on, cutting off circulation until the leg couldn't be saved. It wasn't the leg that bothered her. It was his face. Sonny had changed. He looked old and eyes that once were intense but kind, had become wild and crazed. A smile that used to call you and open your heart had disappeared behind words that were profane and senseless.

Juanita stayed in Japan with Sonny for two weeks. Slowly, he began to respond to her conversation and to her touch. Slowly, he began to relate to information she gave him about Billy and what was going on back home. Slowly, he began to smile at her when she walked into the hospital room. Slowly, he began to reveal pieces of the man she loved. When she left, the doctors told her it would be several weeks before he'd be sent home. It was another eight months.

When Sonny came home, he couldn't work and spent time in and out of the veterans hospital getting physical rehabilitation and psychological counseling. Five years after Sonny came home, their second child, Carolyn, was born and Juanita tried to rebuild a normal life for all of them. Sonny was not the same. He would have moments when the nineteen-year-old, concerned college student, full of love and fire, would shine through his madness. But the madness kept showing up more and more frequently and so did the police. Finally, death showed up.

One day, Sonny got angry at a liquor store owner for charging him too much money for cashing his government check. He pulled a small pistol from his pocket, chased the owner out and began destroying the store while repeating quotations from Frederick Douglass, David Walker and Sojourner Truth. Barricading himself inside the store, he refused to surrender and held off the police for twelve hours while they tried to negotiate with him. When he finally came out, he came out shooting and was killed in a storm of gunfire.

Juanita had watched the slow demise and sudden death of the only man she'd ever loved and was faced with raising two young children by herself. She got her degree in nursing, remained active in community affairs, educated her children, occasionally went on a date, had a few lovers over the years and one day met Lonnie Carlton.

Lonnie had entered her life under sudden and strange circumstances. Juanita never talked about it, his presence was just something she accepted.

He had been good to her and her children. She loved him for being good to them and also felt guilty that she could never love him from that place inside her where the heat was, that place that Sonny had touched. No man since Sonny had felt or seen that heat, but Isaiah Bishop had ignited a fire in her from the first time they met.

Now, in the midst of all that was swirling around them, she felt drawn to Bishop and knew Lonnie was going to be hurt. Sooner or later she would have to take Bishop into her life. Her feelings were throwing her life off balance. It reminded her of a line from a Ron Milner play: "Some people with problems try to subtract by adding and wind up multiplying."

Juanita had just finished washing her hair. She sat in her kitchen, drinking a cup of tea, twisting her locks, thinking about the past and the future. She thought about Sonny's death and Lonnie's friendship and her long suppressed feelings for Bishop. She thought about her son, King, and that the men she knew and loved were all caught up in some strange, violent confrontation that was kept hidden from the women.

It reminded her of the secrets of war that Sonny had kept from her and that had driven him crazy. She thought about the world that black men live in, full of mystery and violence and silence and how they go out to face a world hostile to their existence and come home with blood on their clothes and their conversations reeking with the smell of battle, yet they continue to pretend that they can fight alone. They delude themselves into thinking that manhood demanded that they not show their fear, their confusion or their wounds. Mistakenly they believe that women must be shielded from the conflicts they face. She thought these things and whispered to herself, "Our entire history says you are wrong. Only the women can help you reconcile your manhood to a world that attempts to destroy your being. Only your women have always stood with you and continued the fight. Only the women."

CHAPTER TWENTY-ONE

When Bishop jumped off the second bus two blocks from Juanita's, it was just after nine o'clock. The crisp night air reminded him winter was on its way and he pulled the collar up on his coat and leaned into the wind. About halfway down the first street, he approached a group of teenagers talking loud. A couple of them recognized their teacher and tried to quiet the others. As he got closer, they opened a path for him to walk through and greeted Bishop with the questions and sarcasm that teenagers are famous for.

"Mr. Bishop, when you coming back to class?"

Bishop walked slowly through the group and answered, "Next week."

"They said you was sick."

"You don't look sick to me."

Bishop pointed to the girl who'd made the last comment. "Look, I'll see you next week." Then to the whole group he said, "Just make sure you've kept up with your assignments."

They rolled their eyes and sucked their teeth and pretended to be disgusted at his instructions as they walked on. The volume of their conversation increased as they moved further away from him and he wondered where they were headed since there was no place in the community for them to go.

He continued walking until he came to the corner of Juanita's block and saw that the police car was still sitting outside her house but Lonnie's car wasn't there. Bishop circled around through the alley to her back door. The rear of the house was dark. The lights were out in the kitchen and the back porch light was also out. Knocking lightly so as not to draw the attention of the neighbors, he listened for some movement inside when the back door swung open.

"Come in, Bishop."

The voice surprised him and at first made him hesitant to enter. It was a man's voice, a familiar voice. It was King. "Come in. We've been waiting for you."

Stepping inside the dark kitchen and quickly surveying the room, he made out Juanita and Catrell seated at the kitchen table. King walked over and joined them.

"We were just telling my mother what happened."

The light in the living room fell into the hallway that ran from the front of the house. It stopped short of the kitchen but provided just enough light to navigate around the table to the empty chair beside Juanita. While passing her, Bishop touched her shoulder and she embraced his gesture by squeezing his hand briefly. He grabbed a chair and joined them at the table.

"King, are you all right?"

"I'm fine."

"Catrell, you got my message."

"That's why we're here."

Juanita watched them silently. She frowned, listening closely, analyzing what was going on, studying her son's face in the shadows. King continued the story he had been telling when Bishop arrived.

"Like I was saying, after being in the mayor's office for a couple of weeks, Lonnie started asking me to look out for certain things. He wanted to know about meetings the mayor had and people who came around his office. Then he started asking me to look for notes and files, anything about zoning issues, real estate development projects and things like that. He wanted copies of some of the notes and files. He told me to have Stacey get them for me, that she had given him information in the past. It was weird, because he never said why he wanted the stuff. He just asked me to do it as a favor to him, so I did. After this man Greg Gatson showed up and Stacey got that file on ENTAC Enterprises, all this crazy stuff started to happen."

They listened in the silence of the kitchen, King's voice echoing off the dripping faucet. The phone rang and broke their conversation, causing them to jump a little at the unexpected intrusion. Juanita picked up the wall phone over by the refrigerator.

"Hello....No, I wasn't sleep...Where are you?...Sure, I'll see you when you get here." She hung up the phone and returned to the table. "That was Lonnie, he'll be here in about twenty minutes. You should leave before he arrives."

Juanita came around the table to her son and embraced him. "Billy, are you going to be OK?"

"Yes, ma'am, I'll be fine." He kissed his mother on the cheek. "Don't worry, everything's gonna work out."

Juanita turned to Catrell, took his hand in hers and said, "Catrell, protect my son."

"I will, Ms. King." He squeezed her hand then headed out the back door with Billy King right behind him.

Bishop was about to follow when Juanita grabbed his arm. "Bishop, can you help him?"

"I think so. Right now, I need to talk to Catrell. I'll be back later tonight, listen for me. All right?"

"All right."

He kissed her forehead and left to catch up with Catrell and King who had already reached the alley. Two other young men had joined them. As Bishop came up on them, one of the men turned around sharply and reached inside his coat, ready to confront whoever was approaching. Catrell stopped him and stepped forward toward Bishop.

"Catrell, listen. Can you find Greg Gatson?"

"We're already looking."

"So am I. If you find him, let me know. We should talk to him together. Meet me at the river tonight around one o'clock. I might have some other information."

"Yeah, all right."

They went down the alley in opposite directions. On the bus ride home, the events of the past few days flew through Bishop's mind. He wondered. What was on Lonnie's mind? And why would he put King in this kind of predicament? He couldn't have anticipated all of this shit.

Arriving home the same way he'd left, he was starting to get used to coming in the back door of places. After walking through the house, turning on lights and checking to make sure everything was secure, he went out to his car. The unmarked police car was still there. It looked like the cop was still asleep. Back inside the house, Bishop checked his messages. Vincent, Lonnie and his mother had called. He made a mental note to call his mother tomorrow. He didn't want to talk to her right then for fear that she would detect the stress in his voice and it would worry her. He found Lonnie's business card, called his pager and put in the code he'd given him. Next he returned Vincent's call.

"Hey, Vincent, what's happenin'?"

"I have some documents that may help you out with your problem."

"Good. I'll come around the office tomorrow to pick them up."

"Come early, before noon. I'll be out all day after that."

"All right, see you tomorrow."

Lonnie answered the page as soon as the phone was back on the hook.

"Bishop, I've been trying to reach you."

"I'd turned the phone off to get some work done. Where are you?"

"At Juanita's. I need to talk to you right away."

"Meet me at the Southside Bar, 11:30 tonight."

"See you there."

Bishop could tell Juanita hadn't told Lonnie anything. His voice had an urgency in it, but not alarm like there would be if he knew who'd just been over there. Lonnie was becoming predictable and Bishop was beginning to feel some sense of control over what was happening. He had figured that Lonnie would want to talk to him and that the longer it took for him to find King the more he'd start giving Bishop information. It was about 10:55. The Southside Bar was ten minutes away. He decided to leave right then, get there early and establish position before Lonnie arrived.

As he pulled out of the driveway, the cop in the unmarked car didn't move. He was definitely asleep. Or dead. That thought made him pull alongside the cop and blow the horn. If he were dead then he was useless as a deterrent to someone else attacking his house. He wasn't dead. The horn made him bolt up in the seat. Bishop told him that Lonnie had just called and they were going to meet. The cop waved him on as if he'd been on top of things all the time.

When Lonnie arrived at Juanita's he could sense something was wrong. There was something slightly different in her greeting. Something distant, even angry in her eyes. He tried to read the warning in those eyes and wondered what she knew. He didn't have to wait long to find out: as soon as they sat down in the living room she wanted answers.

"Lonnie, tell me what's going on."

"About what?"

"Look, my son is in trouble and I don't want to play any games. Just tell me what is happening."

The tone of her question demanded an answer. She was King's mother and had a right to know. Lonnie loved Juanita and didn't want to add to her anxiety or deceive her. If his response was wrong, if she sensed he was lying, he might lose her. He might destroy whatever trust had been built over the years spent trying to assure her that his love was genuine.

Lonnie contemplated his answer. He had to satisfy more than one need. In addition to giving Juanita a sufficient answer, there was also a need to protect the secrets he carried and the knowledge he had accumulated about what really went on in the city. He had to answer carefully. Everything was at stake.

"King is in trouble because he discovered some information at City Hall that could implicate the mayor in a scandal."

"What did you have to do with it?"

Juanita had laid a trap. Lonnie sensed it, but didn't know how to respond. He'd spent years interrogating prisoners, tricking them out of information and now he was being questioned, being led down a road that could cause devastation to the one relationship he valued above all others. He had to disguise the truth without lying.

He looked Juanita directly in her eyes and said, "I asked King to check something out for me."

She studied his face. "Why? Why would you use my son to spy for you?"

"It was a mistake." Lonnie looked up at the ceiling. "I didn't think it would put him in danger."

Her voice was becoming more angry and her need to know became more urgent. "Who is after him? What is so important that he would have to fear for his life?"

"Don't know yet." He took her hand in his and continued, "I'm trying to find out now and put a stop to it."

Juanita jerked her hand away and said angrily, "Lonnie, you'd better help my son. I don't care what you have to do. You protect my son and get him out of the shit you got him in!"

Her words were like spears hurled into his heart. The tone of her command was threatening. It was a directive that he had already heard in his own head. He knew that everything important to him depended upon stopping the madness and preventing harm from coming to King. As Lonnie left Juanita's to meet Bishop, for the first time in his life he felt as if his power was slipping away, being stripped by some unseen force. He'd always been the politically connected cop, commanding his men and putting out fires for the politicians. They all had admired and even feared him, because he knew where all of the skeletons stood and the ghosts gathered.

Lonnie had begun his career under the first African American mayor,

150

Sam Page. He'd joined the force thinking he could contribute to the new black political power sweeping across the country. Mayor Page had spotted the bright, well-respected, young cop early and made him a member of his personal security staff. From that position, Lonnie learned the intricate politics of City Hall and government. He witnessed the relationship between the white business community and the newly elected black officials. He watched the rise of the few black businessmen who obtained government contracts in joint ventures with their larger white counterparts. He saw Mayor Sam Page struggle to change the relationship between government, business and the African American community. He also saw him destroyed.

The second and third black mayors were decent men but lacked vision or fire. They were able administrators but didn't lead the city anywhere. They were safe functionaries elected by a coalition of black and white businessmen who wanted political peace after the sweeping reforms of the Sam Page era.

The fourth and current mayor was Floyd Packard and Lonnie despised him. To him, Floyd Packard was an opportunist, a young ambitious politician who had not come up through the Civil Rights Movement or the struggle for black political power. Packard was just a typical American politician with a black face. Educated at Morehouse and Harvard, he made it a point to get himself appointed to the boards of the most important volunteer organizations but did very little to help them. He wrote editorials in the newspapers about community issues, was never involved in any real community activity, but had a knack for being be photographed at key events. Packard cultivated relationships with powerful north side businessmen and powerful south side preachers. When he ran for mayor, he'd accumulated a war chest of over two million dollars and an impressive resume. He'd obtained popularity through visibility, but nobody knew what he stood for.

Once elected, Mayor Packard expanded the minority business program started under Sam Page. But it didn't reach more black businesses or help more black people. It became the private feeding ground for a handful of his cronies. Millions of dollars poured into the bank accounts of nine or ten businesses. Every year, some investigation, some scandal, some bullshit erupted involving the questionable practices of the program or one of his political appointees.

Simultaneously, conditions in the African American community deteriorated. Fewer black students, especially males, graduated from high school and even fewer went to college. More drugs, crime and violence spread over the inner city. Homelessness grew, the infant mortality rate increased, unemployment soared. And, as confidence in black political leadership crashed, disillusioned young black people became enraged, hopeless and too often fratricidal.

Lonnie was caught in it all. He had become cynical about what was possible. He was frustrated and it often erupted when he would talk to Juanita or one of his few close friends. "Those motherfuckers don't want to solve the problems of the black community or the city. They just want to line their pockets, living off the pain of their own people. Fuck them. Fuck the mayor and all of those like him. Mayor Packard is like that clown Bokassa in the Central African Republic or some of those other assholes in Africa who kicked the Europeans out just so they could murder and rape their own people. Fuck them. Fuck them all."

His frustration ran deep, but Lonnie was trapped by his own relationship with the betrayal. He, too, had gotten fat and comfortable as one of the highest ranking blacks on the police force, watching over the inner city as it choked on promises never delivered. He wanted to break the shit up, to find a way to expose the corruption, maybe as a last act of whatever conscience he still had. He wanted to bring down Mayor Packard and his gang but and instead had unleashed more chaos and murder on the black community and especially on the people he loved. There had to be a way to stop it, to prevent more death. He had to find it and the only person he could trust to help him was Bishop.

every time we kill or die
our men are lost
our families cry
our fathers weep
our mothers wonder why
our lives are cheap
in each other's eyes

CHAPTER TWENTY-TWO

He sat at a table by the window in the Southside Bar waiting for Lonnie. Eryka Badu played on the juke box, a few folks sat at the bar and Bishop sat there by the window facing the door looking at his watch. Lonnie was already ten minutes late and Bishop was getting nervous because he didn't want to miss Catrell and King down at the river. At 11:45, just as impatience was starting to take hold of him, Lonnie walked in. He looked beat down. Still well dressed, but weary, worn, even older.

Bishop gestured toward a chair. "Have a seat, Lonnie."

"Thanks." Lonnie loosened his tie and took off his jacket.

"You want something to drink?"

"Naw, I'm cool."

"So, what's up?" Bishop lifted his almost empty glass of beer and indicated to the waiter that he wanted another one then returned his attention to Lonnie. "What do you need to discuss?"

Lonnie laced his fingers as he laid his hands on the table in front of him, then asked, "You ever hear of ENTAC Enterprises?"

Weighing his words, Bishop wanted Lonnie to believe his answers. "I don't think so. What is it?"

"It is a business of sorts. It's run by a cat named Greg Gatson. You ever hear of him?"

"Yeah. Isn't he the young guy who worked for some big engineering company? Used to be in the paper all the time?"

"That was a while ago. Now, he's the secret business partner of the mayor in a consultant firm called ENTAC Enterprises."

The waiter set another beer in front of Bishop as he asked, "What does ENTAC Enterprises do?" He paid for the beer then looked back at Lonnie.

"Basically what it does is take bribes from companies who want to do business with the city. It also puts together deals between large white owned businesses and the circle of black businessmen around the mayor. All of it is done for consultant fees or commissions."

"Isn't that illegal?"

Lonnie reached in his shirt pocket and took out a fresh cigar. "Quite. Packard secretly co-owns ENTAC and he and other officials in City Hall are taking money to ensure these people get their deals through the various committees, City Council and final approval by the mayor. The cat who set it up and the one making the payoffs is Greg Gatson." Lonnie clipped the end of the cigar and lit it slowly.

"So if you know all this why don't you bust them?"

"I was getting ready to when Stacey Freeman was killed because she discovered a file with information about ENTAC. She gave me the information in that file before her death, that's why I was at her house the day I say you there."

"What was in the file, Lonnie?" Bishop set the beer down and listened closely trying to make sure all the pieces fit.

Lonnie blew smoke into the air and watched it float in front of the dim lights before he continued. "Records of payoffs, who was getting what, when."

"Why are they after King?"

"Because they think he knows what Stacey knew."

"Did you find out how Stacey really died?"

"From an overdose of heroin."

Bishop frowned quizzically. "She was an addict?"

"I don't think so. It looks like somebody pumped enough shit in her to get the whole south side high. We think the plastic bag was just to send a message about what could happen."

Bishop had seen such a terrorist tactic before. Like sometimes after a soldier was killed, he'd have his dick cut off and stuffed in his mouth as a sign of what was possible if you got caught by the enemy.

Lonnie watched Bishop digesting the information he'd just given him. He puffed on his cigar then added, "One more thing about Greg Gatson. He's also been associated with some money laundering and has a reputation for violence. When needed he uses cats from the Zulu Nation for intimidation."

Before he'd finished the sentence Bishop was already thinking about the two who tried to burn his house. He hoped the motherfucker who'd sent them had gotten his message. He'd had enough shit. He also needed to leave the bar and head to the river. It was already 12:30, and it would take at least twenty minutes to get to the river and that was if nobody followed him.

"Lonnie, why are you telling me all this now?"

"I'm setting up a meeting with Gatson tomorrow and I want you to go. I figured you wouldn't do it if you didn't know what it was about."

"A meeting for what?"

"I'm going to give him the file if he will agree to leave King alone."

"Why do I need to be there?"

"Because you are the neutral party in all of this. The only one that all sides can trust. I want you to deliver the message about the deal and make the arrangements."

Bishop didn't agree or disagree. His face didn't change. His head didn't nod up and down or side to side. He sat motionless, expressionless, staring at Lonnie.

"What time and where?"

"I'll call you in the morning to let you know."

"Yeah, all right."

They stepped out into the street where the cold October wind blew through the city. Lonnie got in his car and drove off. Bishop got in his Volvo, made a U-turn and headed the other way. It was time to go to the river.

Catrell Merit was skipping rocks in the river just as Bishop had done as a boy. He seemed lost in his thoughts and didn't turn around right away when Bishop's car pulled in next to his. There was a car on both sides parked a short distance away. Both had four occupants. King was sitting in the back seat of one of the cars listening to Israel Vibration. He flashed a peace sign greeting to Bishop, but did not get out. Catrell was waiting to talk to him alone.

As Bishop approached him, Catrell scooped up a handful of rocks and tossed them sidearm one at a time and watched them bounce across the water. Without looking at Bishop he began to describe how standing there at the river brought back memories of a game he played in his youth.

He told Bishop, "My brother Julius and I used to come down here on Saturdays when I was a shorty. We used to compete to see who could skip a rock the most times or make it travel the greatest distance. I only won twice and I think he let me win both times. He was like that. Man, I really miss him. Back then, everything was different. I didn't have to deal with so much shit."

Bishop listened closely as the young gang lord opened up in a moment of introspection. "I'm not proud of this life I live. But I'm not ashamed of it either. When I started out, I didn't think it would lead me here. It just did. There weren't a whole lot of options and I decided early on that I wasn't going to live like the other people in George Washington Homes.

"I watched my mother struggle to raise us on welfare and odd jobs where she could be paid cash. She worked her ass off and still managed to be a good mother. She instilled in us a love of knowledge and of books. My moms exposed us to great literature, especially her favorites, the writers of the Harlem Renaissance and Shakespeare. She took us to all the free shit. Jazz and soul concerts in the park, the museum, art galleries, the library. Occasionally, when she could save the money, we'd go to restaurants with linen table cloths and napkins, so we could practice the table manners she taught us at home."

Bishop watched the water flowing in the river and glanced at Catrell when he asked, "Where was your old man?"

Catrell tossed some more rocks in the river and started talking again, "I never knew my father, but it didn't matter much. I had my brother. He was ten years older than me and much wiser than his years. Julius was my best friend, my mentor, my teacher. There is nobody in the world I loved more than him except my mother. He was a good son and really tried to help my mother out. You know, when he was in school he worked a full-time job at McDonald's and still kept a B average."

"What's your brother doing now?"

Catrell was winding up to throw another rock when he paused for a second, "He's dead." He tossed the rock and watched it skip three times before sinking from view.

"I'm sorry."

"Yeah. It was a long time ago. I was twelve when it happened."

"When what happened?"

"After Julius graduated from high school, he wanted to be a doctor. So he took a job as a welder in the auto plant to make money to go to school. The money was good, too good. He said he would only work there a year. One year turned into two and was headed for three. You know how it goes.

"On his way home from work one night, Julius and some of his co-workers stopped at a Benny's to eat. After sitting there for a while, it became obvious that they were being ignored. Julius called a waiter over and demanded to see the manager. An argument started. The manager told Julius and his friends to leave, then fucked up and said something about not serving niggers.

"Julius clocked the manager. When the waiter tried to intervene, he blasted him in the face, too. The cops came, arrested Julius and gave him a beating that put him in the hospital with a fractured cheekbone, a broken nose and severe damage to his kidneys. Julius was tried and convicted of assault on the manager, the waiter and the cops who arrested him. He was given ten to twenty years in the state penitentiary where he survived four years before he was stabbed by another inmate. He died waiting to be taken to the hospital."

For years Bishop had heard the stories about Catrell. He'd heard how a twelve-year-old boy who liked books, began spending more and more time in the streets, fighting, stealing, running errands for drug dealers and associating with the older criminals who populated his neighborhood. At fourteen Catrell joined with other boys his age and formed the Egyptian Cobras. Their activities ranged from car theft to running drugs. Under Catrell's leadership, they fought rival gangs. When crack cocaine and Ronald Reagan hit urban America in the eighties, Catrell began transforming the Cobras from a street gang into a deadly corporation.

By the time he was twenty-one, Catrell controlled all of the drug traffic in Washington Homes, had established several legal businesses and was slowly spreading his influence over the whole city. He moved his mother out of the projects, into the suburbs and away from the criminal life he lived. A life that broke her heart while she waited for the inevitable, the day she'd have to bury her second son.

Standing there at the edge of the river, skipping rocks, Catrell wondered how his life would be different if Julius had not gone to prison. "You know, Bishop, if things were different I might be a teacher like you. I used to want to be a college professor.

"That sounds funny, don't it? Most people look at what I do and think I like this shit. It ain't that. It's just the life that chose me."

"Yeah," Bishop said. "But you can make other choices now, Catrell."

Catrell shook his head. "Not now."

"You never know."

"Maybe. It's kind of weird though. I do what I do but I know that the cats like King are the ones we've got to look out for. Young brothers like him are our future. Isn't it ironic that he has to be protected from society by someone like me?"

"It just shows you how fucked up things are right now. Catrell our people aren't supposed to be living like this."

"I know."

"And we shouldn't even be having this conversation. You should be a college professor somewhere."

They both laughed, but the laughter was filled with sadness because they both knew that he was a drug dealer, a murderer, a young black man whose choices all but insured he would be dead or in jail eventually.

As the two of them stood there illuminated by the moon, their bodies reflected in the water moving slowly beneath them, their thoughts roamed through the past and speculated on the future. King walked over. "Bishop, ain't this some wild shit?"

"Real wild. You OK?"

"Fine. I just want this to be over. My mother must be scared."

"We all are. But I think we can work it out."

After throwing one last rock into the river, Catrell finally turned around and looked at Bishop for the first time since he had arrived.

"Mr. Bishop, we don't have a lot of time. We should discuss the business."

"You're right. Look, I just finished talking with Lonnie Carlton."

"I know."

Bishop wasn't surprised by his knowledge of the meeting. He had become very aware that Catrell's eyes were everywhere. Bishop recalled his conversation with Lonnie. "Two things. First, Lonnie says he has the file on ENTAC Enterprises. Second, he believes he can trade it for an agreement that King will be left alone. He's set up a meeting for tomorrow where I will deliver that message to Greg Gatson."

King stepped up closer to Bishop and said, "Lonnie thinks Gatson is the man behind all of this. You think he's right?"

Bishop answered, "I don't know. Gatson obviously plays a key role in this shit. But I don't know if we can make a deal with him."

"Fuck a deal." Catrell said as he pulled out his cigarettes and lit one. His eyes were cold and his voice was calm. Bishop knew what he was thinking. It was time for war not for deals. Greg Gatson was responsible for causing the death of Stacey Freeman and launching an all-out war on the Egyptian Cobras. He was hunting King, Catrell and Bishop. Catrell knew his options were limited. He could not negotiate his way out of the situation. He could not make a deal that would pardon him for his past, prevent prosecution for his present, or free him for the future.

Catrell had survived as long as he had because he understood how to maintain the balance of power and had no illusions about why he or others did what they did. People acted based on their interests. Throughout history, wars had always been fought according to that principle. It was never a moral question for those who initiated war, even though they always tried to convince the people that there was some important and virtuous reason for sending millions to kill and die.

As Bishop looked into Catrell's eyes, it was evident that Greg Gatson had miscalculated. Gatson did not understand a young man like that. Catrell was not a Stanford educated, former corporate executive turned money launderer, bag man and political pimp. He had waged war all of his life. To him, this was just another battle and he was planning carefully how to fight and not just survive, but win. He had the mind and patience of a general. Catrell was going after Gatson and whoever else was responsible for what had happened in the last few days. All hell was about to break loose.

King watched patiently, studying, analyzing the conversation. Bishop wondered what he thought about all that had happened and whether he was really just a spectator or whether King was involved in it on some deeper level.

Bishop asked, "Catrell, what are you going to do?"

"I'm not sure yet." He flicked ashes from the cigarette and stared at the river.

Bishop wanted to know what Catrell was planning but didn't want to ask again. He tried to bait him. "Lonnie's going to call me in the morning to let me know details of the meeting."

Catrell didn't take the bait. Instead he said, "I'll have somebody get in touch with you. Let me know when and where it's going to happen."

"All right, but there's one more thing you should be aware of." Bishop reached in his pocket and pulled out his car keys preparing to leave. "Lonnie told me Gatson has a relationship with the Dexter Avenue Zulu Nation."

"Yeah, I know." Catrell thumped the remainder of the cigarette into the river and walked away.

There was a casualness about the way he said it that confirmed Bishop's thoughts. Catrell was quietly preparing the defeat of his enemies. Someone was about to taste his full wrath and power. His troops were heavily armed, willing to kill and unafraid of prison. What made Mayor Packard and Greg Gatson think he would just accept their attacks upon him? It was reported that the Egyptian Cobras controlled a multimillion-dollar-a-year drug business. What lapse of judgment would make them think Catrell and the Cobras would walk away from their money and power without a fight? Bishop got in his car and drove away feeling like he was getting closer to the answer but knowing all the questions hadn't been asked yet.

CHAPTER TWENTY-THREE

When Bishop arrived at Juanita's, it was almost 3:30 a.m., and because it was so late he pulled his car into the alley directly behind her house and parked. He figured it would be safe and undetected at least until sunrise. Even before he reached her back porch, the door opened. She stood there waiting for him. It was good to see her, even under those circumstances. Wearing jeans and a black cashmere sweater, her hair was down, accentuating her features, framing her face, a face tense from constant uncertainty about the fate of her son.

Cassandra Wilson's smoky voice filled up the space in the house and the space between them. Silently, Juanita studied Bishop's weariness, then took his hand, led him out of the kitchen, down the hallway and upstairs to her bedroom.

At the foot of her bed she took off his coat and laid it on a chair then whispered to him, "Bishop, I need you to hold me tonight."

He reached for her. In the darkness of her bedroom, the street light tumbled through the window and draped shadows across their bodies. His hands stroked her locks and back. She kissed his neck, reached for his face and drew his mouth to hers. That kiss took him away from everything else in the world. The softness of her full lips and the sweetness of her mouth fed Bishop, filling him with hunger until he was starving for her. They lay down on her bed and Juanita whispered her needs to him.

"Bishop, I want you inside of me tonight. But I need you to wait until I fall in love with you. It's been so long time since I've made love with a man I was in love with. Just hold me now and let me fall in love with you before it happens. It won't take long. I know it won't take long."

Her words sang promises to him. She had whispered his future as if they'd shared a secret forever. He would wait as long as it took and told her, "Yes, come close. Let me hold you."

It was enough for that moment, that time, that place. Suddenly the bond between them was all he needed and all he wanted. To be close, to wait until she was sure that she loved him, was enough to fill the space inside that only she could feel. Juanita fell asleep on Bishop's chest and he held onto her, staring into the darkness, drifting off into his dream of a time when they would greet each morning together.

While Bishop dozed peacefully with Juanita beside him, across town Lonnie Carlton walked into his home exhausted from the day, the week, the decisions he had to make and the lack of control over a dangerous situation that could change his life dramatically. He fell into the soft burgundy leather chair at 3:45 in the morning.

Lonnie's condo was elegant and tastefully furnished with modern furniture, but it seemed cold and almost lifeless as if no one really lived there. It resembled a furniture store showroom. The only art on the walls were two pieces Juanita had bought him. There were no plants or pets, and it was always clean and neat because he was hardly ever there and a housekeeper came twice a week.

He liked to sleep there when he was really tired. It almost reminded him of sleeping in a hotel room. He wished it had the warmth, the life, the spirit of Juanita's house. Maybe he'd never cared to make it that way because he always hoped that one day they would live together and her touch would color everything for him.

As he sat in his favorite chair, Spike Lee's *She's Gotta Have It* played on HBO and he sipped his beer and smoked a joint, trying to unload the pressures he'd carried home. He thought about calling Juanita, but decided to wait until the morning. Instead, he called the station, checked his messages, then asked the operator to patch him through to the officer watching Bishop's house. The officer reported that Bishop hadn't come home yet and that nothing new had happened there. Lonnie called and left a message on Bishop's answering machine.

After taking one last swig of beer, he went into the bathroom and turned on the shower to let it warm up. He stepped into the bedroom, took off his holster and laid his gun on the night stand. Reaching in his shirt pocket, he took out a computer disk marked ENTAC Enterprises that he had taken from Stacey Freeman's purse when he discovered her body. He laid it next to his gun.

Lonnie undressed and headed across the hall toward the bathroom that was hot and steamy the way he liked it. Just before he reached the doorway, he felt a sudden moment of panic. He looked over his shoulder and a burst of adrenaline shot through his naked body as he tried to run back toward the bed-room. He heard vile, hateful, vulgar phrases and opened his mouth to respond, but his thoughts never made it to words. His head slammed into the tile floor just inside the bathroom and the last thing he remembered was how much love he had for Juanita.

Billy King watched the street lights pass by from the back seat of a black Lexus. In the front seat, two Egyptian Cobras, both around his age, sat silent-ly but alert as they drove King toward another safe house where he would spend the night in hiding. It'd been a week since he became a hunted man and every night he had moved in the shadows to various secret locations that Catrell had all over the city.

The Fugees bounced off the tinted glass windows as the Lexus glided through the darkened streets and King counted the faces of those who roamed the night. Some were homeless, haunting the hideaways they'd fashioned out of boxes, doorways and alleys. Some staggered through alcohol-induced haze or drug-inspired hallucination. Others were like those driving the car, powerful young men imposing their will upon the concrete castles they con-trolled.

The men of his generation were divided by their vision more than by cir-cumstance or choice. What they saw as possible in their own country, a place that remained foreign and hostile to their existence, dictated how they would fight. King studied the young men driving the car. They were around his age. The Cobras had chosen to accept America's definition of them as outlaws, criminals, the enemy. They saw no other way. If they were able to survive by slinging drugs and imposing their will on those weaker than them, by outthinking the police and outfighting others who'd chosen the same path, then they thought victory was theirs. Underneath all the bragging, the baring of teeth, the ranting about their physical prowess, they knew that in spite of their boasting, in spite of their hardened faces and I-don't-give-a-fuck atti-tudes, there was no real victory. There was only battle. There was only wait-ing. There was only time. Prison and the morgue stood ready to embrace them like the fulfillment of prophecy.

Billy King leaned his head against the back of the leather seat, closed his eyes and thought about the young men who went to college with him. Many came from neighborhoods like his, others from quiet middle-class communities. Some were much like the brothers driving the car, but what they saw was different. They didn't accept their position as outlaws and refused to be treated as criminals.

The car stopped at a traffic light and King opened his eyes to see what had caused the delay. It was late, four o'clock in the morning, and he was tired. Fatigue hung heavy on his athletic body and his mind was exhausted from the hurricane of events that had swept him along for the last few days. The driver waited for the light to change then slowly accelerated. The car moved easily through the almost vacant streets. King caught the reflection of the vehicle in store windows then closed his eyes again to wonder about the young men of his community.

They wanted peace and they wanted to know where their place was. But for them there was no peace. There was no place. That reality was causing him to get angry when he opened his eyes again as the car pulled up into the driveway of a beautiful home in an affluent neighborhood. The garage door opened and the Lexus pulled in next to a Range Rover. The three young men exited the car and entered the house from inside the garage.

King recognized important original paintings by Romare Bearden, John Riddle, Jacob Lawrence, Aaron Douglass and Elizabeth Catlett, and the young artist Radcliff Bailey. He also noticed the work of several lesser-known African American folk artists. The rooms were beautifully furnished and the hardwood floors glistened, accentuating the furnishings and the art. One of his escorts retreated to the kitchen, while the other one walked through the house admiring the decor and checking the surroundings. King waited in the living room until they directed him to a bedroom where he would rest for the night. He surveyed the room, took out the 9mm Glock Catrell had given him when the trouble started and laid it on the bed. He undressed, showered in the adjacent bathroom, then fell asleep immediately. For the moment, he was safe from the forces outside the door who wanted to kill him.

Bishop had drifted off to sleep for a couple of hours. When he opened his eyes, the clock radio showed it was 6:00 a.m.. They were both fully clothed. Juanita's back was to him and her body was nestled up against his. As he moved to get out of the bed, the shifting of his body awakened her.

Juanita rolled over to face him and asked, "Are you leaving?"

"Yes. I better go now. Go back to sleep, I'll call you later."

He kissed her forehead and walked gently down to the kitchen where he peeked in the refrigerator and grabbed an orange before leaving out the back door. There was a calmness about him as he peeled the orange and sucked its sweet juice. It was that time of morning where the darkness was just giving way to the light and Bishop began to think about the battles ahead. Violence scared him because ultimately it could not be controlled and its damage was always greater than the perpetrators expected. As Bishop reached his car, he began to feel lightheaded and his stomach felt queasy and his breathing became difficult. He fumbled around with his keys, finally got the door opened and sat down in the driver's seat trying to collect himself before driving home.

When he arrived at his house, the sickness was gone and so was the unmarked police car. The cop's absence unsettled him. Any change in the patterns of the previous few days made him anticipate the worst. Cautiously he got out of the car and approached the house feeling something was not right. He reached down to grab the newspaper off the porch and saw a business card stuck in the door. It was from a Detective Maddox. On the back he'd written a note that said call him immediately. When he entered the house the phone was ringing and it was not quite 7:00 a.m., which made him speculate that he was about to get some more bad news.

"Hello."

"Bishop, it's Vincent. Did you hear the news?"

The place in Juanita's bed where Bishop had been lying was still warm. She could still feel his presence. She knew that it was the day when she would have to tell Lonnie that their relationship had to change. Juanita didn't go back to sleep after Bishop left. Lying in bed, staring out the window, she watched the sun slowly reveal the trees with their leaves turning colors.

The doorbell rang, breaking through her thoughts. It was 7:15. It had to be Lonnie. Because it was a little early, it made her think he hadn't been home yet. After working all night, he would usually stop by for breakfast.

When he'd had a chance to go home and get some sleep he didn't get to her house before 8:00.

Juanita washed her face and laughed when she looked at herself in the mirror because she was a mess and looked just like she'd slept with her clothes on. She was aware that the laughter was also a result of nervous expectation. She had to tell Lonnie then, that day. It would hurt him and she didn't want to, but there was no way to continue in the relationship even though it was comfortable and convenient. She was not the kind of woman who could have two men.

Lonnie had been around for almost twelve years. She knew he loved her and even asked her to marry him twice. Juanita couldn't–she didn't love him like that, even though she once considered it because he was a good man and was good to her. He understood but hoped that one day she would believe that no man would treat her and her children better than he did.

He was a good lover, but she never felt drawn into the delirium of deep emotion that only love brings during sex. Sometimes when Lonnie was inside her, he would confess his feelings and Juanita would silently pity him because she knew it would never be reciprocated. Many times she wished she felt differently, that one day she would receive him and give to him completely. Over the years nothing changed and she couldn't settle for less than what her heart needed. She knew how it felt to be in love. And she knew that after all the years since Sonny died, she was finally falling in love with another man. She was falling in love with Bishop.

When she got downstairs to the front door, Juanita was prepared for the conversation she and Lonnie had to have. She hesitated a minute, took a deep breath, opened the door and was startled to see someone else standing there. It was one of Lonnie's men, Detective Maddox.

As soon as he woke up, Greg Gatson grabbed the remote control and turned on the television in his bedroom. He flipped through the channels until he found the local news just in time to hear the report.

> "Early this morning police discovered Detective Lonnie Carlton dead in his house. Around four o'clock this morning, a neighbor heard a series of shots and called police. They arrived to

find Detective Carlton lying on the floor apparently shot several times. Police officials have not released any additional details pending further investigation. Detective Carlton was a well-known figure in the city and just last week was assigned to lead the mayor's attempt to break up the notorious drug gang, the Egyptian Cobras. Although no suspects have been named, sources inside the police department are talking about a possible link between the campaign against the Cobras and the murder of Detective Carlton."

"Hello."

"Bishop, it's Vincent. Did you hear the news?"

"What news?"

"Lonnie Carlton was found murdered this morning."

"What?"

"Yeah, a neighbor heard gunshots and called the police. When they went there to check it out, Lonnie was dead, lying naked in the bathroom, shot twice in the chest."

"Fuck!"

"You all right?"

"God damn it! Vincent, when is this going to end?"

As the news of Lonnie's murder sunk in, Bishop thought about Juanita. He had to call her immediately. The police had probably already told her. "Vincent, I'll call you later. There's something I have to take care of."

"All right. Don't forget to come by here before noon."

Bishop's thoughts were consumed with Juanita and King and their safety. Without Lonnie and his power, who would protect them? Everyone was in danger. There would be no checks and balances. Gatson had them all on the defensive. Lonnie was dead. King and Catrell were on the run. Juanita was vulnerable and Bishop was uncertain why Gatson had come after him.

He ran upstairs, packed some clothes, inspected the Baretta, made sure there were some extra clips in the bag, secured all the doors and windows, made sure some lights were left on and checked his messages right before leaving. His mother had called again. He'd forgotten to call her back the day before. Lonnie left a message at 3:28 a.m., shortly before he was killed.

Vincent called twice, once at 4:30 a.m. and again at 6:00 a.m. He was about to walk out the door when the phone rang again.

"Hello."

"Bishop, this is Juanita. Something terrible has happened."

Her voice resonated with restrained grief. Bishop's heart cracked open and bled for her. Lonnie was her friend, her lover, her protector. Bishop had envied his place in her life until last night when she promised to give herself to him. They had lain there in peace, holding onto each other in the comfort of the darkness, while Lonnie was being murdered. Already their peace had been shattered.

"Juanita, I heard what happened. I'm sorry."

"They found him early this morning."

"I know. Where are you?"

"At the police station. They picked me up and brought me here about a half hour ago. Can you come and get me?"

"I'm on the way."

"Bishop."

"Yes."

"Thank you."

He could hear her tears falling as she spoke. His own were locked away behind the numbness that engulfed his body when Vincent told him the news. Somewhere behind the veil, those tears were dripping like the faucet in Juanita's kitchen, breaking the silence that surrounded the sickness that surrounded their lives.

Before he left the house, Bishop called his mother.

During my year in Nam, I only called home twice. The first time was shortly after arriving there and my virgin experience in the field caused me to freak out. What the fuck was I doing in a war? Eighteen years old, thousands of miles away from home, running from death, I needed to hear my mother's voice. Only her words could comfort me. Only her voice could cause me to get control of the confusion crashing around inside my head. Why was I there? Why was my life being sacrificed? Why was my mission to kill, to take the lives of other human beings? Why? I knew she could not answer those questions so I didn't ask. I just needed to hear her. If her voice could just reach me, it would wrap around me like a spirit and I'd wear it like a flack jacket into the killing zone. It worked. I listened to her instruct me to remem ber that she and my father loved me, to be careful, to come home safely, to remember that she and my father loved me, to pray, to eat right, to be careful of venereal disease, to watch out for racists, to remember that she and my father loved me. I needed her to protect me but I knew all she could do at that moment was lift my spirits.

The second time was months later when it felt as if the war had sepa rated me from my soul, turning me into a vicious animal. After months of committing and witnessing tremendous violence, I was ashamed because I'd killed not only to defend and preserve my own life, but also to assert my will upon others. We and the Vietnamese were prey and we both had become effi cient predators. The numbness that at first protected me from sorrow, had begun to hide my humanity. I justified murder as necessary to complete assignments. I tried to convince myself with the lie that torture was a tool to triumph over people who'd been classified as the enemy. The thought of what I'd done, of how hideous I'd become, was repugnant to me. One year of hat ing the darkness.

My mother never knew the details of my ordeal. She never knew the internal war being waged between who I was and what the war had turned me into. During that second desperate call, we only discussed mundane things. Before hanging up, she brought me back to life and peeled away the numbness that had become a barrier between me and my soul.

"Never become that which you hate."

That was all she said at the end of the conversation. Those few words pierced my mask and revealed the face of my disgust. What was destroying me came clearly into focus. I had become a killer without a noble cause. (Is there such a thing as a noble cause to kill for?) I was a machine that felt no compassion, that had no conscience, that contained no connection to the value of life. Since becoming a thing that I hated, a twisted thing so full of self-loathing, my mind neither confirmed my complicity nor condemned my conduct.

Her words and her voice called me back. My heart began searching constantly for what was good in me, but those memories had become distant and difficult to discover buried under so much pain. I wanted to go home as a human being but, after a year of war, it was doubtful. I needed to be saved and wanted to be rescued but there were no secret remedies for absolving my bloody sins.

When I returned home, surrounded by people who loved me, I fought my way back to life. It took years. It required constant vigilance. It demanded sacrifice and service to heal my spirit. All those years of working on my wounds, of fighting against the vicious, hateful thing I'd become, made me finally understand that no one should have to enter manhood while wrestling with the demons of war.

CHAPTER TWENTY-FOUR

Heading toward the police station, Bishop recalled the brief conversation he had just had with his mother before walking out the door. As always, she was just checking to make sure he was taking care of himself. She asked about Sheila and whether she was coming home for Thanksgiving and she wanted to remind him about his father's birthday in two weeks. Bishop had never forgotten it, but every year his mother always reminded him. With that mother radar working she said he sounded tired or upset and uttered a sarcastic "uh-huh" when he replied that he just needed some rest.

Fortunately, she didn't pry, even though it was obvious she had detected something was wrong and wanted to investigate further. He promised her that he would go out to her house the next weekend and clean out the basement. His mother always put him, and everybody who came through her door, to work. Recalling the conversation gave him some comfort even though the closer he got to the police station the more uncomfortable he was becoming.

When Bishop pulled into the parking lot of the police station, his stomach knotted up. The combination of seeing Juanita in pain, anxiety about the deadly crisis they were in and being in a police station caused a great deal of tension throughout his body. He took a deep breath, gathered himself, went inside and asked the officer at the front desk where to find Juanita. The desk sergeant directed him through the metal detector, down the hall to the left and to a Detective Maddox. It was just what he didn't need, more tension. The person he was looking for was also the one looking for him.

Marching down the hallway, his footsteps echoed off the tile floor and his thoughts echoed off the stories of black men who had moved through those halls. In his mind he saw them handcuffed and hardened, frightened and fragile, insulting and impertinent. They came in by the thousands every year, some cooperative, some combative, but all cautious, knowing that from the day they were born black and male they were already condemned. He wanted to leave. There was too much pain haunting those halls.

Standing at the door of Detective Maddox's office, he witnessed two young brothers in handcuffs being brought down the hall. They looked like college students. They were frightened and one of them loudly proclaimed their innocence. The otherone commanded him to shut up and demanded to speak to a lawyer. The three cops escorting them ignored the demand and seemed indifferent to the proclamations. They'd seen and heard it before, every hour of every day.

Every instinct told him to walk out of there, to leave before being swallowed up by the sickening smell of the future dying in jail cells. Unfortunately, there was no escape. Juanita needed him, so he pushed through the door ready to take her away from there.

When Bishop entered the office of Detective Maddox, Juanita looked up and spotted him first. She was on a small tattered sofa that faced the door. Detective Maddox was behind an old wooden desk. The desk was cluttered with paper and a dirty coffee cup sat on top, waiting to be used for the tenth time that day.

Maddox stood up. "You must be Mr. Bishop," he said and extended his hand. "I'm Detective Maddox, have a seat."

Bishop shook his hand but said, "I'll stand."

Maddox was an older black man, maybe sixty, a bit overweight with a paunch. He was clean shaven with dark brown skin, salt and pepper hair and a white shirt that was heavily starched. He had a pleasant, almost fatherly air about him. Hanging on the wall in back of Maddox's desk was a framed, blown-up but faded newspaper clipping from a 1963 copy of *The Crusader*. It showed a group photo of the original six, the first black officers hired on the police force. A young Maddox was in the picture wearing a crisp blue uniform. The six of them were hired back in the late fifties and assigned to walk the beat in black neighborhoods and told not to arrest white people. Bishop didn't know Maddox but remembered his parents talking about the original six. He was surprised that Maddox was still on the force and had not retired.

Maddox resumed his seat, looked over at Juanita then looked with concern back at Bishop while trying to figure out a way to interrogate him. Bishop watched him closely and thought Maddox's paternal presence and reputation as one of the original six had probably served him well in conversations he had had with other black men who were suspects. Bishop had no intention of letting Maddox have his way with him.

Before the older man could say anything, Bishop stated, "Detective Maddox, I'm here to take Ms. King home."

"Yes. She's been waiting for you." Maddox opened a drawer in his desk and pulled out a notepad and placed it on the desk. "I assume you've heard about Detective Carlton."

"Yes," Bishop answered and walked closer to the desk.

Maddox scribbled something on the pad and continued his attempt at interrogation. "Well, before you leave, I'd like to ask you a few questions, if that's OK."

Bishop shrugged his shoulders and said, "I'm not sure. What do you want to know?"

"Last night...uh, late last night...where were you?"

"Why? Am I a suspect?"

"No. I'm trying to figure out who killed my friend."

"Then we both seek the same information."

Maddox tapped his pen on the desk. "You're smart enough to know you don't have to answer me...at least...not right now. But don't worry. I don't think you had anything to do with the murder of Commander Carlton. I sort of have to ask certain questions. It's my job to cover all possibilities. You can appreciate that, can't you, son?"

Bishop thought the old man's attempt to question him was funny, but he kept a straight face while he played with Maddox's words in his mind, "He called me 'son'. That was good. He intended to use that fatherly shit to the max. I didn't have to answer. At least not right then. The implicit threat. You can appreciate me doing my job. Ha-ha, very funny." His mind was saying to Maddox, "Fuck you and your job." His mouth was saying something else.

Bishop rapped his knuckles on Maddox's desk and said, "I'll tell you what." He walked over to Juanita who had been angrily observing the sparring between the two men. "I'm going to take Ms. King home and we'll talk later. I'll call you."

Maddox studied the situation and Bishop. He wondered if he should let him walk out the door or hold him there and conduct a formal interrogation. A slight smile formed at the corners of his mouth while he weighed the options. Either way, he knew Bishop was going to have to respond to him sooner or later.

"You're right, son. Ms. King, I don't want you to have to sit around here any longer. Please forgive me. I hope you understand I just want to find out who did this terrible thing."

Juanita stood up and Maddox came around his desk and placed a fatherly hand on her shoulder, causing her to look up into his eyes so deeply, so intensely, that it made him drop his hand and take a step back. The look on his face was confused, as if he couldn't figure out whether it was hostility or grief that she slammed into his face. Maddox turned to Bishop and extended his hand again as if looking for an ally. He was uncomfortable, almost like a child caught in a lie, trying to grapple with feelings of shame and fear. Juanita didn't speak, but walked past him, out the door and into the hall where she waited.

Maddox walked toward the door behind Bishop saying, "Take care of her, Mr. Bishop. And give me a call so we can have that talk."

Without responding, Bishop walked out the door and joined Juanita in the hall where she stood listening to the ghosts of black men gathered to warn them.

I learned a long time ago that the anticipation of combat was always the moment when your mortality was made clearest. The absolute worse time was when you were waiting, contemplating an attack, considering the forces arrayed against you, concerned that perhaps your luck had run out. Once battle actually began, so much was happening that you operated on survival instinct. In the middle of a fight you responded to the need to kill or die, but the hours before that, the seconds of silent, solemn preparation for con frontation used to torment me. I'd study the faces of the other teenage men who might die. I'd think of my mother and father and friends and the life back home that might never be resumed because of the war.

You could almost hear death laughing at us during those moments, as if it knew the feeding time was near and before the day was over, some young men would enter the dead world and their bodies would become food for some evil feast. The air would smell with fear and anxiety and sometimes with piss and shit. The virgin soldiers, those who'd never been in battle, would try to remain cool in spite of an overwhelming urge to run. The veter ans who'd seen the blood and tasted the fire before had learned to suppress that urge even though it raged within them, too.

Chapter Twenty-Five

Sitting in Juanita's house, preparing for the battle that must be fought, Bishop knew that there was no place to run, no way to escape the inevitable. Battle awaited and he had to fight it. He had to kill again or die. He had brought in his bag that had his gun and a couple of clips in it. He took the pistol out, laid it and the ammunition on the table and examined them.

A sudden soft knock on the back door startled him. Juanita was lying down on the couch in the living room and didn't stir. He moved to the door with the gun in his hand. Through the window he saw Catrell standing there alone.

Catrell was dressed in a black pinstripe suit and a black shirt. He seemed very poised and business like when he said, "Bishop, I need you to go somewhere with me."

"Wait here, I'll be right out."

Bishop set the gun on the table and went into the living room to see Juanita. She was sitting up, watching curiously as he entered the room and asked, "Who was at the door?"

"Catrell." Bishop grabbed his jacket off a chair and put it on.

"Is Billy with him?"

"No, he's alone. I've got to go out and talk with him for a while. Are you going to be all right?"

"Yes. Bishop, I need you to help me do something."

"What is it?"

Juanita stood up and faced him. "Will you take me to go pick up something when you get back?"

"I'll be back shortly, then we'll go, OK?"

"Be careful."

Bishop grabbed the pistol on his way out and stuck it in his belt. He and Catrell left Juanita's and walked to the alley where a cream-colored Lexus waited.

Before they got in the car, Catrell said, "Bishop, the cops that Lonnie had watching out for you and Juanita have been pulled off."

"What?"

"Yeah. My folks told me that they snatched them off right after they found his body. Don't worry, I've got men watching out for her and for you."

"Appreciate it."

The two of them got into the car. Catrell usually had one of his men drive him around but this time he slid behind the wheel and Bishop sat in the passenger seat. As they pulled out of the alley and onto the street, two other cars joined them, one in front and one in back. There were four men in each of the other cars, but Catrell and Bishop rode alone.

"Where are we going?" Bishop asked.

Catrell turned the corner and said, "I want to show you something."

As usual Catrell's answer did not lend itself to further questioning. He wanted Bishop to wait to see whatever he had to show and did not intend to spoil the surprise.

They rode in silence for a few minutes until Bishop asked, "Where's King?"

"He's safe, but he's shaken up by the news of Lonnie Carlton's murder."

"Catrell, do you know who did it?"

He glanced at Bishop quickly, but didn't answer his question. Catrell pushed in a tape and they traveled to the music of the Modern Hip Hop Quartet until they pulled up in front of some vacant old warehouses. Catrell cut the engine off and watched the young men in the other two cars get out and survey the surroundings. He looked over at Bishop and seemed to be contemplating a response to the question that was asked at least five minutes before.

"Bishop, why did you kill the two men who came to burn your house?"

His question caught Bishop completely off guard. His face must have registered the surprise because Catrell turned away to give him time to compose himself and the answer. Bishop knew he couldn't lie to him. It would be a waste of time because he obviously knew what happened that night, plus he needed Catrell's help and protection. It was important to figure out what he was really asking or saying. Before Bishop could answer, Catrell fired another question.

"Do you know why they were sent?"

"No."

Catrell stared straight ahead through the windshield. "It didn't matter did it?"

"Not at that moment."

"They attacked and you responded in the only way that made sense."

"You're right."

"Why weren't the police watching your house that night?"

Bishop looked at Catrell and said, "You tell me."

"Do you think Lonnie Carlton pulled them off?"

Catrell didn't wait for an answer. His words hung in the air like smoke as he opened the door, stepped out and walked over to one of his men. Bishop was stunned and confused by the question. "Was he implying Lonnie set me up? Why? Did Catrell have Lonnie killed?" Catrell's words rang like a refrain in his head. *They attacked and you responded in the only way that made sense.*

Catrell motioned for him to get out of the car. Bishop hesitated for a moment, trying to get control of the numbness that was rising inside him again. He had to get control. His heart started to race. He pulled the Baretta from his belt, popped the clip out, checked it and slapped it back in. Before opening the car door, he chambered the first bullet, eased the hammer down, put the safety on and stuck it back in his belt. Catrell walked toward the car as Bishop stepped out to meet him.

"Bishop, you were in the war, right?"

"Yeah." Bishop looked around nervously. He felt that Catrell was too calm, like an assassin. Whatever was about to take place was happening because Catrell thought it was necessary. There was no emotion, no nervousness, no fear. And that's what made Bishop worry about what he was about to see.

Catrell continued his questioning. "What was the worst thing about being over there?"

"Catrell, the worst thing about any war is it forces you to commit murder in order to live. Your spirit can never recover from that. You spend the rest of your life searching for moments of peace."

"Bishop, I've always been at war." He turned away and started toward one of the warehouses. "I don't even know where to look for peace."

Bishop followed Catrell toward the warehouse. There were Egyptian Cobras posted all around. The closer they got, the more he realized that there were suddenly more than the eight that drove in with them. He counted at least thirteen as they entered the building. Inside there were maybe a dozen more. They stood around casually, but all were strapped. Some looked to be in their early twenties. A few were teenagers.

Catrell, Bishop and a few of the Cobras approached some metal stairs leading to the second floor. Catrell went up the first two steps then turned around and said, "Y'all stay down here. Bishop, you come with me."

On the second floor they went through a small narrow hallway that emptied into a large room that at one time must have been an office. It was filthy inside. Dust and trash covered the floor. An old metal desk was stained from water that had dripped from the ceiling. There were large industrial windows along three of the walls, yet it was semi-dark because they were so filthy that only small specks of light poked through tiny spots where the dirt was not as thick. Bishop had no idea what to expect. He closed his eyes for a few seconds to try to adjust them to the darkness then tried to make out the few shapes in the room. The only thing he could see was Catrell walking to the opposite end of the room where he flicked a switch, illuminating the room with a lamp that had a cord running out of one of the windows to a pole nearby. Something stirred in the light, something alongside the back wall where Catrell stood. At his feet were three bodies. All of them bound, and their faces covered by pillowcases.

Catrell held a pistol in his right hand and beckoned with his left. "Bishop, come here."

It was a non-threatening command and that made it more frightening. Catrell stood there like a hunter over the bodies of captured game. Bishop approached with caution, visualizing his own actions if it became necessary to draw his own pistol and fire. Details of the room were important in case he had to kill Catrell. He stole quick glances around the room searching for another exit, knowing the stairway would be blocked by the Cobras. He saw no other way out and it frightened him because he was trapped.

Catrell must have read his face or his mind. His eyes had become acutely focused on Bishop's. There was something different in his look. He was still calm, but something just behind the eyes was boiling. Fire was rising. A cold fire. The fire of rage and contempt.

He reached down and snatched the pillowcases off each of the prisoners. They were all young black men. The oldest looked about twenty-five, wasn't wearing a shirt and had multiple tattoos of what appeared to be gang symbols covering his muscular arms, shoulders and chest. His head was shaven and his brown face was swollen and bloodied.

The second one looked slightly younger and was caramel colored. He was skinny, but must have lifted weights because his body was cut, defined. He had long limbs and even on the floor seemed tall. He had the look of a distance runner, very lean and fit. There were no signs that he had been beaten.

The last one looked nineteen or so with beautiful dark chocolate skin stained by blood that had run down from under his braided hair along his neck and onto his bare chest.

Catrell gestured toward the men. "Bishop, do you know any of them?"

Bishop looked carefully at each one for some sign of familiarity. "Uh-uh. No." He answered.

"The skinny one calls himself Acid." Catrell pointed the gun at him. "He is the leader of the Dexter Avenue Zulu Nation."

It was just as Bishop had thought. Catrell was going after everyone who had declared war on him. Already, Lonnie was dead, so the head of the police action against him had been removed. Now he was cutting the heart out of the forces attacking him on the street. Greg Gatson would be next and maybe even the mayor. They'd underestimated him and they'd all made a deadly mistake.

Acid and his boys sat quietly. There was no defiance in them. They did not appear afraid. It definitely was not fear. It was more like resignation. They gambled and lost and waited to find out the price for attacking Catrell and the Egyptian Cobras.

Bishop studied the men and studied Catrell who seemed lost inside his thoughts. Catrell had walked away from the three men and was pacing the floor on the other side of the room as if he were trying to solve a puzzle. Suddenly, he stopped, walked back over to them and kneeled down in front of Acid. "Tell us why you killed Detective Carlton."

Bishop was surprised by the question and that Catrell seemed to ask it to reassure him that he wasn't responsible. Acid looked him in the eyes then looked away saying, "I ain't telling you a mutha fuckin' thang."

Catrell did not continue the interrogation. Whatever he needed to know he already knew. He stood up still brandishing the .357 Magnum revolver with the three-inch barrel and walked back and forth in front of the men on the floor. Bishop and the men from the Zulu Nation all watched him, bracing themselves, anticipating the first shot. Acid dropped his head and stared at the floor. The young one sweated profusely and his eyes were big as he strained against the rope that had his hands and feet bound. The older one assumed a more defiant posture, sitting straight up, looking at Catrell directly as if daring him to go ahead and pull the trigger. He was obviously going to kill them. They all wondered what he was waiting for.

After a lengthy pause, Catrell stopped pacing in front of them. He examined each of the men individually, hesitated, then said, "One of you can live if you kill the other two."

A death warrant had been issued and it squeezed into every corner of the space until there was no place to escape the power that had just been unleashed against the three men. No one said anything. The musty, dirty smell was overcome with the stench of fear. The proposal was so horrific that the men were speechless and soundless.

Bishop had been standing off to the side, watching the whole thing. He could see the look of pure terror on the faces of the members of the Zulu Nation and the look of victory on Catrell's face. The offer was so cruel it even shocked Bishop, although he was compelled to admire the genius of a move designed to emphasize Catrell's absolute control over all of them and all the violence and all the gangs and all the streets of the city.

A long minute of silence passed before Acid finally raised his head toward Catrell. He strained against the ropes holding him and against the fear gripping him and said, "Fuck you, nigga. Zulu Nation rules!"

Catrell chuckled and dismissed Acid's bravado with a wicked smile. He pulled a knife from his pocket and cut the young one loose. Catrell held the gun out toward him and said, "Here. If you kill them, I let you live."

The kid stood up on shaky legs. His breathing was heavy. Tears and sweat streamed down his face like the blood that had been trickling down his neck. Acid and the older one were now visibly afraid. Their eyes were wide and they had pushed themselves backward, cowering against the wall. The panic came partially from the looming violence. It was also fear of betrayal. Fear that the loyalty that their organization was built on could be broken so easily. Fear that they had lived in a world of lies and crime and murder and now the truth was staring them in the face. There was no refuge from retribution.

Catrell handed the young brother the Magnum and commanded him. "Do it quickly. In the head."

He stepped back and watched the young man tremble with fear for his life and shake with shame that he would violate the code that he had lived by. Bishop's hand rested nervously on the handle of the Baretta while he watched the young man wrestle with the possibility of turning the gun on Catrell to free his brothers. The young brother was trapped. He knew he would be killed by the Cobras at the bottom of the stairs. There was no way out. There was no way for him to live except to kill the men who were supposed to be his family.

Catrell was relaxed, his eyes focused on the young brother but he

182

seemed unconcerned about the potential for the young man to turn on him. He knew that he had broken his spirit. He also knew that he had destroyed his will to resist and that the only thing that mattered to that young member of the Dexter Avenue Zulu Nation, at that moment, was to walk out of there alive.

The brother took a deep breath, stepped quickly to Acid, placed the gun next to his head and fired a shot that exploded like thunder sending blood and brains crashing against the wall behind him.

The older cat recoiled, slamming his body back against the wall. He screamed, "FUCK!!! MUTHAFUKA YOU DEAD!!! YOU DEAD NIGGA!!!" He scrambled along the wall, trying to crawl away like a rat caught in a trap, injured but not yet, dead. After realizing the impossibility of escape, he started pleading for his life. "PLEASE!!! DON'T DO THIS!! DON'T..."

The young boy grabbed him. His young face was contorted with madness and coated with Acid's blood. He fired a shot directly into the older man's mouth, snapping his head back, flinging pieces of skull across the room in a spray of blood. Then as if released by some demon, the young man collapsed on the floor, vomiting, sobbing and mumbling, "God, please forgive me...please, God, sweet Jesus...forgive me...forgive me."

Unperturbed, Catrell walked over to him, picked the gun up off the floor, turned the light off and headed toward the stairs. Bishop stood there for a moment in that filthy room and listened to the young distorted voice of a distorted life and watched a lost and defeated soul wailing against the emptiness.

Nothing was said between them as the car cruised down the street back toward Juanita's. This time Catrell had one of his men driving. He sat in the passenger seat with Bishop in the back. Bishop wasn't sure why he had wanted him to see that act of revenge. Maybe Catrell wanted him to understand that his power, his terrible power, was not just an urban folk legend. Perhaps he wanted Bishop to know that he didn't kill Lonnie. Whatever the reason, Catrell obviously wanted him to know that he was capable of and willing to wage war. The car pulled up in front of Juanita's house and Bishop started to get out when Catrell looked back over his shoulder. "It is almost over, Bishop."

Bishop pulled the handle, swung the door open and said, "I hope so."

CHAPTER TWENTY-SIX

The front door to Juanita's house was slightly opened. Catrell and his entourage had driven off and there were no signs that any of his men were around. Bishop pulled his pistol and slid in quietly. Inside the house nothing seemed disturbed and the only sound he heard was the water running in the kitchen. When he reached the kitchen, Juanita was standing at the sink washing some collard greens. Her back was to the doorway and she didn't know Bishop was standing there watching her.

He called to her softly so he didn't scare her, "Juanita." His voice was drowned out by the running water. He called out louder, "JUANITA!"

She turned around sharply and jumped back a little when she saw him. "Bishop! You scared me."

"I'm sorry but the front door was opened and it made me kind of nervous."

Juanita saw the gun in his hand, but didn't seem shocked and calmly watched him stick it back in his belt as he asked her, "Juanita, are you OK?"

She turned off the faucet and said, "Better. But there is something I've got to do. Remember?"

"Yeah. You want me to ride with you somewhere."

Juanita finished washing the greens and put them in a big pot that was sitting on the counter. She grabbed a leather jacket out of the closet, grabbed Bishop by the arm and they left out the front door, locking it behind them. Still shaken from the scene at the warehouse, Bishop tried to sound relaxed when he asked, "Where are we going?"

"Up to Southcity Lake." Juanita detected something wrong with him. "Are you OK?"

He took her by the hand and led her to the car saying, "I'm all right. Come on, let's go."

When they got in Bishop's car, Juanita fumbled through his tapes and put in D'Angelo as they headed south on the expressway. It would take about forty minutes to reach the lake. Juanita was pensive and Bishop tried to distract himself by listening to the young man croon while they drove toward the country.

Two cars pulled onto Juanita's street and rolled slowly toward her house, stopping a few doors away on either side. At each end of the street other cars parked near the corners at angles where they could see her house and also see anyone approaching her block. A van pulled in the alley directly behind her house and Billy King and three Egyptian Cobras got out. They went in the back door of Juanita's house and the Cobras immediately walked through checking to make sure it was secure. Afterwards they took up positions outside, leaving King alone.

Billy King saw the greens on the counter and decided to cook them for his mother. He seasoned them, put them on the stove over low heat and wandered into the living room. Looking through his mother's collection of jazz and soul music, he chose Earth Wind and Fire, Al Green and Funkadelic. It was the music that reminded him of his parents when he was a boy.

Stretching out on the sofa, King relaxed in the rhythm and remembered his parents dancing together in that room, to that music. He recalled days when his father seemed happy and his mother laughed because daddy's smile was like a familiar friend who hadn't been around in a while. Even though days like that were infrequent breaks from his father's madness and his mother's sadness, those snapshots remained strong, loving images from his childhood.

He thought of his sister Carolyn taking her first steps in that room and his father running to tell Juanita to come and watch. He wondered if his father would be proud of the man he had become, if he would appreciate his son's accomplishments. King wondered what he would think of Carolyn, all grown up, beautiful, educated and headed to medical school in a year. He wondered how his father would save him from the forces outside their house that wanted him dead.

While Juanita and Bishop drove toward Southcity Lake, someone walked up on Greg Gatson's porch and rang the bell. "Just a minute." Gatson shouted through the door to the visitor. He was on the phone with Packard, trying to calm his fears about the events taking place. "Look, you've always relied on me to work things out and I've always come through. It's going to be fine, we're almost there."

"Greg, this is getting out of control. We have to do something." The mayor responded on the other end.

Gatson walked back and forth in his living room. "I know. It's going to be fine, just trust me. It's almost over." He was tired of the conversation and wanted to get off the phone.

The mayor finally said, "All right, I'm going to let you handle it, but you keep me posted. Hear?"

"I'll call you in a couple of hours." Greg Gatson hung up the phone and thought about how pathetically weak and scared Mayor Floyd Packard was. Greg was pissed that he had to constantly reassure him that everything was going as planned with only a few minor problems.

Nine times the administration of Floyd Packard had been investigated by state and federal agencies. And nine times he had been cleared of any wrongdoing. They had survived each accusation of conflict of interest and every complaint of ethics violations. Each time Greg Gatson had secretly worked things out and the mayor's image and reputation had remained intact even though someone in his cabinet usually took the fall and a few even went to jail. His core constituency, the African American community, had always rallied around him whenever he was attacked. Gatson made sure they felt like he was being targeted because he was a black man in a leadership position and unless there was irrefutable prove that he was a crook, the white folks should just leave him alone.

After hanging up with the mayor, a frustrated Greg Gatson went to his front door and saw a familiar face standing there. "Detective Maddox, what are you doing here?"

The old detective looked down at his shoes then back up at Gatson and said, "There's a problem. I need you to come with me, you've got to see something."

The somberness of his tone told Greg that something serious had developed. He grabbed his jacket and his cellular phone and headed out the door behind the old cop. He didn't ask Maddox where they were going or why; he'd find out soon enough. Whatever the problem was, he'd deal with it when he had to. That's what he got paid for, dealing with the mayor's problems. In the meantime, he made some calls trying to stay on top of everything.

In about fifteen minutes they arrived at an old warehouse district near the railroad tracks. Most of the buildings were vacant. Most of the businesses had moved out to the suburbs. Maddox turned the car toward one of the loading docks where there were six or seven empty buildings. Several police cars were there, including the crime scene unit.

Gatson got out of the car with Detective Maddox and went with him up the stairs to the loading dock and into one of the warehouses. Uniformed cops and plainclothes detectives stood around. Some recognized him as an important friend to the mayor and nodded his way. Others looked at him with casual interest. Greg followed the old cop up a flight of stairs, down a hall and into a dirty room that looked as if it used to be an office. Crime scene experts combed the place. Greg surveyed the scene in the dirty room until his eyes settled on two bloody bodies tied up lying on the floor near the back wall.

"Someone made a call to 911 about an hour ago."

"Who are they?"

"We think one of them is Acid from Dexter Avenue; not sure about the other one. We'll get a positive i.d. later. But I thought you'd want to know."

Gatson did want to know. He just didn't need to see it. Acid's head had a small hole on the left side and another one on the right about the size of a fist. The other man's face was blown open and the back of his head no longer existed.

Greg's stomach started churning and the acidic taste of bile surged upwards into his mouth. He fought hard to suppress the urge to vomit and turned back toward the stairs saying to Maddox, "Take me home. I've seen enough."

Maddox walked casually behind him. "All right, but there is one more thing."

"What?" Greg said angrily as he made his way down the stairs and out into the fresh air where he began to feel some relief.

Maddox followed him outside and answered, "Since last night, thirteen key members of the Dexter Avenue Zulu Nation have been killed."

"What!" Greg spun around and faced the old man.

"Yeah. We've been picking up bodies all over the city. All of them tied up and killed like this. And we got a call telling us where to find each one."

"Take me home, Maddox. Now!"

The old veteran cop walked him to the car. Greg was shaking, his legs were weak and he felt like he would throw up any minute. Maddox wondered what was going on inside his head. He'd known Greg Gatson about five years and had never seen him like this. He'd never known him to be rattled by anything.

As they rode back toward the house, the cellular phone rang and Greg hesitated before answering it. He tried to gather himself, searching for that authoritative voice, trying to put on the face people were familiar with. The face of the man always in control of every situation.

"Greg Gatson here."

A voice on the other end said, "We need to meet."

Greg paused, not saying anything. He looked over at Maddox. The man on the other end of the phone had broken Greg's game face and cracked his confident voice.

"Who...who is this?" Greg asked.

Maddox cut his eyes toward Greg and saw the game face falling to the floor. He noticed the voice quivering and caught him slumping further down into the seat. Fear was pouring down on him like a waterfall.

The voice on the phone continued, "Motherfucker, you know who this is. In an hour, a car will pick you up in front of your house. And understand this, you can not run from me."

"I...I understand." Greg hung up the phone and buried his head in his hands. His mouth was dry. He was sick and sweating, watching his world spinning faster than he had intended.

Maddox dropped Gatson off at home and watched the fear follow him like a shadow into the house. Afterwards the old veteran drove down the street to the convenience store at the corner. He took his time, bought a box of cigars, some doughnuts and a scratch-off lottery ticket, then he used the pay phone.

"Tell Catrell I just dropped him off... Naww, he ain't going nowhere, he's scared as hell."

Greg Gatson was an African American success story. He grew up in a blue-collar family with four brothers and two sisters. His dad was a welder and his mother labored in a food processing plant. All of his sisters and brothers followed their parents into the factories except him. They were proud of him for being the first and only one in his family to ever go to college.

Unlike his brothers, Greg was not athletic, and in spite of a small wiry frame and average height, he worked hard at sports but was not very good. What he lacked in size and athletic ability, he made up for in competitiveness, drive and discipline. Greg went to Stanford on an academic scholarship where he made the Dean's list every year. After getting a master's degree, he was hired by a powerful Fortune Five Hundred company. His talent, ambition and hard work pushed him rapidly up the corporate ladder until he was the youngest vice-president in the history of the company. But something happened to him. After five years of countless cocktail parties, lunches at private clubs, company charity events and kissing the asses of the senior officers, he hated his job and the way corporate shit tasted on his tongue.

On his job and around his colleagues, he spoke their language and played their game the way he'd been prepared to. In private discussion with his friends and other black corporate executives, he voiced his disgust at the way he was invited to be the special negro, the acceptable black man, the different African American.

In spite of his talent, education, ambition and acquiescence, he found himself crashing into a wall that wrapped around him like a vice and stomped on his desire to become more than the brother in charge of community affairs, the liaison to the black political establishment. It angered him to realize that his only value to the company was that he fulfilled their affirmative action requirements and could be used to get important contracts from the city. Early in his career, he'd been told by some of the men and women who came before him that the price of success inside the corporations was very high and few black people ever broke through the wall. He was disappointed to realize he was trapped even though he had thought of himself as special and dreamed he'd be one of the few they spoke of.

Greg Gatson made a lot of money in his position as the negro vice-president. He'd also become well connected with the black folks who were running City Hall. After several attempts to get the company to move him into the mainstream of their operation and give him responsibilities commensurate with his title, he finally quit. If he was going to make them money by setting up deals with black politicians, then he'd make them pay for it on his terms.

He negotiated a lucrative consultant contract with his former employer and began lining up other potential corporate clients who needed a well-connected black man to represent their interests. It was perfect for him. He'd make use of the contacts, earn even more money and wouldn't have to deal with their shit every day.

He also made deals on the other side with the politicians. Many of the elected and appointed officials he knew would steer their corporate friends to him so he could lobby on their behalf, receive payments as a consultant and kick some of it back to them in campaign contributions, cash or gifts. After a couple of years he was rolling in money and growing in influence. He knew everybody's secrets and all of their scams. Behind the scenes he'd become one of the most powerful men in the city.

As Greg Gatson became stronger, he also became more ambitious and angry. There seemed to be no limits on how many deals he could make. Opportunities came his way every day. Payoffs, percentages, kickbacks, bribes, consultant fees, lobbying fees, gifts, perks. It all flowed his way. He became a master deal maker once he realized almost all of those people were corrupt. The politicians, the lobbyists, the corporations, their lawyers, the system itself, all were corrupt to him. He had decided to play the game on his terms and now he was getting paid. His motto was "Fuck them."

His lifestyle was what he used to imagine when he was a teenager. He cooked gourmet meals in his million-dollar home and dined in all the best restaurants in the city. His corporate clients provided him with first class trips to Europe and the Caribbean. Politicians gave him box seats at all the sporting events and concerts. Professional athletes and entertainers hung out with him, impressed that a young black man would have as much money as they did, but didn't dribble a ball, sing, dance or work for the white man. He dated and slept with beautiful women. Young, budding entrepreneurs sought his advice. Operating in the shadows, Greg Gatson had become one of the most powerful men in the city.

It wasn't enough. His success was limited by the fact that he was a black man. He wanted bigger deals and more power. He wanted to sit down at the table with the white businessmen who ruled the city. He wanted to be treated as an equal amongst them, and not looked at as just the black man who could help them. Even though he was worth three or four million dollars, he wanted fifty, a hundred, two hundred million.

Greg Gatson developed and implemented a plan to achieve his American dream. A plan that would have worked perfectly, if Lonnie Carlton hadn't fucked it up.

CHAPTER TWENTY-SEVEN

Catrell Merit had been up for thirty-six hours and could feel the strain as he stared in the mirror. Stepping into the shower, the heat and pressure of the water relaxed and refreshed him. He was ready for some rest, but it wasn't time to rest yet. All of his enemies had not been dealt with.

After showering, he stretched his long body across the bed in the hotel suite. For a few minutes he reflected on the action he had initiated, making sure there were no holes, no mistakes. Occasionally, his concentration was broken by images of the young men who had been dying all night. He had killed before, but never so many at one time, in one day.

He tried to justify it in his mind by claiming he'd only done what was necessary. You could not have his kind of power and be afraid to defend it. In the life he'd chosen, his men expected him to lead them into battle and win. They'd always followed him and never doubted his ability because they'd learned to trust his strength. Unfortunately, he had to periodically exercise his bloody power to affirm his right to lead.

In the past, other gangs had attacked the Cobras and he defeated all of them. This was something different. The Zulu Nation was acting on behalf of other people and for purposes beyond just control of the drug traffic in the streets. Whatever the reason, Catrell knew that he had to deal with it in a way that would bring an end to the attacks on him, the Egyptian Cobras and his friend Billy King.

He laid there recalling events and reviewing his plan in the luxury of the finest hotel in the city. The bed felt good and invited him to close his eyes and escape from everything. It made him wish he could stop moving around night after night and was back at home in his own bed, surrounded by his own familiar things. It had been over a week since he'd been there, but the fatigue made it feel much longer. He rested there for twenty minutes but refused to let sleep take over. Catrell struggled out of the bed and took some fresh clothes out of a garment bag. There was still business to do. There was still one more thing to take care of.

He put on a dark blue Armani suit and light blue silk shirt, re-packed his bag and stepped out into the hall where two of his men had been waiting for him. As they walked through the lobby of the hotel, one of them discreetly handed the concierge an envelope full of cash. Two cars waited at the door. Catrell ordered them to head for George Washington Homes.

Greg Gatson sat in his living room for forty-five minutes, trying to decide a course of action. As soon as he walked in the door the damned phone was ringing and he heard the mayor's voice pleading through the answering machine. "Greg...Greg...this is the mayor. Greg, I need to talk to you...If you're there, please pick up the phone."

He'd called back twice since then, each time sounding more desperate, more scared, more pathetic. Greg couldn't talk to him right then. What was he going to say? Surely, the mayor had been informed that a blood bath went on last night and at least thirteen members of the Dexter Avenue Zulu Nation had been executed, including their leader, Acid. How could he reassure him that everything was under control? It wasn't. The shit was completely out of control.

Greg had gambled that the combined pressure of a police assault and the attack from the Zulu Nation would be enough to defeat the Egyptian Cobras. It was a key part of his plan, but it had failed. He had underestimated how powerful and ruthless Catrell Merit was. No, he couldn't talk to the mayor then. His life was at stake. He had to deal directly with Catrell. It was the only way to save himself and salvage what was left of his plan.

Still disturbed from the scene at the warehouse and the call from Catrell, Greg struggled to regain control of himself. In a few minutes, members of the Egyptian Cobras would be there to get him. He wondered why Catrell wanted to meet with him. Why didn't he just have him killed? He obviously executed all those members of the Zulu Nation to demonstrate how easily he could take someone's life. Catrell had to want something. Being a deal maker, Greg knew he had to figure it out before time ran out.

He looked out at the street, saw an unfamiliar dark blue Range Rover with tinted windows parked in front of his house and wondered how many more of Catrell's men were around. It would be stupid to try to run. He was certain Egyptian Cobras were everywhere. No, he had to go with them, meet Catrell face to face and, hopefully, cut the most important deal of his life.

The loud knock on the door caused Billy King to jump up from the sofa in his mother's living room. He'd fallen asleep listening to Earth Wind and Fire and was dreaming that he was standing on a stage, wearing a cap and gown, graduating from law school and his mother was in the front row giving him a standing ovation. She was the only person in the audience, but it didn't matter; she was all he needed.

Trying to clear his mind, he stumbled to the front door and without thinking about his safety, snatched it open without first looking. Standing on his porch, flanked by two of the Egyptian Cobras who had been posted outside the house, was a well-dressed middle-aged man.

One of the Cobras spoke. "He says he's looking for Mr. Bishop."

King squinted and tried to focus as he looked at the vaguely familiar face trying to remember where he'd met him.

The man leaned closer to King and said, "I'm Vincent Daniel, from the *Crusader.*"

"Oh yeah. Mr. Daniel, we met before. I was with Bishop."

"You're King, right?"

"Yeah."

"Do you know where Bishop is? He was supposed to meet me earlier."

"No. Nobody was home when I got here."

"Well, do me a favor." Vincent handed King a large envelope. "Give this to him and tell him to call me."

Still trying to wake up, King said, "I'll write him a note."

His escorts walked Vincent to the sidewalk then returned to their posts. As Vincent drove away he looked back at the house being protected by gang members and thought, "What has happened to us?"

Inside the house, King took the envelope into the kitchen, put it on the table and checked on the greens that had been cooking slowly while he slept.

Southcity Lake was about forty minutes south of town. It was a beautiful country place that had become a favorite spot of the black middle class. Still relatively undeveloped, in the last few years it had sprouted quaint little cabins that were used as weekend getaway spots for doctors, lawyers, business owners, a few entertainers and athletes.

Juanita directed Bishop onto a dirt road that wound along the edge of the lake. The lake was supposed to be a good spot for fishing and it reminded

Bishop of going out into the country with his father and grandfather, climbing into a boat and pushing out into the middle of a lake to spend the day catching Bass.

As they wound their way around the lake, Juanita and Bishop saw very few people there that day. It was the middle of the week and most of the folks who owned those cabins didn't start coming up until Thursday or Friday. It was nice, beautiful, peaceful, a refreshing break from the pace and noise of the city. Bishop spotted only one boat on the lake with an elderly black man sitting with his pole in the water. He was a retiree who got to enjoy the stillness of the lake when no one else was there.

As they rounded the water to the other side, Juanita pointed to an isolated cottage on a slight hill looking down on the lake hidden behind several trees. They pulled up in front and Juanita sat there staring at it for a minute. From where they were parked you could look across the water at the road they'd just driven but still stay hidden from view. It was the perfect spot. You could see someone approaching from across the lake and had at least three to four minutes before they'd arrive. Even then, if they didn't know you were there, they might drive right past the cottage. Lonnie had picked that spot for its strategic setting.

Bishop looked over the cabin and the view and asked, "Juanita, what are we doing here?"

"Lonnie owned this place," she replied. "We used to come up here sometimes."

"Why'd you bring me here?"

"I have to get something," she said, then got out of the car and walked toward the cottage. Bishop followed her, curious about what could be so important and concerned that whatever it was held more trouble. The cottage was a simply decorated but warm space that made you want to sit down, relax and let all the pain of the city float out the window.

There were only three rooms: a large kitchen with a wooden table and four chairs; a living room area with a huge fireplace, a big comfortable-looking sofa and two chairs; and a bedroom that had a beautiful wooden bed and a dresser that looked as if it were hand made. Juanita had furnished the place. It had her touch. There were shelves full of books along one wall of the living room and old photographs of black life from the early part of the twentieth century decorated the other walls in wooden frames. There was also an antique desk with a big leather chair in the corner. A fax machine, computer, printer and a cellular phone sitting in a battery charger rested on top of the desk.

While Bishop walked around surveying the place, Juanita stood just inside the doorway. She was still, almost as if something had frozen her there and she couldn't move another step or say another word. He watched her, trying to decide whether to say something or not. She felt him trying to reach her and reached for him.

"Bishop, I have to tell you something." With his hand in hers, Juanita walked to the sofa in front of the fireplace. She seemed so serious that it made him afraid to hear what she wanted to tell him. But he had to hear it, whatever it was. Bishop chose to sit in one of the chairs so that they faced each other.

Juanita began, "Lonnie used to bring me up here sometimes to spend the weekend. It was his secret hideaway. He'd always come and leave in the middle of the night so nobody would see us. This place isn't even listed in his name."

Bishop asked, "None of the other folks up here recognized him?"

"He rarely went out," she said. "And I never saw anyone talking with him while we were up here."

"It's not unusual for someone in his position to want to be alone."

"It's more than that. He brought all his secrets up here."

Bishop slid to the edge of the chair so that he was closer to Juanita. "What are you talking about?"

Juanita took a long look and a long minute before answering. It was almost as if she was trying to decide if Bishop needed to know what she was telling, even though she knew that she had to share it. She continued, "Lonnie hid important information in this cabin."

"What kind of information?"

"Files on politicians and businessmen involved in corruption and murder and all kinds of illegal activity."

"Did he tell you that?" Bishop shifted in his chair.

"Sometimes he'd tell me bits and pieces. He never showed me the files, but whenever we came up here, he'd spend hours on that computer, transferring information he had written down in notebooks. Now that he's dead I feel I should get his files before someone else does."

They were sitting in the tomb of Lonnie's power. All the secrets he'd seen, all the stories he'd heard, were recorded right there, always available to him. It was what he had done all those years he stood by as the trusted silent sentinel of the powerful. He never divulged their deals. He just made notes and kept them for future reference. Bishop wanted to see those files.

Juanita watched him walk over to the desk, turn on the computer and wait for the screen to give up some answers. It wouldn't be that easy. He needed a code to get in.

"Juanita, do you know the password?"

"Carolyn."

He typed in Carolyn while thinking about how much Lonnie had loved Juanita and her children. The computer responded. He pulled up the files and opened the first one, "Abbey, Walter." There was nothing incriminating, or even that interesting. It was just personal data. Date of birth, address, occupation (lawyer) and a list of corporate clients.

The second file was the same "Ackworth, Melvin." Nothing special, just personal data again. Bishop typed in his own name and his address, phone number and occupation were listed. That was all. Going through several other files, it was the same over and over again. It was just a directory. He wanted the information.

Bishop looked over at Juanita and said, "There's nothing here."

"There must be," she replied.

"Did he keep anything on disk?"

"I think he put some of it on disk. I'm not sure."

Bishop started looking through the house. He searched the bookshelves. There was nothing. In the cupboards, the dresser in the bedroom, under the bed, the medicine cabinet, under the cushions in the couch, nothing. Rummaging through the closets, the pockets of Lonnie's clothes and trash cans yielded no clues, no disks.

Juanita watched him tear up the cottage. He got frustrated and came close to being out of control as he repeatedly asked himself, "Where would Lonnie hide that kind of information?" There was something there. He could feel it. It had to be there and he had to find it.

Retrieving a knife from the kitchen, Bishop cut open the backs of the chairs, the couch and the mattress. Juanita watched him become more obsessed and frenzied in his attempt. He took all the pictures off the walls to find nothing behind them. Finally exhausted, he slumped to the floor with his back against the wall next to the fireplace and it was then that his mind had a rational thought.

Lonnie was a cop, an experienced detective. He'd seen and participated in hundreds of searches and wouldn't keep something that important in the usual places. The cabin had to be just a diversion. He had to think, look for the clues.

"Juanita, what did you and Lonnie do when you'd leave here?"

"He'd usually drive me home."

For the first time since beginning his mad scramble to find the files, Bishop took a long look at Juanita. She had moved off the sofa and was sitting on the floor next to the fireplace with her legs crossed, staring at him almost as if watching a stranger. It made him laugh.

Juanita gave him a curious look and asked, "What are you laughing at?"

"Me. I can't imagine what was going through your head watching me tear up this place."

"I'm trying to figure out what set you off. You seemed possessed."

"Juanita, if Lonnie kept files on all these people, something in one of them will help us. I'm sure of it."

He got up off the floor, shut the computer down, unplugged it and carried it to the front door.

"Come on, let's go."

She stepped around the mess he'd made, opened the door and helped load the computer into the car. She took a last look at the cottage. It was the last time she would ever come there. Memories provoked tears and she shut her eyes for a moment to both remember and to hold back the flood.

Bishop was focused on trying to solve the puzzle as they rounded the lake again and pulled onto the road leading out of Southcity. He was frustrated, bewildered and agitated. They drove about half a mile before they came to the only gas station and convenience store in the area. Bishop pulled in to get gas and some juice. Juanita sat in the car while he pumped the gas and then went in to pay. There was an old black man behind the counter who said hello as he came through the door. The interior was set up like one of those old general stores and the whole thing reminded him of the two-pump gas stations in rural Alabama his grandfather took him to when he was a little boy. He grabbed some juice from the cooler, paid for the gas and turned to leave when the old man spoke again.

"It's a shame what happened to Brother Carlton."

"Excuse me?" Bishop was thrown off by his comment because the tone seemed so familiar.

"It's a real shame, that a decent young man like that would be murdered in his house." The old man talked while wiping the counter with a towel.

"Yeah, it is," Bishop said. "Did you know him?"

The old man threw the towel somewhere under the counter and said, "Since he was a little boy. His family and mine own all the land that is now Southcity Lake. His grandfather and me used to fish together down there."

Bishop thought, "Lonnie and his secrets." The information helped Bishop understand why Lonnie always looked like money. It was a relief to know it wasn't from taking bribes. Bishop wanted to know more and asked, "How'd you figure I knew Lonnie?"

The man smiled and explained, "I saw Miss Juanita in the car when you pulled in. She holding up OK?"

Bishop realized that the old man was trying to feel him out, trying to determine where he fit in all of this. He responded, "She seems to be holding up all right. Do you know her well?"

"Met her once or twice when they stopped here at the store, but Lonnie talked about her a lot."

"Forgive me for forgetting my manners." Bishop walked back to the counter. "I'm Isaiah Bishop."

"They call me Papa Hines," he said smiling. "And this is my store."

"Well Papa Hines, why don't you come out to the car and say hey to Juanita."

"Actually, son, I'd appreciate it if you'd ask her to come in for a second. I'd like to talk with her."

Bishop walked out of the store and toward the car somewhat dazed. Juanita watched him coming toward her and thought about how she would reconcile her past to a future with Bishop.

"Juanita, there's an old man in the store..." Bishop said as he approached the car.

"Papa Hines?" She jumped out of the car and started toward the store.

"Yeah. He wants to talk to you for a minute."

Bishop debated whether he should go back in with her and decided against it. He assumed the old man wanted to extend his condolences to her. Bishop leaned against the car, inhaled heavily to smell the fresh country air and waited. It would be dark soon and he wanted to get back to the city. Through the window he watched Juanita talking to Papa Hines. She came back to the car and her eyes were damp when she turned toward Bishop and seemed to speak not just to him but to anyone in the world who would listen, "Lonnie was loved by a lot of people."

◈

Greg Gatson made one final phone call that he hoped would give him something to negotiate with when he met Catrell. As he left the house the men in the Range Rover did not move. Through the tinted windows, they watched him come toward them and flashed their headlights to signal another car a few doors down. Greg opened the back door and climbed in next to a young man about twenty years old. In the front were two other young men.

For reasons he could not explain, Greg was not afraid. He didn't speak to the men in the vehicle and they said nothing to him. The driver pulled off slowly. Through the darkened windows Greg saw cars with two or three occupants pull away from the curb. He noticed well-dressed young men strolling casually down the street. They were all unfamiliar faces in his upscale neighborhood, and even though they blended right in, he knew they were Cobras. He was right not to try to run.

Watching those men move with purpose, discipline and organization, Greg understood that Catrell's Egyptian Cobras were much more sophisticated than the Dexter Avenue Zulu Nation. That was where he had made the mistake. He knew that the Cobras were the largest and most powerful of the black gangs, but he'd looked at them as just a street gang selling drugs. He didn't understand that Catrell's reach extended into politics and the legitimate business world, much like the Italian, Irish, Jewish or Asian underworld. He thought, "Shit, I should have aligned myself with the Cobras."

Greg Gatson's association with the Dexter Avenue Zulu Nation had begun ten years earlier when he was still a corporate executive doing community service work. He was a board member of the Neighborhood Youth Association and a participant in their mentoring program. During his first year with the program, he became the mentor of a skinny thirteen-year-old named Johnny Wells.

Johnny was extremely bright, especially with numbers. In fact, one of the few classes he attended in school was math and he always excelled. Like a lot of the kids in the program, Johnny was on the edge of a life of trouble. He lived with his aunt in the John F. Kennedy Homes projects on Dexter Avenue. His father was doing life in the state prison for killing his mother.

199

In thirteen years his senses had been filled with the smell of rat shit and dead bodies, fast food and television, alcohol and Philly Blunts, gunfire and gang wars, crackheads, candy diets and rotting teeth. In thirteen years of life, his body had lived in a world of pain and his head had been seduced by the world of pleasure shown so beautifully on television.

Greg Gatson and Johnny Wells became friends. It was difficult at first to win Johnny's trust. Greg was an outsider, from a different world. He wore nice clothes, worked around white people in business suits and had been to college. When Johnny went to Greg's condo for the first time he thought he'd fallen asleep and awakened inside the world he saw on TV. When he went to work with him, he couldn't believe that Greg was a vice-president and had a white assistant.

They went to ball games and to the museums. Greg introduced the young man to jazz, taught him how to do research in a library and how to use a computer. Johnny started attending school more frequently and for several months stayed out of trouble. For the first time in his life, there was a man who paid positive attention to him. He liked hanging out with Greg and visiting that other world, the world he saw on television.

Five and a half months into the program, the two of them seemed to be forging a friendship and Greg was proud of the progress that his young protégé was making. Seeing the impact his involvement had on a young person's life was one of the rewards of that type of program.

In the sixth month, Greg Gatson was told by the program director that Johnny had killed another boy in a dispute about a pair of sneakers. Greg was shocked to hear that Johnny Wells, the young man he mentored, the boy who loved math, had pulled a gun out and took the life of an eleven-year-old who wouldn't give him his shoes. It disturbed Greg to realize that the museum, his plush condo, his vice-president's office, the library and all the other things in his world, meant less than some sneakers Johnny saw on TV and knew he couldn't afford, but had to have.

Johnny went to Juvenile Hall for five years until he was eighteen. During his first year of incarceration he corresponded with Greg. While he was locked up he became a member of the Zulu Nation and the correspondence stopped. They had completely lost touch until a few years ago when Greg Gatson needed help.

About three years ago, Mayor Packard was approached by a developer who wanted to build condos on some prime land owned by mostly elderly, poor black people. As usual, he sent him to Greg who told the developer that they would arrange for the people to sell their land inexpensively and guarantee the zoning, but that he'd have to pay a large sum of money to a black company as a joint venture partner, a company that Greg would designate.

The developer understood how business was done in the city and resented having to do it with niggers. There were millions of dollars at stake and he wanted to make the deal, but not at the price they set. He thought, "Just who the hell do these niggers think they are asking for a half million dollars?" He had a series of meetings with Greg Gatson and sometimes with the mayor where they haggled over price and terms. Finally, the developer consented, convinced that without paying them, the project would never happen.

They got together for one final meeting to work out the details of the deal. Instead of discussing the terms of the venture, the developer played a tape of a previous meeting where Greg threatened to kill the project if he and the mayor weren't paid. Greg didn't blink or lose his composure. He remained calm and continued the conversation as though nothing unusual had happened. This was just a negotiating ploy. The developer was just playing hard ball.

Greg asked, "What are you going to do with that tape?"

"Nothing, if we can work out a deal I can live with," the developer replied.

"What do you want?"

The developer was sure he'd made his point and continued, "Look, we can do business, but I'm not about to pay you a five hundred thousand dollar kickback."

"What are you proposing?" Greg asked solemnly.

"I'll pay fifty thousand dollars if you convince those people to sell me their land." The developer stated confidently. "And another fifty if my project is approved by city council."

Greg stood up indicating that the meeting had come to an end. He smiled at the developer and said, "Let me talk to the mayor about it and I'll get back with you."

"You do that, Greg. This can work for everybody. We do this deal and down the road I'll throw you something else."

It was that last statement that reminded Greg that in their eyes, he was nothing more than a bag man, a political pimp procuring prostituting black politicians for white businessmen. As his anger rose, Greg thought, "Fuck him and his project. This is a black city and a message needs to be sent to all of those motherfuckers. We run shit now!"

Through contacts he'd cultivated in the police department, Greg had periodically gotten reports on Johnny Wells. He'd had no contact with him since he was released from Juvenile Hall, but he knew that in the years since he'd gotten out, Johnny had become the leader of the Dexter Avenue Zulu Nation and was now known as Acid.

The Zulu Nation was a younger and smaller gang than the Egyptian Cobras. They had staked out a small section of the city around the John F. Kennedy projects. The Zulu Nation had aligned themselves with the Asian gangs that were beginning to move heroin into the city. The Cobras had long been associated with the Colombians and for years had dominated the cocaine and crack market. As of yet, there had been no open conflict between the two gangs, although the police kept an eye on the situation given Catrell's history of brutally suppressing his competition.

Greg needed help and also saw an opportunity. He set up a meeting with Johnny "Acid" Wells, his old protégé. When they met, the men embraced as old friends. Greg couldn't believe that this tall, six-foot-three, slim but muscular man, was the little skinny kid whom he used to mentor. Acid still admired Greg and told him how he'd followed his career and liked the way he was moving behind the scenes. After spending time revisiting fond memories, Greg got down to business.

"Johnny, this is not exactly what I'd hoped you'd be doing by the time you reached twenty one."

"Yeah, back then I thought it was gonna be different for me, too."

"It could be worse. You could be standing on the corner slinging crack and running from the police. Instead you're running the show."

"I gotta run shit. I can't be working under some fool."

"Look, I need your help, and I've got a proposition for you."

"Let's talk..."

That discussion, between Greg Gatson and Johnny "Acid" Wells, started an association that greatly expanded Greg's power. He enlisted Acid and his Dexter Avenue Zulu Nation as his enforcers, his collectors, his underground army who would attack, terrorize, hurt or kill at Greg's command.

The first victim of this alliance had his right knee shattered with a baseball bat. He was a real estate developer who wanted to build condos on some prime land owned by elderly, poor black people. After recovering, he walked with a limp, but eventually got the land and built his condos. Greg Gatson got five hundred thousand dollars and became a joint venture partner in the project.

Using the Zulu Nation as enforcer was just part of the deal. Greg knew that with the rise of heroin in the city, the Zulu Nation could potentially make millions of dollars. They were young and unsophisticated, so through various lawyers and businessmen that he knew, Greg set up a money laundering system for them and for doing so was paid a percentage. Through his contacts in the police department he bought protection and information for them. He had the best of both worlds. He made his deals with politicians and businessmen and he enforced his will and made money through the Zulu Nation. He was building an empire.

As children they suffered
as men they sin
and now they
see
no reconciliation
no solution
no redemption
offered
to them

CHAPTER TWENTY-EIGHT

When they headed back into the city, it was dark. The quiet starlit two-lane road gave way to congested highways, urban noise and streetlights. Bishop felt a strange tension traveling with them. It was not between them. It was wrapped all around them. He wondered if Juanita felt it, too. He didn't wonder long.

"Bishop," she said in a low deliberate voice. "This is the last night of this madness."

Her statement spoke his thoughts and confirmed his feeling that whatever was going to happen would take place that night. There was no proof of that. It was just a feeling. Bishop took her hand in his and held onto it the rest of the way home.

When they pulled into Juanita's driveway, King was sitting on the porch. Two Cobras sat with him and Bishop was certain more were stationed around. King waved to his mother and the sight of him sitting there as if he were making a casual visit on a normal day upset Bishop. He wondered what he was doing there when Catrell had told him that King was in a safe place. King and his mother embraced before the three of them went inside. She looked relieved to see her son there, still safe. Juanita and King moved directly to the kitchen where she checked on her greens and directed him to start seasoning the chicken she had thawing in the refrigerator. On the box, King was playing Me'Shell NdegeOcello. For a moment the danger around them felt far away. For a moment, things felt normal and Juanita and her son were smiling.

Bishop tried to hide his discomfort at King's visit and annoyance that Catrell would have him there and went into the living room, removed the pistol from his belt and took a seat on the couch to let the music soothe him. On the end table next to the lamp he noticed a photograph of Carolyn and his daughter, Sheila, together at spring break in Atlanta. He examined the picture of the two girls sitting on the hood of a car and was glad that they were both far away from the evil their families were facing.

Bishop shouted toward the kitchen, "Juanita, how's Carolyn doing?"

Juanita came into the living room and saw Bishop looking at the photograph.

"I hope she's all right," she replied. "I told her about Lonnie this morning and she didn't say much. She just asked me to call her with information about his funeral." Juanita took the picture out of his hand and studied it. "Did you know Carolyn and Sheila are driving home for Thanksgiving?"

Bishop chuckled, "No, I didn't. But, then again, I'm just the father, usually the last to know."

Juanita sat the photo back on the table and said, "Well, Carolyn just told me a few days ago. It'll be good to see them."

"Yes, it will."

Juanita put on an Aretha Franklin song and went back into the kitchen and Bishop rested his head against the back of the couch and thought about Lonnie and how he had known Carolyn since she was a little girl. He had been like a father to her. The thought of Lonnie's death saddened Bishop as he lay back into the music and the aroma from the food filled up the house and his head filled up with thoughts about the possibility of a future with Juanita.

After a few minutes, King interrupted his daydreams when he handed him the envelope that Vincent had left. Bishop had completely forgotten their meeting. Inside the envelope was a handwritten note from Vincent attached to a memo on stationary that said, Office of the Mayor, Floyd Packard.

"Bishop, this might have something to do with your problem. Let me know what you think." Vincent.

The memo read:

Based on extensive study, it is the recommendation of this office that the public housing development known as George Washington Homes be con demned and its remaining residents be relocated so that the buildings can be destroyed and the land used for purposes that would better serve the economic development plans of the city. I will introduce legislation to this effect at the weekly meeting of City Council on Nov. 2.

The memo had been circulated to five of the nine city council members. Bishop recognized the five names as the key allies of the mayor who always voted as a block for him. With their five votes he controlled the outcome of all the council deliberations.

As he looked at the five names Bishop recalled how every one of them had been involved in some kind of scandal. It was a pretty widely held view that they were basically a corrupt group. A couple of them had been accused but never convicted of embezzling money from the city. One of them, who was married, got caught in his office with his mistress bent over the desk. Another one was charged with bribing a group of black ministers to guarantee the votes of their senior citizens. They were an embarrassment to the black community, but somehow continued to get reelected. They were a reminder that the black community needed to grow up politically and stop excusing their bullshit.

King called into the living room from the kitchen, "Bishop, dinner's ready."

"Thanks. I'll be right there. I just need to make a call."

Bishop phoned Vincent and left a message for him to meet him at Juanita's. He washed up and got pulled into the kitchen by the smell of collard greens, baked chicken and rice. Juanita took a plate to the extras on the porch, then she sat down with King and Bishop and they ate like a family. The food was delicious and it reminded Bishop that he hadn't eaten all day. King seemed more relaxed. Juanita tried to appear calm, but there was worry on her face. Bishop's fear and history kept pushing toward the surface, struggling against his will to suppress them. Without voicing it, they all anticipated the reckoning that loomed in the air.

They supplemented the meal with conversation about King's return to law school, Carolyn and Sheila's visit in November, new movies they wanted to see, new music they wanted to buy and the coming winter. Their words didn't really protect them from their thoughts, but they provided a distraction for the moment, allowing them to enjoy the food and the company. After dinner, Bishop was about to ask King to play a game of chess when the doorbell rang. They all hesitated, conditioned by the uncertainty and tension that had invaded and dominated their lives the last few days. Finally, Bishop went to the door and found yet another surprise. Standing on the porch was the old man, Papa Hines with a shoe box under his arm.

Bishop swung the door open. "Papa Hines, what are you doing here?" He waved off the Cobras who were standing nearby watching the old man.

Papa Hines said, "I brought something for Juanita."

Bishop led him back to the kitchen where Juanita jumped up and hugged the old man and pointed to King. "Papa Hines, this is my son, Billy."

Papa Hines took a long look at King and said, "You have a fine looking son, Juanita." Then to King he said, "Brother Carlton was very fond of you young man. He told me you were going to law school."

King replied, "Yes, sir. I hope to be in by next September."

"Won't you stay for dinner?" Juanita asked.

"Juanita, thanks for asking but I've got to get back out to the lake. I just wanted to bring you this." He handed her the shoe box saying, "Lonnie told me to make sure you got it if something happened to him."

Juanita took the box, handling it gently, eyeing it curiously, wondering what was in it, and trying not to let the memories of Lonnie that were rushing to the front of her consciousness make her cry. She looked at the box tied neatly with a shoe lace and said to Papa Hines, "Well, I hope you come back and have dinner with us some other time."

Papa Hines patted her gently on the shoulder and said, "I'd like that. I'd like that a lot."

Bishop walked him back to the door and asked him again if he wanted to take some food with him. He just shook his head no, smiled and said, "Take good care of her, Mr. Bishop." And then he was gone. Like a spirit or an unknown person in a dream, he'd walked in and floated out. Bishop went back to the kitchen with the same dazed feeling he'd had at the gas station.

Bishop sat down at the table and watched Juanita open the box. The first thing she pulled out was a handwritten letter to her from Lonnie that she glanced at quickly then folded it and laid it in her lap. Then she reached in again and pulled out eleven stacks of computer disks. Each stack was held together by rubber bands and contained five or six disks.

Bishop gave a puzzled look to Juanita and asked, "Did you know he had this stuff for you?"

"Not this," she answered. "When we were at the gas station he said Lonnie had left something for me. I thought it was just some personal things."

"Why didn't he just give this to you when we were there?"

"He told me he had to go get it because it was locked up somewhere." Juanita lifted up a group of disks and said, "From what it looks like, Lonnie probably told him to hide it."

Bishop reached into the box and picked up a batch of disks and said to King, "Would you mind going out to my car to get the computer on the back seat?"

King hopped up from the table and headed out the front door. Juanita picked up the letter and Bishop left the room to give her time to read it privately. He felt bad for her and for them. He loved her and wanted her, but their future together was being born out of so much tragedy.

He heard King coming back through the door and went to help him. When they got to the kitchen, Juanita was wiping her eyes gently and went into the bathroom while they set everything up. She returned a few minutes later.

"You all right?" Bishop asked, putting his arm around her shoulders.

"I'll be fine," Juanita said. "Let's see what's on the disks."

With Lonnie's computer on the kitchen table, Bishop sat down in front of the keyboard and Juanita and King pulled up chairs alongside him so that all three could see what came up on the monitor. Anxiously, they began reviewing the contents of the disks. As they unlocked the secrets of the most powerful and prominent citizens of the city in those files, it was as if they were being initiated into some covert voyeuristic club.

The first disk contained notes about a police captain's theft of money and drugs from the property room in the First Precinct. There were forty-one files on it. The second disk had ten files, all of them about liaisons a prominent minister had had with several prostitutes. It had names, dates, places, times and costs. Several other disks contained similar information on local and state politicians, business leaders, labor leaders, preachers and state commissioners of various departments.

There were disks with records of kickbacks and bribes, gang slayings, mob hits, spousal abuse by important civic leaders and illegal business deals by respected executives. One disk contained twenty-eight files, all with information about Mayor Packard's "gifts" from various developers and the favorable City Council votes that followed those gifts.

It was a sordid record of what Lonnie saw in his twenty years as a cop. It was a disturbing comment on the city and the people who were trusted to govern and lead it. It was the shit in the sewer underneath the clean streets and freshly paved sidewalks.

For more than an hour they raced through the disks, glancing quickly at the sickening list of files on each one until finally, Bishop put in a disk that had only one file. It was titled Juanita King and when her name came up on the computer screen, she raised her hand as the commands rolled off her tongue. "Bishop stop! Billy leave the room. NOW!"

The harshness of her tone startled both of them. King obeyed his mother and Bishop awaited her instruction.

"Bishop, destroy it." Juanita commanded.

"Don't you want to see what's on it?" He asked.

Angrily she answered, "No!" And repeated her command. "Just destroy it!"

Without questioning her further or opening it, he typed in the command to delete the entire file. In a few seconds it was erased and he popped it out and broke the disk. Juanita sat in the chair next to him, sullen and silent. Billy was outside on the porch. Bishop stared at the now blank computer screen. Minutes passed without any sign from Juanita on whether they should proceed to review the rest of the disks. There were about seven left. She sat there with her head in her hands and her locks hanging down like a curtain over her face. Finally, Bishop decided to leave her alone for a while. He walked out to the porch where King sat on the steps talking to the two Cobras.

Bishop sat outside and waited for Juanita and waited for some answers and waited for the fire to stop raining down on them. And while he waited on Juanita's porch, Catrell Merit waited inside a vacant apartment in George Washington Homes.

Underneath the window where he stood, it was quiet in the projects for the first night in a long time. There was no gunfire. There were no screams or sirens. The police, who had been laying siege to the stronghold of the Egyptian Cobras, had pulled out early that morning. There was no declaration from Mayor Packard, no announcement that the war against the Cobras had been successful in running them out of George Washington Homes. The residents were not surprised. They'd seen it before. They were used to the public pronouncements of politicians and big displays of symbolic political actions that yielded little actual results in changing the conditions of their lives.

Egyptian Cobras were everywhere, hundreds of them. They were openly armed, posted along the walks, in the parking lots, in the alleys and vacant apartments. It was a defiant display of Catrell's power. It was not a celebration. It was a gesture to his urban army, a show of strength acknowledging their temporary victory over the police. He had locked down the entire community called George Washington Homes. The residents remained in their apartments unsure of what to expect, but grateful that for the first time in a long time, it was quiet, at least for one night.

From the second-floor window of that desolate place called George Washington Homes, Catrell surveyed his kingdom. It was his home. He didn't live there anymore, but it was still home. It was there that he started life surrounded by men without jobs who drank their dreams in the mornings. It was there that he watched those men spend the day chasing money to get high so the smell of their own flesh rotting on street corners would not offend them or remind them that they had surrendered and accepted those corners as their only place in society.

It was there, in George Washington Homes, that he suffered as a child, watching his mother and other women struggle to raise children without the participation or help of those men. He recalled the welfare checks and social workers, truant officers, cops, paramedics and funeral directors who came often to those buildings.

It was in George Washington Homes that he had sex with a girl for the first time when he was thirteen. Her name was Savannah. She was fifteen and they did it down in the basement of his building on an old mattress. He wanted her to be his girlfriend and two days later she was killed when a stray bullet came through her bedroom window and crashed into her skull.

It was there, in George Washington Homes, that he learned to play sports in spite of a lack of facilities and learned to fight because of a lack of peace. His mother took him and his brother out of those buildings as often as she could to expose them to another life, but it was still home. It was still the beginning for him.

The thoughts of his beginning, of his life there as a child, made Catrell uneasy. He hadn't visited those memories in a long time and had gone so far away from that boy playing four square in the alley behind one of those buildings. It had been a long time since he and his friends taunted police officers and provoked pursuit up into the projects so they could throw garbage down from the windows and rooftops.

It was a long time ago when his mother came home and said she'd been robbed by three drug addicts who lived a couple of buildings over and Catrell took a pipe and beat one of the men into a coma and that incident became the beginning of his reputation and his life of violent reprisals against anyone who attacked him or those he loved.

He stood there looking out on all the young men who followed him, thinking of his life as the ruler of that shit, a life selling poison to destroy the dreams of his neighbors and their children. He was the king of all the killing and all the chaos that permeated every corner of that community. He surveyed his success and knew he was damned for the destruction he'd caused. As a child he suffered, as a man he sinned and saw no solution that could bring salvation to him.

The dark blue Range Rover pulled up into the parking lot and Catrell watched as his men got out and escorted Greg Gatson into the middle of George Washington Homes. He was relieved that they had arrived because he was becoming distracted by his memories and his fear that one day he would pay for all the evil he had done. It was time to do business and he began to focus on what needed to be done.

Only a couple of minutes passed before the door to the apartment opened and Greg Gatson walked into the room. With his back to the door, Catrell continued looking through the window at the men gathered outside in the yard in the darkness. He turned slowly to Greg who had been standing quietly waiting for Catrell to acknowledge him. There was no one else in the room. The Cobras who escorted him there had closed the door leaving the two of them alone.

Catrell studied him for a minute before he spoke. "Greg, do you know why I had you brought here?"

"To make a deal," Greg answered cockily.

"No," Catrell said emphatically. "To give you a chance to save your life."

Trying to maintain an air of confidence, Greg said, "Catrell, what I'm going to offer you is worth my life and more."

Catrell liked Greg's attitude. He understood immediately how Greg could have the nerve to attack him. They scrutinized each other, standing there motionless, almost hypnotized as each recognized himself in the other. They were both intelligent, powerful, young, black men. They had both made choices that took them outside the law. They had both commanded the respect and fear of other men. They were both offended by the way black people were treated in society and yet they both chose to betray their own people. They were the best of what their people had to offer and the worst of what their people had become.

A knock on the door of the apartment broke the trance and one of the Cobras entered the room, went to Catrell and whispered in his ear. "Maddox just called and said that the mayor ordered the police to arrest King at his mother's house. They're on the way there now."

Pointing to Greg, Catrell said, "Stay here with him." Then left the apartment.

Greg watched out the window as Catrell called a group of his men together and gave them instructions. Greg Gatson leaned against the window sill and considered the possible outcome of the explosive situation he'd created. He became nauseous again, his pretended confidence was disappearing rapidly. There was an unexpected anticipation that when he returned Catrell would no longer be interested in making a deal, but would simply kill him. Greg Gatson prayed that the mayor had gotten his message and acted fast enough to give him something to bargain with. Greg needed to capture King.

For half an hour Bishop had been sitting on the porch with King and the two Cobras guarding him. It was a clear, beautiful, fall night that they should have been enjoying instead of worrying about who would be killed. The Cobras had said little since Bishop had come outside. He thought that they seemed strangely peaceful. It was odd because either or all of those young men could be dead by the next morning or any morning. Studying them, watching the defiance that swirled around them, seeing their youthful curiosity explore the world as it unfolded to them, they were like most of the other young people he taught.

Juanita was still in the house. It was dark outside and it was also dark inside except for a soft light falling from the living room into the hallway. Bishop wondered whether she was ready to talk and he was curious about what Lonnie knew that would cause her to react so forcefully when she saw her name in his files. As he searched for reasons, Juanita's voice beckoned him back into the house. Nina Simone was casting her spells when he sat down on the sofa.

Juanita walked over to the stereo and turned Nina down. She wanted Bishop to hear her clearly. With her head slightly lowered and her locks falling forward, making it difficult to see her features from the side, she said, "Bishop, fifteen years ago something happened that brought Lonnie into my life."

She paused and looked down again as if overcome by the memories. Watching her suffer made Bishop think of useless things to say that wouldn't ease her hurt but might make him feel less awkward. He decided not to say anything and instead just waited until she was ready to continue.

She still had her head down when Juanita finally said, "Fifteen years ago, a man attacked me." She paused, pulled her hair away from her face and looked up at Bishop.

Her words had caused a sickening, disturbing sensation in him. He felt as if his breath had been sucked away. His heart pounded and Bishop braced himself for the rest of her story and asked, "What happened?"

"I went out once with this brother and he decided I belonged to him. For weeks he called incessantly, sat out in front of my house, came up to my job, followed me, you know the story." Juanita begin playing with one of her locks, twisting and pulling it while she continued, "It was very scary, but I thought he would realize eventually that I wasn't going to have anything to do with him. But, he wouldn't stop, he kept it up for weeks. My son was only eleven or twelve and one day before I got home from work Billy saw the brother outside the house and confronted him with a hammer, demanding that he leave me alone. That seemed to enrage him even more and made him more persistent."

Every muscle in Bishop's body was tense and when he realized his hands were balled up into tight fists, he released them and tried to control his anger when he asked, "Why didn't you go to the police?"

"I did," Juanita answered. "At that time there were no anti-stalking laws. They told me they couldn't do anything unless he actually attacked me. After about two months it just stopped. I figured he'd finally gotten the message. Life for the children and me started getting back to normal. Then one night he caught me getting out of the car in the garage and raped me."

He had anticipated something awful, but the words, "raped me," pierced his being like he'd been stabbed in the gut with a bayonet. Juanita's head was turned slightly in Bishop's direction and it allowed him to see her eyes when she looked up from time to time. Most of the time she stared down toward a group of brass figures from West Africa that stood across the room. She was waiting for him to say something, to react. Bishop gritted his teeth, his nostrils flared, his blood boiled. He hurt for her, was bleeding for her and also wanted to kill for her. Bishop hoped she could not see the murderous face that he fought to hide. He battled to control himself and asked, "Did you report it to the police?"

"No," she said and sighed heavily.

Her answer astounded him. Bishop's question had been rhetorical. He had expected her, an educated, worldly woman to do the correct thing by going immediately to the police. He didn't know what to say. If he asked her why she didn't report it that might imply that she was wrong. Bishop didn't know what to say but it didn't matter, because Juanita said, "I didn't have to report it to the police. I went to his house and shot him."

Bishop knew it was unnecessary to ask her if she had killed her attacker. The answer was obvious and it filled him with a sadness he had never known. He wished that Juanita had never known what it was like to kill. She was a healer with a deep love of life and to have to kill another human being, no matter how foul and fucked up they were, must have been a terrible wound to her spirit. As Bishop pondered the cost of her killing, it drew her closer to him and calmed his rage before he asked, "How did you meet Lonnie?"

Juanita sat up and said, "He investigated the killing and because I'd tried to file that complaint, he came to talk to me."

"Did he suspect you?"

"I'm sure he knew it was me, but he closed the case after a couple of weeks. I never said anything about it and neither did he. He started coming around once or twice a week to check on me. It turned into once a day, which turned into fifteen years. For some reason, I trusted him. I knew he loved me and wouldn't betray me. He never used it to his advantage. Never asked me for anything. He just wanted to be with me and the children. It was very comforting, but I could never love Lonnie the way he wanted me to love him."

Bishop said, "You didn't have to tell me all of this."

"Yes, I did."

"Are you OK now?"

"I'm fine. It's just that when my name was on one of those files, I was afraid it contained information about that case. And I guess with everything that has happened..."

"I know." Bishop walked over and knelt down in front of her. Juanita looked up at him and he swept the locks back away from her face then wrapped her in his arms and held her for a few minutes, trying to convince them both that there was no trouble in the world, only them. They never got comfortable. The sound of tires screeching to a halt outside caused Bishop to bolt up off the couch and run to the front door with Juanita right behind him.

By the time they reached the porch, the young Cobras had risen up off their seats with their 9mm pistols drawn and aimed at the driver of the car who had jumped out and was coming toward the house. He too was a Cobra and they relaxed once they saw that he was one of their own, but were clearly agitated because his hurried arrival meant he had brought news that couldn't be good.

One of them met the driver on the sidewalk. The other one stayed close

215

to King. The two on the walk conversed for a moment, then both came to the porch. "King, we've got to leave. The police are on the way to arrest you."

Bishop stepped up to the young man while keeping his eyes on the street. "Where are you taking him?"

They were already headed toward the car when one of them shouted over his shoulder, "Catrell said bring him to George Washington Homes."

King didn't hesitate. He hugged his mother quickly then ran out to the car with the three Cobras. They sped off down the street.

Bishop stood on the sidewalk looking down the street into the empty space where the car had just been a moment ago. A distraught Juanita went back in the house. Less than a minute after King and the Cobras sped off to the shelter of Catrell's kingdom, Bishop turned to go back to the house when police cars zoomed in from every direction. Tires squealed on the asphalt, doors slammed, dozens of cops jumped out with weapons drawn. One of them started spitting curses at Bishop, "STOP RIGHT THERE, MUTHAFU-KA!!! DON'T MOVE!! PUT YOUR HANDS ON TOP OF YOUR HEAD AND TURN AROUND!!!"

Bishop raised his hands slowly, turned to face the house so that his back was to the cops who were approaching him with guns drawn. The commotion brought Juanita out onto the porch. A cop yelled commands at her. "MISS, STAY ON THE PORCH AND KEEP YOUR HANDS WHERE WE CAN SEE THEM!" Two cops pointed shotguns at her.

Juanita saw Bishop with his hands on top of his head as they ordered him to his knees and then to lie on his face on the sidewalk. Watching them search him, she protested his treatment but received no sympathy. They cuffed his hands behind his back and pulled him up to his knees. Three officers kept their guns trained on Bishop. Juanita's neighbors began filling the street. Police screamed at them, "GO BACK IN YOUR HOMES...THERE'S NOTHING TO SEE OUT HERE!!" The people didn't move. Some brought out video cameras and began taping but were pushed back from Juanita's and blocked by several officers.

Five or six cops ran into Juanita's house, obviously hoping to catch King. Others were in the back, searching the garage and alley. By then, several officers had Juanita surrounded on the porch and you could hear the sound of things being thrown about and broken inside her house. Still on his knees, legs crossed at the ankles, hands cuffed behind his back, Bishop tried to remain calm, but he was worried. The cops seemed particularly agitated and hostile. Anything could have pushed the situation over the edge and someone could get killed. Someone like Bishop.

"I KNEW I'D SEE YOU AGAIN MUTHAFUCKA!"

Bishop looked up at the loud voice moving toward him and saw it was the Superfly-looking cop who'd had him by the throat the other night at King's apartment. He was one of those sadistic ass, self-hating psychos who joined the police force or the army or became a security guard so he could have some authority to fuck with people. The military was full of them and Bishop had seen a couple of officers like that get taken out by "friendly" fire when they fucked with the wrong person over in Nam. But they weren't in Nam, they were on the street in America and he was the prisoner of a psycho cop.

Knowing that that sick bastard was about to interrogate him and there was no telling what was about to happen, Bishop glanced up at the porch to see Juanita. He knew it might be the last chance to look at her. Standing there surrounded by uncertainty, in the middle of confusion and confrontation, she was beautiful, angry and afraid. There was no outward display of what was going on inside her. But when she looked back at him, Bishop saw the eyes of a million African American women watching a million incidents of their men handcuffed and held hostage by certain humiliation and potential homicide. From behind her eyes came flying a million tears never shed and a million things never said and a million prayers for black men who are dead.

Only a few seconds passed while he looked at Juanita, but his response to the tirade of that cop screaming obscenities must not have been fast enough. The cop stepped directly in front of him, blocking his view of Juanita.

"MUTHAFUCKA, WHAT THE FUCK ARE YOU LOOKING AT? WHERE IS THAT LITTLE NIGGA WE BEEN CHASIN'? ANSWER ME MUTHAFUKA! I'M SICK OF THIS SHIT AND WILL FUCK YOUR ASS UP!"

Bishop stared straight ahead. His posture was not submissive, but not defiant either. Still on his knees, he sat back on his ankles waiting for the cop to decide what to do with him.

Suddenly, a shadow, an object, something came flying over Bishop's right shoulder. His peripheral vision picked it up, causing him to swing around to the left, attempting to duck, but it was too late to avoid the blow from the baton that crashed into his face, knocking him to the ground. His eyes watered and blurred. His brain felt like it was sloshing around in mud. He heard cops laughing, and one saying, "DAMN! You hit that motherfucker like you was Albert Belle."

Juanita's voice cut through the laughter, "STOP!!! PLEASE DON'T HIT HIM AGAIN!!!" She was joined by her neighbors screaming for them to stop. "THAT'S RIGHT!!!STOP THAT SHIT!!!WE WATCHING YOU!!!SOMEBODY GET THEIR BADGE NUMBERS!!!"

Then there was more laughing and cursing, "FUCK HIM UP!!! GET THAT BLACK BASTARD!!!" Bishop felt feet stomping him and more blows to his back, shoulders and head. He curled up, trying to pull his knees up into his chest to protect his vital organs when the revelry of the cops was interrupted by that familiar urban sound. TAT-TAT-TAT-TAT-TAT!!!! It was the sound of automatic gunfire. The police who were stomping and beating him ran for cover, drew their guns and waited.

They had only been on him maybe ten seconds. He was still laid out on the ground, in pain, but not seriously injured. He tasted blood and dirt and heard the neighbors say what a shame it was for the police to act that way. Through his swollen right eye he searched for Juanita and heard the police on their radios calling for backup and he hoped that whoever fired at them was a good shot.

The shooting had stopped as quickly as it started, but no one had moved in the few minutes since it stopped. The police looked around cautiously, discussing what they should do. The consensus seemed to be to take him back to the station because it had become too dangerous out there deep in Cobra territory. Bishop wanted to stay there surrounded by witnesses.

There was a sudden strange silence in the street, no gunshots, no screaming neighbors, no commands from the police. Everyone seemed to be waiting. Bishop continued lying on the ground, anticipating whatever was going to happen next. The police were extremely nervous and didn't seem to know whether they should come out from behind their cars to get him or not. The wait continued for several minutes.

Juanita called his name. Through his blurred vision, he saw her walking toward him. A cop commanded her to halt, but none moved to stop her. She reached him, knelt down and sat him upright. She caressed his head and whispered his name. She kissed his face. Her hands were the hands of a healer. Her voice was the sound of history, pulling him, through the pain. He rested his injured life in her lap and the feel of her full lips against his forehead was like the kiss of God.

⬧

George Washington Homes looked almost peaceful when Catrell met King in the hallway of the apartment building where he had Greg Gatson.

"You OK, King?" Catrell asked.

"Yeah," King replied. "It worked out just like you said."

"I knew if you showed up at your Mom's, sooner or later they'd come after you."

"How'd you know?"

Gesturing with his hands, Catrell explained, "There are two factions in the police department. A whole lot of them were loyal to Lonnie Carlton. But there is another group. I thought they might be Gatson's so I figured that since we took him, they'd come after you. I needed to know if he was the one they were taking orders from."

"I got out just in time. Thanks." King said, and extended his hand with his fist balled up.

Catrell tapped King's fist with his own and said, "Yeah. They got Bishop though."

"What do you mean they got him?"

"Right after you booked, the cops showed up. They got mad that they'd missed you and took it out on him. Nothing serious. But they beat up on him."

King frowned and asked, "He all right?"

"Yeah. I sent someone to get him." Catrell pointed toward the stairs leading to the second floor and said, "He'll meet up with us in a little while. Come on."

While King and Catrell climbed the stairs, Greg Gatson sat on the bare vinyl floor with his back against the wall and waited, a prisoner of his own ambition. He looked around the empty apartment and thought, "This is where I've arrived. After all my education, corporate success and political influence, my life is going to be decided in this shit hole full of addicts, alcoholics, welfare recipients, minimum wage earners, young single mothers, unemployed men and undereducated youth. Ain't that a bitch?"

The door opened and he jumped to his feet. Catrell and King walked in. "You know Billy King?" Catrell asked as he pulled out a pack of cigarettes and pointed in King's direction.

Trying to remain calm, Greg answered, "Yeah, I've seen him around City Hall."

Catrell put a cigarette in his mouth, lit it and pulled on it deeply. "Well, Greg, as you can see, your attempt to have him arrested didn't work." He blew the smoke out of his nose then took another hit.

Gatson had his own group of cops inside the police force. He'd recruited them personally over the last two years because they had despised Lonnie Carlton for interfering with their corruption. Those cops were a key part of Greg's plan. They were going to be the troops that he would use in conjunction with the forces of the Dexter Avenue Zulu Nation.

Greg stared at King and realized that the mayor had gotten his message and had sent those cops to arrest King as he'd requested. But they were late and didn't capture him and that meant he had nothing to negotiate with. He didn't respond to Catrell's statement. He just studied King, watched Catrell and wondered about the bond between them. It was different from the relationship he had had with Acid. They seemed somehow connected, like brothers, like friends, like destiny.

Last year one of my students wrote in an essay that she'd only slept in a bed once. It happened when she was seven years old and went to visit her grandmother for two weeks down in the Mississippi delta. At the time she wrote about it, she was a fourteen-year-old freshman. When I read her paper, it was hard to believe that in her entire fourteen years of living, she'd only slept in a bed for two weeks. I asked her why and she told me they'd always slept on the floor in their apartment in the projects to keep from getting shot.

I was bothered by her statement and disturbed that she thought it was normal to live with the constant possibility that she could be shot. It's funny because I can remember being in the war and watching children running, try ing to escape bombs and gunfire and napalm and thinking how grateful I was that we didn't have to deal with that shit back home.

CHAPTER TWENTY-NINE

Vincent Daniel arrived at Juanita's about ten minutes after the police arrived. He saw Bishop lying handcuffed on the ground cradled in the arms of a woman. Anticipating the worst, his tongue soured with that strange sickly taste that comes from expecting tragedy. As he walked toward the edge of the neighbors gathered around, his first thought was that his life long friend, his best friend, had been killed. When he recognized Juanita and saw Bishop moving, he sighed with relief and became furious when the neighbors told him what happened.

Vincent was prevented from getting closer by the police who had formed a line to keep back the growing gathering of neighbors and curious onlookers. He had to walk around the edge of Juanita's yard to get close enough to find out what was going on. The press started arriving. A television crew, a photographer and reporter from the daily paper pulled up. Vincent pulled out his own press pass. The police wouldn't let any of them near Bishop and Juanita.

Off to the side, a young uniformed cop who looked like Ron O'Neal in *Superfly* and an older detective were in a heated discussion. Vincent watched them and recognized the older one as Detective Maddox. Maddox had often given Vincent information about cases of particular interest to the African American community. He respected him as one of the cops who had really tried to make a difference in the community.

Vincent watched and waited for the conversation to end so he could talk to the Detective. The uniformed cop was especially animated and angry. He waved his hands around and pointed his finger in Maddox's face. Maddox seemed to be trying his best to restrain the younger man and explain something to him. Finally, as if completely exasperated, the younger cop walked away from Maddox, dismissing the discussion with, "Fuck it!"

Vincent moved swiftly toward the police line where the conversation had just ended. Before he could reach Maddox, the old detective spotted him and slyly shook his head no, as if to say, "Stay back." Vincent stopped and waited to see what would happen. Maddox walked over to Juanita and Bishop, knelt down and spoke quietly, but confidently. "Juanita, I'm the only one who can get him out of here, but I've got to take him now."

With her arms still around Bishop, Juanita replied, "Maddox, I can't. They'll kill him if he goes to the station."

"Listen to me." Maddox put his hands on her shoulders, forcing her to look directly at him. "Lonnie was like my brother and I won't betray him. You have my word that I won't take Bishop to the station."

"Where are you taking him?" Juanita asked.

"To Catrell."

"Then I'm going, too."

"Juanita, no. You can't go with me. Let me take him out of here. I'll deal with these cops later." Maddox dipped his head toward Vincent standing behind the police line. "Do you know Vincent Daniel?"

Juanita looked over at Vincent and nodded her head. "Yes."

"He'll stay with you but you've got to let me leave with Bishop now before they change their minds."

Bishop listened to the conversation, trying to measure the sincerity of Detective Maddox. There wasn't much choice. If he stayed there, Juanita would resist any more police attacks upon him and might be injured or killed herself. If he went to the police station, anything could happen. If Maddox drove him, the situation would at least be one on one and Bishop felt as if he could probably take him if it came to that.

Bishop said, "Juanita, I'll be fine. Let me go with Maddox. If Vincent is here, he'll help you. Tell him everything."

Juanita slowly released her hold on Bishop and Maddox pulled him to his feet and led him past the other cops and over to his car. Once Maddox drove away, the remaining cops began dispersing the crowd. Vincent joined Juanita on her porch and together they watched the cops pull off in their squad cars. Vincent studied the hatred in the eyes of the young black people who were watching the confrontation. He noticed the look in Juanita's eyes and it reminded him of the eyes of millions of African American women and millions of tears unshed and millions of things unsaid and millions of prayers for black men who are dead.

Detective Maddox sped away from Juanita's house with Bishop in the back seat, in pain and still handcuffed. Maddox looked in his rear view mirror, checking first to see if any other cops were behind him and then to see if Bishop was all right. Maddox guessed he looked as all right as someone could who just got his ass whipped. "Were you scared?" Maddox asked.

The question had a signifying tone to it that pissed Bishop off. He looked out the window and didn't answer. Maddox adjusted his rear view mirror so he could see Bishop's whole face. "I've seen some hard men break down with fear from one beating. In a way it helps us do our jobs. Makes people respect us."

He glanced in the mirror to see Bishop's reaction and was alarmed when he found none. Bishop's face was blank like a mask. There was no expression, no fear, no pain, no anger, no hostility. It was just blank and it scared Maddox. He drove in silence, occasionally checking the mirror to look at Bishop. The expression didn't change and Maddox decided to keep him cuffed until he turned him over.

After driving a few blocks away from Juanita's, Maddox turned a couple of corners and headed in the opposite direction, away from George Washington Homes. He drove several more blocks, turned into an alley, cut his lights off and parked. Bishop was jittery sitting in the back of a police car in a dark alley. A gang of cops had just tried to beat the shit out of him. His face was killing him and his jaw felt like it might be broken. His hands were still cuffed and there was no way to tell what the old cop was waiting for.

The wait wasn't very long. After only a few minutes, a young boy about eleven years old came to the car. He looked in the back seat at Bishop then leaned into the driver's window, whispered something to Maddox, then darted back into the darkness and out of view. Bishop was sure he was a young Cobra and almost certain they were sitting in what had been Zulu territory a few days ago. Hopefully, it didn't matter. After the assassination of Acid, Catrell controlled almost all the streets. The thought that he was still in Cobra territory calmed Bishop but caused him to laugh at how ridiculous that was. "You know, this is some strange shit," he said to Maddox, who looked in his mirror and watched Bishop laughing.

"It actually makes me feel safer that the Cobra's are around here. I must be out of my mind. On a regular day, these young brothers are poisoning their own communities and forcing their neighbors to live in fear. But today, I'm glad they were there to save me from being murdered by the police. Tomorrow, one of those same young brothers might murder me. What kind of shit is that?"

Maddox didn't answer. He got out of the car, came around the back, opened the door and told him to get out. Maddox turned Bishop around so his back was to him. He unlocked the cuffs, put his hand on the handle of his pistol and took a couple of steps back uncertain of what Bishop might do. When Bishop turned to face him, Maddox pointed to his left and said, "Walk to the end of the alley and someone will pick you up."

Bishop took one last look at the detective and asked, "Whose side are you on, old man?"

Maddox didn't respond. He kept his hand on his gun and his eyes followed Bishop as he walked into the darkness at the end of the alley. Bishop's face had swollen up. He grimaced from the pain. Each step reminded him of the beating he'd taken. When he got close to what appeared to be a dead end, three young men slid out from the shadows. Their sudden presence made him stop and brace for some new shock, some new assault.

The one in the center said, "Mr. Bishop, Catrell wants us to bring you to him."

Bishop was weary, aching and wanting the whole drama to end. He asked the Cobras, "Is King there?"

"Everybody is there." The other two chimed in, "Yeah...everybody."

Gracefully, silently, they spun around and walked away without further explanation. Bishop fell in behind them. Following the young Cobras into the shadows had become a familiar ritual in the last few days. Perhaps this time would lead to the answers he needed. He asked his escorts, "Everybody is there. Who is everybody?" They didn't answer and kept walking.

Juanita and Vincent went into the house and found some of her furniture turned over and her things thrown about. Other than King, the police weren't looking for anything in particular. Their action was meant to intimidate, to scare, to threaten. Juanita seemed unfazed by their behavior as she picked up the pieces of glass from a broken picture frame and moved things back into their places. Vincent helped her, trying to read her thoughts and feelings. She didn't talk for a while and he didn't ask her to. He helped her put things back in order until finally she spoke.

"I've spent twenty-eight years trying to keep my son from being killed." Moving around the living room restoring order, her voice was clear but low as if she was talking to herself.

"I made sure he was educated. And not just academic education. He knows a lot about the world and who he is in it. He's ambitious and wants to do something with his life, but every day I wonder whether or not the phone will ring and someone on the other end will say that he's been killed. I wonder who will murder him. The police? One of the gangs? Some criminal out robbing folks? Every day I hope the phone will ring and he will be on the other end of the line just calling to say hello."

Her words were depressing to Vincent and caused him to slump down in the chair in the corner of the living room. He thought, "Is this where we have arrived in the last few years of the twentieth century? Is this what our efforts were for, just to keep our children alive? Aren't we supposed to be further along than hoping our sons won't get lynched?"

Juanita sat down on the sofa across from him and said, "Bishop told me to tell you everything Vincent."

"What do you know?" He asked.

"We have a bunch of computer disks Lonnie was hiding. The ones we looked at had some pretty detailed information about the corruption in City Hall and the police department."

Vincent sat up in the chair and asked, "Where are they? The police didn't take them, did they?"

Juanita gave a sort of half smile and said, "No." She reached in the pocket of the jacket she wore and pulled out a group of disks. From another pocket came more and she laid them all on the table in the living room. "When the police pulled up, I grabbed them. But they knocked the computer off the table in the kitchen and I'm not sure it's still working."

They went into the kitchen and Vincent picked the monitor and computer up off the floor. The monitor screen was cracked and the cord to the computer was ripped out.

"Are these all the disks?" He asked.

"Yes."

"Let's take them down to my office."

Juanita grabbed a jacket and they headed over to *The Crusader* offices.

226

CHAPTER THIRTY

Bishop's body had started to stiffen from the beating. His face was swollen considerably on the right side and he wished he had some ice to put on it. The three Cobras with him were all his students. It didn't seem to matter to them that he recognized them. They were carrying out a mission. Bishop followed them through a building and out the other side where a Jeep waited. After driving a few blocks it was clear that wherever they were taking him, it was not George Washington Homes.

Two of the young Cobras were in the front and one sat in the back with Bishop. An Uzi rested on the seat between them. They studied the streets carefully as they drove cautiously out of that neighborhood. Catrell was winning, but they knew it wasn't quite over. There were still members of the Zulu Nation who hadn't submitted yet and who might try to take revenge on any Cobras they could catch. In addition, the police were pissed off that they were run out of Washington Homes and that the mayor had called off the assault on the Cobras. A lot of them were looking for an excuse to fire up some young Cobras. Even though the Cobras had protected Bishop in the past, right then he felt like his ass was completely exposed. His pistol was at Juanita's and the shotgun was in his car. He had been targeted by the police. It was a dangerous ride.

When Juanita entered the lobby of *The Crusader* it reminded her of her childhood and the times she went there with her father who wanted to show her how a newspaper was not only the voice of the community but also provided all kinds of jobs. Her father and Vincent's had been classmates together at Hampton Institute and would occasionally get together to discuss and debate politics, sports and almost every other subject. She didn't really know Vincent. He was a few years older and knew her sisters and brother. She thought it was good that he'd taken over the family business and was doing well with it.

Juanita watched Vincent talking to the night watchman, an elderly, kind of frail gentleman with a warm smile. She wondered how long he'd worked for the Daniel family. After a few minutes, Vincent gestured for her to follow him upstairs to his office. Once there, they began reviewing the new disks. Like the others, those disks also contained information that would prove extremely embarrassing to some prominent personalities in the city and could even lead to criminal indictments. Lonnie kept pretty detailed notes about the various transactions, deals, deviant behavior, murder and all-around corruption that he witnessed. Vincent was amazed. Juanita was not.

Out of all the disks they reviewed, one in particular made Juanita and Vincent especially curious. On it were only three files. In the first file, called "VotinRites," there was a list of about two hundred people who attended the mayor's birthday party a couple of months before. Next to their names were contributions they gave the mayor at the party. The amounts ranged from five hundred to ten thousand dollars. In all, the contributions totaled over one million dollars for that one night.

The second file was titled "NewDeal" and had a list of eighteen names. Vincent recognized them as the most important developers and construction contractors in the city. Next to each of their names, one hundred thousand dollars was listed. That came to another one million eight hundred thousand dollars.

The third file was named 11/2, and had thirty-three names. It included the eighteen in the second file, several key city council supporters of the mayor, a few from the first list, three of the most influential black businessmen in the city and Greg Gatson. At the bottom of the list was the number fifty million. Juanita and Vincent looked at the screen trying to decipher the three lists.

Juanita looked at Vincent and asked, "Does any of this mean anything to you?"

"The only thing that is familiar is the date 11/2," he replied. "The date the mayor is scheduled to make his announcement about tearing down George Washington Homes."

As Bishop rode with the Cobras he thought about Catrell, King and Greg Gatson, the three young men at the center of the conflict.

Although Catrell Merit had crushed his enemies, Bishop was sure he wasn't finished. The night still held secrets and questions that needed answers. Catrell had destroyed the Dexter Avenue Zulu Nation except for a few diehards. He had killed all of their key leaders and their best fighters. Those who were smart enough, came over to the Cobras when he began his assault on them. They realized the Cobras were stronger and Catrell was a smarter and better leader. The Asians, who were allies of the Zulu Nation and their main suppliers in the rising heroin trade, had already reached out to him. He would deal with them later. Catrell knew they needed him and his Cobras to expand into the city and the region.

The thing that bothered Bishop, was why Greg Gatson decided to come after Catrell. The more he thought about it, the more Bishop was sure Catrell had been aware of Greg for some time and had probably watched him from a distance as he cultivated relationships with various politicians and businesspersons. With his vast network, Catrell had to know about Greg's affiliation with Acid and the Dexter Avenue Zulu Nation. He would have studied his relationship with the mayor and how he moved behind the scenes to make various deals happen. If his pattern held true, Catrell knew that there would come a time when they would do some business together. They were a lot alike, young men on the outside of the law, manipulating things behind the scenes and getting rich and powerful doing it.

King had been unusually quiet through all of it. He'd been almost passive in his response to everything. It wasn't like him. He would usually throw himself into a fight if he or someone he loved came under attack. Maybe it was because he was being protected by the Cobras. Maybe he'd lost his will to fight and was sick of the violence. Maybe he just wanted to live another way. Bishop didn't know what King was thinking and it worried him.

Catrell had moved Greg and King and some of his men just outside the city to a small factory used for silk screening T-shirts. It was one of many businesses that Catrell owned. It was getting late in the evening, almost 10:00 p.m. He waited with his men, his friend and his prisoner for Bishop to arrive. He wanted Bishop's counsel before he made his final decision and his final moves.

They'd driven about thirty miles outside the city, maybe less, when Bishop had the Cobras stop at a convenience store so he could get some kind of pain medicine. After taking four extra-strength Tylenol, the pain in his face

229

subsided a little and his ability to pay attention to where they were going improved some. They drove a few more miles into one of those semi-rural areas inhabited by mostly poor whites and blacks who used to work on farms and now work in small factories that employ fifteen or twenty workers at just above minimum wage.

A sign read "Welcome to Stevensberg! Home of the 1985 State High School Football Champions." A few minutes after passing the sign, they turned onto what looked like the main street. They zoomed past the local McDonalds and Pizza Hut until they came upon a row of prefabricated buildings made of corrugated metal that housed the kind of small manufacturing operations that are now the lifeblood of those communities. After a couple of blocks, they turned down a dark street lined with several more of those same buildings.

They glided slowly until several vehicles came into view at a dead end. They brought the car to a halt in front of the last building on the right. Fifty or sixty heavily armed men stepped forward out of the shadows. It was the signature move of the Cobras, part of their tactical method. Even though it didn't surprise Bishop, it still impressed him. They were a well-trained and well-disciplined urban army. Not at all the media image of an inner-city street gang.

Two of the men came over and told him to follow them. They walked around to the side of the building, entered a small door, walked through a large room with several silk screen machines and into a back room that was stacked with T-shirt boxes and racks of used screens. In the corner of the room were Catrell, King, several Cobras and Greg Gatson, whom Bishop recognized from the photos in Vincent's file. Catrell, King and Greg sat on some boxes just outside a small office, while the Cobras stood around casually though obviously strategically placed. Catrell looked very intense as Bishop approached. King was smiling slightly and Gatson seemed very troubled.

King stood up when Bishop approached and said, "We were worried about you for a minute."

Pointing to his face, Bishop replied, "King, I was worried about me for a minute, too."

Catrell got up off a box and walked over until he was close enough to examine Bishop's face. "You all right? It looks like your jaw is broken."

"Yeah…it feels like it is. Hurts like hell." Bishop looked over at Gatson and asked, "What are we doing here?"

Catrell looked at Gatson and answered, "Bringing this shit to an end. Ain't that right, Greg?"

Greg Gatson had remained silent through the brief conversation. He was sitting on the edge of a box looking down at the floor, nervously tapping his left foot and turning the diamond ring on his right middle finger. He looked up when Catrell posed the question, but he didn't answer. Bishop noticed how small Greg was and it surprised him because he looked bigger in the photographs.

Catrell seemed at peace and it alarmed Bishop because it was the same deadly peace that he had shown when Acid and the others were murdered. It was the temporary peace of men in war who justify their acts as necessary to preserve their own lives or their own interests or their own fantasies. Catrell didn't seem to crave killing like some others. Murder was functional and he understood its power and how to use it in ways that created the psychological terror necessary to rule by violence. The peace Bishop saw in Catrell was a wicked peace, a deadly peace.

King looked removed from it all. Even though he acknowledged Bishop when he came in, it was as though he had drifted back into whatever his thoughts were before they were interrupted. Sitting back down on one of the boxes, King looked at nothing in particular, although he seemed to be taking in everything around him.

Bishop turned to Catrell and asked, "How do you see ending all of this?"

Glancing toward the door, Catrell answered, "I'm waiting for a little more information and two more guests. Then we'll work it all out."

"Who else are you expecting?" Bishop asked.

Catrell responded with silence and a smile as a young Cobra came toward him with a box. It was the kind used for storing files. Catrell took it inside the small office and sifted through it quickly before signaling Bishop to come inside.

Opening a folder and handing it to Bishop, Catrell said, "Look at this. These are Greg's records of all the accounts and businesses he set up for the Zulu Nation."

Bishop searched through some of them and saw document after document listing bank accounts, corporations, trust funds and small businesses set up to launder the money of the Zulu Nation. On every one of the records, Greg Gatson was a principal partner. Catrell sat down in a metal folding chair and thumbed through several folders. He seemed perplexed and probably had the same question Bishop had. What did all this have to do with the chaos of the last two weeks?

The fax machine beeped in the corner of the little office. Catrell watched the machine push out several sheets of paper that fell to the floor. He retrieved them and after reading the cover sheet, handed it to Bishop.

Reviewed LC files. Information very useful for upcoming election. Only file of interest regarding current crisis is enclosed.

At the top of the page, the fax machine had the name and number where the transmission originated. It troubled Bishop when he read it. Someone had faxed it from the offices of *The Crusader.* Bishop stared at the page wondering, "Is Vincent on Catrell's payroll, too?"

CHAPTER THIRTY-ONE

For two hours, Vincent and Juanita had printed out key files contained on Lonnie's disks. The elderly night watchman made copies for them and stacked them neatly in two boxes. As they finished up, the elderly gentleman helped load the boxes into Vincent's car and wished them well as they drove off. He locked the door to the newspaper's offices, went into the secretary's office where he had been making the copies, pulled out a neat stack of extra copies of Lonnie's files, typed a little note and faxed a couple of pages from Lonnie's files to a number at a silk screening shop in Stevensberg.

Back at Juanita's house, Vincent and Juanita sat in her living room going through several of the files while listening to Abbey Lincoln. Vincent made notes on some of the pages about the political ramifications of Lonnie's files. Juanita made notes in her mind about the people whose sins were laid out in front of her. Her generation believed in those people, had campaigned for them and defended them when they were attacked in the media. She contemplated past instructions to her children to be politically active, to register, vote, support candidates and empower their people.

Juanita remembered blood spilled for the right to vote. She heard her grandfather's voice painfully describing her grandmother's death in a rural Mississippi church that was bombed by the Ku Klux Klan because they were trying to register black folks to vote. She recalled the humming of thousands of voices walking dusty roads and the rhythm of all those thousands of feet marching to the polls. Remembering the elections of Ken Gibson in Newark, Carl Stokes in Cleveland, Richard Hatcher in Gary, Coleman Young in Detroit, Maynard Jackson in Atlanta, their own Sam Page and hundreds of mayors, council persons, state legislators, she saw the jubilation of election day victories in major cities, proclaiming the dawning of a new day of black power. She watched hope bursting forth, believing that things would now finally change for a people who had been disenfranchised for so long.

As she stared into her memory, Vincent's voice called her name from somewhere in the distance, somewhere in the present. "Juanita...Juanita...are you all right?"

Guided by his voice, Juanita slowly made her way back. She sensed something hot and wet on her face and realized her anger and pain had caused tears to spill onto her cheeks. Vincent listened intently to the words that flew from her mouth when Juanita said, "How could these people betray us? How could they shit on the faith of their own people who are just one generation removed from sitting in the back of a fucking bus? They are worse than the drug dealers poisoning us."

Vincent felt what she felt and added, "Juanita, like you, I despise these traitors. But we've also let some of this happen."

"I know." Juanita wiped the tears off her face with the palms of her hands and said, "I know we elected them and turned them loose and didn't remain active after we put them in office. I know we've expected them to be right. But I'm not going to excuse their shit. Everybody we've elected isn't corrupt. Everyone hasn't sold us out."

"You're right. We can't excuse them. We've got to get rid of them."

Detective Maddox pulled up outside Juanita's house and waited for his instructions. He lit his cigar and thought about how his friend Lonnie Carlton would give him expensive illegal Cuban cigars on occasion. Maddox settled down into his seat, turned the radio on the sports station and waited. Whatever was going to happen, he hoped it was not going to put him in the middle of a gunfight. He was ready to retire and didn't want to wind up dead after all those years.

When Maddox joined the force, it was printed up on the front page of the black newspaper, *The Crusader.* Just twenty-one years old, he was treated like a celebrity in the African American community. He was one of the first six to be hired in the early sixties. He wasn't allowed to arrest white people and his assignment was to walk a beat in the south side black community. Everyone knew him, the barbers and beauticians, the factory workers and janitors, the maids and chauffeurs, the doctors and dentists, the teachers and the tailors, the numbers runners and pimps, mothers and their children. Everyone in the community knew Officer Maddox and the original six.

Back then he broke up a lot of fights, took men to jail to let them sober up before sending them home in the morning, busted thieves regularly, rapists occasionally, and hardly ever dealt with murder. Over the years, he'd watched all of it change and it made him sad that so many of his people now died violently, murdered by the hand of their own.

Back in the early sixties, Maddox used to spend days walking his beat listening to community folk speak with pride about the Rev. Martin Luther King and the Freedom Riders. Sometimes he'd stumble upon a debate in some barber shop about that hell-raising Adam Clayton Powell, or the corner bar would be full of animated discussion about the clean cut young men in the Nation of Islam and their fiery spokesman Minister Malcolm X. The voices in some beauty salon would be raised over the hum of hair dryers talking about whether President Kennedy was really for black folk.

That was a long time ago. He should have already retired, but he liked being a cop. Sooner or later they'd force him to. That'll be all right with him because he'd have his pension and a real good stash saved up from some of his other activities, like doing favors for Catrell. He hadn't thought about what he'd do when he retired. He always thought he'd figure it out then, maybe move to some island in the Caribbean where he could relax and do some fishing.

The thought of just lying back, spending his days fishing, made Maddox chuckle. He hadn't taken a real vacation in a while, but after all the shit that had gone on the last two weeks he needed one. Before the thought could take root, his cellular phone rang.

"Hello...Yeah, I'm sitting outside her house now...He's in there with her...All right, it'll take about thirty minutes."

As Catrell and Bishop stood in that little office reading through the files on the Zulu Nation and the fax that had just come in, Bishop found himself pondering Catrell's accomplishments. He had built the Egyptian Cobras from a group of car-stealing teenagers who ran errands for drug dealers into a multimillion dollar organization with an estimated membership of two thousand, although no one knew for sure. He had informants everywhere in the city, owned all kinds of legitimate businesses and had successfully avoided the traps of the FBI, the DEA and the IRS.

Catrell had had alliances and battles with the Italian Mafia, the Jamaican Posse, and the Colombian Cartels. With his defeat of the Dexter Avenue Zulu Nation it would be expected that he would be involved with the Asian gangs moving heroin back into the city. No one had been able to stop him. He'd outsmarted or outfought them all.

The Egyptian Cobras had several levels. What most of the law enforcement agencies keyed in on was the street level. They mistakenly looked at the Cobras as a street gang. They didn't understand that those on the streets were just the soldiers. They were Catrell's private army, recruited from the projects and poor communities to distribute the drugs, protect the businesses and wage war when necessary. They were heavily armed and existed in every low-and middle-income black neighborhood in the city.

From the soldiers, Catrell drew the brightest and most disciplined members to run the various legitimate enterprises. From this group he chose a handful every year to become the lawyers, accountants and representatives of his influence in society and financed their education. He also recruited from the colleges, just like a corporation. Some of his "legitimate" members have corporate jobs. Others work in city government, the police force, the state legislature and various commissions. It was rumored that one of the black congressmen from the city was handpicked by Catrell. It would take years for the Zulu Nation to be anywhere close to the sophistication of the Egyptian Cobras. And then, only if they had a leader as smart as Catrell.

Bishop didn't ponder it too long and didn't allow himself to forget that Catrell was a murderer. He began studying the printout of three of Lonnie's files that came through the fax: the first one, entitled "VotinRites," the second "NewDeal" and the third "11/2." All three listed major players in the political and business community and large sums of money.

Bishop was so engrossed in those files that he didn't notice that Catrell had left the office and was outside talking to Greg. King still sat on the box, but was paying close attention to the conversation between Catrell and Greg. When Bishop stepped outside the office with the papers still in his hand he heard Greg Gatson bargaining with Catrell.

"Look, you know I have no choice but to sign all of this over to you." Greg said. "But what I'm offering is something more than just the money in those accounts."

Catrell looked impatient and raised his voice to say, "Greg, you're right, you don't have a choice. In a few minutes the papers will be here and you're goddamned right, you will sign all of the stocks, all of the ownership, all of the money, over to the companies and people I tell you." He put his finger in Greg's face and continued, "You're not in a position to make deals with me. You lost. So shut the fuck up before you piss me off. When the others get here all of this will be settled."

Bishop's heart started racing again. He'd witnessed so much killing in his life and in the last few days. As he watched Catrell in action, he knew that Greg was standing on the edge of a grave. Gatson had to be cool. Bishop wasn't sure Catrell had decided what to do yet. Or had he? Maybe he was just keeping Greg alive to use him for one last reason, for some purpose that he wouldn't reveal yet.

King's face was intense. He was the one who had been the pawn in all of this. He studied the situation, watching Catrell, trying to read his intentions, trying to predict the next move. He flashed his eyes at Bishop. There was no emotion, no question, no answer in the look. He just studied them all.

Bishop walked back into the office and continued trying to make sense of the fax. King came in behind him, took his jacket off and laid it across the back of a chair. A 9mm Glock was stuck in his belt. It didn't alarm or surprise Bishop. It did make him wonder if they were losing King to the sickness, too.

King stepped up close to Bishop and asked, "Is it true that you killed two members of the Zulu Nation the other night?"

The question threw Bishop off. It took a minute for him to gather his thoughts. He didn't want to lie to King but was suspicious about his need to know. Bishop wasn't surprised he'd heard about what had happened. One of the Cobras and maybe even Catrell could have told him what happened. He set the fax on the table and turned to face King. "The only thing that happened the other night was two men came to burn my house down and I stopped them. Why?"

King was staring at Bishop and continued questioning. "What'd you feel?"

"King, in war you learn that whoever attacks you is your enemy." Bishop was uncomfortable with the direction of King's questions and said, "It's not about what you felt at that moment. It's about what you feel for the rest of your life."

King lowered his head. "Do you think Catrell is going to kill Greg?" King asked quietly.

"Maybe," Bishop said.

It bothered Bishop that he couldn't tell what King was thinking. His questions were beyond general curiosity and even though he stood only inches from Bishop, he seemed to be far away, reviewing events, assessing possibilities, analyzing the potential for casualties.

All of them, Bishop, King, Catrell, were drained, worn out mentallty, physically fatigued, emotionally confused. The nightmare of violence and corruption and fear and chaos was swallowing them up. It felt as if that night would be over soon, but tomorrow would come with some new or recycled madness. Bishop realized that whatever happened there wouldn't really end it. It didn't matter what happened to Greg. If he died, it just meant his particular betrayal was over. They would still be swimming in shit tomorrow. Bishop sighed as he turned back to the table, picked up the fax and asked himself, "How did the people of the sun sink so far into the darkness?"

Juanita sat in the back of Detective Maddox's Buick sedan. Vincent sat in the front and they all rode quietly to gather the men she loved and to find answers to why her son was threatened and her friend had been murdered.

Juanita closed her eyes and thought of Lonnie and all the years they'd spent together, all the years that she knew one day she would leave him. He had made her feel comfortable and safe. It wasn't enough for her and she wondered if that was enough to make some women happy. Lonnie had loved her, but could never touch her heart, could never reach her soul and feel the fire that lived there. Maybe it was the circumstances of their meeting. Maybe in the back of her mind she always wondered whether the feelings she had for Bishop would ever amount to anything. Perhaps it kept her from opening up, from receiving Lonnie's love. The grief that hadn't spoken since his murder wanted to shout, but she pushed it back and swallowed it, trying not miss him so much. Tears streaked down her face and salted her lips and she was sorry that one of the best men she'd ever known was gone.

As they drove toward her son, Juanita thought of the way she and Bishop spoke poetry to each other and the gentleness of his touch and the way he fought to restrain the violence he'd learned in his life. She understood his need to be rescued, to be healed. Her son was just like him. When they first met, it was obvious to her why King loved Bishop. She understood it from that first moment and knew that given the time and the circumstances, she would love him, too. It was ironic that the circumstances that finally brought them together would be surrounded by so much blood, so much pain, so many tears. Maybe it wasn't so ironic. Wasn't that the way black people had loved for hundreds of years?

Soon morning
will paint the
city
gently pushing
the night
and the deeds
of darkness
into yesterday
calling the people
to stumble
out of their
dreams
into the reality
of a new day
and new ways
of greeting
each other
in the light
that only the
sun sings
reminding us
of the possibilities
of tomorrow.

Chapter Thirty-Two

A well-dressed black man in his early thirties came unescorted through the door to the factory. He carried an expensive, soft, leather briefcase. Catrell motioned him toward them. Greg Gatson looked up nervously as Catrell took the man into the small office where they talked for a minute and the young man handed him a legal-sized folder. Catrell scanned the contents quickly, shook the man's hand and escorted him out of the office. The man nodded at King before walking out the door to the factory. Bishop gave King a curious look. King answered his glance muttering, "One of Catrell's lawyers."

A few minutes later the door to the factory opened again. This time, five Cobras walked in a formation with one in the front, two on each side and two in the back. In the middle of the circle were two men. Bishop was astonished when he saw who Catrell had been waiting for. Greg Gatson jumped to his feet about to say something but the words never made it out of his mouth. King hopped up, too, tense and surprised. Catrell was the only one who was not. He watched the reaction of the others and watched as the two men were escorted toward them.

Bishop recognized one of the men surrounded by the young Cobras as the loud, violent, superfly-looking cop who had presided over his beating earlier. Bishop locked eyes with the cop who was in street clothes instead of his uniform. He noticed that the arrogance and authority the cop had carried on the street was gone. There, in that factory, he was surrounded by young men who didn't give a fuck about putting a bullet in his head. He kept his eyes on Bishop as they approached Catrell. The place was full of heavily armed Cobras. As they came closer, all eyes shifted to the man whose entrance stunned every one of them except Catrell. The other "guest" was Mayor Floyd Packard.

Detective Maddox pulled off the highway and onto a two-lane road, passing a sign that read, "Stevensburg 2 Miles." Juanita saw the sign and remembered when Stevensburg was just a small rural community and she used to go there as a child to visit her Aunt Ellen, the healer, whom people sometimes called a root woman.

Closing her eyes, she recalled the smell of the fresh vegetables, herbs and roots from her aunt's garden and could see herself swimming in the pond that sat in back of the house. The memories refreshed her. She roamed through her past and wandered through her aunt's yard smelling life blooming all around until grief returned, forcing images of her aunt's funeral and the old ladies of the Baptist church telling her how much she reminded them of Ellen, and Lonnie standing next to her, holding her hand while the Minister said a final prayer and she watched the casket lowered and saw the dirt falling across the wooden box.

Juanita opened her eyes as if escaping from a bad dream and saw the dark country road, reaffirming her fear that she was still headed toward a place where she had to learn and witness something dreadful. Juanita stared out the window of the Buick sedan then let her mind roam again.

Every night for the last few days she had anticipated death. She had already lost Lonnie. Her greatest fear was that her son would make the evening news, another young black man lost to the evil that had grabbed the throat of her community and was choking the life out of her people. Lonnie was murdered by this evil. Her son, Billy King, had been running from it. Bishop had been chasing it, trying to find a way to corner it and kill it. Every night she anticipated a call, another knock on her door, another voice telling her that her son or her love had been stolen.

The weariness of wondering about the future dragged her back into the past, surrounding her with spirits of black women singing mournful songs of black men lost in the night. Voices called her from the darkness alongside that two-lane road. Songs and screams, chants and challenges, words and wailing invaded her mind, reminding her that this was not their destiny. She answered them aloud, sighing, "When will this end?"

The sound that had come out of her was disturbing like the low guttural pleading of someone fighting out of a nightmare. Maddox looked back at her in the mirror and Vincent turned around asking, "Are you OK?"

Like someone who had just regained consciousness, Juanita was confused by his question and hesitated to answer as the voices faded away, back into the history on the side of the road. "Are we almost there?" Juanita asked cautiously.

Maddox looked at her in the mirror again and answered her. "We'll be there in about five minutes."

The mayor was wearing an expensive light blue suit, alligator shoes and a red silk shirt opened at the collar to show the gold chain that hung around his neck. He looked like a pimp or one of those well-taken care of preachers. In a way he was dressed appropriately. He could have been either. Arrogance was draped across his body like James Brown's cape. He seemed annoyed that the young drug dealer had summoned him there in the middle of the night. Everyone in the room could see the mayor's attitude was just an act, because although he might have been disturbed, he had no choice but to answer the summons.

As Bishop observed the cop who had beaten him, he noticed that the officer was extremely nervous. He was bigger than Bishop remembered. Solid and muscular, he must have been about six four or five and maybe two hundred and ten pounds. He was big, weight-lifting, mean spirited mother-fucker. Occasionally the cop glanced around at the young Cobras posted throughout the place, but his eyes always returned to Bishop, always speculating whether he planned to retaliate against him. The thought had not yet crystallized in Bishop's mind. Finding out what had caused the war and trying to insure that he and King walked out alive were taking up all of his head space right then.

Mayor Packard and the cop were only there a few seconds but the silence and the fear and the curiosity had already sucked up all the oxygen, making the room tight like the knots in Bishop's stomach. Catrell said nothing, letting the tension wrap its arms around everybody. King's eyes resembled two small pockets of fire as he stared at the mayor. The cop saw it and his eyes nervously darted back and forth between Packard, Catrell and King. Greg Gatson couldn't take it anymore and blurted out, "Mr. Mayor, I've been trying to tell Catrell that we're willing to make a deal with him."

Catrell said sharply, "Shut the fuck up, Greg."

Catrell's voice cut through the air like a straight razor. The mayor recoiled from the sound and the command. The cop took a step closer, reflexively reaching under his coat for a gun while putting his body between Catrell and the mayor. The Cobras in the room leaned forward ready to strike. Bishop pushed back against the wall and braced for the fire. Fortunately, the Cobras were highly disciplined and waited for a signal before lighting the cop up. Catrell raised his hand and gave a sign that made them all lower their

242

weapons while keeping their eyes trained on the cop. Catrell closed the distance between himself and the cop by taking a long step forward. He looked at the cop with such contempt that it forced him to step back. In Catrell's eyes the cop saw that he would kill him without cause or concern for consequences.

Catrell began to pace back and forth in front of Packard and the cop. The cop's action and arrogance seemed to have pissed him off. It was the first time Bishop had seen him display anger like that. He was like one of those big cats in the zoo, a panther or a tiger pacing back and forth in a cage watching the people stare at him, hoping one will make a mistake and come too close. The pacing went on for about a minute until he got control of his emotions. His first words after that were aimed at the cop. Speaking in a low, calm, almost monotone voice, he was direct and cold. Blood chillingly cold. "Remember this." Catrell pointed to the cop. "I am the law here. Don't you ever step to me again."

The mayor and Greg were visibly shaken by the threat. Catrell gestured to them and to King and Bishop. "Follow me. We have business to discuss."

The five of them went into the small office and Catrell closed the door.

Detective Maddox pulled his car into the parking lot of the T-shirt factory. Juanita and Vincent watched as the darkness seemed to move, taking shape when a dozen young men with guns stepped out of the shadows, surrounding the car. As they approached, Juanita noticed that some were in their twenties like her son. Others were even younger, teenagers guarding whatever or whoever was inside. One of the Cobras came to the driver's side of the car and Maddox lowered his window to get his instructions. "Catrell wants the two of them to come inside and said you should wait out here."

Vincent and Juanita exited the car and followed two of the young men into the factory. Maddox found a dark spot at the far end of the building. He backed into the space where he could see the street just beyond the gate of the parking lot. No cars passed by. He looked at his watch. It was 3:37 a.m. He waited in the darkness, in that small town, in the middle of the night, contemplating the stupidity of the war that Greg Gatson and Mayor Floyd Packard started with Catrell and the Egyptian Cobras.

Maddox settled back into his seat and waited. In his thirty-seven years as a cop, he'd waited often. He'd waited on stake outs and for dignitaries he was assigned to drive and protect. He'd waited while doing surveillance on criminals and political activists. He'd waited for the bag men who brought the payoffs and the politicians who pretended to be in meetings at fancy hotels and were really engaged in rendezvous with their mistresses. He was used to waiting.

Staring into the darkness, Detective Maddox thought about his friend Lonnie Carlton and the times they waited together. He remembered Lonnie always taking notes and telling him to remember everything that everybody did. The memories of his friend hurt his mind and he tried to force them away by thinking of what must be going on inside the factory.

Greg Gatson had convinced the mayor that they could do their business without Catrell Merit and the Egyptian Cobras. Maddox had tried to warn them that it was a mistake. He knew that Catrell was watching them, letting them build up strength, waiting for the right time to step in and force them to either include him or fight him and lose. He used the same strategy whenever rival gangs would form. It had never failed him. His experience and patience proved over and over again why he was the most feared and respected underworld figure in the city.

Mayor Packard was corrupt and weak. His only reason for being in politics was to feed his ego and feed his greed. Greg Gatson knew it and played that corruption, manipulating the weakness to expand his influence and wealth. Greg did not have the patience or the strategic mind of Catrell. He overestimated the strength of the Zulu Nation and underestimated the ruthlessness of Catrell. He mistakenly thought that because he'd gathered his own group of corrupt cops inside the police force and had the support of the mayor and legitimate business leaders, he could run the Cobras out of the city and have total control. He should have asked somebody.

It had all come down to the meeting going on inside the factory. If what Maddox knew about Catrell was true, the killing was over. He wouldn't have brought Juanita there if there was going to be more blood shed. He assumed Catrell was inside giving Floyd Packard and Greg Gatson the terms that he wanted. He knew they were defeated and feared him and would give him whatever he wanted. Maddox hoped he was right.

Once inside the factory, Juanita counted at least twenty more young men, all armed, all serious. Seeing all those young gang members, Vincent's hands became cold and sweaty, even though he tried to remain calm. It was a foreign world to him personally, yet had some familiarity because it permeated his community. It was a world of young men who killed for power and money and most of all what they thought was respect. It was a world that he mistakenly thought his friend Bishop could move in without fear. It was scaring the shit out of Vincent and he wished they weren't there.

A thirtyish young man approached them and the escorts deferred to him as if he had some authority. Vincent scanned the large room, looking past the young man and past the silk screen machines and the stacks of boxes, searching for King and Bishop and looking for some reassurance that everything would be fine. Juanita also looked past the young man, searching the room for her son. Like Vincent, she also needed reassurance.

The young man who approached them said something to one of the escorts who then returned to the outside. Turning to Juanita and Vincent, he instructed them to follow him and led them over to the area outside the small office. Through the dingy window of the door, they could see King, Catrell, Greg Gatson and Bishop involved in a discussion with two men who were partially blocked from their view. Catrell sat on the edge of a desk holding his cigarette between two fingers, talking. Everyone else was standing, listening intensely to what he was saying.

CHAPTER THIRTY-THREE

In that small dirty office with one metal desk and two metal folding chairs, the air smelled as if someone had spent years in there smoking and sweating. The light was bad and the five men were forced to stand extremely close. Too close. The space was full of the scent and aroused senses of men ready to kill or die.

Bishop was exhausted. Suddenly, all the weight of the last few weeks pushed down on him and it felt as if all his energy was running down his leg and onto the concrete floor underneath his shoes. He was tired of that shit. All of it. He didn't want to hear what Catrell was going to demand from the mayor and Greg. He didn't want to listen to their bullshit responses. He didn't want to witness King or any other young men like him denied faith in the future. He didn't want to watch any more killing. He was tired of the shit. All of it.

He looked over his shoulder and saw Vincent and Juanita standing outside the office. At first it alarmed him and then he thought maybe it was a good sign. Maybe it meant Catrell wasn't planning to execute anyone else. While Bishop tried to figure it out, Catrell handed Greg Gatson an ink pen and said, "Come over here and sign these documents to turn over the assets of the Dexter Avenue Zulu Nation." Mayor Packard watched and his cop bodyguard shifted nervously, aware that his presence was really useless there. If things escalated into violence, neither would make it out alive.

As Greg reluctantly signed the papers, Catrell picked up the fax he'd received from the *Crusader* office and shoved them toward the mayor saying, "Tell me what this means." Pointing to the parts that read 'VotinRites,' 'NewDeal' and '11/2', Catrell asked, "What are those lists of names and contributions about?"

Mayor Packard reluctantly took the papers and stared at the pages as if someone had handed him pornographic pictures of himself. He felt naked, exposed. His secrets were getting ready to come tumbling out of the dark little corners where he'd kept them. He looked over to Greg with pleading eyes as if to ask for his permission to respond to Catrell. Greg remained quiet and averted the question in Mayor Packard's eyes and another rebuke from Catrell who was focused completely on the mayor. King watched all of them as the room started to simmer. It was getting hot and he felt beads of sweat rolling down the side of his face.

Catrell pointed to the pages in Packard's hand and asked, "What's wrong? You didn't understand my question? What are you raising money for? What is about to happen in the city?"

Packard cleared his throat, his mouth was dry and he wanted something to drink. He licked his lips, cleared his throat again, but remained silent. He was trying to find a clever way to respond that would give him some leverage in the discussion. He was a fool who didn't understand that it was not a negotiation. He had lost. It was a surrender and the only thing left to happen was a transfer of power and money. Catrell grew impatient. He bit down hard and you could see his jaw tighten and the large vein along his temple, pulsating. His contempt for the mayor rose slowly to the surface and having witnessed him kill coldly with no emotion, Bishop was afraid something terrible would happen there if he was enraged.

Bishop stepped toward Catrell, placing himself next to Packard. He took the pages from the mayor's hand and said, "Maybe I can help."

Bishop's words sounded weak as they fell in the space between the men. He wasn't really trying to help. He was trying to prevent more bloodshed. Catrell turned slowly toward him as if the words had broken the spell he was casting. He looked slightly puzzled and possibly pissed that he was interrupted. For the first time, fatigue was clearly visible on his face and his weariness served as a warning to Bishop that they had to resolve things before it was too late. He'd seen it before, exhaustion, frustration, anger and contempt for one's enemy leading to an act of murder that could have been prevented. Catrell hesitated, looked back at the mayor then at Bishop. "Yeah, Bishop, maybe you can help. You know what I'm looking for."

Relief. Everyone in the room seemed to breathe at the same time. Catrell's words were without anger, but the frustration still hung there. He wiped his brow and tried to pull his emotions back in and for a moment he trusted Bishop to speak for him, to interrogate his prisoners, to solve the puzzle. He leaned back onto the desk, ready to evaluate their answers and Bishop's performance. The mayor, Greg and the cop felt the tension ease, but understood it was temporary if there was no cooperation or if one of them made a mistake.

Bishop took a deep breath and a short step to the desk. He examined the pages Packard had been holding and began his questions by seeking clarification about the three lists on the page. "What is VotinRites?" He asked.

Nervously, the mayor answered, "A fund set up for my reelection campaign later this year." He hesitated then grinned nervously and added, "A war chest of a couple million dollars months before election season would make me, the incumbent, virtually impossible to defeat. My reelection would almost be guaranteed."

Bishop tried not to react to what was being said and continued with his questions. "What is NewDeal?"

The mayor hesitated again. Catrell didn't move. King continued to watch intensely. The cop looked at Greg, who lifted his head toward Catrell as if asking permission to speak. Catrell listened with his arms folded across his chest and stared silently at the floor. Greg accepted Catrell's silence as consent and exhaled loudly with relief that he had been allowed to speak. He wanted to handle things. He thought Packard was a weak fool who might fuck it up and get them both killed. Bishop hoped he hadn't misread the situation. It was too fragile. Greg couldn't start giving long explanations trying to cut a deal. Catrell wanted information, not commentary.

Greg turned so he faced Bishop and Catrell and said, "NewDeal is a group of businessmen who give a private contribution to the mayor in exchange for special treatment if he wins reelection."

Bishop was getting pissed. Greg's comments were a confirmation of their bullshit. Even before reelecting the mayor, they would force some of the most respected businesses in the city to break the election laws and cough up bribes totaling almost two million dollars in unreported personal contributions to the mayor. Bishop tried not to let his emotions show but he was having a hard time restraining himself. He wanted to scream at them, curse them out, smash their pious, hypocritical faces.

Bishop ignored the mayor whose blue suit was soaked with sweat and spoke directly to Greg, "On November 2, a couple of days from now, you are going to recommend that George Washington Homes be torn down. Why?"

It was an unexpected question that caused Catrell to raise an eyebrow. He didn't know Bishop knew about that or maybe he thought he'd been holding back information and couldn't be trusted. At that point it didn't matter. Bishop knew he had to proceed. Catrell lifted his head and looked over at Bishop for a second before looking back at the spot on the floor.

Greg was about to answer when Packard interrupted him by waving his hand. It was a practiced gesture, a rehearsed movement signaling his intention to take command of the situation. It was political theatrics, a mayoral response, a move to re-assert his authority. In his most commanding politician's voice he said, "My recommendation to tear down Washington Homes is based solely on the economic needs of the city. The land is underused, occupancy is less than fifty percent and by law, the remaining residents can be relocated so that we can build something else there. George Washington Homes is on prime land right next to downtown. It could be used for something constructive to help revitalize the city."

He sounded just like the politician he was. It sounded as if he was trying to sell a campaign promise. Bishop knew the mayor was a fool, but it was a mistake to talk to Catrell like he was one. Catrell could tell he was dancing around the questions. He understood that Packard's assault on the Cobras was designed to build support for tearing down Washington Homes and place him in a defensive position by destroying the gang's traditional power base, depleting his troops through incarceration or death. He wanted to know what the mayor planned to do with the land.

Catrell hadn't moved. He just stared at the floor and studied the answers. As Bishop was about to ask the next question, Catrell rose up off the edge of the desk and took one step forward bringing him about ten inches in front of the mayor. They were about the same height and Catrell stared right through his eyes. He just stood there, staring into Packard's brain, saying nothing. Mayor Floyd Packard stared back, trying to pretend he didn't fear Catrell. They stood nose to nose like two boxers in the middle of the ring before the fight starts. The mayor perspired profusely. After a few seconds, his shoulders slumped, he lowered his eyes and looked around the room for help. King had grown more tense, poised as if to strike. He watched Greg and the cop. Bishop surveyed it all, waiting, as men do when they are trapped in confrontational situations like that, to see how it would play out.

The cop bodyguard acknowledged the inherent danger to himself. If they murdered the mayor, they would have to kill him, too. His posture weakened. His body subconsciously began submitting to a fate he couldn't determine or control. The cop looked at Greg, then to Bishop, with a subtle, silent pleading. His expression asked for intervention. Greg had moved back about three feet and taken refuge up against the back wall of the office as if to divorce himself from the fate of Packard. King's hand was on the handle of the pistol in his belt. Bishop hoped King wouldn't do something crazy. At that moment, any mistake, any action could set off a deadly sequence of reactions. They all had to wait while Catrell tested the mayor's nerve.

After a tense sixty seconds, Mayor Packard moved back a few inches, giving way to Catrell's power. Although it only took a minute it felt as if they had all aged from the tension. Silently, Catrell had broken the mayor's spirit. There was no need to humiliate him any further. Catrell looked at Bishop and said, "Finish asking your questions."

Juanita and Vincent strained to see what was happening inside the office. Juanita still couldn't make out the other two men. Vincent couldn't either. They caught Bishop looking back at them but he was trying to stay focused and didn't give any sign of acknowledgment. Vincent wanted to leave. His heart raced with uncertainty and fear. Juanita wanted to take her son home.

The last time Juanita had to go get her son, he and Catrell were in a deadly confrontation. She remembered how infatuated her daughter was with that dangerous young drug dealer. Now, to protect her son, she had to rely upon the same young man who wasn't allowed to love her daughter. Nothing made sense in her community. Forces that were supposed to serve and protect the people were responsible for the deaths of her friend Lonnie Carlton and Stacey Freeman, a city hall secretary. A drug dealer was protecting her family. The man she wanted to love stood at the center of all the insanity, navigating through the tragedy, trying to bring order back into their lives. Too much had happened. Too much was crazy in her life and in the life of her community. All of it was wrong. They were not supposed to live like this. It was time for things to change. She wanted to take her son and Bishop home.

Bishop had only a few more questions and Catrell was waiting for the answers. He leaned back on the edge of the desk but his eyes were still burning a hole in the face of Mayor Packard. He had completely blocked out everything else in the room. Nothing mattered to him at that moment, except his absolute psychological domination of the highest elected official in the city. He was amazing to watch. Bishop knew it was crazy to admire him. He was a criminal, but how could he judge him? Everyone in that room had blood on their hands except King and he was an eye witness to the stench of death that they'd allowed to fill the lungs of their community.

Bishop asked, "Mayor Packard, what does this last list mean? The one called '11/2', that has fifty million at the bottom."

Packard took the list from Bishop and looked at it quickly. It was a move designed to calculate his response more than to refresh his memory. After glancing at the page for several seconds he looked up at Catrell and said, "If...if you don't mind, I'd like to have Greg answer this question. He can provide more details."

Packard's politeness was full of acquiescence. Catrell didn't even acknowledge him. He pulled his smokes out of his pocket, lit one and pointed to Greg whose face still registered terror from the confrontation a few minutes ago.

Greg's breathing was heavy, his face sweaty. Catrell said nothing. His expression commanded Greg to gather himself and provide the explanation. Greg stepped forward about a foot from the wall where he'd sought sanctuary. He took a deep breath and spoke in a slow, deliberate manner, calculating every word, trying to insure he didn't incur the wrath of Catrell. "The mayor is currently under a federal investigation and there's a possibility he'll be indicted for accepting bribes. If he is indicted, it probably won't happen until after the election. We don't think they'll be able to convict him, but in the event they do, we are preparing for the future."

Mayor Packard lowered his head slightly and you could see shame dripping off his face. He wasn't ashamed of what he'd done. He was embarrassed that it had to be acknowledged in front of the people in that room. His bodyguard had regained some of his composure and stared stoically at Bishop as if he needed an object of his fear and anger. Bishop ignored him. He was insignificant in the scenario and there was no need to deal with him right then. King listened carefully to everything, taking mental notes. His hands rested calmly and comfortably at his sides while he watched every word form in Greg's mouth. Catrell focused his eyes on the floor and his ears on the answer, while his mind prepared a response.

Greg continued. "'11/2' is a secret plan we put together a year ago. If the mayor is convicted and forced to give up his seat after re-election we intend to have some things already in motion that could possibly make us rich enough from one deal that it wouldn't matter if we lose control of city hall."

Bishop thought, "They've lost control of their minds. For money they'd brought all that death. For wealth they had created all that chaos." A sickening feeling swirled in his stomach. His limbs were becoming numb. One year of hating the darkness.

Greg looked at his watch as if he had some place to go. He stuck his hands in his pockets and took them out as if he were trying to figure out what to do with them. Visibly nervous he said, "We plan to destroy Washington Homes and build a new stadium. To insure that we wouldn't get cut out of the deal, we set up a company called ENTAC Enterprises that would purchase the land from the city and then lease it to the developers. We'd also become joint venture partners in the construction and operation of the stadium. Over a ten year period we'd make about fifty million dollars. The names on the list are all people we have lined up to support the plan. Many of them have paid at least fifty thousand dollars to become partners with us. As a bonus, the mayor would get credit for running the Cobras out of the city and turning a poor, crime ridden community into a viable middle-class neighborhood."

Bishop asked quickly, "Why did you kill Stacey and Lonnie?"

"Because they found out what we were about to do." Greg responded as if it were no big deal.

"And you came after King because you thought he knew, too?"

Greg sighed, lowered his eyes and said, "Yes."

Bishop was struggling to control himself as he listened to Greg talk. He wanted to spit bile and let the acid burn Gatson's face. Old instincts had climbed to the surface. Bishop felt them crawling on his skin and he tried to suppress them, tried to restrain his desire to kill them both right then. Catrell noticed his reaction and stood up. Mayor Packard, the cop and Greg recoiled slightly. They couldn't gauge his reaction to their revelations. King looked at them with contempt, disgust and hatred alternately flashing from his eyes.

There was much to say, but none of it could be said without the words giving way to weapons. Bishop was silent, trying to suppress the deadly signals from his own sinful past. King was so enraged he trembled. Greg Gatson was choking on the revelation of what he had done and the uncertainty of what was going to be done to him. The cop moved away from the mayor slightly, distancing himself from the hellfire that was sure to be directed his way. The mayor pulled on the sleeve of his jacket and adjusted the collar on his shirt. He looked at Greg for a way out, hoping that he could come up with one as he'd done so many times before.

Catrell stared down at the floor again, studied the cracks in the concrete floor then said, "This is what's going to happen."

Catrell's voice cut through the quiet like lightning. Oddly, there was no thunder. He spoke so softly it seemed gentle. It was almost as if he were a pastor about to give advice to a troubled couple. No one in the room was deceived. Catrell hadn't looked up yet and the pause before his next sentence again pulled the tension tight like a noose. King turned his flaming eyes toward Catrell as if waiting for an order to execute the three men before him.

His face had the look of a killer and it frightened Bishop, who hoped they hadn't lost him.

Catrell stood straight up and said casually, "Mayor Packard, you will run for reelection and Greg you will make this deal happen. You two can keep a half million dollars from what you've collected, but the rest you'll give to me. You will also sign over your shares of the company you set up for the stadium deal. After the election is over and the deal is done, the mayor will resign. I don't care what the reasons are. You figure that out. After that, leave town. Both of you. I don't ever want to see either of you again. You will also find a way to exonerate me in the press and in the courts from all of the accusations you've made about Stacey Freeman's murder. And one more thing. There better not be anymore attacks on me, the Cobras, King or Bishop."

It was the smart move for business. Catrell had studied all that was said and in a few minutes had separated his emotions from what was important to him and his empire. It sickened Bishop, but he understood it. Just like that, all of that murder and mayhem, the confusion and chaos, had been wrapped up neatly into an alliance between those two traitors and the young drug dealer and gang leader.

Even though Mayor Floyd Packard had lost, he still walked away wealthier, and more importantly, alive. His corruption would not be fully rewarded, even though Catrell gave him some crumbs to make sure he stayed loyal. He knew that the mayor was weak and would do what he was told. His greed and fear had allowed Greg Gatson to manipulate him. His inflated sense of importance convinced him he was above the people he was supposed to serve. Catrell intended to use him like the whore he was.

Greg Gatson failed at his attempt to secretly rule the city. His betrayal caused sorrow and slaying and poured more grief on the hope of the people who thought he was one of those who would lift them up. His ego made him believe he had the right to get what he wanted even if it left blood on the sidewalks and the black community full of corpses. His education, his success, his dreams were all stained with betrayal and madness.

King watched Catrell's words fill up the room. Shock, disbelief and confusion swept across his face. Catrell didn't look at him. He knew King would not understand his position or accept it. He would not understand that for Catrell there was no choice. It was the world that he lived in. These were the kind of men who had come to rule his life, their lives. King grabbed his jacket, took several quick steps toward the door, snatched it open and left the room. Catrell watched him as the door banged against the wall and rebounded, slamming shut.

Juanita and Vincent watched King storm by them. They looked into the office for the brief moment the door was opened and were finally able to see the two men they couldn't make out. They saw Mayor Packard and Greg Gatson. Juanita ran after King, who was walking, almost running toward the exit as if he would explode if he didn't get outside to fresh air. Vincent was frozen, cemented to the concrete floor. Seeing Packard and Greg in the room caused his head to spin as he said, "What the fuck went on in there?"

After a few seconds, Bishop came out of the office, followed by Greg, the mayor, the cop and Catrell. Vincent watched them parade by him. They were all solemn. Catrell stepped to Vincent and said, "You have Lonnie Carlton's files and Bishop has some more information for you. When I say it's all right, you can do what you want with it."

Vincent looked at Bishop who acknowledged Catrell's order with a nod.

Catrell continued, "Bishop, Maddox will take you, Vincent, King and his mother home. I probably won't see you for a while. Maybe never. Help King understand what went on here, he's one of the few friends I have." He extended his hand and Bishop shook it gratefully but with dread. Catrell had saved their lives, but before the sun came up he would be back at his trade, destroying the lives of his own people.

Greg, the mayor and the cop stood a few feet away, praying that their absolute defeat would be enough for Catrell and he would spare their lives. They awaited instructions from him. He'd said nothing to them since exiting the office. Finally, he turned their way and waved his hand dismissively at the two men and said, "Greg, you and the mayor can leave."

The three men started toward the door. Catrell looked at the cop and gestured toward some of his men saying, "I said the mayor and Greg can leave."

In midstep, the three men swung around trying to understand what he was saying, hoping it wasn't what they thought. Catrell pointed at the cop and said, "You stay. We're not through."

Fear. Desperation. Defeat. Destiny. All of them surrounded the cop like bars of a jail cell, isolating him from Mayor Packard, Greg Gatson and

254

the rest of the world. Catrell's words and his anticipated actions were a reminder to Greg and the mayor that they, too, must follow his instructions or face a similar fate. They knew the cop was about to be executed. Catrell was going to punish him for his brutalization of Bishop and others. He would become a sacrifice to the demons of the underworld to reaffirm Catrell's place as the ruler of that sick kingdom.

Young Egyptian Cobras quickly surrounded the cop, disarming him and forcing him to his knees. Vincent's eyes were wide with panic. The cop looked at Bishop as they cuffed his hands behind his back. He wanted to ask for his intervention, his forgiveness, but guilt and pride wouldn't let him speak. The cop's eyes dripped with fear. Bishop was numb, his expression blank, as a pillowcase was pulled over the cop's face. Catrell watched with detached coolness, but Bishop felt him studying him to see if he would ask that his torturer's life be spared. Bishop said nothing. Catrell turned to him and Vincent, lit another cigarette and said coolly, "You should leave now. This is finally over."

Juanita had hurried past the young Cobras posted throughout the building. She rushed into the parking lot of the factory and found her son, Billy King, hanging onto the fence, gasping for air. Detective Maddox watched from his car parked in a darkened corner. The Cobras outside watched, too. One of them struck a match and lit a joint. Others whispered to each other while waiting for whatever was going to happen next.

King saw his mother coming toward him and turned away. He was so full of anger and pain that tears poured down his face. He couldn't tell her what he had just seen. He didn't want to repeat the words and taste their rottenness in his mouth. Wiping his face as she approached, his mind was searching, reaching, for his heart. He needed to find something, anything that would help him deal with the urge he felt, the urge to kill. He wanted to discover some good in what had happened. There was none, except the fact that he was still alive.

Juanita had finally reached her son after days of following his path. Her clothes were stained with his hurt. She saw his contorted face and hoped she could relieve him from whatever had twisted his soul. She heard her own tears falling on the ground as she wrapped her arms around him, reassuring him, "It's going to be all right. We can get past this and be healed."

King shook his head, choked back more tears and said, "I don't know, Mama. These people are traitors. They are liars and murderers and thieves. They have stolen our future."

Juanita pulled him closer and said, "No son. They can't steal the future. We won't let them." She repeated the words as if it were an ancient chant. "We can't let them...we can't let them...we can't let them."

When Vincent and Bishop came through the door the sky was already becoming lighter. To his left Bishop saw Juanita and King and wondered if she would ever know, if King would ever tell her how he saw the naked face of treachery. Bishop wondered if he would ever tell her himself, or if it would remain locked inside his manhood like so many battles, so many secrets, so much pain? He was guilty, too.

Greg and Packard stood to the right, maybe ten feet away. Two young Cobras were at the door discussing something with one of Catrell's lieutenants. A car parked in the corner in the shadows moved slowly toward them. Another car came around the corner. The first car, driven by Detective Maddox, pulled up right in front of them. Maddox leaned out the window and said, "Bishop, I'm supposed to take y'all home."

The second car pulled up behind him unable to depart until they'd left. It was driven by one of the Cobras. It was Mayor Packard's Town Car. The driver jumped out, walked past Bishop and Vincent and handed the keys to Greg. He and the mayor started toward the car, trying not to appear too anxious while trying to get to it as quickly as possible. King had gotten control of himself and Juanita released him from her embrace and they came toward Bishop. Finally, they could all go home.

A loud thunderous sound from inside the factory startled them. It stopped Greg and the mayor just as they were about to step into the car. Juanita and King were jerked by the sound as if they'd been jolted by electricity. Vincent grabbed Bishop's arm. Bishop was steady. He knew what it was and had expected it. The cop had been killed by the blast of a shotgun. Bishop was still numb, but even the numbness couldn't prevent the sickness. He could have prevented the execution but didn't. There was too much blood in his memory, too much violence in his history. He couldn't deny his feelings, couldn't stop them from pushing through his pores and out onto his skin. After what he'd seen and done the last few days, he knew he had to rescue himself all over again. One year of hating the darkness.

Silence and sadness hung over everything and everyone in that parking lot, maybe in the world. King walked up to Bishop and for a moment they just looked at each other, unable to express what they both felt. Bishop wished there was something that could be said that would explain the actions of war. There was nothing. Not then. Maybe after some time had passed they would talk about it and resolve that night, a night that was now standing between them. Juanita's eyes were swollen from fatigue and tears as she looked at them with a sense of relief that they'd survived it. Whatever it was.

"Come on, Bishop. Let's go." Vincent said, worried that something else might happen before they escaped. Bishop understood his need to get away from there as quickly as possible. The mayor and Greg climbed into the Town Car and waited anxiously for them to get out of their way. Bishop opened the back door to Detective Maddox's car and Juanita got in and slid toward the middle. Vincent and King went around to the other side where Vincent opened the front door and hopped in. King stood at the back door for a minute looking across the roof of the car at Bishop, who smiled quietly. They hadn't lost him. He was the future. Suddenly, King stepped back from the car.

Alarmed, Bishop asked, "What's wrong?"

Juanita's voice called out from inside the car. "Son, what is it?"

King looked at Bishop as if he had something important to say. His mouth was opened like words should be coming out, but none did.

Bishop started walking around the car toward King. "What is it?" he asked again. His question hadn't even reached King before Bishop realized what it was. King couldn't reconcile himself to the deformed, distorted peace that was made there. He couldn't live with himself if he accepted it. He couldn't just get in the car and go home as if nothing had happened. He wanted retribution. He needed evidence that there was some justice, even in the insane world he had inherited.

King knew he couldn't get answers, so no more questions came from his eyes. He turned sharply. His hand reached under his coat as he crossed the five or six steps between the two cars. Bishop tried to catch him, but before he could get there, King already stood directly in front of the mayor's car with the pistol aimed into the windshield, alternately pointed at the mayor then at

Greg Gatson as if trying to decide which one to shoot first. Bishop approached him carefully. King's hands were shaking, his body trembling. Bishop knew what it felt like. He knew King's mind was burning, trying to decide if his heart could be satisfied by taking their lives.

In that moment there was nothing. No noise. No music. No sunlight. No darkness. No feeling. No joy. No hurt. No yesterday. No tomorrow. No time. Nothing. It had all come to a halt as Bishop wrestled with his own conflicts. How could he tell King not to kill them when they deserved it? They'd tried to kill him and were responsible for murdering Lonnie and Stacey. Bishop felt the same way he did, but he knew the price of killing, the price of war. He knew King would be lost and would spend the rest of his life trying to wipe the stain from his soul.

Everyone waited. Packard panicked and screamed, "OH GOD!!!OH GOD, NO!!!"

Greg Gatson shouted at him, "SHUT THE FUCK UP!!!"

Juanita called to her son, "BILLY!!! DON'T, PLEASE DON'T DO IT!!!"

Bishop stood close to him, close enough to touch him and whisper, "King, don't do it. Believe me, they'll pay for this shit." He reached out toward King's hand and pleaded, "Come on, man. Put the gun down. We got to walk away. They lost."

In spite of his pleadings, Bishop watched King's thumb slowly pull the hammer back. His eyes narrowed. His face became a mask of violence. He waited, hesitated to listen to the voices inside him and the voices around him, asking, begging, pleading with him to choose the future over the present. His hands shook. His breathing deepened. His body stiffened.

BOOM!!!

Suddenly there was a flash of fire and thunder echoed off the sky and rattled the silence. The window was pierced, the peace shattered and Bishop stood with King in front of the car while the mayor screamed, "NOOOO!!!OH GOD NO!!!" Greg Gatson slumped down in the seat and a clucking noise came out of his throat in short intervals while blood ran out the side of his neck.

Catrell walked over to the driver's side of the mayor's Town Car, aimed his pistol in the window and fired another shot into Greg Gatson's head. The clucking stopped and Greg Gatson was dead. Catrell turned to King and said, "Now, go home."

King stared through the shattered windshield. His hand was still extended, ready to shoot. Bishop took the gun from his hand gently, grateful that he hadn't fired it. Catrell had stepped in and killed Greg Gatson so that King wouldn't make the wrong choice. He'd spent the last two weeks saving King's life, and then committed one last act of murder to save his soul.

Bishop led King to the car where Juanita and Vincent sat in horror. After placing King in the back seat where his mother cradled him in her arms, Bishop walked around to the other side of the car. Catrell stood a few feet away and their eyes met across the abyss. For the first time since all of it began, Bishop saw remorse on the face of Catrell. And in that moment, that brief, painful moment, Bishop shared his sorrow, knowing how beautiful Catrell could have been. Bishop was thankful he'd saved their son and it hurt knowing Catrell was lost to them forever, because he was their son, too.

In the days after the battle, when our wounds were still fresh and the scars had not yet begun to form, I went to Lonnie Carlton's funeral with Juanita and she went to my father's birthday party with me.

The community grieved for Lonnie and Juanita let it pour over her like rain, but didn't cry in public. Sometimes at night when her head was lying on my chest I'd feel her tears falling upon me. She'd weep in the darkness and the silence and we'd hold onto each other, hoping that there are others in the world like us, others who are trying to love.

In the months after the battle, when our wounds began to heal and our scars served as reminders of our history and our future, we attended the college graduation of our daughters, Carolyn and Sheila. We watched with pride and hope and pondered tomorrow. Juanita and I talked about having another child, but decided to adopt one. Maybe next year.

Vincent wrote about the corruption in City Hall in "The Crusader," ran for council president and won. Mayor Packard was indicted after being re-elected and subsequently resigned. As the next highest elected official, Vincent is now the mayor until a special election can be held. George Washington Homes was torn down and a new stadium is being built.

The Egyptian Cobras now control the cocaine and heroin traffic in the city. Catrell hasn't been seen in months. The rumor is he has AIDS. There is fear that if he dies, there will be another terrible war in the city to determine his replacement.

The music of Leesa Richards is filling up my car as I drive by the hole in the ground that used to be George Washington Homes. Her soulful, young voice is like a light breaking the darkness, pointing us toward better possibilities. And even though it seems as if images of war and madness will remain fixed inside my head forever, because I am with Juanita, the voices of pain that come with it are not as loud as they were. I wonder sometimes, what my life would be, had I not been born and raised in war.

I also question how King deals with those nights of terror that he survived. I wonder if he's tamed his need for revenge, his desire for retribution. Where does he put the violence that curses our lives and causes our young men to kill? He's started law school. We speak often, even though our late night chess games are infrequent. His mother and I are going to be married in a few months. The Super Bowl is coming next year and the people hope that the games will stop and their lives will be taken seriously.

I wonder if this country will ever reconcile itself to our young men who

260

are feared for many unworthy reasons and seldom admired for the right ones. Even the majority of our sons, men like King, the ones who don't fit the stereo types, are treated like outlaws, suspects, potential threats to the public order. Where is their place? When do they find peace? How can they develop their full humanity when they are constantly at war, constantly the object of subtle and direct ways to suppress them? When will this country learn that this shit will never be right as long as they have no place, as long as they know no peace? By now, it should be understood. Generation after generation, these young men will continue to defy the warmakers until the end of time or the end of this. Whichever comes first.

I look forward to going to work. I have students to teach tomorrow.

Acknowledgements

This book is the result of a life that was and is shaped by many people. It is the result of work that was guided and influenced by many hands. There is no way to explain or truly describe the profound ways they have enriched my life and work but I must at least try to speak some of their names and say thank you.

To my mother, Imani Humphrey, there is no way to adequately convey the deep love and appreciation I feel for you as a parent, teacher, friend, and editor. Thank you. To my brother Mosi, sisters Holly and Leesa, grandmother Vivian Humphrey, aunt Malkia Brantuo, Uncle Arthur and all my aunts uncles, cousins, nephews, and nieces (there are too many of ya'll to name everybody) thanks for being a family that encourages dreams and visions.

A special thanks to the men who have become my brothers especially Rasuli Lewis and Sala Udin, Viktor Bouquette, Menelik Shabazz, Paul Robinson, Sababa Akili, Steve Blount, Thomas Jones, Earl Peek, Jeffrey Edison, Geoffrey Grier, Karenga Hart, Anthony Mizell, D'amo Murphy, Seyhoum Tesfaye, Rahsaan Salandy, Kendall Minter and Tyrone Johnson. You have been major sources of inspiration in my life and seed for the positive characteristics for the men in this story.

Many aspects of this book are also drawn from what I have learned from the talents, work and energy of men who are and have been my teachers: especially Amiri Baraka, Ron Milner, Robert F. Williams, Haki Madhubuti, Mwawaza Hollifield, Kwasi Thornell, and David Franklin. I am thankful for the lessons and the guidance.

I feel a special sense of gratitude to my publisher and friend Haki Madhubuti. He has not only contributed a large body of his own work to the tradition of black arts and letters, he has also worked tirelessly for more than thirty years to insure that other writers would have a place to publish their works. The building of Third World Press is a model for what we can do and I am grateful for the entire staff, especially my editor Gwendolyn Mitchell.

Finally, this book and all my work is the result of the support, guidance, criticism, suggestions, laughter and help from my wife, Lita, whose love forgives me and forces me to be better.